The Last Prophet

Tim Heath

Copyright © 2015 Tim Heath
All rights reserved.
ISBN-13: 978-1505448856
ISBN-10: 1505448859

Also by Tim Heath

Cherry Picking (Published 2012)

ACKNOWLEDGMENTS

Writing is a team effort and I'm so grateful for those who are working with me to help get my novels to print. For some this is the second time already.

My wife, Rachel, was once again the first person to read it, giving me helpful advice and making sure I wasn't too wild! I'm so thankful for the encouragement you have shown me and the space you have allowed me to carve out this second novel.

Elizabeth Knight has once again done a wonderful job on the grammar side. Some of your comments made me laugh and I'll have to publish them in their own right some day.

Sylvia Knight and Chelsea Bielskus were both proof readers this time, offering some expert insights. Chelsea remains my number one fan in America and your enthusiasm for my books is encouraging!

Thank you also to my editor, Phil Whittall, coming on board for this latest novel. It won't be the last time we work together. Your attention to detail has saved me from some embarrassing mistakes!

The cover design is once more the work of Taaniel Malleus my designer. It's so much fun working with you on these projects. A truly international team!

Thank you also to those who have already read and written such amazing reviews on Amazon for my debut novel *Cherry Picking*. I hope you love this book too!

Please connect to my Author page on Facebook:

www.facebook.com/TimHeathAuthor

Follow me on Twitter @TimHeathBooks

Chapter 1

Present Day

A high pitched noise broke through his thinking. Distant voices, though he couldn't make out any of it. He had no idea where he was. His head hurt. There was darkness but light, bright light, burst through his eyelids as he slowly opened them, blinking.

This seemed to draw attention to those nearby. The voices increased, in both volume and number. A blurred figure came over to him. A female. He could make out she was leaning over him a little, asking him something. He could see her lips moving, but nothing was making sense. Things went dark, his eyes heavy once more, the sounds drifted away. He was gone again.

The brief awakening had attracted some attention; a nurse came over to check his breathing. His eyes were still distant, as at other times. The frequency of arousings was now increasing, a sign that he would soon start coming around and would soon be able to talk. That would mean the dreams would start. And therefore the confusion too.

It was now late. Lights were on, fewer voices could be heard. People were not in so much of a hurry. Nothing made sense though. Everything felt fuzzy, even the sounds. The light broke in again, as his eyes opened. He saw the light bulb this time; for a moment it was clear, a crisp image. Then it was gone. The light hurt his head anyway, and it was now banging away again. There was movement somewhere, but he couldn't tell where. Someone was putting something metal down, the noise distorted by hitting something hard. An echo. A whistling. The light started spinning. His world started falling. He was now floating, now plunging, his body braced for impact, his legs hurting, his arms hurting. But nothing. He wasn't falling any more, but had not come to land. The light drifted away, the sounds fading slowly as he drifted off once again.

The nurse, Lorna, had seen him flinch as she moved the bedpan. As she turned to put it down, it slipped from her hands, crashing to the floor, rolling in a semi-circle around the end of the bed, before speeding up as it spun around quickly before coming to a stop, the sounds bouncing around the sparsely furnished room. She left the pan on the floor and turned to the patient. His body was starting to shake, his arms and legs flailing, his head rolling from side to side on the clinical white pillows. Then he went still. She checked the monitor quickly, the figures blinking away, reporting no serious change. But it would start soon. It wasn't long now. The eyes would blink rapidly and when that started, she'd have to sit with him, watch over him. Listen to him, and talk when she could. He'd be confused, they all were.

There was no leaving this man on his own, in case he woke up and talked and no one was there to listen. The camera mounted on the wall was recording everything, had been ever since he arrived two weeks ago. It was the procedure now. Everything recorded, everything noted, nothing to be missed. But they knew, from bitter experience, that left alone, the suffering was much worse. They'd risk losing him. That couldn't be allowed. He was far too valuable for that.

It was just after midnight when his eyes started blinking rapidly, so quickly to be done consciously. So quickly that it almost didn't look human. There was sweat now running down the patient's forehead. Drops of liquid fear, no doubt. His first images were coming. This would go on for about two weeks. At least that's what had been the plan with the others, give or take. But there was no telling really. The others had not made it. Left to themselves one way or the other, they'd died. This wouldn't happen this time. They understood now. They needed him. He needed them. He would not be left alone, not now. Not now they were starting.

Ten minutes later he awoke with a start. He sat up with a jolt, nearly sending Lorna flying backwards in fright. She'd forgotten that the first time it was like that. Calming herself, she remembered her training, she regained control, she sat waiting, watching, ready to help.

His eyes were open though he was not sure of what he was looking at or where he was. He turned his head to see the woman next to him, watching him, smiling. Smiling at him. He wanted to open his mouth, but words, he knew, could not come. The words were just not there for what he'd just seen, what he'd just experienced. So real, and yet it had been a dream, a premonition, maybe. Yes, a premonition, that was what it was. That's what it had said. The man in the vision. He'd said something about a premonition; the gift of prophecy. Was that it? Was that what had been said? He was not so sure now.

His mouth was open, but he could not find the words. Could not make himself talk. She kept smiling and then told him it was okay. He was safe now. Her voice sounded like that of an angel. Yet she had no wings. His head hurt, pain from something unknown at the back of his head now making itself known again. He wanted to reach back, to reach inside his head. To scrape the inside of his skull, to scrape that grey matter out, to throw the pain away, to bring relief to his head. He closed his eyes, the room spinning again, the feeling of falling. Falling through the sky, falling into nothing. There was no bottom, no end to the falling. Nothing to end his misery.

She jumped up quickly and grabbed his head, as she saw his eyes losing focus. She lowered his head onto the pillow again, making sure he was comfortable, pulling her hands out slowly from under his head, making sure she didn't touch the bandaged area at the base of the skull, just above the spinal cord. She stood next to him, just watching him; he looked so calm. She wondered what was going on, where he was now, what he was seeing.

The team watching the scene through the camera, reported the status of the patient. Reported that he was now showing signs. Reported all that was going on. This report would get flagged, would get passed on to people in suits, military types as well. Important people. People in a hurry, people under pressure.
The team watched with interest. What had been a rather dull few days was now going to get interesting. Everything needed to be recorded. Documented. Tracked and filed. Nothing could be left to chance, nothing missed. But they were prepared now. This time, they knew what to do.

Her patient stirred again, the eyes blinking, flickering, pulling her back into the room. She looked at the camera almost subconsciously; of course they were watching. She sat there waiting. Smiling.

He could hear some buzzing, but sounds were normal now. The light not so blinding. He emerged from his dreams like a swimmer arises from the warm tropical sea. Now he was awake. Eyes open. The room not currently spinning. The same woman still sitting there. Smiling, always smiling. He wanted to touch her, to see if she was real, but his arms would not move. He just couldn't lift them. What had happened to him? He focused on her, on the smile, that warm, inviting smile. Her eyes were blue, with a hint of green. Or was that just a reflection from somewhere? He opened his mouth. He felt dry, thirsty, for the first time in a long time. When had he last had a drink? These thoughts rushed in and didn't stay for long before the next one came in, pushing the previous ones out of the way. He could not get any answers.

And then the dream came back. The damage. The destruction. What had the man said in the dream? A premonition, or had he thought that? His mind was confused. The word Prophet bounced around his distant memory, but soon faded. He was struggling to focus now. He wanted to say something. He couldn't form any words, couldn't remember any words when he needed them. The only word was hello, and then a smile. 'Yes, let's smile back at the nice woman that is smiling at me.'

She said hello back, but he didn't hear the sound. He saw the lips, and was processing that when things went dark again. His bed opened its arms to pull him back inside, to swallow him once again. It wouldn't let him go. It wouldn't let him out of its reach. Not for now anyway.

Saying his first words was a big step. He was trusting her, he was aware of her. That was a good sign. It was nearly morning. She should be replaced soon, but she knew they wouldn't allow that now. Not with things still early on. He had to see her when he awoke, for the next few times anyway. To change now would only endanger things. She called for a coffee. This was going to be a long day so she might as well settle in for the long haul.

He saw a city, though wasn't sure he knew where. No, he hadn't been there. This was something different. He was aware of it all unfolding before him, before his eyes. In his head. A huge light appeared in the clouds. A fire. A great fire seemed to consume the sky. Now he saw buildings falling, buildings crashing to the ground. Bodies on the streets. People jumping from the higher floors. Smoke rising from lower floors. Smoke everywhere. Destruction, devastation, despair.

Things went black. That buzzing was back. That light, that smile as he opened his eyes. She was still watching him, sitting there. Attentive.

"Hello," he said, his voice sounding alive, sounding fresh and new.

"Hello, John," came the reply. That same soft voice. Those same gentle eyes.

"Where am I?" he asked, glad that the words seemed to be coming back to him.

"Don't you recognise it? You're in the hospital, John. You're in your room."

It made sense. Of course it did.

"Do you want to tell me about what you just dreamt?" she asked, always gentle, always suggestive, never demanding, never threatening. Always soft.

"What I dreamt?" he said, confused, and then it came back to him. The images. The sound. The smell. The fire, the sky of fire. The buildings. The bodies.

"I don't understand. It was a city. There was smoke and fire everywhere. Bodies. The sky, it was as if it was on fire. A giant fire across the sky."

"Do you know where you were?" she asked, but it didn't matter. It would just help him understand she was with him.

She was safe. He could talk with her. He needed to talk with her. To tell her all that he saw so that he could understand it all. Yes, he needed to talk to her, to unload. Maybe this stuff was important? Maybe he was seeing it for a reason? Yes, that is what that man had said, to tell what he saw. To share, to not hold anything back. To speak out what he was going to see. What he was going to experience. To reveal what was to come. To save everyone.

"I don't understand," he said, looking puzzled. He was starting to look troubled.

"It's okay, John. It's okay, you don't need to say now. You'll know more soon. We have time." She had to reassure him, had to calm him. Getting them frightened never helped and might even shut him down altogether. He was too early on with the visions. He needed to feel normal about it. Then he would understand more. To rush him now would not be good. It wouldn't be good for anyone.

It was dark now. John came round and initially couldn't see anything. He remembered where he was. That sinking feeling that tells you your real world is no better than the nightmare you have just awoken from. This time there'd been an air of death about things. A darkness that had been closing in when he once again came up from the depths and now found himself in his new reality, this hospital room that he had no memory of ever arriving in. And yet he knew he hadn't always been there. The shadows of a life once lived floated around his subconscious long enough for him to be aware of them, even if as yet he couldn't get to them.

Lorna, sitting in the corner quietly watching him as always, now made her presence known so that he knew she was there to talk to. To leave him alone might risk everything, though even now she saw John was stronger than the others had been. He was coping so far really well with what he was seeing. He was developing as they hoped he would. Time was against them, but wasn't it always?

The camera on the wall continued to record and document everything. The team monitoring John had grown steadily over the last few hours. Now it was standing room only in the office. The recordings were run through various computers. Each statement that came out of John's mouth was analysed by nearly a dozen different units. They were looking for weaknesses, signs, pointers. They were still learning what any of these looked like. This was just the third live case anyway. There was so much they didn't know. Too much it seemed.

Chapter 2

Present Day

John had not been awake for long before falling back to sleep. The drugs were doing their job. Lorna sat thinking about things. She too was starting to feel the hours now, the first signs of tiredness kicking in. With John now heavily sedated, she would be able to get at least a few hours' sleep. She needed it. They were moving into phase two and that was when things got really serious. She got up and, checking the monitor that hummed away in the corner, was happy with what she saw. John would be asleep for at least five hours. Then he'd have a very strong vision. She'd have to be with him for that. It was important that he talked about it. Important that he saw she was with him, listening to him, believing him.

Lorna glanced up at the watching camera.

"I'm taking four hours' sleep. He's out of it now. I gave him enough to get him easily through five hours. I will report in as soon as I'm back," and out she walked. They couldn't speak back to her anyway. Just watch and record.

At the end of the corridor, a room had been put together for staff members to sleep in. Lorna pulled the curtains shut and more tired than she had felt in months, she took off her shoes and just laid down on the bed, pulling the cover over herself, willing herself to fall asleep quickly, putting her thoughts, concerns and hurting heart to one side. She needed to sleep. She didn't know when her next chance would come. And she deeply needed a break from the burden of sorrow that was now sweeping through her once again, as it did when she got the odd minute to herself. Before too long, she was asleep.

John became aware of the bright light with a start.

He was still asleep. This vision felt different. It felt real. He turned his head. He was in a big room; the walls there somewhere, bright but he couldn't make them out. It was peaceful though. His body was not in pain.

Suddenly into the room came a man. The man seemed to glow, a radiance, but there was a warmth and safety about him. John turned to him and gave him his full attention. The man smiled in return. A gentle, inviting smile.

"Are you an angel?" John was almost too afraid to ask.

"No, I'm not." Still that warm, calm nature.

"Am I dead?"

"No, John, you certainly are not dead. You are very much alive. You have a great job to do."

At this point, John recalled the earlier visions he'd had, though none were quite like this one.

"Am I a prophet? Are you telling me what is to come?"

"You are the last chance, John. It's important that you share all you see. Talk to the nurse. Tell her everything. She will help you. She is your friend."

John thought about the always smiling face, the warmth in her voice. Yes, he would trust her and tell her everything.

"But I don't know anything. I've seen the fire. The destruction. The darkness closing in. But how am I meant to stop it? When does it happen?" John was not sure he wanted to know the answer. He knew he would have to do his part. That was how he was wired. He saw things through. He got the job done. He would do all he could. He knew his responsibility.

"All in good time, John. I can't tell you everything at once."

"Then who are you?" John asked.

"I'm a projection of your imagination. An image

your mind has chosen to display these messages. That's all."

It seemed the best answer to give at that stage. No use knowing what it really was. John seemed happy with this. He felt happy. It kind of made sense to him now. It was one of the few things that did.

The man walked over to a door on the far side. John followed. It all felt so natural, and yet, it was all so strange. Opening the door he walked through it and paused. John felt the chill of death before he was even through the door. Fires were still burning in the distance. A scene of total destruction lay between him and the fires. It was impossible to tell where this was or what great city this had clearly once been. He was certain it was no place he even wanted to be.

"What happens? When does this take place?" John asked, desperation now showing in his voice for the first time.

"Just watch and listen. Your next five visions are very important, John. You can save the lives of millions of people. You can do it, John, we know you can."

The scene before him started to shake, to become unstable. Like tiles falling from a bathroom wall, the scene of destruction, slowly at first, fell before his eyes until nothing was left but bright white light. Refocusing his eyes, he came to himself and recognised the same regulation hospital light hanging above him. He was back.

Lorna had managed to catch just over four hours of sleep when the alarm went, notifying her that her patient was showing signs of waking up. It was in those moments, anything from a few minutes to ten minutes, when the visions were at their clearest. At their strongest and most memorable.

She was back into his room before his eyes had opened, which they did after a couple of minutes of watching him. He seemed to be staring at the ceiling for a little while, fear and a lack of understanding showing on his face. Then he blinked, and his expression changed into one of calm. He was adjusting to this well. Lorna knew those who were watching would be very pleased indeed.

After a little silence, as if still taking in all that he had just seen, he turned his head a little towards her, though his movement was still limited somewhat by his injuries, of which he was as yet largely unaware. She intended to keep it that way.

She smiled at him. He seemed to return the smile for a moment as well. Getting up, she glanced at the monitors checking his vital signs. The drip hanging next to his bed supplied pain relief, amongst other things. She looked at the tubes going into his arm. It had been hard to get a vein at the first few attempts and his arm now showed evidence of this with extensive bruising on his right arm.

"That was something," John said, irony clear in his voice. It was really good that he had spoken first. Instead of shutting down or even denying what he was seeing, he was offering his willing help, involving her. This was a very encouraging sign. None of the others had been like this.

"Tell me what you saw this time, John," she said in reply, so warm and gentle, always inviting and never demanding. Just as she'd been so thoroughly trained to do the day she signed up for this.

"There was a man. I was in some kind of building, but I think that's not important. It might even have been just my mind. The man even said he was just my imagination projecting thoughts into a figure."

"Our minds are very powerful things." There seemed nothing more to comment.

"Anyway, I saw what once had been a city, I guess. It was destroyed now, but you could tell. The bricks and debris. The rooftops on the ground. Bits of cars everywhere. Smoke rising in little columns as far as I could see in every direction. I couldn't tell where it was. I asked when it happens, I remember that now. I didn't get an answer. But there was this overriding feeling. This sense. It was death, I felt it before I even walked out of the door. The darkness was pressing into that room before I laid eyes on anything." He paused.

"I'm scared you know. I don't know why I'm seeing this or where or even when it happens." Lorna just watched him, kept smiling, desperate not to let her own panic and feelings show. He had to go through with this. They needed him to understand.

The moment passed. John seemed to regain a little composure.

"But I must be seeing this for a reason. The man said I could save millions of people. That the next visions were important, that they were going to show me something I needed to see. Show me some way that I could help. I won't let you down. I'll tell you all I am told, all that I see. We'll get there, together. I don't want to do this alone."

Lorna wanted to cry, to shout, to scream. Her heart raced, her emotions flowed. This was a most encouraging step that John had taken. It made what he was about to see far more crucial. Maybe he would be able to do this. Hope started to fill her aching heart.

Chapter 3

Present Day

John found himself standing in the same large room and, as far as he could tell, he was on his own. He took a moment to take in where he was, the reality of it. The smells and sounds. He was aware that this was another vision, and it bothered him. He was still struggling to come to terms with all that was happening, let alone why it was happening to him. How could he possibly be able to help, other than tell some important people what was going to happen?

His own mood was about to change, fear waiting in the wings to come and steal any hope that might still be lingering. As if knowing this, the man appeared again from the shadows, the man John had been seeing in these visions.

"Hello again, John," he said, in a soft, almost fatherly tone.

"Hello." John thought of nothing better to say in response, and was now working hard at burying those thoughts and fears that moments before had been looking for a way in. He didn't want to let on what he was thinking, to tell this man, this stranger, that in fact he wasn't up to the task. That he couldn't do it. That he'd fail them if they carried on pushing him.

"Walk with me," he said to John, leading off to the side again, in the direction of the door that he had walked through last time, the sense of death still very fresh in his memory. He went through the same door he thought he'd walked through last time but it led instead to another large hall, an aircraft hanger. It had that same sense of death but it was less oppressive. Less aggressive, more normal, somehow. Having taken his eyes off the high ceiling where the light was brightest, he took in the floor and could soon see why that sense of death was still so evident. Covering the entire floor space were rows and rows of body bags. The black plastic was fresh, each one sealed, but it was clear what they were and what was inside each one. John looked up at his companion.

"Yes, John, a lot of people are going to die. This is nothing in comparison to who could die. Millions are at risk. And you can save them all."

John froze on the spot with that last sentence. His resolve kicked in again, bringing fresh life.

"How? How can I save them all?" John asked, his head turning, ears straining for anything that he could catch.

"You'll know soon enough," was all that came back in response. John knew better than to reply with another comment or argument. He wanted to drill the guy, to drain every last bit of information from him. He wanted to be told straight what he had to do, when and how. He wanted to be presented with all the facts so as to be able to make an informed decision. That was how he worked and what he most wanted. Not all this guessing. Not all this walking into strange rooms in strange visions, not knowing where he actually was, or when. But in himself he knew it would be pointless to press all this, to ask too many questions at this stage because he was barely dealing with what he was being told, let alone with anything extra.

Besides, he knew he was not really in control of the visions. These premonitions were driving him, he reminded himself.

"You're going to wake up now. Remember to tell the nurse all that you've seen. Don't leave out any details and don't forget to mention something that might be vital. You can trust her."

The room faded, John's vision vanishing and in a moment his own eyes were open. One blink and he went from there, wherever that was, to his hospital bed, which felt as safe a place as any the world had to offer at that moment.

Three Weeks Ago

James arrived home earlier than usual, dropping his bag in the hallway. It had been a tough day. Lorna was in the kitchen but came and greeted him, giving him a kiss on the cheek. Their eyes met but words were not spoken. There had been a silence growing over the last few weeks and she didn't know why. Clearly it was something to do with work or so she hoped. Better that than something more serious. She knew it wasn't another woman. She followed him into the kitchen, the kettle already on. He took time to wash his hands at the sink.

"Tough day?" Lorna said. It had been three minutes since he'd arrived home.

"Something like that," he said, a smile flashing across his face for a moment. He dried his hands on a towel.

When the water came to the boil, she poured two cups of tea and joined him in the lounge. The doors to the garden were open from earlier and James stood looking out before walking through them and going over to a flower bed. He pulled out three weeds.

Lorna placed his tea next to him but left him to it. She couldn't tell what was weed and what was meant to be there. Besides, he always did the garden when he needed time to think. She walked back into the lounge and sat down in her chair, a magazine open on the arm, but she just watched James for a moment. Something had been bothering him for a while and he clearly still didn't feel ready to talk about it with her. That realisation was starting to bother her.

It was the following morning and they both woke

with a start. Their pagers were bleeping, demanding as always their immediate attention. A large scale disaster was unfolding and they were being summoned. A van was on its way to pick them up.

Just one hour later they were both sitting in a army truck with three other passengers. None of them knew what was happening. James and the other three were to be taken to the main crash site, Lorna was to be flown by helicopter back to the hospital where she worked as the wounded were now being brought in and the existing staff were already being overwhelmed by the quantity and severity of their injuries.

"You are about to enter a military secure zone," the soldier shouted above the noise of the armour-plated vehicle that had transported James to the incident site, now being code named Point Zero. "When you get out," he continued, "you are to proceed directly to Major Jeffers in the main hangar that will be in front of you. Here, put on these now." He passed them each a set of chemical suits and the tense atmosphere that already existed got even more tense as each person put on the bright yellow outfits, the boots a few sizes too big but that was the least of James' concerns.

Moments later, the truck came to an abrupt stop and the rear door flew open, orders and noise and shouts filling the small cabin that they were sitting in, kicking them into life as one by one they exited the vehicle. They made their way, at speed, into the large aircraft hangar. The soldiers said something to a man inside before they ran over and turned a corner, disappearing out of sight.

James could now not see the other three, as his mask only allowed him to look straight ahead at the man he assumed was Major Jeffers, the guy the soldier had mentioned just a few minutes before. "Listen carefully," the Major started. "What you are about to be told his highly sensitive information. You are standing on one of the most top-secret RAF sites in the UK. At precisely zero-three-hundred hours this morning, we lost control of a nuclear-powered space probe which we have been testing in partnership with NASA. This was one of four state-of-the-art satellites that are currently orbiting the earth, eight-hundred miles above the atmosphere. We had just uploaded re-entry coordinates to bring it back to this very base. Twenty minutes after losing control, we lost all contact with the probe but had initiated evacuation procedures for everyone on the base. Only priority personnel remained. These include the small team of people responsible for the whole program. They are the only ones keeping the other three satellites in orbit at the moment. The program, shall we say, is far from being bug free." He took a sip of water from the glass that sat on the small lectern style piece of furniture to his right. "Precisely one hour after losing control, the probe crashed to earth right here on the base. It's taken out half of the buildings and is dangerously unstable. We are in contact with the control team but are unable to reach them due to the possible risk of fallout. The collision has put a large split in the main reactor." He paused, as all of those listening looked up at this last piece of information. This was news to everyone in the hanger for there was no public knowledge of this facility having a nuclear reactor. "Needless to say," he finished calmly, "we have a major containment issue on our hands. There is the risk of this getting totally out of control. We can't afford any mistakes with this one."

Lorna was lost in her thoughts since arriving back at work following the helicopter trip to the helipad above the A&E department. The past thirty minutes had exposed her to the worst kinds of injuries she'd ever witnessed in her whole career: severe radiation burns on the sick and dying, and these were just the ones that had lived long enough to make it to the hospital. She was unprepared for it, as were all the staff at the now overstretched hospital. Men, women and children of all ages. Face, legs, torso; there seemed no part where people were not affected. Four people had already died since she arrived. Several more were likely to at any point. Lorna walked around in a daze. Trying to save life was in her blood but most were too badly injured to be saved. Thirty minutes later she was outside, desperately in need of some air, tears running down her face, as deep waves of grief flooded her one after the other.

James had been at Point Zero for an hour when the sirens rang out and an evacuation was ordered. With the chemical suits on and the noise from all around them so deafening, it was impossible to hear the sirens, and James would have been unaware had it not been for the orange light that flashed as well, its piercing spinning glow illuminating the dark corner he was searching for survivors in. He signalled to the other man near him to leave and went off to look for the third person in their party, who was at that moment on the other side of the building.

Major Jeffers met the first guy as he came running out.
"Where are the other two of you?" the Major barked back, not looking at all impressed. He pushed the man in the right direction, sending him on his way and looked up as a giant fireball engulfed the sky, another huge explosion on a site that could bear little more. The building shook and flames leapt across the roof as the explosion intensified into a raging, angry, fire. This was followed by another explosion, this one at ground level. The south wall began to collapse as the Major ran back for cover, narrowly missing roof debris that came crashing down. It didn't matter. Seconds later the first nuclear reactor blew and

obliterated an area the size of a football field on which it was housed. There was very little left of the building James had been in. Smoke was pouring from the debris now lying on the ground, as unseen fires burned. Those that had somehow survived the explosion were at that moment being exposed to extreme levels of radiation poisoning, their fate sealed.

Lorna was ordered into her managers' office as soon as news reached them about the explosion at the RAF base. Her boss's superior was also there. They only got together like this when the news was bad, usually a terminal condition to report to a patient, but anything was possible now.

Over the next five minutes they shared the news Lorna had been dreading. That there had been a serious incident at Point Zero, that one of the main nuclear reactors had exploded and how it had obliterated its surrounding area. They shared how her husband was unaccounted for but as far as they were aware, he had been in the main hangar which had been completely destroyed and was dangerously close to the radiation leak. They shared how the Major, and one of James' party members had been reportedly seen dead, lying on the ground about one hundred metres in front of the fallen building.

"I'm so sorry to be the one sharing this news with you," her manager said.

Tears filled Lorna's eyes. Her James was dead and it felt, in that moment, as if her world had stopped. Nothing seemed to mean as much any more.

Her manager, Alison, touched her gently on the arm and continued.

"There is more, Lorna. The control room for the remaining nuclear probes currently orbiting the earth was also dangerously exposed to lethel levels of radiation. No one but one man made it out alive, and he is in a bad way, though somehow still alive."

Lorna was hearing this but not really taking it in. Why did it matter now, and why were they telling her all this? All she wanted to do was to go and find her husband's body, to be alone, to mourn his death. And her manager could see that in her face too.

"Look, Lorna, take a few moments to pull things together. But we need to talk some more. This is an ongoing crisis and we need every skilled hand that we have. God knows we're going to need it before the day is out. Go get some fresh air. Then come back when you are ready; you have one hour."

Lorna wanted to tell her to shove the job but she did need the fresh air. Suddenly the walls were closing in on her and for a moment she thought she was going to fall, but putting a hand out and touching the wall, she made it along the white walled corridor and out the main doors.

Thick black smoke could be seen on the horizon. She walked the other way, great soundless sobs now coming from her body, as wave upon wave of emotion flooded out of her in an uncontrollable way. She sat on the ground, on a soft patch of grass still wet with dew, and cried her heart out. James was dead. And it hurt. Hurt more than anything she had ever known. A piece of her was now missing, gone. Lost. Would she ever feel complete again?

Back at Point Zero, the RAF base was in total lock down. The full sense of what was happening was beginning to dawn on a watching world, and that day the number of press helicopters and crew was noticeably less. They were starting to understand the danger they were being exposed to. Four reporters had already been killed, dozens more exposed to levels of contamination that would kill them before the month was out. It was all one big mess.

On the far side of the base, over the airfields and about a mile and a half from the incident area, which so far was in the opposite wind direction, stood the main hangar. The offices here stood to serve as the new mobile command centre. The bodies were already beginning to appear on the hangar floor, one hundred so far and counting, men and women, husbands and wives, sons and daughters. Soldiers and pilots. Good people. Alive no more.

It was about an hour after the latest blast that the trucks started turning up from the nearby villages that sat downwind from the RAF base. Three villages in particular had been badly affected. Most of those that had not heard the news and got out quickly, were now dead or dying from radiation poisoning. Some trucks were taking the wounded to the hospital, though many were dead before they arrived. The dead were being brought to the hangar. It seemed the best place to contain the news and fallout.

The scale of the incident was so overwhelming and so many people had been affected that even the Major Incident plan could not be activated. By the end of the day the news was clear to everyone. Row after row of body bags filled the huge hangar. Those camera crews still alive knew that nuclear exposure had been dangerously high already and they carried on regardless, working to record and document what was happening, wanting their last days to mean something, knowing a painful death awaited them shortly. The same went for most of the soldiers and pilots still around. Exposure would kill them sooner or later, but they carried on serving, regardless of the personal cost. The scale of the damage just meant there was nothing else they could do.

The footage of a hangar full of body bags was headline news around the world. Death on a catastrophic level and this was just the start.

Lorna had gone back to her manager's office, as

requested, but in truth she had nowhere else she wanted to be, or could go. The hospital was overstretched already. They needed her, and at that moment, she needed them. The pain of her own loss was very real but in the heat of battle, as her nursing had now become, she could lose herself enough to forget about her own problems, before a pause in the action brought the emotions all flooding back and she'd have to compose herself all over again.

And so she sat there and waited. Alison was busy on the telephone, intrigue in her voice. Putting the phone down, she looked up at Lorna.

"They're bringing someone in who was right in the middle of it all. They say he's in remarkable health."

Lorna didn't know what to say. She'd seen the injuries to the bodies of the victims already here. They'd probably seen as many already die as those they'd managed to make a little more comfortable, but even that was just postponing the inevitable. Quite how someone who was in the middle of it could still be alive, she didn't know. Nor did she dare to think about the extent of his remarkable health.

As with Chernobyl, the effects would surely be felt for years to come, touching the generations of as yet unborn children with all sorts of horrendous side effects.

"Lorna, I know this is a terrible time for you with the news about your husband...."

Lorna looked up at her. Alison trailed off for a moment, not sure how she was meant to finish that sentence, before starting another on a different tack. "We really need your skills, Lorna. To say that we are overstretched would be an understatement. I need to get on with this incoming patient. I've been ordered to give him priority for some reason. They say he is one of the scientists behind the probes. We'll put him in isolation, so it'll take me out of things for a while. I'll need your experience here, Lorna, to cover me while I'm away.

Things will get a lot worse before they get better. Most of the nurses out there are under-trained and under-prepared. They need guidance. You are not the only one whose lost someone today. James was a good man......I'm sorry for your loss."

With that, she headed for the door and was down the corridor before Lorna could mutter a response, not that anything was coming to mind anyway. She let her training kick in, going out of the same door but the other way down the corridor. She picked up the first clip board she found and scanned through the notes of the patient in the bed in front of her, before walking on to the next, having a word with a young nurse in the process, trying to do her best, trying to do something. Trying to save lives.

Lincoln Knowles was the name of the man who was pulled alive out of the control room at Point Zero. He was thirty-eight, slightly overweight, typical of someone his age in a desk job like his. He wasn't particularly active now, but was in reasonable health before the incident. As far as he knew, no one he had worked with had survived. Most were killed in the seconds after the explosion. Somehow, he had survived that and the following hours. Somehow, he was breathing as they brought him into the isolation wing of the main hospital. An eager crew of doctors and nurses waited for him, masks on, protective suits in place, but his radiation output was very low. That part was still a mystery to them all.

Alison Hesse was in charge of Lincoln's care; she was Lorna's manager. Still single and with her parents retired and living in the US, as far as she could tell, she had not lost anyone close to her in this tragedy. That made it easier for her to be professional about it all, and coupled with her experience and senior position, made her the prime candidate to oversee the care and monitoring of Lincoln. This most unusual but vitally important patient was now in her sole care.

He came in confused. Most of the incident had been blocked from his memory. This was not too uncommon in such cases of extreme emotional trauma. He did know his colleagues were dead. Somehow he'd retained that one strain of memory, but aside from that fact, the incident itself was a blank. Everything from that day had gone from his short-term memory. It was unclear at this point whether he would ever get it back.

That was the least of their worries. Keeping him alive was, though it was true that his own body had done a great job of that so far regarding the radiation at least. Because even though the two people sitting either side of him in his particular office had both died very quickly from the explosion and the radiation, Lincoln, though exposed to the same levels, had remained largely unaffected. The test results, which were now starting to come back, reported much the same. Granted, he had some issues. Some internal bleeding. Some burns to the skin. He might not hear out of his left ear again due to a perforated eardrum. His right shoulder was broken after he was hit by falling materials when the building collapsed. But given that he was exposed to an extreme nuclear explosion, the fact that there was anything left at all was a miracle.

Two hours later, when it was discovered that his injuries consisted entirely of physical ones caused by things hitting him or fire, but no evidence at all of any radiation damage, the mood turned from fear to astonishment, and the protective clothing could be removed as he was not a threat to them any more.

Present Day

John had been awake for some time and had told Lorna everything he had seen in his latest vision. He was sitting up sometimes now, though his wounds were still making that difficult. He had taken a little food as well, the first since he'd come in a few days before. That was a good sign, though he hadn't enjoyed the taste of the food nor did it sit well inside him now. He mentioned this to Lorna and she gave him something to drink.

"Tell me, are you happily married?" he said. Lorna almost dropped the glass of water which she had taken back from John after he'd finished with it. He noticed her reaction.

"Forgive me, I didn't mean to pry. It's just you wear that beautiful ring that catches the light so often and the wedding ring next to it, yet you seem so sad. There is sorrow in your eyes. And I know I'm not so unwell that it's concern for me. So I was wondering if everything was okay?"

She smiled at him, just briefly, for his concern for her.

"Everything is wonderful," she lied. Or at least it had been the last time she was at home. She smiled her fake smile to John but that deep knot in her soul quickly wiped the smile from her face, which John noticed but didn't comment on. He could tell something was wrong. It was starting to worry him.

"Look," she said, her tone changed and her lets-get-on-with-it attitude restored. "You need to focus on getting better."

"I still do not know what these visions mean."

"I'm sure it will become clear soon, John. This is happening to you for a reason, so I'd say go with it and know that I'm here for you every time you wake up."

"Yes, thanks. Don't you need somewhere to sleep, or have a home to go back to?"

"That's quite enough talk about me," she said a little too sharply. She caught herself. "Don't worry, I'll rest when you do, and I'm working a long shift so that's why I'm here all the time. I'll get to go home soon, we just need to see some improvements first."

"Look, I didn't mean to be nosey, its just I have no one to talk to. I woke up in some hospital, my body all smashed up but I've no memory of what happened to me. And one more thing, why has no one come to visit me? Was I really the sort of person that no one wants to see?" He stopped himself. Those thoughts had been fighting for air in his subconscious but had now been voiced for the first time.

"Look, John, it's nothing like that. Your family and friends are just away at the moment. We are trying to get hold of them." That wasn't in fact true. They had yet to be informed that he had even survived, and with so much death being reported and the images now being shown on news channels around the world, it was easily assumed he was dead. Him and the thousands of others.

One Month Ago

As Lincoln Knowles drove in to work that morning, the sun was just breaking through the early morning clouds, on what the forecasters predicted would be a clear, fine day. On this particular day, to Lincoln and his colleagues, the weather meant everything.

Twelve years of research, more than half a million combined lab hours and billions of dollars of UK and US investment had preceded this day. The joint initiative with NASA had been the single biggest project ever undertaken by the Royal Air Force. Its future depended on this project producing results and leading, they hoped, to many more collaborations. The International Atomic Energy Agency had been left out of the deal entirely, so that the UK would be the ones to benefit most from the results.

They knew there would be risks involved from the very outset of the giant project. It was such new, uncharted territory. But with the Russians and the European Space Agency getting wind of the possible deal, and then the Chinese too coming looking, the British had moved quickly to tie up the deal with the Americans, much to the dismay, and calls of betrayal, by the struggling ESA.

On the surface of things, that was mostly just water under the bridge, as Lincoln cleared security and proceeded up the main approach on the base. They'd needed to call in the ESA for some specific small scale projects, and Russian technology had also been needed when issues arose about three years before with some of the launch equipment.

As Lincoln parked up and got out of the car, he walked towards the main doors. Two soldiers were stationed either side, and without moving from their posts, they'd checked him out, confirmed his ID and let him walk right past. Only a select few had such privilege. He worked in a medium-sized side office with two others; a man named Robert Quinn, mid-forties, who was moody and kept himself to himself, but was very good at what he did. Also with them was Eleanor Jones, who at twenty-eight was the youngest by far, but managed to hold her own, most of the time.

As Lincoln came in and put his coat on the hook, the other two were already at their desks, Eleanor finishing an apple while reading through some report, large numbers of crisp A4 paper scattered all over her never tidy desk. Robert was tapping away at the computer, the Met Office page showing detailed weather conditions for the next twelve hours on one of his screens, the next five days on another. Neither particularly acknowledged his presence but they knew he was there. Besides working together for the best part of the last decade, none of them really had much else in common. It was a set-up that worked well for them. They enjoyed what they did and got the job done. They produced results and they got very well paid in the process. It was win win.

And in just over five hours, they were launching the first of four state of the art nuclear powered probes that would put the British and Americans way ahead of the rest in defence and surveillance technology.

Lincoln had barely sat down when there was a slight tap at the door as Major Jeffers came walking in. At sixty-three he'd been eligible for retirement for a few years already, but this was to be his legacy. He was determined to see it through and then he could retire a contented man. At five foot eight, what he lacked in height he more than made up for in authority. No one crossed the Major and still had their job the following day. But it was his larger-than-life character that really won people over, and he was highly respected around the base.

He'd taken up a training post, on his way to becoming a Major, a year before Afghanistan, though he'd seen that conflict coming, and the subsequent one in Iraq, long before it was public news.

"Good morning, Major," Lincoln said, turning and standing to greet his friend. They didn't really work in the same fields; Lincoln's was the science and research area, the Major was the RAF base and military side. But this project had brought them together, and there was now a mutual respect for one another.

"Good morning to you, Lincoln. I'm not a scientist, but you don't need to be one to see that it looks clear out there for launch day." He had a smile on his face.

"We look at a little more than the clouds, but yes, we are go for take-off, Major."

"Jolly good!" he said. He then turned, and was off. There seemed no reason to delay them any further and really the Major was just passing the time, increasingly nervous. There was little he could really do about things now. That responsibility was with Lincoln and his team and the teams that were situated in the other offices that were located on that part of the base, away from cameras and watching eyes, kept secret from a world that really didn't need to know too much. And one of the biggest secrets of the last decade was finally about to be launched. There was a real buzz in the air on the base at that moment.

Twenty seconds after noon on that clear Monday lunchtime, the first probe successfully launched, was racing up through the sky. At about half the size of a standard Mini car, and weighing about the same, what the probes lacked in size they more than made up for in power. Their nuclear potential was by far the most anyone had ever produced, and safely up in space, it was assumed their risk would be minimal. Over the next twelve hours the other three would be launched. Each one had its own unique orbit that consisted of anywhere up to thirty-seven loops of the Earth before it repeated the pattern again. Once launched, the four probes would work together, mapping the planet in a whole new way, but controlled centrally from the base-camp computer. It was a technological first, a piece of future-proof machinery that could adapt and develop with breakthroughs on Earth. A triple blend of nuclear science, NASA experience and British engineering.

At half past one the probe entered into its consistent orbit pattern and its feedback showed all systems were functioning well. It was then locked into the computer's mainframe, which acted as its invisible anchor point.

Everybody celebrated the news. High-fives erupted around the office and the press releases were being given one final read through, though they wouldn't be sent until tomorrow, when the final probe had been launched. They were highly censored anyway, reporting the main points but obviously leaving the details lite.

Lincoln left the office for some fresh air. It had gone two and he was hungry, having been locked away indoors for too long, only now appreciating the fine weather for himself.

The Major came walking over to him, also noticeably more relaxed.

"A hell of a job you all did there, if I do say so myself."

"Thanks, Major. Believe me, we are thrilled to have finally reached this stage. It's a huge boost for the UK today."

"Yes, indeed. Well, I won't keep you. I'll come back for the other three when it's time." With that, the Major shook Lincoln's hand and walked away. There were four hour intervals between each of the launches, so it meant there was still around two hours left before the second of the four probes was being sent into orbit. Lincoln hoped to catch a little sleep before then, so ten minutes after going outside, a sandwich and banana successfully devoured, he made his way back in. Finding a quiet corner in a dark room, he lay down for his routine twenty minute power nap.

It had been several hours since the final probe had been launched, all four now locked into position, and the early signs were very promising. The global mapping process was about to take place. It was half past three in the morning. Lincoln lay sleeping on the sofa in the break-out area, a random room put together some years back to give the personnel somewhere to sit in comfort, unwind, talk but mainly sleep.

"Lincoln, wake up," came the call, as someone was shaking him by the shoulder. Lincoln stirred and within a moment was wide awake, a habit all light sleepers pick up only too easily. He could tell by the expression on the face of this young assistant that something was wrong.

"It's the first probe. It's stopped responding," he said. Lincoln jumped up, and having fallen asleep in his uniform, walked straight out of the door and into the main control room, which was directly connected to his office.

Most people were there, moving around frantically or just staring at a computer screen. He could see Robert and Eleanor in the office. Major Jeffers walked over to Lincoln as soon as he appeared.

"They say we've lost contact with one of the probes," the Major said, repeating the only piece of information that Lincoln had been told for certain so far.

Lincoln took in the screens: the monitors recording the feedback, the maps that were tracking the orbits, the latest readings before they lost the signal. None of it added up.

Lincoln put his arm on the shoulder of the Major in a supportive way.

"We'll get to the bottom of this, Major."

"Then what are you waiting for? We have a lot riding on this, you know!"

Lincoln knew that only too well. He walked quickly into his office which was alive with activity. Not looking up but knowing Lincoln was in the room, Robert said from his desk:

"The first probe took itself offline about twenty minutes ago. The other three are still responding and everything is reading normally. We've recorded a deceleration in its airspeed over the last ten minutes."

"It's slowing down?" Lincoln questioned.

"It would appear so, yes."

Eleanor spoke up at that moment.

"I'm looking into the processing side, working with the last recorded readouts from the probe prior to losing control of it. I want to make sure it's not a programming issue." That had been largely her responsibility. It was therefore unlikely to be the case. She carried on typing away, her keyboard speed rivalling that of any touch-typists at over eighty words a minute.

It was going to be a long day.

Chapter 4

Present Day

Lorna sat down in the new look hospital canteen, with a tray of food she probably wouldn't eat and a cup of coffee, if you could call it that, warming her hands. She took a sip and turned her nose up at it as she lowered it back to the table. At least it kept her hands warm.

She had not eaten in a long time, had been working for hours, and yet nothing appealed to her. She felt emotionally spent. It seemed as if she would soon lose the ability to feel anything. Still, she figured, maybe that was better than feeling all the hurt and sorrow that could otherwise overwhelm her.

People were coming and going around her. Two people came and sat down at the spare seats on her table. They didn't say anything. She didn't mind. Their old canteen had been reassigned to accommodate more people, using old military hospital beds. Lorna was doubtful that she had ever been in this room before. It now more resembled a fast food restaurant than it did a quiet and sedate hospital canteen. How things had changed over the last few days.

Lorna let those happy thoughts come in for just a moment. Memories of walking hand in hand with James. The cobbled streets of the Old Town in Tallinn. The medieval cafés and bookshops. The six hundred year old chemist that they'd come across, with an array of dried animal parts that sat in glass jars; ranging from whole hedgehogs and dried toads, to deer penis. They'd laughed so much in that little chemist that day. It was a very odd assortment but such a fond memory. Just another memory. And then came that point of remembrance once again. James was gone. The knot in her stomach twisted and tugged as if to drag her from that happy place she'd been in just moments before. It would not allow her to be happy for long. The pain felt so intense once again.

She got up, not that those on her table really noticed, anyway. Her place was filled before she'd got to the door as the crowds pressed into an area a quarter of the size it should have been.

To Lorna the loss of James felt such a waste. She was aware that he had died doing what he enjoyed doing. He was great at his job and really cared for others. And even though she felt selfish for thinking it, she now wished he hadn't been a man that cared for others as much as he did. He'd died for others and yet it was not them that was hurting, it was her. They'd sacrificed so much of their own happiness for others, that now Lorna was wondering if it had all been worth it.

Had she known the last time she saw him that there would be no more times, she would not have left him. She would have told him how she felt, how she loved him.

Tears were now running down her face again. She didn't mind that others were looking. She wasn't the only nurse crying that day either. She knew life would never be the same again, and that was only too evident from the activity at the hospital that day. What she didn't know yet was the true extent of the disaster. And it was a race against time.

Three Weeks Ago

The main hangar stood eerily quiet on a day that had seen so much death. The body bags filled the giant floor space. With a change in staff and the sheer number of inbound deliveries, the count had been abandoned somewhere around three thousand. It would be confirmed later that there were in fact three times that number at that point.

It would take weeks to fully process all that had

already happened. Months to repair the damage. And years before the legacy would stop claiming lives.

Felix May was a middle grade officer who had just weeks to live. He had been on the other side of the base, running an errand, when the explosion happened that had killed his whole unit. He'd been working almost non-stop since then.

Felix was a bright lad, university educated, a doctor in physics. He'd pursued that path, and the girl he loved, into a bright career. After two years, when it was clear the girl wasn't interested, the career lost interest too, and to the surprise of all at the time, Felix suddenly quit and took a job in the RAF.

His potential had been seen early on, and the Major had him earmarked for big things in the future. He was made an officer and was popular among the guys.

As he stood silently in the hangar at the end of that day, the cameras gone, the trucks now stopped, he looked out upon the rows of body bags. The trucks would be back tomorrow, he was sure. Space was running out.

In his growing role within the RAF, he'd been heading up a team working on a programme that could help pilots who were suffering with a range of post-war syndromes. They'd just been getting to understand the Gulf War issues when he'd joined at twenty five.

Some of his patients came in with little memory of the incident they were struggling to come to terms with. His experiments helped to understand that these were the easiest type to deal with. Memory blackout allowed them to reprogram the mind to anything they wanted, within a strict code of practice that had been cleared at the highest levels with direct intervention from the Prime Minister. It was highly sensitive research and one of the RAF's best kept secrets, along with the true nature of its space probes project.

It was later that night, hearing news about the rising

death toll, and the projections of even worse to come, that Felix first started thinking about making a revised program.

Present Day

John opened his eyes and found himself in a bright room, the walls white, light everywhere. It was hurting his eyes. He was standing up. He put his arms up to his face to shield it. Things didn't hurt any more. This told him, as if he needed the confirmation, that this was another vision.

From the left a figure slowly emerged through the brightness. The man came over to John and smiled.

"Hello, John. My name is Felix. And it's my job to tell you everything that you need to do and the reason why you are seeing these visions."

John fixed him with an intent gaze. There was something different about the figure standing just three feet in front of him. Was it the same guy as before? He wasn't sure nor had he the time to process that. The conversation continued:

"Okay, I'm ready for that now, I think."

"Yes, you are. That's why you've been selected."

John thought about it for just a moment. To be selected means to have been actively chosen for something, him over someone else. Him over everyone, for all he knew. And if there was a selection then someone, or something, was doing the selecting. That thought actually scared him for a moment.

Up until the visions started, John had not been a religious man.

"Walk with me, will you," Felix said.

They walked into the light, towards the walls, but they were actually bright windows, sunlight and floodlights pouring in. John could feel the heat from the lights. He didn't say anything about it. He just followed.

"You have a gift, John. Something you were born

with and didn't know. Something that has kept you alive for this very reason. Something that will save millions of people."

John realised the visions were special and unusual, but to hear them called a gift made him feel an increased level of pride in himself, as if it was all somehow his doing. He ignored the fact that a gift always come from someone else anyway, otherwise it couldn't be called a gift.

"How will I save these people? I really don't know what it is I am to do."

"You will, John, very soon. You will know what it is you need to do and you will do it, because the fate of all those you know and love, and millions of others, rests on your ability to do what you need to do, to do what you must do in order to save these people. What I want to know, John, is, when the time comes, do you have it in you to save these people?"

How was he supposed to answer that question? There was much he was yet to know.

"I will be," he determined. Clearly these visions were coming to him for some reason, some higher purpose that he was yet to be made aware of, but which, he was convincing himself, was all now happening for a grand plan.

"Good, John. You have it in you. You just don't know that yet. But it's been in you for a long time, and is about to make itself known. We are having this conversation because of that fact. You have nothing to worry about. You'll be a hero."

A hero. He'd never been called that before. Far from it. He was the man who got his head down and got on with it. He didn't go looking for fights. He didn't want to win medals or trophies. There were no prizes on display at his home. He was no one's hero. Yet what Felix was saying now had him floating as if he was ten feet tall. Maybe this was his moment? Maybe this was why his life had been so ordinary up to that point. So normal. So boring.

Now that he let himself believe it, he knew he was made for higher things, for greater things. And if he really had it in his power to do this, to save all these people, millions of unknown strangers, then he was game. He'd do it. He was all in.

"Tell me everything I need to do," John said, turning to Felix. Felix smiled, and putting his arm around his shoulders, walked him out through a door into the light.

The sunlight was starting to fade now, but the floodlights were still giving out their full power. Felix and John had been walking and talking for quite a while.

"I'll do it," John finally said. Felix stood there in silence.

Felix had been explaining what would be needed and how the millions would be saved. For this to happen one person would need to sacrifice their own life, to make the ultimate sacrifice and give himself to save the rest. Unless this was done, everyone would perish. There would be no future for anyone.

John was still a little unsure of the specifics, but having been told plainly and matter-of-factly, it finally gave him a handle on things, and an understanding as to why this was happening. He was still unsure when this would happen. But his mind had been made up. He'd taken just moments to process it all.

A large part of him wanted to be the hero. Finally he'd get to be the one others talked about, others praised, others noticed. No longer the quiet guy who kept himself to himself. No longer the last one to be picked for the sports team. This was his moment, his world. Time to be a hero at last. Time to be who he was really made to be.

"I'll do it."

John awoke with a start. Sweat was running down his right cheek from his forehead. Lorna came rushing over to him and with a gentle touch, damp cloth in hand, wiped his face. It felt cool and refreshing.

Nothing like how he was now feeling inside. Focusing clearly again, he looked at Lorna. She herself was starting to feel real concern for her patient.

"I know what I have to do now, Lorna."

She lowered her head a little but then recollected herself and caught his eye once again, eye contact being so important for communicating trust and relationship.

"I'm going to have to die."

She knew it already, but hearing him say it so plainly, little emotion if any in his voice, caused her stomach to turn. Steadying herself, she composed her feelings and responded:

"What do you mean?"

"The man in the vision said that millions would die. He said that I could save them. That it would cost me my life but I could save them through this. He said that I would die anyway if I didn't. He said I was born to do this. And you know what, I feel that now. I still don't know when this will be. And I don't know how I can have a normal life after all this, knowing that one day I will be called to do this. But I'm ready. I'd do it today if it meant being the hero for once."

She took in the way he said that last bit. There was pride in his teary eyes. There was passion. This meant the world to her. Lorna didn't know what to say. She didn't know how to respond. This moment had been everything she had been trained for and everything they were hoping. And yet now it felt wrong. It felt like they were cheating him. Giving him only half the story. She wanted to say something, to tell him what she knew. She wanted to stop what she'd been part of starting. But something in her was stopping her from doing that. Maybe it was the loss of her husband. Maybe it was wanting an end to all the suffering and death. She knew if John didn't do what he needed to do, then what they'd seen up to now would be nothing compared to what would be. What would certainly happen. And that thought alone was enough to keep her from saying anything, even though the reality of her actions now would haunt her for the rest of her life. There had been some who had questioned tricking anyone into anything. Their views had been drowned out by those saying this program gave them a guarantee. End of story.

"You are a hero already, John. I'm glad it's all beginning to make some sense."

She passed him a drink and then placed a tray of food next to him on the table, without saying anything else, and then quickly walked out of the room. Tears were running down her face before she was even through the door and into the corridor. She kept going, looking for somewhere quiet to hide for a moment. Anywhere would have done.

Three Weeks Ago

Lincoln's last recorded status had been stable. His wounds hadn't really had too much time to heal before he was brought into the program that Felix had adapted and put into operation. As his nurse, Alison was not too impressed.

It was getting late in the afternoon when Lincoln had his first vision. He woke with a start, causing Alison to stumble in fright. It was like a corpse rising from the dead. Fear gripped Lincoln's face. Huge beads of sweat sat on his forehead, kept in place by the large wrinkles that were there, a combination of middle age and excess weight.

Alison comforted him, laid him back down, and seeing his eyes were processing and working through what he'd just seen, went to the door where a nurse awaited her.

"We have another one coming in, similar to your patient. No obvious signs of serious injury. They want you to check him over."

Alison glanced back at Lincoln, who while still looking shocked, was at least lying down and seemed to be doing okay.

"Okay, show me the way," she said, following the other nurse down a corridor to another room where the latest patient had just been brought into.

There was blood all over his face, and his shirt was heavily stained. Two nurses were cutting away his clothes to get a better look at him. An open break in his leg would need some work. There were fire burns to his back, but like Lincoln, there were no obvious signs of radiation burns.

As the activity in the room continued, Alison's beeper that all nurses wore around their waist started vibrating away. It notified her that there was a serious change to her patient. She ran back down the corridor to investigate.

She could hear the heart monitor before she got to the room. Two other nurses were also racing in as she got to Lincoln. There was a flat rate on the heart monitor showing no pulse. One nurse was bringing over the ECG, both pads now placed on Lincoln's chest.

"Stand clear," Alison called as the first shock was administered. Plenty more followed, and then Alison took over, doing CPR.

By now the room was filling up. Her manager was also in, a surgeon herself, coming over to check the patient. Still there was no response. They continued for twenty minutes.

"Call it," came the instruction from her manager.

Alison looked up in disbelief. She continued on a little, pressing harder with her hands, pleading for life to return, for his heart to start again. Willing him back to life.

The instruction was repeated, louder this time, and an arm placed on her shoulder, pulling her away from her patient.

"Time of death," she started, reluctantly, then looked up at the clock on the wall, "five fifteen."

She took off her gloves and threw them into the bin. She went to the far wall and pressed against it, arms above her head, unsure of what had just happened. Her manager took charge of the room.

"Take the body to be examined. We need to know what went wrong, why and fast. Alison, come with me."

With that she left the room. They were already starting to wheel the bed out of the room. The machine and wires and tubes, disconnected from the patient, were left hanging. Alison came away from the wall, taking one last look at Lincoln, who now seemed at peace, and went off in search of her manager.

It was only after the second patient died, also from a heart attack, that they understood. In the seconds and minutes after waking up from the vision, there was greatly increased brain activity. This was causing the body to generate huge amounts of adrenaline. This in turn resulted in the heart rate rapidly increasing, leading to cardiac arrest, the heart attacks that killed both the patients.

With two bodies in the hospital morgue, it was easier to see what they had in common, in order to work out what made them special.

Alison was quietly removed from the program. She had been solely responsible for two valuable patients whose conditions had suddenly changed; Lincoln being left in his room alone while he had his fatal heart attack. She'd been made the scapegoat and was angry at being the obvious easy target, but threw herself into the care of the hundreds of other patients they had. Lorna was called into the programme as they rapidly built up a new team.

She spent the next day in intensive training, being

told everything they had learned up to that point, going over all the readouts, looking at how the other two patients had reacted.

It was decided that a constant presence was essential, and Lorna needed no training in this area, as her bedside manner was second to none. She felt it was strange, being taken from hands on work when nurses were already short, and far too overstretched, but she kept her thoughts to herself. She had been made aware of what had happened with her manager Alison.

It was at the end of Lorna's day of special training that news came in about another survivor being pulled from the rubble. It was a reporter, whose whole team had been killed. All of them were in very close proximity to the blast, being situated just a few hundred metres downwind from the main nuclear reactor. They'd all been exposed to lethal levels of nuclear radiation, and all had died, but one.

Because of the location of the damaged news van, it had taken days to get that near, and as the chemically suited clean up crew made a check on the van, body bags at the ready, they were shocked to find one of the guys still breathing. Lacking food and water, and physically thrown about as their van was smashed and flipped by the explosion, he was in a bad way. Quite broken but, amazingly, alive.

An hour after being pulled carefully from the crushed van, John was being wheeled into his own room, Lorna checking the vital signs of her new patient, who remained unconscious.

A crew of two mechanics worked at fitting a camera high up on the far wall, the latest plan to try to record and monitor what was happening to their most prized patient. John would be watched closely by a team of military personnel who were overseeing this project and keeping a watchful eye on everything, and everyone, involved.

Lorna read through her notes once more. It had been the fourth time she'd read them that day. With her patient completely unconscious, there seemed little else to do.

Three Weeks Ago

"I don't understand it," Robert said, charging from their small office, Eleanor barely raising her head. She, meanwhile, continued to work the screens, pulling data and monitoring the situation with all her usual grace and brilliance. The RAF had been very fortunate to have secured her services, their offer coming at a time when she was being head-hunted by some of the largest business empires on the planet.

Robert walked up to Lincoln who was looking at the main output screen, standing there silently, as if words had no way of expressing fully what was now going on internally. He was terrified. His own career aside, this had been a flagship British project and trillions had been invested already, a fact little known by the general public but now sure to get out if anything went wrong. And it had gone badly wrong. The self shut-down of the probe while set in its orbit had been a major failing of its on-board system command. There was, it had been thought, no scope within the system hard drive to have acted like this. It was as if it was creating its own commands and following its own orders. That, they knew, was impossible. And yet, from what they were reading on the many screens, they still had no idea what had in fact taken place.

It was early afternoon on that same day, the day after the initial launches, when the rest of the satellites went offline and then each started slowing down. The original probe was at this point starting to re-enter the earth's atmosphere. There was now a gallant effort to regain control. However, their efforts were fruitless. The base was put on high alert and all non-essential personnel were evacuated, which was still only about a third of the people. Being a closed circuit nuclear probe, there was no real fear of the reactor detonating on impact, but they were taking no chances. What they didn't know was that the malfunction, as yet undiagnosed, had in fact engaged the nuclear reactor, making it in essence a falling nuclear bomb. This would be discovered too late to save anyone.

By half past two the probe had entered European airspace, on its locked-in coordinates that would bring it back to the very base where the concept was first conceived and from which it had been launched just seven days before. It was never designed to return to Earth. There was about thirty minutes left before impact, its re-entry doing very little to slow its speed or change its trajectory.

It was only in the final two minutes, as everyone waited silently, literally holding their breath, that the true extent of the imminent disaster was known. Just ninety seconds before impact, stunning the watching crowd, a message appeared on their main terminal, the last communication they had from the probe – it simply declared:

"THIS WAS NO ACCIDENT - GOODBYE..."

A cry went up, people started running, desperate for a way out, though they had no chance. Significantly, no one reported the message. It would die with them.

The probe impacted the ground just a few metres from where it was launched, in the centre of the base. A small explosion shook the ground, and for a couple of seconds there was nothing, before the nuclear core detonated, the immediate area obliterated as a mushroom cloud rose in the afternoon sky, it's ominous image captured and beamed around the world.

Chapter 5

Present Day

John opened his eyes and found himself hovering over the ground, flying as it were. He was having another vision. As far as he could tell, he was alone. His view was locked onto the ground; it was a scene of destruction. Trees were scorched, blackened and dead looking, some broken in two, as if just tossed aside by some giant force moving through.

Now cars were visible; crushed and twisted, the roads they had been driving on hardly visible under the layers of debris that sat on top. Maybe there was going to be a tremendous storm, the thought flashed through John's mind, but didn't stay for long.

Through the smoke, its dense cloud making visibility very difficult, he caught a brief glimpse of a snake-like river running down below, and froze at the realisation:

"This is London," he said aloud to himself, "I'm looking at London!" The panic was short lived. Up above, to the right of the window he was looking out of, a large ball of fire came into view, dissecting the sky at an alarming angle, showing no sign of stopping, and in what seemed like seconds came crashing down into the smoke and destruction below. A bright flash broke through the smoke clouds, the force of it such that he felt the place he was sitting in shake. Then a mushroom cloud arose in the distance, and his world tumbled, spinning around and around, falling to the ground, heading into the destruction. He closed his eyes, this was becoming too real.

In those final seconds, knowing he was about to wake up, he determined to remember it all, though what he saw was hardly something he could forget. London, destroyed below him, smoke everywhere, and then a nuclear explosion.

He drifted off to sleep at that moment, as the images in his head were meeting the ground, and there was stillness and darkness. Nothing happened for an age, it seemed.

He felt his heart racing, then calming. His hearing came back, his eyes beginning to open. He was back in the hospital room.

Three Weeks Ago

News from London was going all around the world. All flights were cancelled, not that anyone dared to venture to this radioactive disaster zone.

Various news teams were still trying to record the events and an American crew were scanning the city from a four person helicopter.

The scene below them was carnage. The first explosion had destroyed a small area and smoke was pushing up. The camera on the helicopter was beaming live images to its news show, which was being relayed around the world. London had taken a serious blow.

The pilot navigated as best he could, keeping high and away from the huge columns of black/grey smoke billowing in their direction.

The Thames came into sight briefly, its curves and turns picking up reflections of nearby fires burning, and a few boats were seen floating by.

One of the news crew suddenly spotted something in the sky, and directed the cameraman to the fireball that was appearing from the right. Although it was a little restricted by the helicopter's fairly small windows, the camera caught the object descending, as an eerie quiet fell upon the crew. Seconds later, after the object had dropped from view, there was a blinding flash of light, the force of it shaking the helicopter as it hovered there in the sky.

Warning buttons started sounding all over the dashboard and the pilot had to fight hard to keep control. The cameraman picked out, to everyone's horror, a giant mushroom cloud appearing on the horizon. Just moments later, the full force now engulfing them, the helicopter was thrown about violently, the pilot being slammed hard against the control column, losing consciousness. Then the helicopter plunged head first towards the ground.

The last thing the cameraman was able to do, was to point the camera to the ground, so the camera recorded through the front window of the helicopter the approaching ground, and then there was nothing.

The helicopter exploded and the blades were thrown at high speed in different directions, smashing into burning buildings, adding to the carnage.

Felix had been watching the television whilst editing some clips when the news helicopter had crashed. He was one of the millions of people shocked and alarmed by what he was seeing. The screen went blank for a while, before returning to a silent and subdued studio. The two news anchors were lost for words before regaining some sort of composure.

Felix quickly stopped what he was doing and went to work on the most recent footage. He put together the two minute clip in no time, as the helicopter covered the city, then the river, then the flash and explosion.

Felix hoped it would really feel like his patient was flying. Seeing everything that the camera saw, as if with your own eyes, there would be no understanding of what was actually going on.

Felix finished by adding the special touches that he hoped would bring an element of consistency to all the images, these visions that he was putting together, this program he was perfecting.

Running back through it about half an hour after

first seeing it, he was most impressed at his own handiwork. He did a little more editing on it, taking out small bits of detail that might make it look obvious, and ran the final version through once more, just to be sure, before saving it, labelling it clearly, and inserting it carefully into its correct position in the final program.

Felix checked his watch. It said that it was nearly six, though you wouldn't have known that from outside. The smoke and clouds made it much darker than it was, giving everything a night time feel.

His own health was starting to worsen. For him it was now a race against time to get things working; testing, he hoped, could start tomorrow. He'd certainly be around for that. He just wasn't now certain of how much longer he'd be around after tomorrow. Pushing that thought from his mind, knowing it wasn't doing him any good, he returned to what he had been doing before the latest interruption. He'd work as late as he could, before tiredness would get the better of him.

Present Day

John lay awake and conscious on his bed, though Lorna was not initially aware of it as she prepared some fresh sheets and tidied away some of the things that had been brought into his room. As she moved freely, with her guard down, John spotted something in her, something like a deep sadness, and was watching her intently when she spotted he was awake and returned the gaze. Her automatic smile took up its station on her face once again, but what he'd just seen in her eyes, told him a whole lot about the reality of her own personal situation. It was still a mystery to John, but with only Lorna for company, he hoped he'd get the chance to get to the bottom off it.

"How are you feeling, John," she said, trying to shake off the fact he'd been watching her, and sensing he'd probably already read through her obvious disguise.

"I'm doing as well as can be expected, right?" It wasn't really a question and she didn't give him an answer. She instead smiled away, turning slightly as if to continue her needless work, before saying:

"Is there anything I can get you, John?"

He shook his head. What he wanted to know was why was she so sad. Was it his condition, though he felt he was improving all the time? There was certainly something she was hiding from him, and it was obvious now in everything about her; the way she hung her shoulders, the way her body frame seemed to be deflated, as if the life was being drained out of her.

She carried on with what she was doing, but her heart really wasn't in it. What she wanted to do was talk, talk to anybody, but right now talk with John. She wanted to pour out her heart and how she was hurting inside. She wanted to tell him that she didn't want to be there with him. She wanted to tell him all that, and yet that would mean telling him stuff he wasn't yet meant to know.

But what was reality now, anyway? She'd not asked herself about the morality of what she was involved in, she had just followed orders. Still, she was acting under her own control, choosing to use her skill and training to bring something good out of it all. And she'd convinced herself, nearly anyway, that it was a numbers issue and not a point of moral truth. One life for the lives of millions. And yet in all those millions her James was still gone. After it all, if they were even successful, she was still alone. She stopped herself. She hadn't thought of herself as alone at all until that moment. How could she return home and live in the same house? She would be expecting James to put his key in the lock and walk in at any moment. Thoughts were racing in and out in a random fashion. She was just standing there, looking at nothing in particular, when John's voice pulled her back to reality.

"I said, are you really okay? You've been standing there for twenty seconds just refolding that same sheet over and over."

Momentarily embarrassed, she turned and faced John. Changing the subject, as she was now in the habit of doing, she said:

"You need some more medicine. Lets see if I can find a vein, shall I?"

"Look, you can talk to me if you want, you know. I'm a great listener. I mean, lying here, what else can I do?" He laughed, which brought a small smile to her face.

"I'm sure you are, John. I'm sure you are. But you need your rest and must keep your strength up. You don't need me unloading my issues on you, that's for sure."

"I don't know, try me," he said, but it was clear he wasn't going to have any luck, this time. She rolled up the sleeve of his right arm and tapped it with her two fingers, before rubbing a small amount of local anaesthetic on it and then slowly injected him with the latest cocktail of drugs he was being required to take. They would, amongst other things, help reduce the stress on the heart and the overload of brain activity during the visions, which would greatly reduce the risk of a heart attack.

"Look, John, you get some rest now and we can chat when you wake up, okay?"

"Okay, if that's what you want," he said, as the drugs were already getting into his blood system. His eyes felt heavy as the room went dark, the sounds fading as he dropped off once again into his drug induced state of unconsciousness.

Three Weeks Ago

Felix had seen enough of death. His cough was also getting worse. He was under no illusion that his life too had been affected and that he had days, at most, left. It made every hour all the more important. He had to complete the program and get it operational. There might still be a chance that it would help. And besides, he had to do something with his remaining time.

The reality of his situation actually made it a lot easier to proceed. The thought of future ethics committees and court cases held no threat, as he knew he would never be around to face them. It meant he could focus on the pure science of it, a rare opportunity for someone in his field of operation, and he was not wasting any time.

Most of the program had already been written in draft form, though with a very different purpose in mind. Felix had already collected as much material as he could – much taken from the hours of television exposure the disaster had had from around the world. Where those cameras had no access, he'd added his own footage with a simple enough hand-held camera, recording the bodies, the burning, the destruction and death of anything previously living. He had used this footage to create a backdrop in the program, and once uploaded onto the main computer, hoped he would be able to create walk through scenes with these very images.

Present Day

With her patient asleep, Lorna had taken a long walk around the grounds of the facility she was working in, taking in the small pockets of nature that still remained. Nearly all the trees had gone now, but a few smaller ones retained some form of life.

She hadn't been able to really process everything that had happened to her over the last few days and she knew that there wouldn't be a chance now either. If she really walked that path, she did not know if there would be any way back. It was a door she really didn't want to open for fear of it being more than she could bear. It certainly felt like it would be. In her unconscious thoughts, she knew there lurked a monster of hurt, rage and bitterness that she had so far subdued, or more to the point, ignored.

She had always wondered how people dealt with the death of a loved one, having been faced with it many times with her patients, and those left behind. Now she was certain she didn't really want to know. Work gave her the perfect excuse, but it was more than that. This was survival. Not just herself, but for the nation and millions of others affected by this catastrophe. There was so much going on inside the walls of the hospital, that for once she really didn't know what would happen. Humanity, or more to the point, humanity closest to her, was caught up in the same battle to survive, to live, to come out of this thing still intact. And deep inside, she knew that if there was a chance this world would survive, then she would survive it too. She determined that her survival was now intertwined with the rest of the world. If the ship was going down, then she'd go down fighting; but if they were to survive, she was determined that she'd be there with them, not a victim, but a survivor. A winner. The lucky ones that get to see the sunrise after the storm of the night before. The Lorna of one month ago was gone. If she was to come through this, and really come through it, she'd have to adapt, have to change, have to fight. In the natural world they say only the strongest survive; so she would have to be the strongest. To allow her emotions to control her, or distract her, let alone hurt her, was just now, not an option. In those few minutes of walking, thinking, and peeping through that door in her soul, she made up her mind to be stronger, to bury those thoughts and hurts, to lose them and forget them if possible, and then to do what she needed to do. If that was to follow orders, she'd do it. If that was to cause others hurt for the greater good, she'd do it. If it was to let someone die, she'd do it.

Head down and with a speed and purpose to her

walk, she returned to work, in through the main doors, but she was returning as a very different person. The crowded waiting area was full of people, some already checked in, others just waiting. But these were no longer patients – these were victims. They were all victims. And together, they would fight to survive.

Three Weeks Ago

Felix had been working for seven hours straight, unaware that it had been that long, but he'd been left unnoticed and unchallenged. People just didn't know how to deal with the clear-up, let alone ask what he was doing. Many of the first body bags were now starting to be removed, for fear of health issues, and also the need to create more space. The clean-up was greatly hindered by the lack of numbers. Outsiders were now not allowed, and not willing, to come onto the site as authorities started to implement disaster management plans, in limited places, still overwhelmed by it all. The radiation in places was still high, and the risk of further explosions was very high. Those that were helping, the people located on so far unaffected parts of the base, were now starting to show signs of extreme, and fatal, radiation poisoning. Just two days after the initial explosion, there was less than half the manpower there had been. Most were now sick, a small number had fled, but that would not save them, even if they avoided the usual army discipline. They would all be dead in a matter of weeks, if not days. It was not as if breathing fresh, clean, countryside air would be enough. They'd already ingested lethal amounts of poison, alien to the body and killing it one cell at a time.

Felix knew all about the reality of his situation, and if anything, it gave him a certain kind of freedom. Decisions were easier to make when you didn't have to question yourself, or think about the effect on others.

You've just got 'to do'. His involvement in the project in the past had given him a high level of understanding, and his science background gave him a natural interest in what was possible with the human body, and with the mind in general.

After a quick break, where he grabbed some food and a drink of something that slightly resembled coffee, he was back at the controls. The program was largely finished, but now needed testing. He'd been able to use the pre-programmed avatar to do much of the dialogue, but needed to himself record the specific parts that would result in the actual conversation element, dropping the thoughts into the mind. He was still as yet unsure exactly how to play this part, but wanted to test a few options and see what the effects looked like. He was eager to get on with testing and implementation. There was still a long way to go.

Chapter 6

Present Day

John had been awake for about ten minutes and had been discussing in detail with Lorna all that he'd seen in the latest vision.

It had really frightened him. Up to that point, he hadn't been able to work out where this was going to happen. Now knowing it was his own capital city made it all too real.

He was struggling to come to terms with the magnitude of it all.

They'd sat in silence for about three minutes, Lorna keeping herself busy, doing nothing in particular, but waiting for John to continue talking. In the long silences, of which there had been many, she had learned that it was best for him to speak first. She had no idea what it was all doing to him on the inside. That didn't matter, she reminded herself for the hundredth time that day. This is what needed to happen. It didn't matter what he was thinking, he'd soon get through it, soon understand, or more to the point, would soon understand it from his limited point of view. He'd been taken to a place and had no way of knowing it was anything but what it seemed.

"Tell me about your husband," John said, breaking the silence finally and catching Lorna in her thoughts. His eyes fixed on her, willing her to talk about herself a little, searching for some other connection point other than these visions he was seeing.

She moved her hair from her face with her hand, pushing it behind her right ear. It was a habit that occured when she felt unsure of what to say.

"His name is James and we met when we were studying. He's a doctor. He loved to help people. We spent time in Mexico during university. Such fond memories. He was such a good man." She caught herself, realising her mistake and turned away automatically, tears building in her eyes.

"Did something happen to James?" he asked, picking up on the words, processing their application, and any significance they had to him.

"I really can't.....I really don't want to talk about it," she said, holding back tears as best she could.

'Can't or won't' raced through John's mind, but he didn't let it out. 'What is she not telling me?'

Lorna felt she'd said too much already. It made her uneasy, uncertain of what she should let on and what not.

"You don't have to tell me anything if you don't want to. I didn't mean to pry. I'm sorry," he said.

"Don't be silly. It isn't your fault. It's just....complicated."

Three Weeks Ago

The bodies of the first two survivors had been under intensive study for the past day. Foreign contaminants were found to be extensively in their bodies following the explosions and subsequent radiation poisoning. This, mixed with the high adrenaline levels, had magnified the effect and caused the fatal heart attacks. The cause of death had been no great mystery, but everything needed to be recorded and monitored, all information being kept and analysed in depth. What intrigued them most, was why either of them had survived at all in the first place, a fate not shared by anyone else in their situation, besides John, who was only the third known survivor, and the only one still alive. Tests were being carried out on different parts of the corpses, tissue samples being sent to various labs, small teams of scientists mapping the DNA codes, looking for clues, looking for an explanation that for twenty-four hours, had so far eluded them.

To help the heart, they had been using beta-blockers, a commonly used drug to reduce adrenaline levels. John was being closely monitored, and the signs were good. But if they could get a match from these two dead bodies, something connecting them, protecting them, then they could run the test on John and confirm that it existed in him, too.

Something inside these two men had shielded them from the poisoning, a unique and as yet unknown protection. Was it just chance? Some right place, right time scenario that had, in some way, allowed them to live through it. With one survivor, you can allow that in your thinking, even if the odds are millions to one. In human history, as far as they knew, there had not been many precedents set. But with three initial survivors, the probabilities were impossible to calculate and they were searching for some medical, physiological reason. There had to be a scientific solution, an answer for it all, and that was what the small team were diligently, and painstakingly, looking for.

Present Day

John came around, fresh from another vision, to find Lorna sitting there, studying him, waiting. There was something different about her face, so much so that initially, as he started coming round, before he could see clearly, he had thought it was someone else. Her eyes looked changed, somehow, it was just the smile, for the most part, that told him it was Lorna. He was happy it was not someone else, but there was slight fear there at the obvious change that had taken place from the woman he'd last seen.

"How are you, John?" she asked, with noticeable concern in her voice.

"I'm good. I had another vision. Felix, that's the

name of the man I see, showed me more things that will happen. There is so much death, Lorna. I still don't know when this is, but I saw what I think is this hospital."

"You did, did you?" Lorna said with genuine surprise. She had no idea what the program really showed.

They talked freely for about twenty minutes. Lorna was totally engaged in the conversation, her focus never taken from him. John found this strange at first but began to enjoy this new side to her, and relaxed as he spoke, Lorna asking the occasional thing, but he was mainly doing the talking. And it felt really good to talk, to share with her. He knew, from the first moment he had awoken from the first vision, that this was not something he could handle on his own. What helped massively was that she believed him and encouraged him to share. He wondered, at times, if there had been others like him that most people thought were just crazy. People who talked of hearing voices in their heads and having conversations about things that had not happened. What if there had been more like him? Others that did not get listened to, others thought crazy and locked away, others with different pieces to the puzzle, different information that might be vital in order to piece together everything that was about to happen.

As their conversation drew to a close after thirty minutes, he came back to these thoughts. 'What if I am crazy' he thought, dwelling on it for a moment. 'Lorna would have been instructed to listen to everything I told her – and to just smile'. He thought how there seemed to be no other nurses or patients around, how he hadn't actually left the bed, let alone the room. The camera on the wall could clearly have been for security – her security if he turned on her.

Mulling it over a little, he let it drop. It was a door he didn't want to open, for fear of what he might find. And besides, he was in hospital for a reason, even though at that moment he had no recollection of ever arriving, or why he was there, besides the obvious fact he was seeing these visions. These thoughts were now something that troubled him a little, as it became clear to him that there was much more he wasn't being told about his situation. At that moment Lorna came back in from the doorway, though she had never been far from him at all.

"Tell me, am I crazy?" he said, catching her attention.

"No, John, you are far from crazy," she said very calmly, as if it was a silly thought. John didn't want to let it drop.

"Then, why am I here, I mean, why am I in this hospital?"

"Because of your injuries, John."

Of course, that made a bit of sense. Something had happened to him and he knew his head hurt. He hadn't got off his back since he'd been there.

"Can I walk?" It seemed a strange thing for John to suddenly ask, but he clearly wanted to talk. "And why can't I remember anything about what happened to me?"

"John," she said, ever so motherly, "you were in a serious accident and your body has blocked it from your mind. It's perfectly normal for that to happen. Our brains are very complex things. And yes, in time, you will certainly be able to walk again, you just need to recover and get plenty of rest."

He smiled at her. She seemed to be telling the truth, and he saw no reason why she'd have to lie to him, apart from telling him he wasn't crazy. He figured no one would ever really answer that with a 'yes' to a patient if they really were crazy. To do that really would be crazy.

Three Months Ago

James awoke before dawn, though a street lamp gave some light into their room. Lorna was working nights, which was fast becoming the norm, so he was able to turn on the bedroom light without disturbing anyone. They were both working more and more hours with schedules that didn't often complement each other.

After a quick cup of tea, James pulled on his jacket, over his jeans and black polo shirt and slipped out of the front door. His car was parked in front of the house and he was away, off down the road before anyone could have seen him. There was no one around at that time of the morning anyway.

Forty minutes later, the sun still not fully risen, he pulled up to the security gates at the RAF base, two armed guards watching him come to a halt, the taller of the two walking over slowly to him, a sub-machine gun hanging loosely around his waist. James was not a stranger to the base. As one of only three registered doctors used by the forces in the area, he was occasionally called to the site, but wasn't there too often. One of his senior colleagues was generally on duty there, but had been taken ill about a month ago, so his responsibilities had been shared between the other two. James was therefore given more work to fit into his already demanding week. This was his fourth visit to the base that month.

His documents were checked, but it was just a formality. The soldier standing next to his red Mazda recognised him the moment he pulled up.

They exchanged a few words, but James did not want to hang around for too long. Not today. Moments later, the gates swung open and he drove along slowly, careful to keep to the five miles per hour speed limit in force on the base. He didn't need any unwanted attention that morning.

He pulled up and parked about fifty metres from the main doors. Two further armed guards stood there. He'd seen very few people going in and out of those doors.

Opening up a bag on the passenger seat next to him,

he pulled out a camera, the type used by newspaper photographers, its long silver lens making it hard to steady at first, but he soon got it balanced. He took three snaps, unsure whether the camera had actually taken anything until he spotted the digital display still showing his last photo.

He didn't feel comfortable doing any of this.

He saw the Major coming from a building on the far side, talking with an aide as they made their way, slowly, to the main building that he was watching. His car was one of about forty that were parked there. He was quite sure he was relatively hidden, but wasn't going to take any chances. He snapped away again, another two shots: the Major at the doors, entering the building, the aide turning back and heading the way he'd just come.

He sat there another ten minutes but no one else showed. He was starting to think about leaving when two more cars came through the main gates. He watched them carefully in his rear view mirror. They parked about ten cars down from him, so that they wouldn't have known he was in the car. Two people got out: a man whom he guessed was in his early forties, and a woman who was much younger, maybe late twenties. They clearly knew each other and walked together to the security guarded doors that the Major had just gone through. Snap, snap, snap. James took some more photos and watched them through the camera. The guards hardly moved as they opened the doors and waved them both through.

He sat there a further half an hour but there was no more movement. It was approaching eight, the news was just starting on the radio, and James decided he didn't want to stay any longer. Turning up the radio, he started the engine, and proceeded back up the road, through the security gates and was into the morning traffic, heading to a café about four miles from there. It was time for breakfast.

Three Weeks Ago

After much study, the test results had come back on the two bodies that had now been lying in the hospital morgue for nearly forty-eight hours. Due to some rare chemical make-up, each body had been protecting itself from the nuclear radiation by shielding itself with white blood cells and a chemical deposit, which was as yet unidentified. It was nothing like anything they had ever seen before. It would prove impossible to replicate.

But now that they knew what to look for, it was a simple procedure to confirm that John, their latest patient to come through the ordeal alive, also had this bizarre genetic mutation in his system. This Mysterious Chemical Presence (MCP), as they had coded it, was responsible for keeping each man alive, at least at first. As far as they could tell, the MCP absorbed the radiation on contact, sucking it in at molecular level, and breaking it down, with part of the poison left harmlessly stored in the host body, the rest leaked as an odourless gas through the skin. They'd not been able to see this in practice, but it was their best guessed theory at that stage.

Three Months Ago

James pulled up at the café and parked in the car park. There were not many cars around, which was not unusual for the place. It was midweek and early, but they did a good breakfast and it was nowhere near home. He didn't want there to be the chance that anyone would see the meeting he was about to have.

The man was waiting for him when he walked in and James made his way over to join him. This was only the third time they'd met, and he still did not know his name. It was to remain that way. They shook hands warmly enough, though they were not friends. James handed him back his camera bag and the man took a quick scan of the camera, looking through the dozen or so photos that were on the memory card.

"Must you look at them here?" James said, his head looking around, though no one was nearby. He grabbed a menu and looked through the various dishes available to him. A pot of tea sat on the table, his companion already halfway through his first cup.

The man put the camera away again.

"These are good, thank you," he said, looking up at James as he finished with the menu, replacing it on the table. He knocked over the pepper pot, a small pile of brown dust escaping onto the table.

"I don't like doing this. If I get caught, I'm finished," James said nervously.

"Relax, you are not in any danger," came the reply. James didn't believe it, jumping up to go and place his order at the counter. He paid with cash, and came and sat back down. They didn't say another word to each other for five minutes, the man opposite him drinking his tea, before pouring himself another one. James' food arrived, a full English breakfast, minus the egg. He'd never got on too well with eggs. The landlord then came back with his coffee and milk, before leaving them both in peace.

James took a bite of a sausage and had some bacon. He poured milk into his coffee and took a sip. Everything was being done very deliberately, as if every movement was being monitored.

"So, who were in the photos today then?" James asked finally, wanting to break the growingly awkward silence.

"First in was the Major, as you've seen before. He's the highest ranked person on the RAF side there. In these photos," he said, showing the display to James of the man and woman seen entering, "the guy is a scientist, they both are actually. Non RAF personnel but they've been on the base for months. His name is Lincoln Knowles. The chick is Eleanor Jones, very bright girl."

What he hadn't said was the fact he'd met Eleanor before, and they'd dated, on and off, for about six months. Staying there one night, he'd got wind of something, as only a reporter could, and had dug around the flat a bit, but there was very little there. He'd allowed the relationship to go on longer than he'd wanted, though he enjoyed the sex. He'd done some digging and soon got wind of her secretive placement at the RAF base. She had never discussed it with him, though he'd often asked about what she did and her vague answers only left him more intrigued.

They both sat eating their breakfast, the one man watching James while James himself was more aware of who was or wasn't in the café watching him.

Chapter 7

Present Day

Lorna had felt terrible within herself all morning. She'd stonewalled her patient when all he was doing was try to talk with her and help. Besides, the connection would be stronger if she opened up, and most importantly of all, she really needed someone to talk to.

John was finishing breakfast when she came over closer to him and pulled up a chair next to the bed. She took the tray away from him, a bowl and cup stacked neatly in the middle. There was something very organised and orderly about John. She liked it.

"Look," she started to say, not really sure of the words she should best use to describe what had happened, "James died recently. My husband died..." and she broke off, though there were no tears at that moment. They would come soon enough, she knew.

John closed his eyes as if reliving all the things he'd said and asked about, feeling like a fool now for prying on what was this widow's hurting heart.

"I'm so sorry to hear that," he said, eyes opened again looking for her eyes. She caught his glance but couldn't keep it.

"There was an accident. He got trapped somewhere he really shouldn't have been. He was there helping people. He's a doctor, but I think I told you that already." She had, but he wasn't going to comment. Instead he sat there quietly. Now it was his turn to do the listening, to be the listener. She'd been so helpful with everything that was happening to him, though all that, for the moment, was far from his mind.

"He'd made me breakfast before work on the day he died. It's really my final memory of James." She said his name so gently, as if handling a baby, as she trailed off, before coming back into the room, and the conversation. Talking was doing her some good. She felt some of the great weight inside shifting. Maybe some healing would come by sharing her hurts with someone and, at that moment in her now strange world, John was the closest person to her.

"We were happy, really. There was something bothering him at work, I think. But we were happy, we enjoyed each others company. I just had no idea that that morning would be the last time I saw him alive." She paused, already at risk of saying too much. There was still a lot at stake, and she wouldn't be allowed to jeopardise it all, aware that this conversation was no doubt being listened to intently and every word and phrase analysed. She had no way of knowing how close they actually were. Would there be a knock at the door and a bunch of angry suits? Would the army come and arrest her for some hideous crime she knew nothing about. The fear of the unknown kept her boxed in. She didn't want to knowingly overstep the mark.

"We'd had some great times together, some great trips. Central America had been a highlight, as well as cruising around the Caribbean in our own boat."

John saw life in her eyes, a sparkle, that hadn't been there since he'd first seen her. All too quickly it faded, as he guessed the reality of her loss hit her hard once again.

"Anyway, now you know. If I'm honest with you, I've been completely knocked sideways."

It was obvious enough to him, but he smiled and kept eye contact, which she was now a bit better at returning. There seemed a familiarity to her, but he couldn't put his finger on what it was. It also led him to ask something else that was now bothering him, having heard her speak so well of memories and highlights from her life.

"Thanks for sharing that, it couldn't have been easy. Can I ask something totally unrelated?" She nodded, tears fighting to come through, the emotional tidal wave now catching up with the words she'd just spoken.

"As you were talking about those memories, the sights and sounds, the feel of the place. It made me realise I have no sense of that for my own life. I can't remember anything." He paused briefly, before asking his next question. "Will I get my memory back?"

She took a moment before speaking, composing herself as her emotions still battled inside her.

"We think yes, in time, you will begin to regain your memory. When people undergo some traumatic ordeal or situation, the brain acts to protect us, and shuts down."

"What happened to me then? What put me here?"

"I can't say, because then, in the future, you will be unsure whether you remember it yourself, which would be a sign that your memory was returning, or because I've told you, and you've taken that knowledge and made it feel like an actual memory."

It wasn't totally true. They, of course, had no intention of telling him what had really happened to him. The incident part anyway, because of the drugs that were being fed to him, would be permanently forgotten, as his memories of everything surrounding the actual disaster were being erased. But her explanation satisfied John, and he shut his eyes briefly, nodding to confirm his understanding. A wave of tiredness was kicking in. His sleeping patterns were totally messed up and, with no natural light, his body was genuinely confused as to what was day and what was night. Lorna got up from her chair, putting it back against the wall. John closed his eyes again and was soon asleep.

Three Weeks Ago

Felix awoke suddenly from a deep sleep, having

worked late into the night. He'd fallen asleep at his desk and had somehow knocked over a coffee cup during that time, leaving a small stain on some papers, but it was long dry and wasn't anything serious. Light was coming in from outside and, before checking his watch, which said it was already past eight, he could tell it was morning time. He'd had about five hours of sleep.

He stood to stretch, coughing suddenly as he did, his hand automatically covering his mouth. It passed, but then he noticed blood on his hand, not a lot, but enough to remind him of his fate. It was sealed, there was no undoing it. If anything, it focused him all the more on what still needed to be done.

Before finishing last night, he'd uploaded the files onto the main computer and left it running. Going over to the machine now, he could see it had completed. Some testing would be needed, but he'd already done a little on himself, and it was certainly a very surreal experience. He'd messed with drugs when he was younger, and the trips he used to take then had nothing on these visions. The vision that followed felt one hundred times more vivid as there was no sensory input to give him conflicting information about the test he was running.

Felix was well aware that the nuclear reactors on the base had a safety shut off facility, a last resort kind of action, but they were already way past that point. So far beyond it, it seemed impossible to somehow now get to that safety switch and contain the problem. It would take quite something to do that, and he'd need resources. He also knew his program now had the capability to train such a person, should that opportunity arise. He'd heard whispers of the rumours from Russia and Japan about the 'walking dead', people that had some how survived, as if protected from the poison. For Felix this was a golden opportunity to put it all to the test. He had to be ready if that opportunity presented itself and he needed the backing of those above him. He'd written to them the night before, telling them what he was capable of doing, and asking for support and clearance at the highest level.

That morning, however, as he checked the computer, a vague but clear refusal had come back. It annoyed Felix. They were struggling to catch up, he knew. They were fearful. There must have been mayhem going on at HQ, jobs on the line, the government about to fall for having got it so wrong with these probes.

Felix knew they couldn't see it as he saw it, sitting in their safe leather seats miles away, no doubt flown to the other end of the country to avoid being caught up in this mess. They were short sighted. It was obvious to him, at least, that this was going to get a lot worse before it got better. It would be an ongoing nuclear disaster unless someone could do something, but that something was an impossible task, unless of course, you could survive radiation poisoning. And within half a mile, Felix was sure such a person existed. He was a numbers man. He'd done the maths. More people had been exposed in London than had been in Russia and Japan combined. If those incidents had produced freak survivors, then the numbers were good that the same would be true here.

Felix knew he was going to die very soon. That part was sinking in. It also made it easier to do what he wanted, what he knew needed to be done. He would never have to answer for his actions, whatever happened. That would, at worst, be someone else's issue. But there was more. He knew there was a way through, he'd seen it the moment he'd started putting the program together. He knew what he had to do. And if some suit in government couldn't see what he saw, then he'd have to show them. He'd have to prove the point. Some folks, he told himself, can only see something when it's right in front of their faces, so he was going to have to do just that. Opening up the rejection letter that he'd received, he ran it through another program, taking the header and signature, and simply altering the wording such, that once finished, it was a fully supportive authorisation letter from the very top itself, demanding full compliance with Felix's master program, giving him any resources and personnel that he required. However, he would never get the chance to use it, nor needed to. But it felt good to have it, just in case. Today was going to be a great day. He could hardly wait.

Three Months Ago

It had been two days since the breakfast meeting, but James was going to meet the man once again, though he was unhappy about it. This time they were due to meet late morning, in a small village about three miles from where the café was.

James walked into the small coffee shop, a bell ringing as the door opened and then shut again behind him. There were five tables in the seating area, with two or three chairs at each. Only one other table was occupied at that moment, an elderly couple, at least in their eighties he thought, sipping tea from small china teacups, a toasted bun, butter melted on top, sitting on a plate between them. The gentleman had looked up, nodded and returned to his tea. Somewhere out at the back, someone was rattling cups or plates, no doubt the café owner cleaning in the kitchen. Moments later he saw a lady stick her head out through the open door from the kitchen, dish cloth in hand, and she called to him:

"Take a seat, love, I'll be over shortly to take your order."

James opted for the table in the corner, as far away from listening ears as was possible, given the small and cosy nature of the café. Sitting down, he spotted that both of the elderly couple were wearing large hearing aids and he smiled at his own caution. He could probably have stood directly behind them and they wouldn't hear.

The lady appeared again from the back, coming over with a smile on her face and pad in hand.

"So, what can I get you?" she asked. James had not actually looked at the menu that sat on his table, but ordered a pot of tea and a toasted teacake as well. It looked good from what he could see, and it was too early for lunch. 'Elevenses' as his mum would always say.

Moments later when the order had been taken and the lady was back in the kitchen to prepare it, the door opened again and in walked the man he was to meet. A shout of "be right with you" was given from the kitchen, as he walked over and took a seat opposite James.

James guessed his companion was about the same age as him, maybe a little older. He had dark hair, that was kept neat and tidy. There were the beginnings of what were a few grey hairs, but it worked well. It suited him. He wore a smart jacket, a dark blue shirt underneath, without a tie.

They exchanged small talk, obvious stuff about the traffic and the weather. It was awkward and forced, and they both knew it. They were not meeting here as friends, neither was it a business meeting. How had he got tangled up in all this, James started to ask himself, but the reality of the answer came too quickly, and he cut the thought off mid flow.

The lady was back, the tray was unloaded in front of James and the bill was put in the centre of the table, recording the items he'd ordered. She turned to the other man and took his order; he'd gone for the same. The teacakes were selling well that day.

"I need you to do me one more thing," the man said suddenly, his voice calm, a sense of finality to it all, as if James' nightmare was about to be over.

"What is it?" James said, with obvious levels of apprehension.

A package was passed across the table. No one else was taking any notice, but James felt naked. Exposed. Vulnerable. He grabbed the package, feeling its weight, and slid it onto the floor as if it were a bomb or box of Class A drugs.

"What is it?" he repeated, a little more urgently, his blue eyes boring into the brown eyes of the man sitting just a few feet in front of him, the other side of the table.

"It's a piece of clever technology which will give me ears to listen into what is happening." It would give him a lot more than that too, but he wasn't going to dwell on that. It was a remote hard drive, with transmitter ability, and could grab all electronic data within about twenty metres of its location. Telephone calls, video feed, emails. Anything.

"What am I supposed to do with it? he said.

"I need you to hide it inside the main control room at the base."

James' eyes opened wide and he looked around wildly for a second.

"You are out of your mind! There is no way I can do that!" His voice was raised a little, though no one reacted. The lady came back at that moment with the second order, placing it down in front of the man, the paper bill added to the first in the centre of the table. They remained silent for a few seconds, as she left them once again. The pause had been a useful cooling off period.

"I need you to do this, James. You are still on duty there at the moment, aren't you?" He knew he was, but it helped change the subject a little.

"Yes, why?"

"Look, I've arranged an opportunity for you to be able to go to the base later today, you'll definitely be called soon. Someone will need some medical attention, which will be your natural way in." He passed James an envelope which contained a small pouch. A needle and small bottle of medicine were inside.

"You'll need this with you. Its the antidote to what the lady will be suffering from. You'll need to inject her before the shaking stops. You'll be fine. And when you are there, look for somewhere to stash my package. Somewhere central, in the main area, but somewhere well out of sight. It's important that they don't find it. You got me?"

"Yes, I've got you. And I don't like it one bit!"

He took a bite of the teacake and washed it down with some more tea. His phone rang. It was the base, asking him to come in. One of their members of staff was feeling unwell. Could he come at once? James' eyes flashed up to those of the man sitting in front of him, with his phone still to his ear. 'Who is this man?' he thought. 'What have I got myself into?'

"I've got to go. That was the call." James got up, took out a five pound note and dropped it on the table. He picked up the package, putting the envelope inside his jacket, and left the café.

The lady appeared again, hearing the bell, and came over to the table, picking up the paper bill and the money, which was too much.

"He's a doctor. Something came up suddenly," the man said.

"No rest for the wicked," she smiled, taking his dirty cup and plate away.

Before arriving at the café to meet James, he'd been at Eleanor's home. He had called in the night before as she had asked him to come round to pick up some stuff. Hours later, a bottle of wine sitting empty, Eleanor asleep on the bed, he had stirred himself and pulled himself free from the tangled bed clothes, covering up Eleanor again. He went in search of his clothes.

He took out a bottle of powder from his pocket. An

odourless drug that he sprinkled over the coffee. It would take a little while to affect the body, just enough time to make you feel a little unwell, before convulsions, even foaming at the mouth would begin. Left untreated, it was a poison and would kill. But it was easily cured, which made it a very popular drug with police interrogation teams around the world, though it was illegal in the UK.

Having spiked Eleanor's coffee, he watched a little television, keeping the sound down, before undressing and getting back into bed. To be double sure in the morning, he would make her coffee before saying goodbye. Getting under the covers, she turned over in her sleep, her body pressing against his, her breasts facing him, and he ran an arm over her, easing her onto her other side, and then fell asleep.

In the morning, they showered, got dressed. Eleanor was a little foggy about the night before and had quite a hangover, though she remembered the drunken sex they had had. He handed her a hot cup of coffee as she stepped out of the bathroom, a towel wrapped around her.

"Thank you," she said, taking a sip. She felt happy, glad that he was around again, wanting there to be more, a relationship, something for the future. She stopped thinking about it and got dressed. They both left the house before nine, going their separate ways. She was driving the one hour it took her to get to the base and he went the other way but would wait twenty minutes before turning around and also going in that direction, to meet James in the café later that morning. Things were progressing well. By the end of the day, he might actually know what the big secret was; he could see the headlines already. His headlines. It was going to be huge.

James pulled up to the main security gates just twenty minutes after receiving the call for help. He was cleared and drove his red Mazda up the main drive and parked in about the same spot he'd been in just days before. Opening up the boot of the car, he grabbed his black leather bag, the large kind all doctors seem to carry, and started to walk to the guarded main doors. They were expecting him. Inside his bag he'd carefully placed the metal recording device he'd been given, as well as putting the needle and medication in there, now just part of his equipment, as he played the part of the good doctor with all the answers. He'd come to save another patient.

As he was led through the main doors, down the corridor and into the central control room, someone came running to him shouting. The guard left him at that moment and returned to his post.

"Thank goodness you are here, Doctor, she's just in this office."

At that moment, she started shaking violently on the floor. Letting his training kick in, he got down beside her, checked her vital signs, then checked her eyes, which were starting to roll. Opening his bag, he took the medicine and the needle, joined the two together and finding a vein, plunged the needle in hard, giving her the antidote she needed.

Initially nothing happened. This worried James, though he didn't show it. Then calm returned. The turnaround was actually rather dramatic. Just five minutes after convulsing on the floor, suffering with severe stomach cramps, eyes distant, foam building at the mouth, she was moving around, talking freely, feeling no pain.

James was there to monitor her for a while. Business returned to normal in the office, her two other colleagues were now back working on computers, doing important stuff that he had no idea about.

An hour after his arrival, Eleanor was feeling much better and James was leaving. He put his business card with his phone number close by for her, should there be any further signs. He already knew there wouldn't be.

He put his bag in the boot, now empty of the device which he'd managed to hide, quite easily in the end, in the main room. With Eleanor recovered, and things got back to normal, he had been left to himself somewhat, and whilst continuing to 'monitor' his patient, had managed to slip the package into a dark corner, underneath a desk that no one sat at, between wires and cables that went into nearby machines. No one had noticed anything.

Driving through the main gates, only now did he wonder what he'd actually done. He'd taken a brief moment to check the package he'd been given after leaving the café and was certain it wasn't a bomb. Certain, in fact, that it was what he'd been told it was. But still, what really was going on? What hideous crime had he just committed? The gates opened and the guard actually waved to him as he passed. He pulled out onto the empty road and headed back to get on with the rest of the day, to deal with his own patients who needed his time, people who had been put off while he played spy, or criminal. He was not yet sure how this particular role would turn out.

Chapter 8

Present Day

"How long have I been here, Lorna?" John asked, awake from yet another vision. It had been just a flash of something, this time, a glimpse. They were coming more regularly now. Things felt like they were speeding up.

"I've been with you for four days now, John. Before that, I'm not sure," she lied. She knew exactly how long John had been there, but for the first part, he was unconscious and then was kept heavily sedated while everything was set up and tests were done.

"So I've been here for all these days and still no one is here to see me?" he said, back on the theme that he'd brought up the other day.

"It's a little more complicated than that John. What you are seeing, you are clearly seeing for a reason. It's warning us of something to come. We need you to remain here until we are sure what needs to be done. Are you clear on that? So no, we haven't tried to contact your family yet, but you can be assured they are certainly concerned for you."

She had no knowledge about his family. She knew nothing of his life outside of the hospital, besides the situation he'd been in when they found him, in that news van with the rest of his crew, all of whom were dead.

"I guess you're the nurse," he said with a slight smile, the kind that was playful but also showed he didn't really believe a word she was saying. This didn't surprise her. She'd never been a good liar, and wasn't really too happy about all the practice she was getting in becoming one.

Three Weeks Ago

The small team that had taken the program off Felix's hands had quickly brought Lincoln into the new, very experimental, program, and the first vision implant was going well. Their patient was responding. Maybe this would work.

Midway through, word came of a second survivor, and they went to work straight away putting together the paperwork that would give them full control over the patient.

The medical staff knew full well what they were now doing. Just seconds after the vision finished, the patient shot bolt upright, nearly scaring the nurse beside him to death. It wasn't something the team were expecting either, but it created some amusement.

"It works," someone announced to the rest of the team.

That night, by the time the second patient had been put through the program, again reacting after the first vision, again scaring the life out of the same nurse with him, the problems were starting to show. Like Lincoln, where it had been assumed some weakness of the heart had caused the cardiac arrest, the second guy had died. Again it was a heart attack.

Twenty four hours after the second death, and with a team of fresh thinking army personnel in place, the data had been extensively studied, codes of practice drawn up, training provided. Beta-blockers were made available; adrenaline was a huge problem in both men and the visions, brought on by memory replacement had just been too real to cope with.

The nurse in question, a senior manager called Alison, was 'reassigned', and Lorna was brought in to replace her.

She was put through a day of training. It was specific training to this program, starting with an understanding of what it was, what the patient would be seeing, covering areas of psychology, brain function, sensory awareness. It was detailed and time consuming. It was everything Lorna needed to keep her mind from her own loss and sadness she felt. She adapted very well to it.

When John arrived, she was there to receive him, though it was two days before he would be started on the program. He was unconscious and had been found in quite a bad way. He had some serious wounds, including one on the back of his head, but that gave them the idea about connecting directly to his temporal lobe and the visual cortex, two of the main areas active during the visions. Great care was taken and the area was well protected afterwards. A synthetic material was used to fill the cavity, a common army technique for quick patch up jobs on the field of battle.

She came and went, but never went far. Then he was ready for the first vision, and from then on, she was with him for every waking moment. A camera was also installed in the room, just to keep her on her toes. Not that she didn't have enough to worry about already.

Three Months Ago

Back in his office, James' mysterious stranger sat glued to his chair, as the early data picked up by his secret box was starting to come through. Telephone calls, internal memos, blueprints, orbit patterns: the works. He had thought he was onto something big, but had no idea how big. He'd been monitoring all press releases from the base for months and they'd said quite a lot without saying much at all. It all talked of big stuff, but his own observations of the base, watching as much as he could from a distance, showed another secret side which hadn't fitted with what was being openly shared.

Now he knew why. Now he had the inside line, picking up on everything that was being said inside the control room, every message being sent between the teams. Everything. And it painted a very clear picture. He couldn't believe his good fortune.

None of this seemed possible weeks before. There seemed no way of ever getting near enough to the base to really learn anything. That was until he spotted James, one of three on call doctors, when he was actually there for his first visit, as the main doctor had been suddenly taken ill. He had watched him enter the base, through the gates, and walk around freely. He'd watched him walk up to the main building, where he was met and led through the doors.

Thirty minutes later, seeing James get back into his red car, he had followed him as he left the base. It was about an hour's drive, but eventually James pulled into his surgery, a full afternoon's clinic ahead of him.

James didn't notice the stranger walk into the surgery that day; he didn't know all the patients anyway. Far from it. He was one of four doctors working in the clinic, each with thousands of potential patients on the books, situated as it was in a busy part of West London. The man scanned the list of doctors, but was helped by James coming out of his room at that moment, walking over to the reception area, talking with a staff member. 'Dr J A Brookes M.D.' was written on a plaque on the door.

Just a week later, the set up was in place, unknown to the dear old lady involved. Her medical records had been accessed and changed, her allergic reaction to penicillin temporarily removed. She was in for some mild discomfort. Dr Brookes saw her, spoke with her and diagnosed the problem, prescribing her an antibiotic: penicillin. The prescription was written by hand in his own hand writing. She would not actually take them, but it was enough to frame him.

Her records were then put back as they were before, the warning clearly visible for anyone to see, unavoidable really. A lawyer was paid to file a complaint, contact made supposedly on behalf of the family, and a young lawyer from an average London firm marched into James' room at the surgery one Tuesday morning, without the knowledge of the elderly patient, and claimed to be her lawyer. Papers were thrown onto the shocked doctor's desk, with claims of malpractice. He could be struck off for this.

A copy of her medical records was among the papers too, a yellow highlighter crudely indicating, as if it could be missed, the confirmation of her severe allergic reaction to penicillin. A copy of the prescription was also there, prescribing a level of drugs which would be normal in the situation, for anyone who was not allergic.

James felt cornered, unprepared. The evidence looked damning. True, he'd been busy, working often sixty, maybe seventy hours a week. The extra trips to the RAF base didn't help. But still, to miss such an obvious thing, he didn't know how he could have. He was careful, and yet the evidence in front of him looked bad.

It only got worse hours after that, when, as he sat in a local café, a cup of coffee in front of him, James was approached in person by this smartly dressed stranger, claiming to be a reporter. He had wind of the story and threats were made. This was all James needed. He'd left that encounter with the lawyer with some sense it could be dealt with. Now if the press got hold of it, he was finished.

It was a hostile opening to their connection as James wanted to punch the guy for being so sleazy, but he knew that would only make things worse. He was instead surprised when the reporter suggested he might be able to help. He had connections with the family, very good connections. He was certain he could make this go away, but James would have to do something for 'them' in return. He never did understand who the 'them' was, but he wanted his own error kept quiet. He was happy to play their game, for the moment, if it meant coming out of this all with his career intact. And so the plan was put into motion. They talked occasionally, before the face to face meetings started again. First he was to take some photos of the RAF base he occasionally went to. Then finally, after that time in the café one late morning, he was to plant a listening device. After that, it was promised, the allegations would go away. He really wasn't needed any more, but he wasn't told that, as a backup. Always better to keep the threat there, just in case something extra was needed. It wouldn't be.

After everything that had happened, James started to suspect a set up, but had no way of proving it. If the mysterious stranger was to be believed, then his problems had now gone. But it all seemed rather convenient, the otherwise random connection between the potential lawsuit, and this so called journalist, who appeared and offered to make it all better. To make it all better once he'd done something for them. And yet he'd done it. It was just some photos at first, but then that device. He felt nervous, feeling that in his last action he'd overstepped the mark. Surely, once they found it, they'd be able to check the CCTV or something? Surely there'd be some record of him being the one planting it? Surely he wouldn't have actually been that lucky as to get away with it, when he had no real idea what he was doing?

And if it did come out, he knew for certain he'd be on his own. The stranger would be gone. Out of sight. And James couldn't accept that. He arranged one final meeting, where he pretended to make demands about wanting confirmation the issue was put to bed then they'd gone their separate ways. James was the first to leave but he waited in a hire car, a black Laguna. He followed the guy all the way to his office, which was indeed a sleazy tabloid newspaper. 'No surprise there then,' he mused to himself. It fitted. He'd obviously been set up, but if he was at risk of going down, he wanted his own piece of backup information. He needed to know the name of the guy who had suddenly dropped into his life, whom he'd worked hard at keeping away from everyone close to him, especially his wife Lorna.

Walking in through the main doors, he'd chatted up the girls on the front reception area, playing it cool, going on to ask about a reporter who once interviewed him for some big piece, saying he'd like to get in touch. He described the man as best he could, from memory, but there was still a look of confusion on the younger of the two girls' faces, not much more than twenty, she'd only worked there for seven months.

"Oh, I think I know who you mean," the other said, as a look of recognition spread across her face, her eyes sparkling. 'How typical,' James thought to himself, 'putting two very attractive women on their front desk.' The older one, who was maybe just twenty-five, cleavage showing, a red bra strap visible on her right shoulder, continued:

"The guy you're after is called John...something....I remember now. John Westlake."

Present Day

John Westlake lay awake in bed, as Lorna came over to check his condition. His wounds were starting to improve, the dressings changed every day. They still had some way to go, and one wound on his left leg still required antibiotics. But apart from that, progress was good. He'd survived a nuclear explosion; anything else was a bonus.

John still had no memory of anything before waking up in that hospital room. A doctor had come to him, on John's request, and they'd chatted about the issue of memory loss. When ready, it was agreed that he would be given help, professionally trained experts to come in and work with him, in the hope of getting his long term memory back. His memory of the disaster and what followed were being kept subdued, controlled by the constant drugs being fed to him through the tube attached to his left arm. They hadn't told him that, of course. But there seemed no harm in him having his long term memory restored. In the moments before death, what else would he have to think about?

Two Months Ago

It was a fresh morning, a slight breeze blowing, leaves moving around carefree on the ground, like little children playing chase in the park. Dark clouds sat on the horizon, looking ominous, threatening a soaking at some point. John would keep an eye out for them.

He pushed that thought from his head and started his jog. It had been too long, and just thirty seconds into it, he could feel it. His engine inside, heart, veins, oxygen supply, just wasn't up to it. After two minutes at a medium pace, he paused. Catching his breath, he started again, slower this time and more steady. Fitness was going to be a much slower process than he had hoped.

Running through the country tracks, over fields and through the occasional wooded area gave him time to think, to process. It was now a welcome escape from the pressures of life, his working world in particular. Everything in him was telling him he was onto something big. Part of him, and something he was trying to suppress, to deny, was telling him to walk away altogether. To leave it. To not get involved with something so top secret, so high level. He knew it was the kind of situation, in the films anyway, that ended in a killing here, murder there. He could just imagine a team of hit men waiting for him behind the next group of trees. And who'd know? Who'd ever find him out here, even if it was noticed he was missing. He didn't dwell on that thought for long, but did start watching the path ahead of him, just in case.

His more ruthless nature wanted answers, though. Opening the situation up to an outsider, and one he assumed was currently unnoticed, would mean the public could one day know the truth. But what truth was he going to uncover? That was the real question that had kept him awake most of the night. Full of nervous excitement, and fear that kept him from sleep, he finally gave up as dawn broke. Pulling on his running shoes, he thought the fresh air might give him some respite. And it was, in a way. It was giving him time to slot his thoughts into place, to align his priorities and hopefully allay his fears.

Thirty minutes was all he could manage, and he walked the final bit back home. He'd made it back without fainting, he congratulated himself. And no sign yet of a kill squad. For all the good the run had done as he walked through the front door again of his pleasant and cosy cottage, it all came back to him, like a mantle that he was wearing. He needed some answers, and he needed to pass this on to someone else, someone who could share the load.

Twenty five minutes later, after a shower and hot drink, he walked into his home office area, and sat down to start listening to and reading the latest output from his listening device left in the control room at the RAF base. The box was transmitting constantly, whatever it was picking up. That message was sent out to a hub, which was then relayed to his own computer sitting in front of him. It wasn't totally untraceable, but it would take some time. He really didn't know how long he had. He assumed, if they were onto him, the signal would stop first, proof that they'd found the box. That would give him advanced notice, long enough to get away from there, but it was a scenario he hadn't thought much about. He had no idea where he would go, apart from just driving as far as he could.

His main problem was that it was such time

consuming work. He needed to bring in others, maybe a team to work with. While there was only one of him, the stuff coming in was hours and hours of information from many people. Telephone conversations into the base, internal chats between offices there, emails, memos. The lot. John quickly found that much of the information was unrelated. He had no access to actual files. All source documents were no doubt already planned and locked away. Therefore often, without reference to what was being discussed, it was hard to really understand what was being talked about. But anything new, and he'd know. Left long enough, he knew he'd come up with something. And he now knew he needed some help. The newspaper did have two teams, usually only working with the main lead reporters, on the massive stories. Sitting there with a notepad full of notes already, he thought he could have a shot at getting his own team, but would have to share a little information with his boss later that day, to know if it was possible. It would all take him longer than he wanted, but at the end of it he would get what he most needed.

Chapter 9

Present Day

    Lorna had dropped off to sleep when John awoke from his latest vision, the sixth that he'd had in the last two days. She stirred quickly, a small alarm making her aware that he'd woken as the vision finished. She stood up, straightening her uniform a little, and went over to switch off the sound. John looked in good shape, though a little sweat was on his forehead. She wiped it gently and he thanked her.

    "How are you doing, John?" she said. He knew the routine by now.

    "It was much like the other ones, though this time I saw a building. It was burning. The walls looked like they were melting, or that they had been melted at some point. There was no roof, but it must have been some type of office or something. It led into another area. Then the vision changed. It was all new again. Like nothing had ever happened. Like this was before the disaster, maybe in our time now? A long corridor led into some sort of industrial area. There were tubes and pipes, huge pipes everywhere. There were large white cylinders, about six of them, standing end to end. They each looked about thirty metres in diameter. Give or take. The vision took me half way down the long warehouse or building. Maybe it was some type of power station. It was massive. Between the middle two cylinders, there was housed a control unit behind a solid metal door. It was open. And in the bottom of the unit, under another solid metal protector, there was this big red button. It had the words 'SAFETY SHUTOFF' written around it, in a circular fashion. I had the urge to push it, but then it all faded and the vision ended."

    Lorna had listened carefully, actively nodding to show him she believed him.

"What do you think it all means?" she asked.

"I don't know. This one was different in that it was showing two different times, I guess. One time before, and then another time, in the same place, but after. I think the button is important. I think it needs to be shut down before this incident takes place. I think that's why I'm being shown this." He remembered back through his first few visions. The destruction and death, the body bags. Then he remembered about his own life being given, a necessary sacrifice to save millions. The man in the visions, this Felix, had been very clear on that. This thought now unsettled him. If he was just to shut off this button before the incident, where was the risk? Maybe the shut off was the risk, but why would he need to do that? And who'd create a safety shut off anyway that blew you up? It didn't make much sense, but then nothing was making much sense. Life, as he knew it, was very different. Though he had no memory of the time before waking up in the bed he was now in, he knew that there must have been a normal life somewhere back there, a simple daily routine that he had followed. And yet, something had intervened. Now he was stuck here, seeing visions, talking with some strange man that didn't seem like an angel, and being given the task of saving millions of people.

That part he was sure of. He was prepared to save them, though the last vision had actually confused him. He wasn't expecting to see anything normal looking. Before that, it was only an apocalyptic world of death and destruction, and that was a very clear message: to prevent it. Now he wasn't really sure what to think.

"If I'm honest, Lorna, I don't really know now," he said, a blank expression of hopelessness and questions on his face.

"You've come this far, I'm sure it will soon become clear to you. I'm sure you'll know soon enough what it all means and what you have to do."

"I guess you are right. Look..." he said, changing the subject. "I'm sat here all day and night, there is no television. Can I have something to do? I mean, a book to read or anything?"

It had been discussed, though the issue was of course not to allow him to see anything from the news. One of the channels was gone altogether, their transmitter, as well as most of their production crew, destroyed in one of the explosions.

"I'll see what I can do for you, John. Maybe we could get a DVD player and put on some films or something. I'll see what books I can get hold of as well."

"Thanks."

It was the least she could do.

Twenty Four Days Ago

There had actually been four different launch sites, allowing the team to better synchronize the operation, each probe autonomous in its operation. However, it had caused extensive damage when the probes went offline, each returning to its own original launch coordinates, each a mini nuclear bomb. This was the worst man made disaster of all time. For the UK it already felt like the end of the world. There had been no evacuation plan, as the control room, the location of the original probe and therefore the first one hit, had been destroyed. It was only at that moment of impact that they knew for sure the remaining probes were armed. Over the next two days all three final probes eventually came down, exploding on impact, a medium sized nuclear explosion each clearing about four square miles. Every probe, as powerful and state of the art as it could be, had a relatively small payload of 50 megatons in comparison to the main reactors on site. That was the equivalent of 50,000 tonnes of TNT. The bomb dropped on Nagasaki by the USA at the end of the Second

World War was about 21 megatons. The damage done to London by the probes was already more than nine times the destruction caused in Japan's second city when it was hit with a bomb all those years ago. What had happened so far would be a mere drop in the ocean compared to what would happen if the main reactor at the RAF base exploded.

Housed in the main power plant, there were six state of the art and highly secretive nuclear reactors, a set-up that was so powerful, that it had to be kept secret. Done properly, it would provide much of the country's power in the years to come. It would be a perfect solution to world energy requirements so they would have power left over to sell to Europe, and blueprints for the scheme to sell to the highest bidders.

The outside two cylinders, the ones at either end, had similar levels of power to the probes. Their scientist had found a way of packing an explosive power of about 52 megatons into the small spacecraft. The spacecraft that had been funded in part by outsiders, including NASA. The Americans had been kept from knowing what was really happening. The fact was that the technology was also being used to build a super facility, to make Britain the market leader in energy production. It was one of these two outer reactors that had exploded, killing James and others, just hours after the probe had hit. However, the risk was far greater than that. Cylinders two and five had been the result of three years of further development and each had 15,000 megatons of power equal to the highest payload that the Americans had ever tested. The British scientists had not stopped there though, continuing their scientific explorations to create the two central cylinders of the row of six. Cylinder three was made with a depleted uranium tamper. The Russians had once tested a bomb with a lead tamper, but now the British had taken it a step further, producing 100,000 megatons of power. That was the equivalent of 100 million tonnes of TNT. Cylinder four, the last to be finished, one year after number three, went even higher, at 120,000 megatons. Nothing like it had ever been produced before. There was no nuclear reactor on planet Earth anywhere near as powerful. After the Sun, it was the second most powerful energy source in the solar system. Combined, they had the power to destroy most of Europe. The radiation would make the rest of Europe impossible to live in. It was thought it could trigger a nuclear winter like nothing ever seen. Its potential scared them. Like the young scientist Frankenstein, they wondered if they too had created a monster.

Built inside the facility was also the ability to shut it down. Between the two most powerful cylinders sat a metal box. Housed inside was a button which would close all six reactors down and drop the uranium rods into pre-dug underground chasms, deep and heavily protected by 10 metre thick walls.

It was to be a last resort, and of course no one ever spoke of it. It was an unthinkable final solution, and they boasted about the actual safety of nuclear power, their ability to harness it in a safe way and their track record in terms of safety. And it was well founded. There had been no real safety issues. Still, it could not get reported to the world. Better kept secret and useful, than public and vulnerable. There would be a storm of protest if it were public knowledge that a potential time bomb was situated in the middle of half the country's population.

Three Weeks Ago

Putting together the final part of the program had not been straightforward. Footage of the inside of the facility was not easy to come by. The main control room had been easy. News footage had been shot briefly after the first explosion, before the reactor blew. The film going in through the doors showed the metal walls literally melted where they stood, as if made of wax, molten metal obviously running down the walls. How hot had it got?

There was no further coverage of the rest of the facility though. The nuclear radiation prevented anyone from venturing further in. This caused Felix a problem, but he was lucky to find the solution. Stored inside the offices were archived footage of the base not long after it was completed, and long before the last four cylinders were ever finished. Clean and clear, the presentation video had walked the viewer slowly through the facility, into the main power plant, taking in the giant white cylinders. It was perfect. Midway through there were recordings of the safety features, and especially the cut-off button.

"Perfect," Felix had said aloud to himself. With some editing, he'd been able to stitch both clips, old and new, together into one flowing movement, as if it were one continuous shot. He could do nothing about the new, cleanness of the second half. It might confuse, but it would show anyone exactly where the button was. They'd seen it now. They'd been shown where it was. It might work. Maybe someone would be able to walk in there and close it all down, to put the uranium out of harm's way, to silence the risk. Maybe there would be hope. Besides that, there was nothing they could do. Left untouched, the reactors were on, working full power, producing huge quantities of energy that was going nowhere. It was just building up. The five remaining cylinders were effectively ticking time bombs, each with power to destroy, but combined, the impact was unthinkable. Life on planet Earth, as they knew it anyway, would be changed forever.

Present Day

John was asleep again, and once more seeing a vision. He'd been walking with Felix, following him around a building, walking nowhere in particular, just talking.

"That button you told me about?" John said.

"That is an important thing. Very important. That is your way of saving everyone," he said.

"I see. I felt I saw it for a reason. But why was it so new? That part seemed more like it was now, I mean, not destroyed. Not part of some disaster that is about to happen. Can't we find out where it is now, and stop it?"

"It's not that simple. Your mind sees things how it wants to. You made it new." There didn't seem much else John could say to that. "But you are getting close. Time is nearly upon us. You now know what to do. The challenge remains; will you do it?"

"I will," he said, without a moments hesitation. "I'll do what's needed. If there is a way to do this and survive, I'll do it. I'll find a way."

"It will cost you your life. You already know that."

"But there must be a way. Maybe I'll be okay? Maybe God will save me. Maybe this is what I've been made to do. My calling?"

Felix was silent. There was no response. For once, there was not an answer to John's comment.

"You now know what you need to do," Felix repeated.

The room shook, darkness fell, and then there was light and he was once again awake, once again going to process and discuss what he'd seen. The routine was becoming a little tedious, though he didn't want to say that to Lorna.

One Year Ago

It had been a heated and uncomfortable day of discussions. The British were holding their ground and keeping their cards very close to their chest. There was too much they were not letting on. This annoyed the other groups present. The Russians, for obvious reasons. They'd been called, and were offering some assistance, but they felt they were just being used. The Europeans were fuming, angry at the blatant rejection being shown by the UK. The Chinese knew they were outsiders. They were there to listen, but had failed at the first round of negotiations twelve years before when plans were first discussed. Their spying network went on to confirm theirs had in fact been the highest bid. Its rejection, and their exclusion, had been for other, as yet unknown, reasons. They were a non-player, but were far from happy. Even the Americans were angry, the day's plan not going as they had envisioned. A break was called, each party needed to regroup, to assess how they now stood, to work out what they needed to do next. There was a long way to go if things were to progress.

Refreshments were brought in. A much more elaborate dinner was planned that evening at the American ambassador's residence. No one was totally sure, at that moment, if they would go.

Thirty minutes later, the food going down nicely, there was a different atmosphere in the room, for now anyway. It was calmer, less conflicted. The various parties knew each other, or knew of each other, well. Some had worked together on other projects for years. Relationships aside, with something of this magnitude, this potential, they all knew especially well that politics was playing a huge part. Each party knew that the others were spying on them, if not personally then certainly government to government. It was possible there were double agents in the room at that moment, with twenty-five or so men and women there, making up five nations or group of nations. None would suspect it in their own ranks, but they certainly thought it of the others.

Over the last twelve months, a group of four Chinese businessmen, a Russian diplomat, even a French and German chemical research team had all been 'asked' to leave the UK. They had all been spies. Everyone knew it. An American CIA field officer was 're-assigned' when his cover was blown. It wasn't, of course, just one way either. The British Secret Service had been just as active, and just as devious. Trust, in international relations, was a very fluid currency. It changed as much as the wind did, one time this way, then just as easily going the other way.

They ended the evening on easier ground, talking about security and safety, and an agreement regarding nuclear behaviour. All superficial stuff, all a smokescreen to what was really going on, and what soon, if not tomorrow, would have to be properly discussed. They left for dinner, the British taking up the invitation which they couldn't really have turned down on home soil, plus the Americans were the ones they were most in partnership with. The Europeans declined, angry at playing second fiddle to the US in the partnership, as did the Chinese. The Russians agreed, which would add some fun to the evening. If anyone knew how to party, it was the small team of seasoned Russian representatives. They even had their own special vodka with them. Maybe they could get someone to talk after all, they mused amongst themselves, chatting quietly as they were led to the venue for the evening meal.

Winfield House, the home of the Ambassador of the United States of America to the United Kingdom, was your classic English 'country' home situated in Regents Park, London. Fresh security sweeps had been done during the day before the first groups arrived, but that night was largely about dinner. Business would not be discussed, attitudes left on the doorstep, further conflict, it was hoped, left for tomorrow's full day of discussions.

The Russians were the last to arrive, which didn't surprise anyone. All three cars had left from the same place, heading for the same destination, and yet that journey had taken nearly sixty minutes longer for the car containing the five Russian members of their group. They had already started drinking, already ahead of the rest. Soon there was an easy attitude flowing between all three groups, a skilled group of waiters moving around the room, almost unseen, refilling glasses with the various wines available, taking away empties, passing around food. The Russian Ambassador was also there, though neither he nor his American counterpart were anything to do with the discussions. However, they were fully aware what was going on. Two senior British figures were there, once Ambassadors themselves, in both the USA and Russia. It seemed only right for them to be involved, and they helped to balance things out a little, as well as dilute the crowd enough to keep things peaceful. The Europeans not being there helped in that regard, and both the British and the Americans were wary of the Chinese, so their absence was a relief too, though an ominous one at that. Chinese counter-intelligence was growing around the world. They had more known spies operating than the British, US and Russians had combined. Their exclusion from the deal had been one made at government level, with huge pressure applied from foreign sources, most noticeably the White House itself in Washington, DC. It wasn't totally justified and the Chinese had come up with the most cash, certainly when taking into account trade and economic deals thrown into the mix as part of their package. True, they didn't have the breadth of experience that the Americans could offer, and that had been the party line when the announcement was made, confirming the initial partnership with just the Americans. The Russians had been brought on side later on, of course, when problems arose, and basic technology was needed. It was an unusual connection for them as well, in third place behind the other two. They were not happy with it at all, and their goal from the talks was to become an equal in the process, sharing their part of the cost, but more critically, benefiting from the results. For their part, the Americans were there to get an agreement on the nuclear power plant. The probe technology had been the key, it opened up a wide range of options for them, and they were surprised it was the British who discovered it. They hadn't known the Brits were a player in that particular field. However, it suited the US. It was far easier for them to come alongside the UK and negotiate what they wanted, than it would have been with nearly any other nation. The British knew they were onto something special, a breakthrough that would put them number one in the world in regards to energy supply. They had to keep the plans secret, for fear that they would be stolen from them. The truth was, though no one currently in Winfield House knew anything about it, that it had not in fact been a British invention, but a British theft of the highest magnitude. It was thought that only three people on the planet knew of its true origins, and none of these three was in a place to be able to say what they knew, their situations far too delicate, or isolated, for that. Because of the advanced nature of the final design, it wasn't obvious how it had started. The secretive nature of the Chinese scientists who first worked on the idea, meant that Beijing could only have their suspicions in regards to who was behind the theft. They'd actually have to see the plans themselves before being able to accuse the British. And so far, they'd been sidelined. Which only made them more suspicious of this revolutionary British breakthrough.

The Chinese were therefore at the talks to get whatever they could out of the process. Anything to work on, anyone who'd be prepared to talk. Chinese secret service personnel had been digging around for people they could turn. They had had many conversations with unsuspecting people who were unaware of what was actually being attempted. They had yet to find anyone who was high enough to know anything important or, equally, willing to betray their country. They remained in the shadows, constantly active, but invisible.

The four men and two women from the European Space Agency were there just to show their disgust, to look both the British and the Americans in the face, as if to say 'how dare you do this to us.' From the European side, they felt betrayed by the British, who chose the US over them, though they were geographically much closer. British/US relations were not what they were fifty years ago. A strong Europe made for a strong UK, if they could only see it that way. And they were equally mad at the Americans, for doing cross Atlantic work, yet picking a partner as small as the UK and ignoring the rest of Europe. European/American cooperation would have been huge. It would have seen the strongest possible common market and together they could have controlled the world. If there were to be any cracks in the age old 'special relationship' that both the British and the USA claimed they had, then the ESA were going to find it, and failing that, they'd make their own crack and drive such a wedge into it, that it opened up a huge rift.

The stage was set for an even more heated second day of discussions in the morning. Each group had its angle, each side its own agenda. They all knew something had to give, but none of them wanted to be the ones to give. There was too much at stake to show weakness. This was a time to be strong, to make strong demands, and be prepared to back that up with whatever seemed necessary.

Chapter 10

Thirty Days Ago

John had been able to obtain one of the two teams that he needed to help him gather data, his boss having finally been persuaded after weeks of effort. The more information that came through, the clearer things had become. John had needed to give up a lot of his information, which in his position made him feel vulnerable. He had, though, managed to keep hold of enough so that he remained the one calling the shots. Daily reports would have to be made and the team were on lease to him for only a week. Unless strong results were being shown, he'd been warned, then they were coming back. But in truth, it was a slow week for news. His boss sensed, as John had done at the beginning, that they were onto something huge. A team of four had been made available, along with an unmarked news van from the vehicle pool. Fifty-five minutes after finally being granted the help he'd been in so much need of, they were all driving back out of the city, towards the RAF base. John was keen to show them the sights and bring them up to date. He'd shared with his boss what he had found out and now he was sharing this news with the crew. Traffic was slow, queues common, as they made their way south. What John hadn't said, and wouldn't, was how he was getting the information. John liked to keep his cards close to his chest. That was why all the best reporters were also great poker players; it just came naturally.

Two hours later they had seen all they could at the base, which was very little. Besides, John felt even more conspicuous in a transit van than he did in his car. It had given the crew an idea about things, but really John needed them for their ability to help analyse everything. The data was more than anyone could handle on their own. Every time John had tried, there was always more at the end of his session than there had been hours before when he'd started. And this had been building to an uncontrollable level over the previous six weeks. He was worried that he would miss something, miss a vital piece of information that would give him clues as to what was really going on. Miss a vital piece of the puzzle.

John decided against bringing them to his home. The van was spacious, though with very little airflow. It was well equipped, and for short periods, with only about three people working there at a time, it was bearable. Much of their time would be spent sitting in a café, processing things, drinking coffee, having a cigarette. Usually in that order, though not always, and frustratingly for John, usually in cycles of only thirty minutes.

After two days, with fresh data pouring in all the time, they were starting to get through the backlog a little and making some excellent progress. John's boss had already seen enough to grant an immediate week's extension to this project, even with five days left to run on his initial week. John felt encouraged, and the crew were good at what they did, being a specialist unit with a lot of experience, though they usually worked on some celebrity or a sleazy politician and occasionally a Royal. Still, the process of listening and waiting, recording information and processing data, was all the same. Now it was an RAF base; next month it could be anything.

Present Day

John lay in his bed, encouraged for the first time in a week. He'd just seen the specialist, a doctor who had come to talk with him about his long-term memory loss. He'd left now, and Lorna was back in the room.

"How did it go?" she asked.

"He says there is a chance that I will be able to

regain my memory at some point. He's going to try some prompters on his next visit, things that might cause me to remember. He said the mind shuts down when we hurt ourselves, as the body's way of dealing with the situation. So we're going to have a go, but he did warn me not to get my hopes up or to think it'll be a quick, easy process. He also said that sometimes the memories are troubling. He once had a patient who had been this crazy, angry guy before he had a car crash. His post crash self was peaceful and happy, getting on with people. When he first started getting his thoughts back it was hard for him. He saw that he'd been a monster, beating his wife. He understood why his family had not come to see him." John paused at that, Lorna looking up at him, though his eyes were distant.

"You are not a monster, John. That was not your life then, I'm sure of it."

"Well, the truth is, I guess we don't know. Not until I get the thoughts back, if that is even possible. He did say they might not come back. The brain can cut these off forever, burying them so far that I'll never reach them in my conscious thoughts, only maybe in the occasional nightmare."

Lorna was listening as she got a needle ready, another injection needed for something, and he automatically held out his arm, as she injected him with the latest batch of drugs.

"What about you, Lorna? Who are you?"

Lorna smiled.

"We've talked a little bit about this already. But..." and she pulled up a chair and sat next to him. "I travelled a bit, certainly when I was still studying, and a little since. Central America was my favourite, working with street kids. These little ones had nothing. Dirty, and with no one looking after them. Some slept at the dump, some in parks, some in buildings. They grouped together, but this was more for protection than real companionship. Too many of them got into drugs and crime. Many were trafficked. It was horrible. There were five and six year olds looking after their younger siblings. It was heart wrenching. We live in such wealth and yet this is possible in the same world." She was talking with real passion, with a freedom that John liked. She'd often been so careful and reserved. The good listener. Now it was John's turn, and he was enjoying being on his side of the conversation.

"The job now means we travel less. We managed getting out to Venice, in Italy, some time back." He knew where Venice was. "It was only a few days, but was such a welcome time. The challenge with these breaks was that they were always so few and far between, and we were just getting rested, just getting into the holiday when it was time to come back, and work hit us once again with a vengeance. One week back and you'd feel like you'd never been away." They both smiled at each other. It was nice to be talking about something other than their present situation.

"Did you always want to be a nurse?"

"Actually, when I was little my parents tell me I first wanted to be fairy." John laughed out loud.

"What's so funny?" Lorna asked with a grin.

"Nothing really. It's just I didn't have you down for the fairy wings and magic wand type. Thought you'd always been clear about helping people, like being a social worker or doctor, I guess."

"That came soon enough. When I was nine we were out for food somewhere, when my big brother just started choking and coughing. He went blue, and fell to the floor. He couldn't breathe. The look on my parents' faces was horrible. I was crying so much. Then a doctor came forward and just acted. She knew what to do. What she did saved his life that day. And from then on, I knew that was what I wanted to be. I wanted to know what to do if something like that ever happened around me. And so it's what I became from that moment on, and all I ever wanted to be. I guess it was when I stopped being a little girl and started thinking like a grown up."

"That sounded horrible. And you were only nine? What about the rest of your childhood?"

"As I said, that's when I started thinking like a grown up. Doctors don't play with Barbie dolls, they save lives. So that's what I was going to do." She caught herself, in how intensely she'd been speaking, how serious it had all become. John was a good listener but she knew she needed to stop.

"But, look at me, making you all sad now for the girl who grew up before her time. At least you know that I've been training a long time for this moment!" She was smiling and joking with him. It lightened the mood and now John was smiling again.

One Year Ago

The second day of negotiations were well under way, with most of the delegations in for the nine thirty start. The excesses of the previous night still showed on some and had kept some others away, but only temporarily. The previous night's gathering had broken just after midnight, the glasses no longer being refilled, and the crowd, which had remained peaceful all evening, getting the hint. Tired from their long day anyway, and with another full day ahead of them, it was a welcome end to what had been a non-stop roller coaster. They'd get what rest they could, their convoys taking them to the various hotels where they were staying. Talk had been slow on the way back and on the way in that morning.

In the morning session there was a break for refreshments around eleven. Freshly brewed coffee sat in jugs on a red covered table, and the Americans were at least satisfied with what they were drinking. Usually coffee was quite bad at these type of meetings, and the Americans knew that Brits preferred tea instead, and therefore did not understand what decent coffee was. The coffee was African, as were the catering team. It had escaped everyone's attention, including the British who'd hired the caterers, as well as the Americans who'd been taking care of security, that about half of the crew of caterers were South African or Nigerian Secret Service, working together as a powerful African coalition. With food and drink abounding, the conference room frequently replenished with plates of food and bottles of water and juice, it was easy for them to listen in on something they'd been left out of altogether. Their cover was good as this was the first time they'd ever met as a whole and each agent was only aware of maybe one other agent in the crew. This was the way they worked and it was proving very effective. Three years back they'd infiltrated an Indian run operation in Colombia, which had been working with drugs, amongst other things. Three Indian agents were found dead, the drugs gone and a warehouse full of weapons was handed over to local government forces. No one knew that the whole cartel had been drugged and secretly smuggled back to Africa for interrogation to an unknown location, which was just the way they liked to work. The Indians had been warned off, and now Africa was learning how to make more money from it.

The next session before lunch was easy going. They all knew that the financing section and product review, which was happening after lunch, was going to be where things got really interesting. The British knew this was going to be hard. Costs were rising, with the Americans already putting in much more than their share, but the UK had nothing really left to give. They were most nervous about the information relating to the product. The Chinese had to be kept at arm's length and it was being worked out how this was going to happen. It was deemed best if they could be removed from the day altogether, but that was just wishful thinking. It had been the British who'd invited them in the first place, though of course they had no real choice. To have done anything else would have been to have admitted what they'd done. If the Chinese were to accuse the British of theft, it was possible that anything could happen, even war.

"Quite a time we are having," said the head of the American delegation to his British counterpart, as they stood next to an open window, a plate of sandwiches in their hands.

"Yes and we all know what's coming next," he replied.

"You know we will not put any more money into this?" the American said.

"Who says we'll need it?" came the unconvincing reply.

"We know where things stand. Our question is, who are you thinking about bringing into this thing? Because that might cause us a problem."

"I don't know what you mean, and you should check your sources. Last time I looked, you weren't doing too well either back home. You know what they say about a house divided."

The American smiled for a moment, but only to acknowledge a well delivered counter.

"I'm just saying we need to work together on this and tread carefully."

The British knew this only too well.

"I think we know what we are doing."

"Do you?" came the challenge, the American raising his voice enough, a flash of red coming across his cheeks. He held his gaze on his counterpart for a moment, his face fixed and giving nothing away, before he smiled a little, and just like that, moved on to lesser things. They finished what was on their plates, both excused themselves, and went their separate ways. Ten minutes later the discussions were back under way, though as soon as they started to talk, there was a call put through to the room, and it rang for a few moments before the Americans, acting as the chair for this session, picked it up slowly. The room was quiet.

Present Day

John was awake and reading through a novel he'd been given, though he wasn't looking too impressed at it as Lorna walked in.

"This takes a bit of getting used to," he said, putting the book on the bed. Lorna knew what he meant, but said anyway:

"What the book, or me walking in on you?" She was smiling at him, he knew what she meant.

"I really appreciated our conversation earlier," he said. Lorna paused as she was folding some blankets, putting them back where they belonged. "It was good hearing about your adventures in Central America, working with the street children. You took me to somewhere else, somewhere far away, anywhere but here. It was nice." She could imagine anything was better than where he was.

"Well, you have the book," she said, subtly diverting the conversation away from herself.

"Yes, it's a slow starter but I'll read it through. You never know, it might pick up. Are there any more from where this came from?"

"I'm sure there are. I'll ask around for you."

"Do you read much?" he asked.

"I have been known to, yes. However, it doesn't always fit with my working life. My mind gets too crammed with everything, so I tend to wait for a holiday and then read a good book I've heard about."

"By good book, you mean something mushy, I

guess?" John was smiling up at her.

"Not always," she replied, leaving it at that.

Grabbing some fresh bandages, she came over to him.

"I'm going to need to change these again today, to see how you are healing."

"Okay, thanks. Can I get a wash or something? A change of clothes? I feel very grubby in this same stuff all day."

"A bed bath you mean? Why, of course." She smiled at him, a little sparkle in her eye, but only briefly.

"I didn't quite mean that, nor to put you to any trouble."

"It's no trouble, it's something that needs to happen, I just wanted to make sure you were well enough. I'll get it sorted for later tonight, before you go to sleep. Change the bedding as well, while we are onto that."

"Thanks. Look, Lorna, I do appreciate all that you are doing for me. Not just the routine stuff, but the talking, the book, everything really. You might just be the one friend I've got left."

"Look," she said, choking back the emotion in her throat. "Don't you get all soppy on me now. It's me that reads that stuff remember, you're the thriller reader. And besides, its who I am. I get to do a job that allows me to be myself."

That wasn't of course entirely true for her in this latest role, however. It actually cut right across a lot of who she was and what she felt was right, but she buried that thought, not allowing it the air to breathe for fear that it would take root in her head and make her start to ask the difficult questions she knew were there.

"You continue reading," she said, and John obediently picked up the book once again. "And I'll go and start preparing everything I need for later to get you cleaned up a little bit more. Do call me if you need me, but

I'll see you again shortly."

Twenty Six Days Ago

It was the start of John's fourth day with his crew of guys from the paper. They'd each settled into their own working patterns. Time in the van meant that, because of the space shortage, at any one moment one guy was resting, usually smoking a cigarette. The café, which offered much more space, had become the venue of choice, though the frequency of going outside for a smoke had not altered one bit. The café gave them a little more comfort, though not much more, and the owner loved the extra trade and the impression it gave that business was good.

John had been getting on with the guys well. His 'A-team', as he liked to call them, Alan, Aaron and Andrew, were keen workers, and it didn't help that their other colleague, the butt of many jokes was called Bradley; he became the sole member of the 'B-team' once the phrase was coined. In truth, mostly it was healthy banter, at least from the A's. However, Bradley was a less than forgiving man. He'd been overlooked for promotion several times and was one of the longer standing employees of the newspaper. Only Alan from this team had been working longer and Aaron had been with the paper for just a little over a year, yet all were now in the same position, and on the same salary, he imagined. Bradley dreamed of something more, of moving up to the major leagues, not sitting with juniors as he was currently, with boys half his age so green out of university that it made him sick. Like the rest, he too had picked up on what was unfolding, aware that there was more to this latest story than met the eye. He'd been around the industry long enough to pick these things up, to sense them, to know when something wasn't what it seemed. They'd tracked royalty with fewer security problems than this army base were showing.

There was a story here, possibly the biggest one he'd ever worked on, and he had an inside track. Maybe after all these years, this could be his big break. Maybe he'd be able to beat the rest of them to the story, to go and define his career by selling the story to a rival paper: his story. The thought made him feel alive inside, but he needed to stay controlled, to stay focused, to run with it all until he had enough information. He was so distracted in his own mind, dreaming about what could be, that he had not noticed the others calling him until John shouted the loudest:

"I said do you want another drink?" he repeated, angrily and showing it.

"Oh, yes please," Bradley said.

John turned away and went to place the order, the word "Prat!" said loudly enough for all to hear, including Bradley. There was a grin on everyone's face, a laugh somewhere, which only made Bradley more determined to outdo them all. He'd take their laugher for now, the butt of their jokes. What he was planning would take the smile off every face. He'd lose his job, that was obvious. But in a cut throat industry such as news media, it could also be the start of a blossoming new career somewhere else.

John was at the counter ordering the drinks while the owner of the cheap but tasteful café was making small talk, trying to understand a little of what was going on, and why the sudden invasion, welcome as it was, into his café:

"I guess you are not monitoring the weather," he'd said. John hadn't liked the suggestion.

"Who said we were monitoring anything?" he shot back.

"No, don't get me wrong," he said, his right hand coming up and waving around as he talked. "I wasn't saying anything, I just meant it looks interesting, that's all. Anything juicy I should know about?"

John could see the guy was harmless and just looking for some gossip, and instantly changed his tone, which noticeably relaxed the owner, his hands less animated, less defensive, as he placed the last hot drink on the counter and gave John the change from the note he'd dropped down to pay.

"You can read about it soon enough, like everyone else," John said, this time with a smile. The smile was returned, as the owner moved out the back once again. John placed the drinks onto a tray and brought them over carefully to the waiting men. He passed them around, with care, though he banged Bradley's down with enough of a thump to keep him on edge. Bradley's hand came up to grab the cup and there was no word of a thanks from him. John let it drop for now. He'd keep his eye on the rogue member, the one guy that didn't fit. He liked his 'A-team', even the fact that they fitted the title, because they *were* great. Had there been another guy; an Albert, or Anthony or even an Abigail, he'd drop the loner and get them in. He thought he'd let Bradley see out the week, but after that, he'd look to replace him. Of course, John wasn't going to let that be known, and what Bradley lacked in personality and team dynamics, he made up for in attention to detail and the ability to read between the lines. So at that moment, he was a necessary hardship, and as the butt of most jokes, it also kept team morale up, for the rest of them at least.

It was just after lunch that they made their first big breakthrough. Having ploughed through data for days, the speech and conversations often in code, they had picked up a framework, without knowing what it meant. Their detailed system of tracking and recording meant that everything was there, accessible for all, a shared document making collaboration easy. It would also form a background on what they had pieced together and, when key clues were uncovered, they could look back and fill in some of the missing pieces. It was a tried and tested system. For the old timers like Alan and Bradley, they'd first started using written notes, boxes and boxes often, and when later on, a key reference point was understood, someone would have to work through hundreds of sheets of paper looking to make sense of it. The age of the computer, and with it the Internet, had changed all that. Though the information was just as plentiful, even more so maybe, their ability to search and cross reference was made much simpler, easy with the brilliance of something like Google, where they could all view and update the same reference source in real time.

  What they had already picked up was a reference to a specific date and key time, though there were three additional possibilities. It had been thought it was for a press release, or information update. They had speculated on a wide range of ideas and none were near the mark. But on that day, as Alan was scanning through a chat message between two office staff, he'd picked up the word 'launches' being referred to, and it started a frantic look through the information to see if it fitted with what they knew. And it did. The slip, which went unnoticed on the base, though was itself against protocol, meant John's team were able to start filling in the gaps, looking back over many of the coded messages, and now understanding they were talking about a launch of something. It started making a whole different level of sense. It was not yet clear if the four options were for four possible launch sites, or for four launch events. But they'd made their first major breakthrough. They'd got wind of something so secretive, that as far as they were aware, no one else outside the base knew anything of it. It gave them a sense of power. As six o'clock approached, the usual finishing time for the crew, no one was moving anywhere; only at half past did any of them look at the clock above the counter. More drinks were ordered as the early evening crowd started to come into the café and take the remaining available tables. Business was good for the owner, who opened until eight and wasn't about to ask his now permanent guests to leave any time soon. They were good for business, and quite a few of the other customers, usually through whispered questions, were picking up on the sense of a developing story in their neighbourhood. How little they all knew at that moment.

Chapter 11

Present Day

It was in the early hours of what would have been the weekend, though days came and went, each like the one before it and certain to be like the one following. Lorna checked once again on her patient, who was sedated and due another vision really soon. She'd not been able to sleep herself, her mind too active though her body was too tired. She'd contemplated taking some sleeping pills later, if needed. But right now sleep was far from her mind.

Today would have been her wedding anniversary. And she was well aware of that fact as she went about the early morning routine. It wasn't that she felt sad, just empty. Emotionally she was spent. She felt like nothing was in the tank, neither joy nor despair. She hadn't been able to cry for days and had actually spent a few minutes in front of the mirror the night before trying to make herself cry. To have a tear run down her face. To emotionally come alive because, with the way she was dealing with things, she wondered if she could ever feel anything again. Her one slight change in the last week had been her conversation with John the previous day, where she'd let go a bit and the hint of feeling, of being human, appeared on her soul's horizon, though it was short lived. Later that day, when John was sound asleep, she'd had a briefing session with the special unit monitoring the progress so far. The doctor who'd spoken with John about his memory situation was already there. The tone had been sombre. Lorna wondered what she had done wrong, but it wasn't really anything like that. The conversation had been based around the risks involved in memory recovery. Anything that would make the patient more unstable was deemed too risky. They knew there was no danger of his immediate memory being restored, as that was being subdued by the drugs he was being kept on. So the debate had been proceeding as Lorna sat quietly, wondering why she was really being involved in all this, though as she was obviously the closest person to the patient, on that level alone, it made perfect sense.

When asked her opinion on certain elements, she'd shared what she felt. Notes were being taken, and for all she knew the meeting was being recorded. It wasn't, in fact, this time. Finally they came to what she felt was probably their agenda all along and talked with her, but didn't lecture her, about her sharing her personal history with the patient, though on that point opinion was divided as to whether in fact it would be positive for the patient and should happen more. After all was said and done, it did nothing to change her mood, just the reminder, that even a simple conversation with a patient was not something that happened just between two people in a room, but was being listened in on. That anything she poured out from her heart was also being poured out onto a group of strangers sitting in some room somewhere. People that she might never meet, yet knowing things she hadn't told her own parents. It seemed wrong.

As the morning wore on, it was her family she most missed at that point. Her brother, a few years older than her, had become a great older brother once the last few years of childhood had passed. He had his own family now, with three lively little children. She'd loved being an auntie even if she hadn't yet been able to be a mum. And in that moment the thoughts came back that now, widowed, maybe she never would be. Maybe she'd only live a few more weeks or months anyway. That was what most people faced unless things could be stopped. And so she came full circle. It all rested with her and her patient. As crazy as it sounded, as unlikely a solution as it seemed, this really might be their best shot at ending this disaster once and for all. Walking back into the room, John, her patient, lay in his bed that he'd been strapped to for many days now. Peaceful and sedated but far from free. His physical wounds were starting to heal, though once some of the swelling had gone down, the odd cut or two might well need some further work, and certainly a few stitches. Soon he was about to see another vision, a routine one, further confirming, encouraging his mindset, showing him what would need to be done, talking him through the need to sacrifice, to give himself in order to save everyone else.

For Lorna personally, she'd made a conscious effort not to think about the ethics of what she was involved in. She herself had only come into the program late, fresh on the loss of the first two patients and the errors and mistakes had been the basis for her own training. No one had raised the higher issues with her. She knew not to go there herself, but was just following the natural course of things. She felt she was living in a nightmare, so might as well go along with the things until their natural conclusion. Then she could just wake up. They all could. Then it would all be changed again. Not undone, far from that, but there might be hope again. The calm after the storm. The chance to get the help she needed, that everyone needed. Help that would finally make a difference.

She touched John's head, stroking his forehead gently. He seemed at peace, though there was an unguarded roughness to him. She wondered who he was really, and what type of man he'd once been. Now he seemed very accepting of this imposed situation. He was caught up in it like a child playing a video game. For him, this was real. He could become the hero, he was the hero. But there was no extra life, as if after it all he could carry on. Game over for John really was game over for him, but for her and the rest of the world still alive, it was game on. That glimmer of hope was knocking at the door, crouching and waiting to be let in. She could sense it but knew it was not time to open that door. Not yet. There was still too far to go. But she knew, even in that moment, snatched from her husband, a widow before her time, on her anniversary and yet away from family, she knew: when the time came, that door was going to be flung open. If there was hope for anyone, she was having her fair share. She'd wallow in it, embrace it, swim in it. She'd allow it to engulf her. She needed to believe that better days were just around the corner. That things would not always be as they were. But for now, that door had to remain closed, those thoughts kept at bay, for fear that it would never happen and everyone's final hope would be lost.

John came to not long after that, as Lorna was still standing next to him, but no longer stroking his forehead. He'd once again seen destruction, death and the despair of so much suffering. Once again he'd seen the shut off button, the sense that this was the way out. Once again he'd been faced with the question of whether he would do it, could do it. Once again he'd been told to talk with the nurse. He'd grown in a sense of destiny in the vision, of purpose. Waking up and finding Lorna just standing there, so gentle, but a deep sadness, a distance, showing in her eyes, he turned his head to face her and softly spoke the words:

"I have a lot to tell you." She pulled up a chair, and he began.

Three Weeks Ago

Felix had finished the program the previous night and had been testing it throughout the dark early hours of Tuesday morning. In days gone past, he was an early to bed, early to rise fit and healthy young man. Often he was up before dawn, his five o'clock runs a well established habit as he'd been going out for years. He'd loved the stillness of the world at that time of day. Regardless of the events happening around him, or the busyness of the day, or the troubles on the news, at that time of day, when it was just him and nature, the roads still quiet, the world seemed totally peaceful. It was people that took that peace away. It was a special time for him, and those memories came back now for Felix, as he stood, looking wearily out the window as the first signs of dawn appeared. He was no longer the fit and healthy man he once was and that old self certainly felt a lifetime ago even though it was only a few days. He doubted if he could run half the distance now that just days ago would have been no problem. He could feel the effects of radiation already taking hold of his body. He knew he had a matter of days left, if he was lucky.

The coffee had run out the previous night. He was in no position to complain, and no one was there to listen anyway. He'd always been around people, had needed some attention and company in life, and didn't really enjoy his own space, and yet, now, that suited him. But the thought that he'd die alone, without seeing another person, did bother him. Still, he'd put himself into the program that he'd adapted, so his image and legacy might live on beyond him.

On his messy work station sat a photo of much happier times. There was a group of young people, all in their early twenties, with Felix himself in the centre, looking young and free, as indeed he had felt at that moment. The photo had been taken in Spain, a group holiday he'd taken with twelve friends, six guys and six girls and they'd all had a great time together. He looked at the photo and allowed his mind to wander, just for a moment. He remembered the warm sun and the easy days, walking around the coastal villages or just lying on the beach. He'd also had a thing for one of the girls they travelled with and a relationship had started to blossom in the sunshine. It went on to fade out when back home, back to reality, but it had created some great memories. The thought occupied his mind fully for a few moments, until reality set back in, and the seriousness and permanency of his situation came back to the very front of his mind. The moment was gone, the happy, carefree memories put away, maybe never to be revisited. Now, there was nothing like that to look forward to. In the end, life hadn't been what those early days had promised. No one could have foreseen what had happened. Life itself was hanging over the edge. It made what he was doing all the more important. If the main reactors blew in the facility then it was all over. No one could live through it. No one in the northern hemisphere, anyway. The world would be a very different place. The reactor had to be shut down and for that to happen someone would have to be the one to go in there. That itself presented a lot of issues. The radiation and exposure, the closer you got, was enough to stop even the strongest man. No radiation suit could protect someone from the lethal levels being released all over the base. But they'd have to find someone. Felix knew there was just a matter of weeks before the whole place would be obliterated. He hoped they'd find a way of making his program become the life saver. It was to be his legacy. Now he needed to get word out to others that it was finished. He'd test it more later in the morning but he was now desperate for sleep. Since the incident he'd only managed sleep in four hour blocks. So he lay down on the sofa, a paper plate falling to the floor, but he was too tired to notice, his body spent, his energy gone. Sleep was needed to get him through the rest of the morning, to do what needed to be done. Just moments after lying down, he was sound asleep.

One Year Ago

On the morning of the second day of talks, a small team of three agents had been tracking a number of key Chinese personnel. It was a Black Ops MI6 operation. The twelve high profile Chinese personnel were from a wide range of backgrounds and industries, though three were also known to be spies. They were all of great value to the Chinese state. They were quite unaware that MI6 was taking their photographs and recording their details and so they just carried on their usual routine.

At eleven the photos were delivered by courier to a London newspaper with UK coded security alerts, threatening the lives of the Chinese personnel photographed, which included those currently at the ongoing talks that the British were hosting. The newspaper, having long since been used as a contact point for the IRA to give coded warnings of attacks on the mainland during the time of the Troubles, had immediately passed what they had onto MI5, the UK based Security Service. A call was put to the Chinese embassy in London and an agent was on his way with the photos and a strong suggestion that all personnel be removed until the threat was dealt with.

The Chinese had been grateful for the information, but included within the list, as well as spies of their own, were high level business leaders, a diplomat, as well as the team currently meeting with the various space agencies trying to get to the bottom of this UK/US cooperation. They were therefore reluctant to move everyone out, instead insisting on greater security, the time to work on things themselves, and assurances from the UK that everything was being done to stop this threat. The MI5 agent had been unhappy at this, but she assured them they were doing their best; she herself was unaware of what was going on. They'd do their job to the best of their ability, but were frustrated at the Chinese reluctance in the face of a serious known threat to this group of high profile Chinese nationals currently in the UK. MI5 knew enough about the potential targets to know they were all of great value to China.

With the situation unchanged at the talks, the Black Ops team, working on orders given before, had located their first target, a sleazy Chinese businessman, currently in London to finalise a takeover, but also there to sign an arms deal with an Afghan contingent. There was a lot they had on him, and he was shot dead just before one o'clock as he left his hotel in West London. MI5 had yet to locate him but were on their way as soon as they got the call, worried now that this was an ongoing terrorist operation against a number of high profile Chinese targets in the UK. Calls were made and pressure applied by the British government to the Chinese. It was ordered that all the identified targets be pulled into hiding immediately, for their own safety. MI5 jurisdiction prevailed and the calls were made to all those under threat including the ones in the ongoing negotiations. An American voice answered the phone and after clearance was confirmed, the details were quickly relayed to the people concerned. An MI5 car was waiting at the venue, and with their Chinese bodyguards, the small Chinese team were being taken away at speed, running from this unknown, but apparently deadly threat.

"I don't know what you did," said the head of the American delegation to his British counterpart, as he leaned over and quietly whispered into his ear, "but it worked."

He smiled at this, but only briefly, before raising his voice to the whole table.

"I do hope they will be okay and maybe join us again at a later point, but for now, I suggest we get on with this session, as time is pressing and we have a lot to discuss." With that he turned to his American counterpart, who opened up the files in front of him and started the detailed look at finances, as planned. With the Chinese now away from the table, it was at least going to be a less difficult afternoon session.

Present Day

Lorna was grabbing five minutes of air, as her patient was reading another book in bed. They'd found an old stash of novels stored away in what must have once been the hospital's attempt at a library. John had been delighted. He loved to read, though couldn't tell if that was just now, because he had nothing else to do, or if he had always loved to. Regardless, he'd already worked through one book and was well on his way through a second.

Earlier, they'd talked for a long time about what John had seen. About how it had made him feel, the emotions and connections made between what he was seeing and his readiness, his willingness, to do what was being asked of him. About what was being demanded of him, and what he needed, no, want in fact he wanted, to now do himself. It had been a poignant moment, all kinds of thoughts racing through Lorna's mind, but she did well at not showing them, only occasionally breaking eye contact as she listened, and this just for a brief second, desperate as she was not to give John a hint of her inner turmoil.

Now outside, she was struggling to come to terms with everything in her head. The ethics of the situation were not clear, had never been clear, and therefore she was struggling for total peace about what she was involved in. On many levels, it just felt wrong, and yet for so many people, millions and millions of people, it would mean everything could be made right. In her moments with John, she could push the thoughts, as best as she could, to one side, but in the cool air outside, and on her own, they were waging war with her conscience. She'd been raised better, she told herself again and again. But this was another level and this was not just for her now. It was for everyone else. But as a nurse, every natural instinct was to take a patient out of danger, not to keep him in a place, a situation, that would lead to his death. And in John's case, a willing death, a sacrifice, he thought, but then he didn't know all the details. No, he was being fed a cocktail of drugs to keep his body and mind subdued while being shown things that looked so real he assumed they were. It was telling him he was someone that he actually wasn't. And by assisting with all this, by being aware and yet going along with it, she was by definition agreeing to it. So in this moment, she was questioning a lot of things in her life. True, it had to be said, she had not been given much choice in the matter, her grief and the loss of her husband originally clouding her responses early on so that she was in the program before she knew what it really was all about. But she also couldn't stand up in court and deny she made an active choice to stay in it. There had not been any threats to her, neither had she attempted to get out. Maybe if she had, if she'd forced the situation earlier on, she'd have been threatened and made a prisoner in the role herself. That way she could have shifted blame, and therefore the guilt, onto others. But she had not done that, nor felt like she had the resolve to do that now. If she was honest with herself, although she had many misgivings about how it was being done, she was in a way glad that at least something was being done.

Her loss aside, which she hadn't really started to deal with, there had been far too much death and loss already, and yet if the reports were to be believed, those that had lost their lives would be nothing compared to the millions that would die if the situation escalated out of all control, as it was threatening to do. Some were saying that it was an 'end of the world type scenario', as most knew it. Like something out of a Hollywood blockbuster and yet sadly not. This was going to happen unless something changed.

Lorna had thought back to the Vicar that married her and James. She had not really been a church goer, but had gone along to their local Church of England church in order to get married. Their banns were being read, and as a result, they needed to attend for six months before. It seemed a good way for the church to get young couples into the congregation that mainly consisted of pensioners, and they'd enjoyed the experience, for the most part. He was a younger clergyman and this was his first job as Vicar. He'd been a good listener, getting to know them both as they approached marriage, and then he took the wedding service himself. What Lorna was now thinking was that she wished she could now speak with this guy again, to talk through life and the decisions she was making. Lorna wasn't really a religious person, though she felt in herself she was not a bad person. The words of that Vicar came back to her; sitting in the cold, but friendly church building one Sunday, he'd addressed everyone as bad people. That the church was for bad people, and in fact no one was good. Everyone made bad choices. He'd talked about another man, the Jesus from the Christmas story and what he'd done. How he'd been the only one to actually live a good, sinless life.

  How funny, she felt. In this moment, when faced with life and death, and the ongoing consequences of the decisions she was now having to make daily, that in this moment she'd wanted to talk to this guy, someone from a church that she didn't really understand, and had only been a small part of for six months so that they could get married there. They'd said about going back again after they were married, but hadn't ever done so. Life seemed to take over, and even when they did have a Sunday off, it never really crossed their minds to get up and go. Neither of them had been particularly religious, and yet here she was, now, and this was the one person she wanted to talk with.

  Of course, the chances were high that he was already dead; or would certainly die soon. And what would death really mean? She had so many questions. Even for a nurse, the reality of death as a certainty for all, at some point in life, had really only recently come home to her. Before the loss of James, she'd never faced the loss of anyone she knew, and even now was not really dealing with the matter. But it was obvious now. Death was certain. No one could live forever. If John was to make this sacrifice, at some point in time everyone he saved was going to die anyway. Maybe from natural causes instead, granted, but it would only postpone the inevitable. It was a strange thought. Did the fact that, what they were doing would only buy people a little more time on Earth but ultimately not save them from death, mean it was all futile anyway? This seemed ironic for Lorna, in the mood she was in. She had never really contemplated life and death as much as she had recently, and understandably so. People don't talk about the things they don't understand. As her five minutes' break ran into ten, she had started opening her mind to one of the biggest questions of them all: what is the meaning of life and is death the end?

After thinking nothing for nearly a minute, a silence in her head as she just pondered the weight of those questions, she laughed out loud, a brief outburst, but releasing all the same. She was amused at how serious she'd become in her thinking. The air was doing nothing for relaxing her mind, but the thinking was doing something to move her along emotionally.

She did want to talk with the people from the unit monitoring her and her patient. She wanted to raise these questions, ones of ethics, with them. To sound them out, to make her thoughts known, even recorded, in case at a later point this would come back to hurt them all. Walking back towards the hospital, she sent a message to the one contact she had, asking to have some time to talk with them. Before she got back to the room, she'd had a reply, setting up a time and place to chat things through, once the patient was comfortable. It could happen straight away if she wanted, so once she checked in on John, who was enjoying the latest novel, well over half way through it already, she went on to meet with two people from the training program, while another monitored the patient for her on the screen.

Twenty minutes later, she was on her way back to John; it was time he ate. She'd shared her concerns, wanting to go on record to state her position. If anything, it had gone a long way towards building relationship between her and them. Communication had improved vastly, it felt they were all on the same page now, and they'd appreciated her honesty and boldness, her willingness to work on something even while she had her own concerns. She was putting professionalism over individualism. They'd congratulated her for that, though she wasn't there for their praise.

They'd finished by thanking her for raising a real issue, something they too were working through, and they would certainly use her thoughts as they started to draw up an ethics policy for not only John, but the entire program. They encouraged her to continue to talk with them, to make time for it. They were there for her to talk to, though they cautioned her from saying too much, certainly in this regard, to the patient. It wasn't her place to find out where John stood on these issues of faith and the questions of his view on life and death.

Walking back into the room, Lorna felt that a lot of emotional baggage had been shifted in the last hour or so. It was far from being got rid of, but well on the way. John put his book down, folding the corner of the page he was on in the process, nothing more than about fifty pages left to read, it seemed.

"Good book?" Lorna asked.

"Yeah, I'm enjoying it. You can read it after me if you like. I think I'll be finished with it this afternoon."

Lorna brought over some food.

"Here, take this," she said, placing a tray in front of

John, who positioned it in front of himself and took a look at the day's offerings.

"Looks good," he said, a little too sarcastically.

"You know hospital food. We have a reputation to maintain."

They both smiled. John started to eat slowly, as Lorna took away some dirty towels and generally made herself useful. The hard part was almost done. Her patient was healthy, improving all the time, physically recovering. He was dealing well with what he was seeing, his heart rate after each vision was almost unchanged, there was less stress on him. In all regards, he was doing well. The most important part was yet to come. Could he do what was being asked of him, and could she watch him do it without saying anything she shouldn't?

Chapter 12

Twenty Three Days Ago

It was the end of the first week with the news crew. They'd been learning a lot from the base over the last two days, and there was a noticeable increase in communications to work through. It was clear, that as the launch dates approached and intensity increased, people were becoming surprisingly less guarded, maybe even saying things they shouldn't in their internal memos. These were deemed to be a safe form of communication, unaware as they were of the prying eyes of this intrepid news team. John had shared some of the highlights from the last few days with his boss at the paper and, unknown to John, draft stories were already being worked on. It seemed everyone wanted a piece of the action.

If they were correct, the launches were to be in the coming week and, with no real releases from the base to the various news agencies, it made the nature of these launches all the more intriguing. They'd picked up some of the details for the probes now too, as changes in the probes' make-up meant a late revised plan was sent around. It was picked up by the spying device, and greeted with a stunned silence by the crew. It was bigger than they thought. They'd also nearly been hacked, or at least the army base had. They'd monitored the response, and the securing of the attempted pathway that the would-be hackers had tried to use. From their end, they were left unnoticed. It was not clear who the hackers had been. The news crew had no way of knowing since they were not on the inside. But the fact someone else was looking in, made them all the more alert. They could only speculate as to who it was. Another government, another group from the UK, maybe even another newspaper? Ironically enough, that last option made them more nervous. This was their story, their effort and handwork. For another crew to sneak in at the end and see everything, grabbing their own story and ruining all that they'd been working for, was unthinkable. The team's work was prioritised, extra resources were made available and people were on hand at the head office to be called on as and when needed.

John was now under a lot of pressure to produce results, to bring this through into a fully formed story. They'd break it the day the launch was made. It had the potential to be massive, and was certainly an exclusive. They had just three days. Having worked seven days solid, he had allowed the crew to stagger their days off, each member of the A-team having had a day off in the last three, and that day it was Bradley's turn. John himself had not taken any time off. He dared not risk losing this one, like a fisherman battling with some monster catch, he knew he couldn't let up for one moment. He was in this until the end. He wanted his catch. To let it get away was unthinkable.

Bradley, a day to himself, was far from resting, however. He'd got everything he needed, and had copied what he could. He'd pieced together what was happening when and he had already written half of a draft of his own exclusive story. Using a pre-paid mobile phone as he was naturally the very cautious type, he'd arranged a meeting with another national newspaper. He'd flashed his credentials around in an email to the owner and claimed to be bringing with him the biggest story of the decade. It was the type of story that paper specialised in, and was far from the first time they'd coaxed in a juicy story that was jumping ship from a rival paper. They'd let it be known, not publicly of course, that they were in the market for such stories, and paid well for those that ran this particular gauntlet. It was dirty work, but then again it was an industry, certainly at that level, that lived for dirty. And someone had to do it, Bradley told himself, as he walked into the paper's London office. Now it was his turn to shine, to make the kind of breakthrough that would elevate him to where he wanted to be, where he needed to be. This was his moment. However, his nerves were shot. Looking constantly over his shoulder, he was starting to fear his own shadow, certain that someone was on to him, that his magic moment would get stolen from him. He made it to the lifts and selected the twelfth floor, getting into the lift alone. No one was following him, but in his own head he was now a walking target, vulnerable at any moment, and certain to be found out.

Thirty minutes later, he felt a lot happier about the situation. He'd shown them the outline, running off the highlights, without giving up his source. It was clear to them that Bradley was well connected, either directly with the base or through someone else who was. They'd been excited by the information they'd seen, the make-up of the probes, the launch information. They'd then talked about a million pound contract for the story and the promise to keep him on the staff as a senior reporter after it broke. Memos were sent. It could go live that week, the paper was keen to break it at least a day before it would otherwise break with their rival paper. Bradley left with instructions to put the finishing touches to the story and to have it back with them by the end of the day. He left to go and find somewhere quiet to sit and write, though he needed some lunch first, so he headed for a restaurant.

Picking up on the newspaper's internal memos was a team of two South Africans, working as part of a bigger team that saw Nigerian and South African secret services joining forces. They'd been monitoring a couple of the major newspapers for anything relating to the probe mission. This news changed their mood instantly and once the two of them had found the information and reported it, they were out onto the streets, keen to talk with this mysterious reporter looking to turn traitor on his current employer. From the little they knew, this man was clearly in contact with a real source for the level of information he had far surpassed theirs. Their own attempted hack into the army base the other day had not been successful and now that weakness in the system had been repaired and fortified. Posing as high level employees from the newspaper Bradley was doing a deal with, they'd met him in a restaurant and started up a conversation. For Bradley, as he had been so secretive and it had only just happened, these people could only have been who they said they were. He wasn't willing to talk about sources, but their probing was starting to get to him. They threatened to pull out of the million pound contract altogether. They kept asking about who it was, whether it was someone on the base. They'd stated it was important this was reputable, that the paper had a right to know, especially if they were paying out a million pound fee for the story. On this note, Bradley realised they had a point. He did not want to say too much, but made it clear his source was direct and was not a person. When he was quizzed a little more, their persuasive nature eventually got through to Bradley and he let on they had a listening device stashed safely away that was picking up everything and was totally untraceable. He lied about that last bit as he was getting worried that he was revealing too much.

It was maybe ten minutes after sharing this that his two companions left abruptly and Bradley felt a little confused as to what had just happened. The two men reported in with the information and were told to wait outside the restaurant until they received further orders. Bradley, meanwhile, continued to work on his article, potentially the crowning moment of his career. He was already starting to spend the money. It made it harder than usual for him to concentrate.

"Focus, man! Focus!" he told himself. "You are nearly there. Don't mess it up now."

One Year Ago

The second day of discussions had long been finished and most of the delegates had left. There were no formal plans for that evening, each group free to find their own entertainment, and some just went back to their hotel, tired from what had been a difficult day.

The British and Americans had remained and both parties sat in the lounge area of their rented conference facility. Drinks were served regularly by the catering team, who had been asked to stay on a little, with the promise of a large bonus.

"We really are going to have to talk about what happens after, you know," the Americans started, laying right in with their sole agenda. "We have poured in millions for this and our goal all along has been the power plant blueprints that we agreed to share."

The British snarled at this, three of the group falling back in their chairs, each looking annoyed but not rattled by the statement.

"This was a space probe agreement and you all know it!" the British said first.

"Quit playing games with us. You'd have got nowhere without us. Your space program, if we can even call it that, was a joke. You have no experience, no expertise, and yet you needed us to get you where you are. All the time we've worked on the technology together, building and developing the nuclear capability, something we know for sure that you've developed and extended into practical applications for use on a ground based power station. You can't pull the wool over our eyes. We know what's going on."

"And what is going on, please tell me?" The British were getting angry now, and it showed.

"You needed everything we could give you.

Technology and the experience of NASA, the mighty US dollar. Investment and trade. It was us making this happen for you and without us you were nowhere. It was our government agreeing with your government that it was in everyone's best interest if we could do this together. And while the space probes are revolutionary and brilliant for what they are, they were just a smoke screen. You needed us to help you to see if we could get them to work, so that you could profit from the rest. So we are here for the blueprints. We too are equal partners in this. We can agree to split the world how we want so that we don't both sell power to the same countries. We can reach a solution. There is no way you can hold onto this thing on your own."

"Is that so? I'm not really sure you know how business works."

"Don't patronise me, you stupid Brit!" Everything went silent for a few seconds. The emotions calmed a little before the American continued: "We knew all along what kind of deal this was."

"So I won't need to remind you that our deal was to launch four state of the art space probes that will revolutionise our ability to monitor, record and track anything and anyone we like. And on that front, we are partners."

At this the Americans collectively grunted.

"You surprise us," the Americans said, "to think that we'd be so naive as to not know this was your smoke screen all along. Had it been us you stole this from, it would already have been over."

Both teams locked eyes with each other. It had been said. The Americans knew that the British had stolen the idea. Did they know from whom it had been stolen? It was probable they could now guess, anyway.

The conversation paused as a fresh supply of coffee was brought in, though nobody wanted any, nor had it been ordered. The waiters removed the empty cups, before exiting back into the kitchen. It was here that the team of caterers made their first mistake. They sent a call to their section head who was also based in London at that moment, reporting news about the power plant blueprints. These seemed to be the hot property now at stake between the Americans and British, though the news of the space probe program had also been of great interest. This call had been tracked by the same MI6 Black Ops team who'd been busy earlier that day. It was the first sign that anyone else had been keeping tabs on the talks. It became a major security alert which needed dealing with quickly. And they knew exactly what needed to be done.

Twenty Three Days Ago

The two South African secret service agents had been in conversation with area HQ for thirty minutes, through coded messages.

"We need to be careful about what they are picking up. It's possible they will be able to monitor any message we send," came the latest reply.

The two guys looked at each other. They'd been going around the same issue for some time now. Still there had been no reply to their main question.

"Has the virus already been uploaded," they repeated.

"We are unclear on that," came the automatic reply. They were staying silent, it was becoming clear. Over half their questions that day had been answered the same way. In other words, 'we aren't going to tell some low-ranking field agents like yourselves.' They got the message.

What most people at the time had not known, apart from those in the African secret service, was that the attempted hack had not been without some success. True, the team from Nigeria that had carried out what they thought was the main hack had not been able to find out what they were after. This had been to look for the plans for the power station as well as to understand the true origins of the breakthrough. That information had very explosive potential and was clearly highly valuable if traded for money or other trade links. That attempt was really just the smoke screen, because unknown to that team was an Indian genius who was also working for the service. He'd managed to piggy back his way in during the attempted hack and had successfully uploaded a worm that would sit dormant in the computer system but kick in once the probes were fully operational. It would effectively give him full control, and he'd use it to send the probes back to Earth. The Indian young man also worked for the Chinese. Why earn from just one side when two were paying top dollar? The worm was therefore more destructive than either side knew, and included a message that would appear in the final seconds before impact. It was the Indian technician's way of showing ultimate power; to laugh in the face of those who were paying him, to prove he was the best and feared no one.

Back on the street once more, the two South African agents were given orders to just watch Bradley. At that moment he was paying up, having packed up his things into his bag moments before, and he was now heading towards the main doors. They were in a small park across the road from the restaurant, and it was a busy day in London. Cars, buses and taxis moved in every direction. Bradley was outside and on the street, deciding which way to turn. The two agents, safe in the crowds, left the park, keeping him in eye-shot the whole time. They agreed to split up and one started to cross the road as two shots rang out. Their eyes went instantly to Bradley who fell to the floor. Blood was visible on the pavement where he lay. Screams could be heard, as people ran for cover. Cars stopped. The two agents froze, then quickly backtracked. A crowd of people were starting to approach Bradley, but even from a distance, judging by the expressions on the faces of the gathering crowd, hands coming up to shocked mouths, it was clear that Bradley had been killed. Back together again, having moved further along the road out of sight of the incident, the two agents sat on another bench in a small green area. Police sirens could be heard approaching and two cars travelled at speed past them, their blue lamps flashing and bouncing light through the darkening evening. One of the two agents opened his phone again, keying in his message in code:

"Was it us?" he wrote.

"We are unclear on that," came the instant response.

Present Day

The hospital had continued to be busy, with all staff continually stretched and run off their feet. This was apart from Lorna, who was to remain exclusively available for John. The nurses were running out of steam, their energy levels dropping, as patient after patient came in, the majority of them beyond hope even before arrival. It was more a matter of making them comfortable in death rather than keeping them alive.

What the hospital was struggling to cope with was the number of visitors arriving, who were desperately searching for missing loved ones. Despite the warnings and potential danger to themselves, hundreds of people had still travelled from far away and were searching the hospitals. It was impossible for the hospitals to keep on top of all the patients. Many of the victims were brought to the hospital in a dreadful physical condition, so identification was becoming a real issue and many came with no documentation on them at all. It was becoming a logistical nightmare to keep track of who was who, and where anyone was. So now, many days after the initial incident, and adding to the chaos already going on, there were hundreds of visitors, each demanding answers, each desperate for news on lost loved ones. Sadly, however, it was rare for someone to actually find the person they were looking for. News spread, of course, of those rare reunions, and hope rose in the many more still searching. Some visitors just walked around the hospital, going where they shouldn't, often dropping in on rooms at the worst possible times and often seeing something they would later wish they hadn't, but it did not stop their pursuit for information, for news, for any kind of hope.

On a few occasions the visitors showed genuine concern for the nurses, asking how they were coping. You could tell those that knew what they were talking about, and understood what it was like in a hospital when trauma hit, though even they were really just after news.

Alison was walking around, taking note of the situation around her, and saw one of her young nurses being given a hard time by two male visitors. As she went over, the guys spotted her coming and turned to her.

"Can I help you," she asked them; the young nurse was clearly grateful for the rescue, and quickly made her escape.

"Yes, we are looking for a colleague of ours," the taller guy said. A strong accent came through, though it wasn't clear if he was trying to hide it or emphasis it. "He was a reporter with our paper, we thought we lost the whole team but apparently he's survived. Do you know if he's here or not?"

Alison looked at them both, and trusted her instincts.

"Look, I'm really sorry, but I don't think we can help you. We have over three thousand patients here, most of them are in a very bad way, and we have no idea of who most of them are. I am not aware of any journalists here, maybe you should check another hospital?"

They both looked noticeably agitated by her reply

and her unwillingness to help. But since they were getting nowhere, they thanked her and turned away, walking back out of the main doors, before stopping, now out of sight, to work out what they were going to do next.

Alison, meanwhile, went to find the young nurse who had been talking with them before she intervened. She didn't have to go far before she came across her.

"Nina, can I have a word?" she asked, pulling her to one side, as a trolley was being moved down the busy corridor. "Those two men, what did they say to you?"

"Same as the rest. They were looking for a relative of theirs, a guy in his thirties named John Westlake. They had a photo but I knew nothing about him, and then you came over."

"Thanks, Nina. Leave this one with me," she said and continued on her way.

During her next coffee break, Alison took time to go and find Lorna, to have a catch up, but also talk about the day's events. Finding her on her way out for some fresh air, they walked together and talked. Eventually the conversation turned to Lorna's special patient.

"Talking of John, there were two guys in here today looking for him. Said they worked for him and had heard he might have survived."

"How did they hear that?" Lorna said. "I thought nothing had been released about him because it was best his family assumed he was dead?"

"Yeah, that's what I understood too. They were South African, I'd recognise that accent anywhere, but something didn't sit right about them. They first told Nina that he was a relative before I arrived, and then they talked to me about working with him."

"Seems strange. Did you say anything?"

"No," Alison replied. "That sixth sense us nurses have in these moments. You know what I mean, when what they are saying doesn't fit with what we are seeing and reading from their body language. There's no way they could have known he was here, or alive, if they were with the paper. Not unless someone has been talking."

"Okay, leave this one with me, Alison. Thanks for letting me know. I'll take it to the team monitoring this all and see what they have to say."

"Thanks. So," Alison said, changing the subject, "how are you bearing up since you heard about James?" She knew it was a raw subject but they had talked briefly once, the other day, and Lorna was handling things quite well, even then.

"I've not really had the time to process things if I'm honest. You know how it is here, too much to do." That was an understatement if ever she heard one. Alison nodded but didn't comment. No comment was needed. They were both in the same place, unable to talk about what was really happening, barely coping themselves.

Lorna continued:

"Yesterday would have been our anniversary, so that brought a few things home, in their own way." Alison looked to Lorna, a tear in her own eye already but nothing showing on Lorna's face.

"One month ago I was as happy as I had ever been. And now......" Lorna didn't know how to finish the sentence, so Alison spoke for them both.

"Now, girl, life just sucks."

They both looked at each other, weighed down for a moment with the seriousness of it all, before each one smiled, almost at the same time, as if to say 'that's right, we'll just have to shrug it off and carry on regardless.'

They looked out over the fields, the trees that once stood so tall, their autumn colours so bright, now just adding to the scene of despair. Beyond them, the fires still burned, the sky line filled with towers of thick black smoke, the distant sky itself a dense mass of smoke and fumes. A darkness was covering them, as if to symbolise what was also covering their emotions. It was a cloud that would not be easily moved. They stood next to each other for what seemed like ages, not saying anything, just watching, looking, thinking their own quiet thoughts. After some time, Alison put her arm around the shoulders of Lorna and spoke softly:

"Look, I think we'd better head back in, but I've enjoyed this. Please know that you can talk with me about anything."

"Thanks. I've needed this too. I'll certainly take you up on that offer. Tell me though, how has it come to this?" She was pointing to the horizon that once boasted a superb view over London.

"I really don't know, Lorna. I just don't know."

They started walking back towards the hospital, slowly but steadily, before Alison finished:

"But whatever caused this, it doesn't have to be what defines how it all finishes. We've survived, and we'll go on fighting. It's all we can do. It's all we can ask our patients to do. And if your patient is really able to do what we hope he can, then one day, that view, that city we once looked out over, could be rebuilt. And out there somewhere, ahead of us in some unknown future, are also the building blocks for our own lives to be restored, one block at a time. You'll see."

Lorna pondered the words for a moment, and held onto them, but there seemed no obvious reply, so she didn't offer one. They went their separate ways, and returned to the roles in which they were most needed: Alison to the busy and hectic wards, Lorna to her patient John, on whom now rested so much. The hopes of the nation. Yet so little did he know.

Chapter 13

Twenty Two Days Ago

It was two days before the first launch and day eight of John's team project when news first reached them about the shooting of Bradley outside a London restaurant. They were all deeply shocked and surprised; there was no obvious motive. It wasn't too long before they all started to see the possible connection, each in his own way, but nobody said anything out loud. They had no idea as to why he had been killed or what he'd been doing in London that day. It was his day off, so perfectly understandable that he might have gone somewhere to eat. The team had not picked up any hints that Bradley was involved in anything unsavoury, though no one knew him that well. He was the outsider in the group and had grown increasingly more so over the previous few days. In some ways, him being off the previous day had been easier on them all.

Now, of course, came the guilt and remorse and they'd taken time away from all the monitoring to talk through and process what had taken place, to mark the passing of a colleague and accomplished journalist, even if not the loss of a friend.

After the thirty minute pause, there was a distinctly more sombre mood, a deeper recognition that they were now a man down. Had what they were doing got him killed? This was the thought on John's mind as he cautiously started working through things again, looking at his notes, reading through the documents, piecing together the story.

Across the city, at the rival newspaper Bradley had approached the day before, there was also a tellingly downbeat mood in the office of the editor. He'd been told the news by his boss, while we was working on a draft of the story based on what Bradley had already given them.

They were now rather cautious about proceeding, aware that what he'd told them had almost certainly caused his death. They'd been at the scene within minutes of the shooting, as the office was close by and it was central London after all. A shooting was a big event. It was clear it had been a professional hit: two shots fired from some distance, from an as yet unknown marksman's gun, hitting the same spot on the victim's forehead. An assassination. It added to the story, but also brought a sharp reality to it all. They were being pulled into something far bigger than usual and it had got their source killed. Was it the British cleaning up, or Bradley's source killing him for leaking their information? There were too many questions and it was too hot to touch. Crucially, they were ordered to shelve the scoop until further notice. The paper didn't want the fight coming to them if they published what they had. They recognised when to back away silently, and this was certainly that moment. Security was stepped up around the building, as well, just as a precaution. If the killing had been a warning, for them it had worked. They had the outlines of a great story anyway, ready to be used when the time was right. It would certainly hurt someone, but continuing to publish it at the moment, could end up hurting them the most. That wasn't something they were willing to do.

    As lunch time approached in the café where John's team had largely based themselves for the previous week, the usual trade was starting to come through. Passing customers were obviously aware of news reports about the journalist as his picture had been splashed across many front pages, and most locals had recognised him as a regular visitor to their local café. And with the team's number obviously reduced that day in the café, the gossip was beginning to spread fast. Rather than stay away, people were going out of their way to drop in on the tired looking café. It had never done such a good trade as it had in the previous eight days.

John rounded up his A-team and decided they'd move out for the afternoon. They could all now fit comfortably in the van, and maybe it would be quieter for them. He was aware of the increased traffic through the café and didn't want to attract any more unwanted attention. It was also getting nearer to the launch of the first probe and they wanted to be as near to the site as possible.

They were starting to pick up a lot more relevant information from the base. Internal memos between various departments, weather readouts, guidelines, as well as all the inconsequential chat about weekend activities and such. They had already figured out which people to focus on as they had already worked out a system and understood the obvious hierarchy working within the base. They would prioritise the information coming from certain areas of the office or certain people over that of other, less senior, people. That way they were able to keep up with the information, even though they were now a man down.

Later that evening, as their van pulled back into the car park at the café, they got out and returned to their own cars. Alan took the van home himself as they'd agreed to meet early the following morning. John saw the owner of the café doing the final clean up as the café was closing. There was no one left in the place after what had been a very busy day for him. John walked in, the door making a ring, and the owner peered through from the back, thinking he'd have to tell someone it was closed, only to see John. He smiled.

"Quite a day!" he said, coming out with a cloth in his hands.

"I'd say we've been good for business. Maybe we should work on commission," John said with a smile.

"The gossip has been flying around here, I can say. Lots of folks have made the connection. I'm really sorry for your loss."

"Look, don't feel sorry. In truth, we have no idea what happened. Maybe just some random act of terror? Maybe someone paying some revenge for something from before?" John didn't really know what more to say.

"The folks in here today have been genuinely sorry with what happened. Most had made the connection, for the rest they soon heard the rumours when they arrived here."

"You've got your own little thriving gossip mill all of a sudden," John said.

"I know. Who'd have thought it!" the owner said, a smile crossing his face. "One more thing. A couple of strangers came asking around as well, just moving through the crowd. White guys with an accent. Australian or South African, I can't always tell. They weren't American, anyway, that's for sure. They mean anything to you?"

"No," John said, a little concerned. "What do you mean they were asking around?"

"Just that, really. Turned up around three o'clock. Ordered a coffee each, and sat there watching the door. I was in and out of the kitchen but it seemed they got into some of the conversations going on around them. They were asking about the dead guy, asking what they all thought and had they seen him here. Most folks played it dumb, but I don't think they bought it. They left suddenly, and a few of the people talked with me after. They wanted to know who he'd been working with. They wanted to know about you and your team."

John looked even more concerned now. So the owner added:

"I didn't say anything. I don't think anyone really did. But I thought I'd mention it to you in case."

'In case what?' John wanted to ask, but let that thought go. "Thanks," he added and turned to leave. "Look, you've been great with letting us use your café, and I'm glad it has been good for business. But I think we're done now with this phase of things, so we won't be back tomorrow. All the best. And I hope to see you again at some point." John turned and left, not knowing if he would actually try and come back to the café. It had made a really useful base for the week, but the food wasn't much to write home about. And now someone had come snooping. That made him a little cautious. Fear now rose in his stomach like bile. He looked around the empty car park but was alone. Pulling away, he kept checking his mirrors, watching for any tail, but the roads were quiet and as far as he could tell, no one was watching him.

Back at the cottage, he once again checked around, remaining seated in his car for five minutes just watching the road behind him as well as for any movements coming from inside his home. There were neither, so he slowly got out, locked the car and walked over to the front door. He was like a man with a death sentence hanging over him. That was certainly how he was beginning to feel.

"What have I got into?" he said aloud once inside, having checked every room twice just to be sure. Taking a bottle of whisky from the cupboard under the stairs, he pulled out a glass and sat down, turning the TV on. There was an old British comedy just starting. The perfect end to a troublesome day. Sixty minutes later, the bottle half finished and the comedy programme only just ended, he was already asleep.

Three Weeks Ago

Felix managed just over three hours' sleep and he woke with a start just after ten on that bright, fresh Tuesday morning. The program was finished, some further testing was needed, but he'd get that done straight away and aimed to make it available to others before the day was out.

The great challenge would be to get it to the right kind of people and, more importantly than that, to find someone who could be the person to make the journey back. There was no way of knowing how possible it would all be. Unknown to Felix at the time, two attempts had been made to go in and close down the system. The first guy, in full chemical suit, had been so disabled by the weight of the suit that he'd become unsteady working his way through the debris, the same rocks and bricks and metal that made a robotic operation impossible. He'd caused a long tear to the suit that had caused severe radiation burns which killed him. He was still over three hundred metres from the site when he fell down dead. At the next attempt they got within one hundred and fifty metres, but even without a tear in the suit this time, the level of output from the leaking nuclear reactors, as well as the general heat and difficulty of the situation, had stopped that attempt. There were no further volunteers to try again nor was there an obvious solution to protect them from the lethal levels of radiation anyway.

In the early evening of that Tuesday, a day that had been like all the others since the incident with many deaths reported, fear growing, worldwide support being offered but from arm's length, of course, Felix deemed his part in the program to be concluded. It was time to bring in others, fresh people who could take things on from him. He would have liked to have been involved further but he knew his time and energy were now running out. Far from resting and maybe having a few more days or weeks to live, he'd burned himself out by working non-stop, sleeping very little, in the vain hope that he'd be able to see the issue resolved. To die trying was better than to die doing nothing at all. That was his state of mind. There was no escape for him, so why not work hard and hasten the inevitable rather than stop and feel sorry for himself, and have it all happen to him anyway.

At six that evening, as he finished a telephone call with the army, the officer stated that they were very keen to speak further with him and someone was already on his way. The military realised they were fighting a losing battle. The clean up problems were getting worse by the day, the death toll was rising inexorably, with no hope of the containment or isolation that was desperately needed. So when Felix had rung them, talking about this mind control program that he'd been perfecting, it gave them ideas and hope where up to that point there had been nothing to go on. So someone came round to discuss his ideas.

By nine that evening Felix was feeling more exhausted than he'd felt before. After a long discussion the man from the base had gone and so had his pride and joy. He'd been cut from future involvement which had been a problem to him at the start of their talks. He'd wanted to see it in action, to be an adviser, to talk and work with them as they tested it and, hopefully, put it into operation. But he was a liability now, they saw. Sick beyond recovery, the last stages of the illness were already starting to become visible. Felix was suffering from nose bleeds and his hair was falling out in large clumps. The official who took the program away then left him alone. Now there was nothing to do but die and the end was very swift. Just thirty minutes after the man had left with his legacy in his possession, Felix fell unconscious on the floor of the room that had been his workstation for the past week. He was not to regain consciousness, drifting deeper and deeper away, though it would be three days before his body would be discovered. His time had come and his passing was as peaceful as was possible.

The special unit from the army who were now in possession of the program would start testing straight away that very night. Its potential was seen for what it could do, blinding the mind of its victim and making him do whatever they wanted, in the belief that it was some premonition he was seeing, some higher calling being given to him to save others. If they could get someone to willing make the walk and shut down the reactors, then the world had a chance to recover. The UK might survive this disaster, England could one day come alive again. Controlling the mind was one thing. The limitations of the human body remained, and that would take further testing. With so much widespread death and destruction, it was hoped, with justification as it turned out, that there would be someone, or something, that would come from it all and give them hope. If someone was somehow less affected by radiation, or showed the ability to survive, it would give them a window. They were aware, after all, of the secret stories from Japan and Russia after nuclear explosions of the 'walking dead'. Tales of survivors being found, of living beyond what was normal, when everyone else around them had died. These stories were hidden and the people in question had long since died. It was already estimated that millions were potentially affected in the south of England. Unconfirmed reports had it that the death toll was already at three hundred thousand and this was rising by the tens of thousands each day. With such a huge number of people, it was surely a matter of probability that soon, as in those other countries from years before, there too would be unlikely survivors, and if that was the case, then maybe this program was the lifesaver they were looking for. Maybe Felix, this strange young man who'd called them out of the blue, had given them one last hope of coming through this nightmare. The only obvious prediction now, with the reactor likely to explode at any time, was that life in and around England would not survive if the whole plant was to go up. It would be very soon that the opportunity would present itself, with the first of three survivors pulled from the debris, wounded, battered and bruised but importantly, very much still alive.

Chapter 14

Present Day

It was night already before Lorna got a chance to chat with the army team behind the program she was assisting John through. Her patient was now asleep, his third book already looking well read lying beside him on his night stand. Before getting some sleep herself, she'd wanted to inform them about the two visitors, she wanted to check to see if they were who they said they were, though she had come to doubt that more and more as the day had gone on.

Taking a few moments to share what she'd been told, she outlined what had happened, and what they'd said, giving the two accounts of who they said they were, and stating she didn't feel either was true.

"Thank you very much for letting us know," they said.

"I thought nothing was being said about him being here?"

"As far as we know, nothing has been. We are going to step up security just in case. We'll post two men outside his room at all times and look to increase security going forward. There is no way they could have heard anything from us, though we'll run an internal investigation to be totally sure of that."

"Who do you think they are then?" Lorna was a little concerned herself now.

"At this moment, we really can't say." Lorna looked like she was being shut out. They picked up on this and rephrased the response. "By which we mean, we really don't know who they are or what their intentions are if, or when, they find John. We will go after them and try and find out who they are, but that will be another team, and we'll brief them tomorrow. For now, the patient's continued good progress needs to be our number one concern and we'll therefore watch his security very carefully. If anything further develops or if you hear about these men coming back again, or anyone else, please alert us straight away."

"I will." Lorna got up, and after saying goodnight, went off to find some much needed sleep.

Meanwhile, outside the hospital the two South African secret service agents were still monitoring the situation, having reported back to HQ their earlier encounter. They were unhappy at how things had gone and concerned that they'd made things worse. It wouldn't be allowed to happen again, they'd been told.

It was assumed, correctly as it happened, to be a very good sign that the South African involvement in the affair was still largely undetected. If there were any exceptional survivors, they were either too unwell, or too unconscious to speak. Or they did not know, or could not remember, anything important anyway. Since the South Africans had been made aware by Bradley some two weeks before that a team had been listening in on all base communications, the obvious assumption was that they must have also picked up on the message that had been uploaded, which was meant to have died with everyone. A survivor might therefore cause huge problems. The incident was so far being treated as a huge accident. That is what it was meant to look like. If it was found to be otherwise, it wouldn't take long for the warships to set sail and full-scale war to break out. There was no way any African country could stand against a British backlash. As a precaution, there had been lots of information planted, conveniently hidden, to make initial blame hard to find with China, Russia and even the Americans all looking a bit guilty. Little did the Africans know that the Chinese were already very much under British suspicion. It had been their invention that had been stolen. It seemed likely that the Chinese would want to discredit any future British energy breakthrough, delivering a blow of such magnitude that the country would collapse. The truth was that neither China nor the Africans had known how bad the incident would be, but far enough away from it all, with a Europe no longer in the picture, it would make the world once again a level playing field. America would lose one of its closest allies, who were also its strongest economic partner. The market was open for a new superpower and the main players were already fighting to get into pole position.

The African continent certainly wanted its part in that. Their joint secret service efforts had got them a long way and gave them a chance for their own shot at glory. The two South African field agents, one of about a dozen teams currently on the ground somewhere in the UK, were told to stay in the shadows for now, to keep watching the situation and gather all the information they could. If there was any chance that this man was still alive, and knew something, then they were to make sure it never got out. Containment was to be the main goal; at this moment, they just had no idea of the complexity of the situation they were walking into.

One Year Ago

The true identity of the African secret service team, which was largely operating undercover as caterers, was leaked by the Black Ops team to MI5 shortly before midnight. Evidence had been planted following the earlier shooting of the Chinese businessman to lead the British Security Service to find and trace those responsible. MI5 moved fast, arresting everyone within a few minutes of each other, but still shooting erupted at what turned out to be the Africans' base camp. Three men were killed and two others wounded. Another two were taken into custody for questioning. As was normal in the situation, the Chinese were told about the attack, that the three terrorists solely responsible for the earlier attack had been killed and that the risk was now gone. The other targets were free to go and could continue whatever it was they were in the UK to do. MI5 did not tell the Chinese about the two wounded and two held captive. It was better they thought they were all killed. MI5 could therefore interrogate them all themselves and learn properly who they all were and how they had come to be spying on them. In time, they would be released back to Africa and denied entry back to the West. But that would be some months away. For now, the word was that all terrorists had been killed. The security alert had been reduced. Things could return to normal and the Chinese contingent could be around the table again tomorrow for day three of the talks. A new team of catering staff, British nationals, would be sourced and used for the remainder of the talks. It had been a successful closure of the risk of anything more getting out, but had also made the British aware of this otherwise unknown threat. How much else the Africans had learned was also a worry. They'd been nowhere near this deal before, but now potentially knew as much as anyone.

Present Day

The two South African agents had spent the last day coming and going from the general hospital area. They'd checked out another nearby hospital, just to be sure, but that had almost nothing happening in terms of patients that might be talking. That place had been for the palliative care of people who would soon be dead from their injuries.

Once again they were outside the same hospital they'd been at that morning and they'd seen a few nurses come and go, one or two of whom they now recognised. They also had confirmation that this was the right hospital as their sources were picking up on various communications. A special British army security unit was reported to be on the way for the following day. It was too much of a coincidence that it had happened the day after they'd both started asking questions at the hospital and got nowhere with either of the two nurses they'd questioned. For the time being they needed to keep a low profile. Like one of their native big cats in Africa, they needed to watch from the tall grass, bide their time and, when they saw their chance, go in for the kill. The element of surprise was still with them and maybe they'd been lucky so far. Now they would have to wait.

Deep inside those same hospital walls, the small specialist army unit monitoring the progress of John in an otherwise secretive operation, were themselves working with a few extra personnel. A briefing had just finished; the four men from the SAS army unit deployed to help the team had been given the information as it currently stood.

Nothing had yet been discovered on who the visitors were, the face matches not producing any results so far. It was widely decided that they were undesirables and therefore everyone was on high alert. The SAS team were ordered to find and locate these two South Africans. They were needed alive in order to try to find some answers to some vital questions: who were they working for, what were they doing, why were they here and what they wanted with John? It had been confirmed that no such men worked for the newspaper that John had spent his professional life with. Nor were any of John's family from outside the UK. Since the only information that the South Africans had given was that John was a colleague or a relation, along with the name of their patient, it was a good guess that they were highly trained and working with others. Security was reviewed, passwords changed. A new level of encryption was added to all communications and that would keep any prying eyes out, at least for a time. Unknown to the unit, the SAS were also carrying out background checks on each member, in cooperation with MI5, in order to reveal any possible leak, though nothing would be found in that regard. It was getting dark when the four man SAS team left the hospital the way they had come, in an unmarked white van from a rear entrance.

It was an entrance the two South Africans had been watching for some time, aware of the standard issue van, void of any type of marking, which ironically made it stand out for them all the more. Having had their communications channel broken, a first sign that greater encryption was now being used, they'd seen all they needed as the four men came quickly out of a fire door in an empty part of the hospital and got into the van. Even in those few seconds, you could see the army discipline in their stride, the fact they walked straight forward, in perfect pace, not looking around them, all getting in the van at the same time, the doors closing at the same millisecond. This was special forces if ever they saw them. At that moment, they both looked at each other and physically moved back further into the shadow of their vehicle as the white van came round and passed them, still some distance away. They were unnoticeable in their current spot, but still felt very vulnerable.

"We'd better call this in. Those guys were British special forces. The SAS don't mess around. We need to get out of here for the time being."

"I'm with you," the other guy said, a little younger than the man now driving, but with more field experience. He was calling in with the news as they moved off into the night's traffic. Though there were still cars moving around the edges of the city, it was obviously nothing like it used to be. Delays were now unheard of. Those who were still alive were doing their best to stay away. And at that moment, their radiation injections aside, the two South Africans wondered what in the world they were doing anywhere near this mess.

Later that night, they would face a grilling from their superiors. How had they been so stupid as to just walk into the hospital and start throwing questions around. They'd blown their real element of surprise and brought upon themselves their own search party. While they themselves were looking for someone, they would now have to watch their own backs. It made their involvement risky and for a time they were going to be redeployed. However, they were still high ranking and highly experienced. If things needed to get dirty, they were both the best that the Africans had to offer. It would not be possible to keep them on the sidelines for too long. But for now, they were to lie low. Another two teams were deployed to watch the hospital. Head office was trying once again to get through the new encryption, to learn what they could that way. They'd faced a setback, but if they were careful, it would still prove impossible for anyone to discover their involvement in all this. Time was still on their side. Any more failure would not be tolerated.

One Year Ago

The rest of the talks had progressed well, without much more drama. The Chinese were back around the table, though they were quiet after everything that had happened. The Americans had an obvious objection to the British but no one was sure what it was, or why, apart from the British themselves. The Russians were able to offer more help and some finances. This had brought them into things a little more. But they wanted greater involvement and that would have to come at a later point. First they needed to show the others what they could do. They would have some bargaining power when the others saw what they had to offer. With technology now also coming from Russian factories, that opportunity would soon present itself. The Europeans had been the ones who had gained least. And just being there was like watching a love affair blossom before their very eyes, with the British coupled with the Americans in the way that they had hoped they would have been. They still felt cheated. They'd also picked up a change in the relations of the two so-called partners, a friction that had been growing over the course of the last few days, both parties sitting further from each other, acting more aggressively towards each other, often cutting in on speech, questioning, challenging, even acting quite rudely. They knew something was up. It seemed a crack in the special relationship might be presenting itself. Now they just needed to find the right kind of explosive to blow it all apart.

The Chinese had not learned much more about how things stood. Their agents had not been able to turn anyone onto their side nor get to learn anything of any real value. The terror attack and the potential threat had been news to them at the time. That was unusual. Usually they were the first to know and passed on what they knew, some of the time, to those at risk. But they'd been unaware of any threat in the UK and didn't really see anything to be alarmed about, even after the photos were sent to the newspaper, until a key agent, in deep cover, was killed outside his Kings Road hotel in Fulham, West London. After that they'd agreed to the withdrawal, not wanting to risk the lives of their other assets, some of whom were planted at the highest levels, deep undercover, and not in any of the photos: enough had been shown to make them heed the warning. They had learned that there was a team, much bigger than just three, working in the UK from an African coalition. They had not bought the UK story about the three dead being all that MI5 caught, though they had no way of being sure. Either the British were hiding something, or there were others still on the run. The Chinese were checking the latter possibility with teams covering the country and all airports. The former was also being worked on, with undercover agents inside the government and security services pressing to discover all they could.

The talks concluded in the afternoon of the fourth day of discussions. Farewells were said, and they were courteous, if not warm. The Americans were last to leave, and one of them grabbed his British counterpart firmly by the arm and said:

"This is not over if you think for one minute we've been silenced on the energy issue. We've gone to war for much less. You think about that one for a minute while you drink your milky tea and eat that disgusting fruit cake you all love."

With that, they left the building, travelling in three black four-by-fours that left at speed and disappeared into the early evening traffic.

Chapter 15

Present Day

John woke up in a dark room. It felt cold, but he wasn't sure if that was more the darkness or the reality. There was no sound. On the far wall there was now a window. He was moving towards that light, though his legs were not moving. He was in another vision. As he approached the window, there was an empty chair. From the shadows appeared Felix, his constant companion through the last week or so. The truth was, John had lost all sense of time. He had no idea of how long things had actually been taking. He was not too concerned about it however. Here he was, injured and recovering in hospital, with as yet no memory of who he once had been or why he had ended up in the hospital in the first place. The longer it had been, the longer he feared that he didn't want to know who he was. He'd struggled with the fact that besides Lorna, his trusty nurse, no one had come to see him. Once, as Lorna left he had glimpsed two army personnel outside the door standing guard. Keeping him under guard, no doubt. He was beginning to believe he was a monster. He was starting to fear the return of any memory, like the light being turned on to a scene of terror; images that you wish you never saw, but have no way of erasing. And as Felix approached, in this latest vision from the darkness, those thoughts were racing around in his head like motor cars on a Grand Prix circuit. The darkness seemed to be hiding a lot and also seemed to be loaded with fear, it was starting to get too much for him. Little did he know but this was to be the last vision of its kind.

Felix walked over slowly, deliberately taking the chair, moving it around a little. It seemed very exaggerated, very intentional and yet at the same time quite frustrating. Nothing was said for a long time. Felix looked up at John, straight into his eyes it seemed.

"We've reached the end of things now," he said and the words hit John with almost physical force. His mind started going wild, his heart-beat rose noticeably. While many things were still uncertain in John's mind, the end of this experience felt like a bad omen. John had been aware of this from just the first few encounters. Being told it was about to finish, meant that his part would be about to start. That thought scared him. He still had no idea about timing, or when this would all happen. Was this a vision with years to wait or had he been told this just moments before it was to happen? Either way, in that instant, he knew things were about to change dramatically.

"I need you to listen to what I have to say, as I will not have another chance," Felix continued. "My time has come and this is the last occasion when we will be together."

"Please tell me when this is going to take place. Please give me some idea of how long I have." John was sounding desperate, his voice doing nothing to mask his inner feelings.

"I can only give you so many answers. I can only show you what is to be and what you need to do. And I have shown you that. You've seen what will happen and you've seen that you can stop this. It remains in your hands to save everyone. Timing is not important, as it will all be clear to you. It is not something you have to trouble yourself with, or to think about. It will be obvious to you soon enough. And then you will need to act."

John sat there silently though his mind was far away. He was recalling much of what he'd seen, as if his brain was in video playback mode, retelling the story so far, the death and darkness, smoke and fire. That feeling from the first moment of a dark shadow, maybe death itself crouching, even lurking in the background. The body bags. The first time he'd understood that it was London, when he'd seen the snake-like river, because nothing else had given him any such clarity. Before that, it had just been some destroyed city that could have been anywhere. But it wasn't anywhere. It was his own capital city, the place he'd always lived, as far as he knew. But then there was so much he didn't know. Felix was speaking again, and it took a moment for John to refocus. His mind was tired. It had put a lot of strain on him, incredible as it all was.

"You need to know you can do this. You need to know that we believe in you. You have been seeing these visions for a reason. You are the last prophet, the only one who can do what you need to do. Without you, the world is doomed. Without you, everyone dies, including you. But you've been chosen because there is something special inside you." Felix wasn't going to say what that was, it was best to let John think that it was something more spiritual than the physical, chemical reality.

"I am ready," John said, the first words he had spoken for a while. There was some resolve starting to show in his voice now.

"Good, and very true. You were born ready. This is what you were made to do. This is your destiny, your calling."

Felix, knowing he was about to die, had put everything into the final recording, saying as much as he could without saying too much. Now he was coming back to the heart of what the program was to achieve, what it was all designed to communicate. He was not going to hold back. He knew that this recording would outlive him, that it would be his legacy, his final words on the Earth. Whoever was watching it was therefore also with him in his final moments. Felix was therefore making this clip for his own reasons too. He was unaware of who would be listening, who exactly would be seeing the vision, but aware enough, or hopeful enough, that it would be someone. It was Felix's way of dealing with his own mortality, his imminent passing. Felix knew what it was to look death in the face, to know its inevitability, to know there is nothing you can negotiate your own way out of, no way of avoiding it. So it was fitting that both men, though never physically meeting each other, were spending this final conversation facing the same outcome. They were about to die.

"I need to be sure that you have understood me," Felix said. "Please talk me through from the beginning what you have to do. Please run it by me one more time just to be sure. I will go very soon, and it will be left with just you. It will be up to you." Felix fell silent. John closed his eyes and started saying what he was recalling, from the very beginning, the scenes around him, right through to what he needed to do. He was still speaking, it seemed, as the room fell dark, as Felix disappeared, as things started spinning, shapes coming and then going, and once again he arrived back in the hospital room, his bed feeling warm around him. In his mind he was still speaking, still saying the words:

"And I need to make a sacrifice. I need to give myself to save others. I need to shut that button down and stop all the death. It's my calling, it's my role. I am the last prophet. And I will do everything you've asked me to do."

Twenty One Days Ago

John awoke late in the morning, still on his sofa, the television playing quietly in the background. His mobile phone was ringing. It was Alan, and they were wondering where he was. They'd agreed to meet in a lay-by just a mile from the RAF base. John had overslept. Jumping up, he'd told them he was on his way and that they were to stay where they were, that they'd be working from the van today, and not to bother going to the café.

It was not even twenty minutes later when John was

out of the shower, cleaner, if not totally sober. He drank a mug of strong coffee as quickly as he could and the effect was almost instant, though he still didn't really like the taste. He often wondered why he drank the stuff and yet consume it by the bucket load he did. Grabbing his jacket and keys, he was off out of the front door and into the car, watching around for any other sign of life, but so far all was quiet which suited him completely. He'd decided against mentioning anything to the others in the team about the two guys who'd come looking for them. Chances were, he now hoped anyway, that their paths wouldn't cross again, he had no intention of ever going back to the café, certainly not with the team. And the café was a long way from where they were now headed. Although, if the killing of Bradley had been linked to the base, then potentially the nearer they got to it, the nearer they got to real danger.

Today was the date of the first launch and it looked a dry and clear day for it. John hooked up with the team less than one hour after Alan had called and they were now approaching the base. They parked in a viewing area that had been made a few years before for the avid plane spotter, though thankfully they were alone that morning. If their research was accurate, today should see the launch of a space age probe, right from the very base now in front of them.

The events of the day unfolded very much to plan. It was as if they knew the story before it was being told and they were the only reporters to witness that historic launch. The rocket was much smaller than they'd expected and the launch seemed successful as it shot fast into the sky, soon out of sight. John wondered what the UFO freaks would make of it, realising that there was probably some truth behind their sightings even if they were misguided as to their origins. What they'd just witnessed was the launching of a space probe from UK shores. To their knowledge, this was the first of its kind. And if it was to be believed from their findings, three more were to follow from different bases over the next few hours. They would not be able to see them from where they were, but they were seeing the output from the main control room display, so they were easily able to keep up to date with everything.

The information output following the first launch was amazing. They'd seen the drafts for the media, which they now knew only told half of the story. Obvious, by its absence, was any talk of the nuclear capabilities of each mini probe that was being sent up into space.

During the morning and afternoon, a few cars came in out out of the viewing area, the drivers all middle aged, on their own: anoraks. None of them particularly noticed the van and, for all of these late comers, there was nothing for them to see. They'd missed the real action; John just didn't know whether they were there at that moment because they heard about something or just to watch for planes that day. Maybe it was something they did all the time. John took note of each car, recording its registration number before each one left, but he felt there was nothing to fear from any of them.

Late that night, food was ordered in, and they were just starting to dig in, unsure about how long the night ahead was actually going to be, when the first warning signals came through from the probes. Everyone forgot about the food and watched the output. From the sudden flood of phone calls in the control room in the base in front of them, they could tell that something was wrong. The first probe had stopped responding and there were the beginnings of a mild panic. It was to be the start of a long night for them all.

At some point in the early hours the base was put on full alert, and it was clear that the probe was heading straight back to where it had come from. Personnel were recalled and, in the chaos that followed, even the main gate was left momentarily unguarded, so they took a chance and moved their van, with the lights off, onto the main base. This was going to be the scoop of the century.

John had asked Alan to get the camera working and the equipment assembled in the van which now sat, quietly and out of view, on the base. They had a perfect line of sight to the launch area from the previous day. The crew were busy with the equipment, the camera now in position and working. John himself sat watching the main output screens. It was clear from what he could hear from the control room, not far from where they were sitting, that the scientists were bracing themselves for an impact. It would be a loss of a very expensive and high spec space probe, but beyond that, nothing too bad. The area had been cleared and the nuclear core was deemed to be safe, its reactor not engaged and there was thought to be no danger from the impact.

Three minutes before impact, the communications went quiet, as if they were holding their breath in there, which many of them actually were. John took a look out of the van's window but it was impossible to see anything, the speed of the descending probe meaning it would probably not be visible until the last few seconds.

But it was with about ninety seconds to go that John saw, for the first time, what was really happening. This was sabotage. The one piece of communication that came from the base, now written across his screen, had reportedly itself just come from the probe and was being read by all in the control room on their big screen. It had the message:

'THIS WAS NO ACCIDENT - GOODBYE...'

John jumped up from the terminal, hitting his head on the ceiling, nearly knocking himself out. His crew turned to him in surprise, concern showing on their faces, but they did not want to miss the impact. John could not breathe, the words just not coming out. He'd semi-concussed himself and the van was now starting to spin around him. Alan turned to him from the camera asking:

"Are you okay, man? That sounded quite a bang."

Still the words would not form so John started pointing at the screen. Alan had turned away so that he could start working the camera again. There was silence for a few seconds. John started hitting the screen hard with his hand, the sound bouncing around the small van. Two of the men turned, but neither could see the screen from where they were sitting. With real urgency John continued to point, frustration more than anything being shown through his strange, silent actions. Aaron got up and moved over to the screen, reading loudly as he got there:

"THIS WAS NO ACCIDENT - GOODBYE..." The others turned to him and then they all looked at John. He was starting to lose consciousness from the blow to his head. Just then there was a bright light in the sky as the probe came into view. The three members of John's A-team froze as they watched from the van, like rabbits caught in the headlights of an approaching vehicle. The probe smashed into the ground, an instant explosion erupting, bright light swamping the van as it was lifted from its place thrown through the air across the car park. It crashed into the ground, rolling over and over. Fire burst all around them. John lay buried in one corner, the rest of his crew already dead. He was buried, but still alive and now just waiting to be rescued, though he was unconscious and unaware of it. He would wake up in a hospital bed a few days later, with no memory of how he had arrived there.

Present Day

John was physically doing well, though his wounds were still a few weeks from healing. Lorna had spent a long time with him following his latest vision and he'd talked for ages about it all. The truth was, for the last few days they'd been going round in circles. Their starting points were different but they were concerned with the same central issue, and ethical issues at that. Both were dealing with the bigger questions in their own way, and importantly, they were both in agreement that what needed to happen, would happen. She'd left the room briefly as the doctor came in and another session regarding John's memory got under way. She would be back before long and she needed to be too. The doctor only knew so much and could say even less. But it was safe for him to at least start the session with just the two of them.

"Okay, so how do you feel?" he started, giving John his full attention.

"Still nothing has come back. The visions are taking my sleeping moments, and there are no flashes of anything that resembles a previous life I once had. And if I'm honest..." he said, pausing a little, suddenly wanting a drink of water from the glass that sat next to his bed. The doctor let him take his time, sensing what the next statement was going to be, as they'd talked about it quite a bit last time. "If I'm honest, I'm still not sure that I want to remember. I'm afraid of what I will find out. At the moment, I feel like I mean something, that I have a purpose. What if I find out I'm some very different person? Was some very different person?"

"Who you were and who you will become do not have to be the same, you know."

"Yeah, I do see that," John said. "Its just, I don't know really." He was struggling to form the sentences that best described his inner feelings. "Its just, what if the reality of what I once was...why I'm alone here in hospital. What if that reality so shocks me, so scares me, that it reawakens something and I change back to that person? That I put aside all that I know and become him again?"

The doctor took some time to think and looked over at Lorna who had returned to the room. He continued:

"This isn't something you need to do at all. This is something you wanted to explore and for that I am here to talk with you. There are probably lots of reasons why family haven't come. Why friends aren't around. Its not been possible to contact too many, and with all that's happening to you, probably not the best timing for you anyway. If you turn to me and say you don't want to continue, that is okay with me. I'm here to help you, to talk with you. I'm here because if you want to try and restore your memory, or at least some memories from before, then I can help you with that. I can give you some tips, some advice. There are some exercises we can do. But I'm here on your request, and until you feel happy one way or the other, we won't start with anything."

"Thanks, Doc," John said, feeling a little less concerned than he had a few moments before.

"Change is not easy to handle, for anyone."

"What do you mean by that?" John asked.

"I mean, in the here and now, this is all you know. To remember some of your life from before, as you said, is to risk changing the way you feel about yourself, or maybe changing the decisions you want to make for the future. Change is difficult to handle at the best of times, and yet, here, you are far from your best of times. But that's just the point. Change has already happened. Something changed for you. Something happened. So you are already in change. So to be afraid to change back from this current strange situation to what was once normality is not logical." He stopped talking, a puzzled but open look appearing on John's face now.

"I think I get what you mean. You're saying that I'm fearful that finding something out will change my world, but this very world I'm trying to protect by not opening that door, is already a change in my life."

"Yes, so on many levels, you are already a changed person. And just because you have no memory, does not mean you are now better off not remembering that previous life. In your final moments, to have those memories to look back on, happy times, better times, I'm sure will be of some relief for you."

"I hadn't thought about it like that, I guess. I mean, besides our conversations in this room with the pair of you, and these four books I've read this last week or so, I don't have any happy memories. Don't get me wrong, I have enjoyed our chats, Lorna," he said, turning to her, not wanting to offend her by that last remark. She smiled and nodded, too caught up in everything to want to voice a response. It felt like thin ice that they were all walking on and she didn't want to be the one to risk breaking it.

"So tell me, Doc," he said, turning back to him. "What things are there that I can do? What might help me remember something? Anything?"

"The brain is an incredible organ, John. Way more advanced and fragile than the best of the supercomputers, its full mystery is still a long way from anyone's understanding. From my professional background and experience, there are some mind mapping exercises we can do, but results vary greatly from person to person. On some these exercises don't work at all and, on a rare few, it has resulted in an almost complete memory recovery. The most effective way is to find triggers. And by this I mean things that cause you to remember something based on a smell, a familiar place or a situation, or anything really. A trigger could come in a million shapes or forms, but is that moment when so much of your surrounding situation is prompting brain activity, like *deja vu* it would seem, that it compels the brain to dig deeper and brings back that connection. What often follows as that part of the memory is restored, is a flood of associated memories from the same time."

"So what are the best triggers you've seen?"

"For helping victims deal with a terrible crime that

might have been inflicted on them, or around them, it would be to walk them around the crime scene again, and deal with the issues that arise. It's hard for them, but brings healing. For most others it's talking, going through photos, and voice recordings are also great. Sound seems to penetrate at a different level. Of course, a bit of all these areas would be ideal and could help memory recovery. The challenge with people in your situation is that, because of the memory loss, we can't tell where those trigger points are, or those key locations that might restore some thoughts." The doctor was unaware of where the patient had been rescued from so for the doctor this was true in John's case.

"Okay. With all you've said, I do feel like I still need a little more time, but am coming round to the idea of giving this a go soon. I just have no idea where to start."

"Of course, I understand that, John. It seems like an ocean but you can leave that up to me. Clearly, you are some weeks off being up and about. So that takes out the chance to go to a location, for example, even if we knew where to go. At the moment, we can start with some of the exercises when in a semi-conscious state. I ask you some questions about things. We could start that this afternoon. Do you think you are up for it?"

"Thanks, Doc. Give me some time to chat this through with Lorna here, and I'll get her to pass you on a message later. Is that okay, Lorna?" he said, turning to her.

"Yes, of course it is," she replied.

The doctor made his exit and it went back to being just the two of them in the room once again. That was a memory John was only too familiar with, though far from unhappy about.

Chapter 16

Present Day

The news was dominated by just one story: the unfolding disaster, the consequences of which one one could foresee.

The city was struggling. Many businesses around the city, if physically still intact, were effectively closed, government departments were struggling to keep up. Police and armed forces were stretched, hospitals were overwhelmed by the dying, the remaining fire fighters were exhausted.

For the media it was the biggest story they'd ever covered, or ever would get to cover. It was a story the world needed to know. A number of reporters and teams had already been killed, not to mention John's team that had witnessed first hand the original explosion.

The African secret service had decided to change tack and went back after the former employers. So when two well dressed young ladies walked into the main doors of the newspaper's offices, no one was really too bothered. They were yet another team who worked for the secret service. Having spoken with someone on the front desk, they were led into a waiting area. They were offered a hot drink, which they both accepted and took a seat on a black leather three seater sofa that seemed to dominate the room.

It was a few minutes before someone came in to see them both, and he apologised for keeping them waiting as he shook each hand and took a seat opposite them. They exchanged business cards; John's boss took in the names and tried to link it to the faces.

"So ladies, you said to our receptionist that you had some information you were following up on and that it was of a sensitive nature that would require someone senior. Well, I'm the best we could find I'm afraid," he said with a smile on his face. "So, tell me, what is it you are following up?"

"We think we came across one of your teams investigating the RAF base before the incident."

"Go on," he said, wanting to keep his cards close to his chest and hear what they had to say before he said too much himself, if anything.

"John once contacted us, as he needed some help. Nothing to concern you, but we were just aware of what he was starting to work on."

"Is that so?" he said, looking down at their business cards again. The made up name of the business on the card did not mean anything to him, of course, but at any rate it did not look like another rival newspaper. The thought that John had involved anyone outside the paper was difficult enough to hear.

"Look, you don't have to worry. We are on your side in this," the shorter of the two said, picking up on the obvious thought patterns now going through his head. She had shoulder length brown hair that she was wearing loose and no hint of an accent. She continued:

"Its just, we heard that John Westlake was found alive and is being treated in hospital. And if that were the case, we'd like you to pass on our regards."

The man sat back in his chair at this point, showing clearly to the two ladies that this was the first time he'd heard about it, as they expected.

"That's news to me. Are you sure? Who said this to you?"

"It was something random really, just word of mouth from someone at a hospital, mentioning a journalist named John being found alive. The rest of the crew were found dead, of course."

"I know that for sure. But I was told they were all killed. We ran a story the following week naming all our staff that had been killed and he was on that list. How can you be sure?"

"Well, that is why we are here. I'm sure that if this is true, like us, you'd want to know. If one of your guys made it against all odds, that's the good news story we've all been waiting for," she said.

"Yes, indeed. But I just can't believe it. They were right on top of it when it happened."

"That is what we heard, too. Look, here are the details of the hospital we heard this from," she said, handing him a printed sheet of paper with the basic information listed. He knew of the hospital once he saw the name. She continued. "By all means go and check this out for yourself. You guys are the investigative reporters. We are just the messengers. But we really do hope you find your man and, if you do, please do call and let us know. It would be nice to know he survived, unlikely as it sounds. It would also make a nice story."

That part was becoming only too clear to him at that moment. The cogs of his editor's mind were already turning and he was thinking through the possible angles. If someone had been that close and lived, it was an amazing story. The two ladies got up, clearly indicating that they were bringing this brief meeting to an end.

"What did you say John was asking of you again?" he asked. They both stopped, the taller one, with longer black hair tied neatly to one side, turned back to him.

"We didn't. Let's just say we were offering operational relief, and leave it at that, shall we?" That was one way of describing paid sex that he'd not heard before.

"Oh, I, erm, see." There seemed nothing more to say, and neither did they give him the chance, as they walked out of the room and left the building.

Clive headed for the lifts that would take him back up to his top floor office on the fifth floor. Though not the largest of the London based papers, they once had many hundreds of staff, scattered around the country, if not the world. Still, the office had always been the hub of the operation, the engine room of the whole paper, and yet for too long now, it had been but a shadow of its former self. Clive was a seasoned reporter. Sniffing out a good story was in his blood. And the country needed just that. If there was any truth in what these two women had shared, he was going to dig and find out. Walking into his office, having grabbed a couple of staff members on the way in, he set to work straight away on the phones, trying to find out what he could, arranging to get someone to the hospital, as well as finding out if John's family had heard anything.

Once more back in the car in which they'd come, the two African secret service ladies reported what had taken place to their contact at HQ.

"We'll keep tabs on movements from here on. If he calls, we'll let you know. I don't think he will, unless he wants sex. We led him to believe we were call girls, so I think the connection to us and John is broken. I don't think he'll come calling, though please monitor the number and if he does call, you can put him through."

"Very good. We have another team at the hospital. He isn't likely to go himself, not at this stage, but will surely send someone else quite soon. They've started making calls already. They certainly believed what you told them. They'll lead us right to him, the perfect shield for us. Stay where you are and we'll be in touch."

They ended the call and sat there drinking coffee from tall paper cups that they'd purchased from a street side coffee booth on the way back to the car. They were parked in a quiet side road, about sixty metres in direct line of sight from the newspapers front doors. If anyone of interest was going to leave, especially Clive, they'd be onto them. The day was going better than hoped.

Present Day

Lorna had made a cup of tea for them both and came over to put John's cup next to his bed. He thanked her. They'd been talking a little since the doctor had left, not just about the memory loss, but things in general. They each took a sip from their cup. Lorna was aware that she was now enjoying the company. It was unlike anything in her nursing career before, to spend so much time with one patient. Going through a difficult time herself, it meant she had grown an emotional connection with the one person that was listening to her, and it was true the other way round as well. They continued to take small sips of tea, as if knowing what the other person was thinking, or at least having an idea. John valued the conversation more than ever. She'd become his one support throughout the whole ordeal, he knew he could trust her. If she was happy for something to happen, then it was fine for him too.

He placed his now empty cup on the bedside table, making sure he didn't knock over his growing pile of books. The latest one had been a space adventure, and though not his usual read, it was enjoyable all the same. One thing he did have was time, so it was good to be able to indulge in reading; of course he was not sure if he'd ever done much before but he doubted it. Who would have the time unless they were lying in bed all day long. Lorna finished her tea now as well and placed her empty cup next to his.

"I'll have to clear some of these books out, otherwise it'll become a hazard," she said with a smile, breaking the silence and moving back into a normal conversation.

"Thanks. This last one is quite something. I find myself lost in another world: literally in this case," he said, tapping the cover. She laughed a little. Her James had loved those type of books and the type of films that came from them. It was certainly not her favourite genre.

"Tell me," he said, noticeably more serious now. "If you could have your memories wiped, now, as you are, with all the hurt and regret you have, would you do it?"

"That'd be like saying we should delete all our photos on the computer because we don't like the last few. But it's my whole life, and to lose all the good memories because of the harder ones, would be to lose much of myself. And besides, it's more the emotions now than actual memories. Does the sadness go away when the memory does?"

"I guess I don't really know. I mean, I feel as I do at the moment but is that normal or not? Was I sad before, or happy? I really can't tell. Is what I'm feeling now real, is it a happy time? Am I my real self? These are questions I really don't know how to answer, because I have no background, no history to refer to. Do you think I was happy?"

"I think you were like anyone else, certainly. No one is happy all the time, but life for you certainly would have had its highlights, yes."

"How can you be so sure?" he said.

"Honestly, you're not that special." She was smiling at him as she said this.

"Thanks!"

"What I mean is, why would it have been any different for you compared to nearly every single person who has ever lived?"

"Yeah, I see what you are saying. So do you think I had a family?"

"A wife you mean? No, I don't think you do. Of course, maybe you didn't ever wear a ring, but there certainly isn't any sign of one. You can tell when someone who normally wears a ring doesn't have it on. The finger is a different shape, usually a different colour where the ring once was. It's of course impossible for me to really tell.

You seem like a nice guy, so there is no reason why you shouldn't be. Maybe it was your job, maybe that got in the way?"

"What do you think I did?" he asked, enjoying the conversation.

"I have no idea," she lied. "Maybe you were a pilot?"

"No, I can't see that really. Can you?" He laughed as she did. A shared joke.

"Do you think there was something about my life that meant I was chosen to have these visions? Do you think it was because I was a good man?" The atmosphere in the room suddenly got a little more serious. John picked up an instant awkwardness in Lorna.

"I honestly have no idea and really don't want to talk about that." It didn't make sense, but John let it ride. There was an uncomfortable silence for about a minute. Lorna collected the empty tea cups and put them back on the tray by the door. She came back and took some old books from the bottom of the pile next to his bed, leaving just the one he was reading. She left these also by the door, before coming back and sitting down next to him once again, ready to move on from their last moment.

"Why do you do what you do?" John said, looking up at her.

"Nursing, you mean?" she asked, John nodding his answer. "I told you, it was the moment my brother was choking and that lady came and saved him. From then on I always wanted to be a nurse, always wanted to help people. To know what to do in an emergency."

"Yeah, I know that. That's why you got into nursing. I mean, why now? Why are you still doing this, when you've so recently lost your husband? Why are you working when you've not even got through grieving? Why this much dedication?" The discussion had become rather heavy. Lorna knew she needed to dig deep and move things away from this region, otherwise it could lead to problems later.

"I guess I just can't stay away." The smile on her face looked real enough. "Anyway, you need some more medicine really soon and I do need to take a look at the wounds before dinner. So while it has been good talking, you need to let me be the nurse again and do what I need to do."

"Yes, ma'am," he said, a jovial tone returning back to their conversation. The moment had passed.

Lorna stood up and straightened her uniform, before going over to prepare the latest batch of drugs that her patient needed. She'd then redress his wounds. John picked up his book and opened it to where he had left off. He was soon lost in his new world once again.

Present Day

Back at the offices of the paper, Clive had a notepad already half full with snippets of information. Together with his team which had grown steadily during the course of the day, they'd tracked down as much as they could about the family. They had carefully found out that his relations had heard nothing from John for weeks before the incident and evidently nothing since. They were parents mourning the loss of a child they saw all too infrequently. Part of that had been because of his job, and though they were grateful their son was working, it was a difficult issue. It was the job that had ultimately led to their son's apparent death and that of the rest of the team working with him at the time. It was a delicate conversation.

Nothing had been said to them at that moment, for fear of giving them false hope. A reunion story also held much greater power if the parents were the ones being surprised. Clive could imagine the look on their faces, with the cameras rolling, as their son was brought out to them, literally back from the dead.

A check of the hospital records gave no mention of John Westlake being admitted, but then again, there were only just over three hundred names listed, and it was common knowledge that the three thousand bed hospital was way overstretched. The majority of patients were either yet to be processed, or as yet unidentifiable. The thought was shocking enough. If John had survived, what kind of state was he in? And then Clive came back to what had been said by the two ladies who had been to his office earlier that day. They said it was word of mouth, that John's name had been mentioned. And therefore they knew his identity, or at least had something with that name on, and yet the hospital records were showing blank.

Of course Clive could well imagine there just weren't enough staff to update records. The team came up with the idea to go and offer their help to the hospital in relation to data entry, helping to get patients listed and put onto the empty data base, to start the process of connecting loved ones to the sick and dying. Most families hunting for relatives did not find them before they died. There was just too much destruction, too much change to get things happening as they needed to be done. People were being transported all over the country to hospitals that had space. Nearly every bed within about 100 miles of London was occupied. There were calls for mass evacuations into the northern regions of the country, where hospitals had some capacity. Many people had made the move themselves already, staying with relatives and friends and getting as far away from the disaster area as possible, though ultimately not far enough to be out of harm's way.

A pair of young reporters left the offices and took a company car to the hospital hoping, as a natural part of the sorting process, that they would be able to locate John, if he really was there.

Watching the two reporters leave, the African secret

service agents reported this to their HQ and pulled away slowly to follow them. Another team were on their way to the newspaper, and would continue to monitor what was being done. Traffic was heavy enough to go unnoticed. They drove the fifty minutes it took them to get to the hospital and only then did they stop following. Instead, the other African secret service team were told who it was that was approaching and they took things on from there. A computer at the hospital was hacked to monitor any updated information, as they assumed the young pairs offer of help would be accepted. If they were fortunate enough, John's status would soon get updated, his room listed, and then they'd send in a team to take any appropriate action deemed necessary.

Chapter 17

Present Day

John delayed his decision until the morning, but finally asked Lorna to pass on a message to the doctor that he'd like to start the memory exercises.

The small monitoring team, together with Lorna, had the previous night discussed the issue. They had agreed there was no danger in him having some of his long term memory restored. It was highly unlikely that anything would change. From what they could tell, he lived a very ordinary life. Nothing since the disaster would come back, as his memories of the time immediately after the incident were being suppressed and slowly destroying themselves. Clearly he was creating new memories well now, so there seemed no serious damage to his memory's functionality.

The doctor came not long after breakfast and they talked a little, like old friends, which for John was partly true. Besides Lorna, the doctor now helping him did represent the only other person he currently remembered knowing, though maybe that was about to change. John realised that maybe he was just about to get some of his life back, to meet some people he knew, if only in his mind. The thought of that thriller him.

Lorna left them to it as they started a few simple warm up exercises and headed towards the nurses' station, in search of Alison, her previous manager. Alison was a friend, a listening ear. They both needed each other and over the past week they had actually grown closer than ever before. She could be herself with Alison. There were a lot of thoughts going through her mind.

"So how's our star patient getting on?" Alison started in a friendly manner, as they walked slowly around the edge of the hospital car park.

"He's in with the doctor now, going through some

memory stuff. We see no problems with him regaining some lifetime moments. The team actually think it has helped him feel more connected to me, the fact I'm willing to help him in this way. They also feel it will help him with what he needs to do; in the final moments, he will have something to think about. Someone to be there with him."

"Yes, that seems sensible. Of course, there are no guarantees he'll get anything back."

"No, he knows that. We've talked a lot actually, about many things."

"You like him, don't you?"

Lorna looked at Alison, but could see she wasn't making a joke.

"Not in that way, no. It's too early for that, anyway. I'm not sure I could love again. But yes, I've grown close to him. It's like I'm his sister or something. I'm not quite sure what the fit is. Sister sounds a bit wrong now that I say it."

"And he trusts you?" Alison continued.

"Yes, I think he does." Lorna paused. "Am I a bad person for doing this to him?" They had stopped walking and Lorna was now looking Alison in the eye, but she couldn't keep eye contact for long and she looked off into the distance at nothing in particular.

"I think you are being very brave. I mean it." There was no reaction with Lorna. "I mean, look at what you've gone through."

"We've all gone through this."

"Yes, I know, but the loss of James... I mean, you've not had a chance to pull your own emotions together, to get into that good place. I'm sorry for my part in that. I hated sharing the news with you. Hated the way we did that, so clinical, so final. Not giving you a chance to pause. We were all struggling to keep up, we still are."

Lorna turned back towards Alison and put her hand on her shoulder.

"It's okay, I don't blame you. It's been good for me. What else would I have done? It has allowed me to get through it all. If I'm honest, there have been days when I haven't thought about that life at all. Moments where I'm just in the here and now, almost forgetting that the world's falling apart; that my world has fallen apart."

They stood silently for a while, Lorna's hand still on her shoulder. She then turned again and they continued their slow walk, going nowhere in particular, not that there was very far they could go. There were, however, noticeably fewer cars parked there than when things were normal. From where they were, they could not see the destruction of the city. In their random wanderings they had unconsciously turned the other way, as if to deny what had happened. But what they couldn't see was certainly making itself known in the sky above them. It was as if a layer of blackness had set up home, like some invading force had come from outer space and had blocked the sun from them all. There was also this smell, this stench in the air. It was unmistakable. Neither of them commented on what was obvious to them both.

"So, do you think John is ready to do this?" Alison said, breaking the brief silence, and indicating more accurately where she wanted the conversation to go.

"I think he will. We've created a world for him which he thinks is real. We've convinced him that he is somehow different. I've been there all along to listen to him, to encourage him, to make him feel this is all normal. That he is special. That he is seeing something that hasn't yet happened, and he's ready to take that step. We've got there, we've done what we set out to do. Physically, he's still not quite ready to start walking. In some way they maybe started things too early with him. There will be some time before he gets to do it, though of course the sooner the better, I know. So in the meantime, I will have to keep talking with him. Keep up the show, the pretence."

"You'll be great, Lorna, he trusts you. He's your friend."

"I know that, but doesn't that make me the monster? The evil villain?"

"It makes you a better woman than most. You've put everything you are facing on hold. You're serving for the greater good. For the good of the majority. For the continuation of life as we know it, too many have died already; hundreds of thousands of people are dead. Many more are going to die from the radiation. But not as many as those that will die if those reactors all explode. We'll die. If we did nothing, we would have been dead. We still might be if John changes his mind, or proves unable to do what we hope he can. What we all need him to do. Yes, we are all asking a big thing, an awful lot of him. But better one man dies believing he's the hero, than everyone dies. We've given him this chance. This moment to step into human history as a champion. A victor. The man that saved the day. We've given him his shot at glory."

"But it's all unreal. For him, there need be no dying. He'll recover. By some freak outworking, he was exposed and yet has lived; is living. His wounds will heal, he'll eventually walk away. And we are asking him, no tricking him, to trade that in, in order to save us. That doesn't seem right."

"It isn't fair. None of this is. I wish with everything in me that this thing never happened. But it did happen, and we've got to contain it, we've got to stop it claiming even more lives. Our lives. The lives of everyone we know still living. We've got to do whatever it takes to stop it, to end it, once and for all. And for that, it takes one man; this stranger, this freak for want of a better word. He does have a gift, his body does hold something special that has kept him alive, more than that; has shielded him from the poison. It doesn't affect him. He's immune to it. And that does make him special. It makes him very special, unique in so many ways. And so when he walks up to that reactor, the radiation isn't going to stop him. The heat from the building fires we can protect him from, but the poison we couldn't; and yet he is already protected. If it really works, he gets to walk right up to that button, to shut it all down, to deactivate the reactor. He really is special."

"Will I regret it, one day, Alison? Will I look back, and wonder what I allowed myself to do? What I allowed myself to be part of? Like some Nazi party worker, following orders. When all is said and done, will I look at my life and ask 'what have I become?'"

"We all have regrets. Things we should have said, things we shouldn't. People we should have spent more time with, or less. Things we should have seen, places we should have gone to. You've got to see that this is totally different. It's the life of one man for the good of the world. One man with an amazing ability, to soak this poison in and yet it would not kill him. One man that is now willing to sacrifice his life, knowing the cost, for the good of us all. You've got to look beyond this situation and think about the bigger picture. You still have the chance of a family."

They paused, realising how intense it had all become. Alison changed her tone and continued:

"I'm here for you. I'm on your side. We can do this together. We can talk about anything. You are not alone in this, you do not have to carry this solely on your own two shoulders. As capable as you are, you do not need to do this on your own."

Lorna smiled. She slipped her arm through Alison's as they started working their way back towards the main entrance. It had been long enough, but the chat had done her some good. Done them both a lot of good. She didn't want to be alone in it, especially now that things were getting to the final stage.

Walking back in, they spotted the two reporters working through the database, entering the names of those that they were being told of. So far, John's name was not on that list neither would it be. Alison said goodbye to Lorna, before going over to check briefly on the two of them working away on the computer. Everything was fine, they needed nothing, and she left them to start her next session of rounds. It was going to be as busy as any other day.

****

The doctor had been gone some time and Lorna had finished with the latest set of new dressings for John's wounds. Her patient seemed in good spirits, which was nice to see, a good sign. She was still processing her chat with Alison from that morning, but her head felt quite clear for a change.

"So tell me how it went this morning with the Doc."

"Nothing has happened so far, if that's what you're checking. He did say it might take a few sessions before we even know how successful it might be. We talked a bit, and then I had to relax my mind, imagine a warm, sunny place and he talked me through what it felt like there, what I was feeling etc. He set the scene well. It was very relaxing. He then dropped in some questions, some promptings, random things really. Nothing resonated, however, not this time anyway. In some ways, if I'm honest, that was a relief. I thought that maybe all the memories would jump back at me and suddenly I'd have them all to deal with at once. I'm not sure if I could cope with that, on top of everything else, at the moment."

"Well, I don't think that was ever going to be a possibility. You do need to know that it might be that nothing happens."

"Yes, I am aware of that. Part of me wonders if that would be the best thing anyway, but a larger part now also wants to know who I was, who I am. To have some recollection, some understanding of the journey I've made, of the people that have been around me before all this."

"Do you think it will make it any easier knowing all that, with what you have been shown?" she asked, bringing it back to what lay ahead of them both.

"You mean the visions, and what I need to do?" She nodded. "I guess I don't really know. I've not really made the connection with what I was seeing and what happens in reality. What if it doesn't make sense, doesn't mean anything at all?"

"But you know it does. Something amazing happened to you. Something unique." Given her patient's situation, she was now surprised at how easy it was to bring him back on track, to make him do what deep down she now wanted him to do; wanted with everything within her. She admired him so much, but she would think much less of him if after all this, he walked away. That couldn't happen, nor would she allow the thought.

"Lorna, I've not left this room in a long time. I can't remember ever being outside this room, besides these visions I've been having. What if they were memories? What if they were my brain's way of bringing back to mind things that have happened? What if there is no safety switch? That I'd just be waiting for this thing to happen, and nothing ever does? What kind of life would that be?"

"John, this way of thinking is not helping you. I can see it's confusing you. You've been through something different. It's left you wounded, but somehow, you've been spoken to. You've seen what needs to be done, you've been told that you, and only you, have the chance to stop it. Have the power to prevent it. To save everyone. To be the sacrifice to save those around you. To save me." She stopped as John looked at her, real emotion in his eyes now. Had she said too much?

"Look, okay, I get that. I'm sorry," he said.

"No, I'm sorry. I didn't mean to say it like that. I

went too far."

"No, you didn't. And you are right. I guess I just have so many question, which I don't know the answers to, that I'm starting to doubt what I've seen, what I know. But you are right. It might save you. You are younger than me. If I'm to do this, clearly it's got to be in my lifetime, otherwise what's the point? If I'm the one to do this, therefore, you'll still be around. It helps me to think of it like that. Being a sacrifice to faceless people, millions of people at that, doesn't really equate. How can it? I would have no way of ever knowing them. But to think of some people, someone, like you. You are someone worth saving." He reached over and touched her hand, though she pulled away momentarily, mainly out of self preservation. She patted his hand with hers. There certainly was some kind of connection between them, but she feared they didn't both see it in the same way.

"Look," she said, changing tone as easily as anything. "We need to focus on getting you better. On taking some steps, and sooner rather than later. Spend too much longer in bed and your legs might stop moving!" She was smiling, so John knew she didn't mean it literally.

"That would be good. I'm in your hands, so when you say I'm ready, I'm ready. And thanks. Thanks for everything you've done for me. You've kept me alive, kept me going. Without you, I don't know if I could have come through all this."

"Rubbish," she said, not at all convincingly. She felt a knot growing in her stomach and needed to get out of there. 'Thanks for everything I've done for you' she thought over and over again, the words smashing around her mind, doing damage on the way. 'I've made you a prisoner, I've kept up a lie. What I've done to you is made you swap your life for mine.'

She realised she needed some more air and made her escape. The guards on the door were told to call her if the patient needed anything, but he was already reading the book again, drawing towards the final chapters, lost in space.

****

The joint MI5 and SAS task force had been working hard together since being handed their assignment. The files and reports, both open source and security service documents, were spread out evenly around the giant conference table at Thames House. They had been going over everything documented from the previous year's negotiations when the world powers had come to England and talks had taken place. There were a lot of things that made more sense now. The actions of the Chinese, Russians and even Americans made all three of them look a little guilty. There was the surprise African involvement at the dinner reception. Little more was known about them.

As they dug and tracked various comings and goings, there was enough of a trail to assume a mainland operation was being carried out by a foreign intelligence agency on British soil. Surveillance was stepped up on the various embassies involved, agents now tracking each coming and going. A control room was set up, too. More agents would be pulled into service as the need arose and it was highly likely that they would.

Section heads had been called and they were now all sitting around the large table, each man a seasoned professional with significant experience. The conversation was loud and open.

"We need to know who is behind this," one said.

"It's a breach of trust, especially if it's the Americans."

"However, we must tread very carefully."

"Agreed," and that was echoed by every one of the five men around the table.

"When the time comes, and when we are clear who it is that is involved, we need to act ruthlessly. We are all aware now of what is required. If the Chinese were to find out what happened, we'd have big problems. If the Americans got wind of something themselves, they could use it against us."

"They wouldn't dare," came one reaction. The rest were not so sure.

"Once the level of involvement is assessed, we'll meet again to decide on action. We need to know what they are after. We need to know what they know. And we certainly can't let them anywhere near our man."

It was unanimously accepted, and a team from the SAS would base themselves at the hospital to watch the patient and watch for anything suspicious. Visitors would be monitored, the hospital put on shut down. It didn't matter what the outside world thought, John's safe little haven was all they needed to protect. His existence affected the existence of all. Now their lives all depended on him finishing the job. Little did John know, lying in his hospital that night, that so much was resting on him. Without knowing it, the nation needed him alive for just a little bit longer. It was only a small group of people, working around the clock, who needed him dead.

Chapter 18

Clive was walking the streets that surrounded the newspaper's main office just after four in the afternoon. That morning he had met someone, but unknown to him, each step he took was being watched and followed by the two African secret service personnel. They followed him into his first meeting, actually sitting on a table next to his, though hidden behind a pillar so that they got a good listen in on what he had talked about. If they'd been speaking in code, it was a highly elaborate routine, and had them fooled. No information had come to light from that particular source. In reality, Clive had darted around a conversation, digging without making it look obvious, seeing if his usually good source had anything, but getting nowhere. After only thirty minutes, he called it off, much to the annoyance of his table companion, who'd been looking for another handsome pay-off but clearly hadn't produced the goods, that time. They went their separate ways, the two women looking at each other for a moment, wondering if they'd missed something. It could have been an elaborate smoke screen, though they would never know for sure either way.

They followed him to lunch, this time keeping watch from afar, as the restaurant he was going to was far too small, and far too overbooked, for them to sneak in unnoticed. Sitting outside and across the road, in perfect line of sight, they ordered coffees at a boutique café, sitting at a table for two on the street itself taking in the warm sun, while they kept an eye on events across the road. Nothing dramatic seemed to happen. The man Clive met had been about his age, dressed the same. It seemed, from the body language, that there was a mutual respect, but no close friendship. They would get a photo of the companion, and get the guys at HQ to dig up who he was, just to be sure. It was thought that it was largely social, and nothing relevant to their case, as the two hours pressed on. Between them, the two men had drank through a bottle of wine and then some after lunch whisky. How they would work that afternoon, it was hard to say.

Leaving the restaurant, they followed him back towards the office, before Clive had made a phone call, stopping in the street. On finishing the call, he turned around suddenly and started back in the other direction. The two ladies, who had been following him only about twenty metres behind at that point, thought they'd been caught as they quickly took in a shop window of a local travel agents. However, Clive's mind was on other things and that soon became clear when he arrived at a café not ten minutes from there. The two ladies saw him meeting with a young woman, probably half his age, and she'd kissed him on arrival, Clive's hand on her backside pulling her tight in towards him. This was no business meeting.

As the two flirted with each other in the café, the African secret service were running through the photo of Clive's lunchtime companion, and it was confirmed he was Editor-in-Chief of another British paper, though they were at different ends of the gene pool. That paper had class, while Clive's tabloid paper was not interested in class of any sort. It made an interesting contrast, but for now, they couldn't see any angle on it that would make further investigation on the companion necessary. They preferred to keep the field tighter and stick to the main players. At this stage, anyway.

Clive and his young love parted company, with a passionate embrace, just before four. He certainly walked with a spring in his step after that, once more on his way back to the office. The two ladies kept a greater distance, sure that he was actually heading back this time, but not risking another close encounter. Next time they might not be so lucky. The two secret service personnel waited outside, at a distance, looking like tourists, but always watching. They were sure Clive was going to lead them to something soon.

Back on the fifth floor, his office at least was starting to show signs of how things had once been. There were a team of five now working with him. Priority at that moment was to get some results. So far, the young pair at the hospital had nothing to report. They'd successfully identified around eighty five percent of the patients at the hospital, and while not finding their man yet, it had brought great joy to many who were searching for loved ones. On the back of this good news, three similar projects were happening at three other hospitals, as people volunteered to document who was where. The country, as best it could, was slowly trying to get back on its feet.

It was just before five when Clive took the call he'd been waiting for. As chance would have it, the guy he met for lunch from the other newspaper had connections with a firm of architects who, as well as overseeing a major extension to that newspaper's head office just over a year ago, had also built the hospital where John was supposedly being kept. In the few minutes after taking the call, Clive had been emailed the plans. He was a happy man. That would mean the records could be matched to what his two young reporters were finding out, and certain sections of the hospital could then be searched once they realised the holes in their information. If John was there, it was hoped that tomorrow they'd find him. Clive called his team working at the hospital and told them to wrap things up that night, as best they could, and to bring everything with them to the office tomorrow. They said there was still some way to go, and that it would take them too long to finish that night. Clive finished by telling them to do as much as they could.

The call was listened to by the African secret service, a team having bugged the telephones in the office the previous day. The two ladies looked at each other with interest. It seemed Clive had found something. It was not totally clear what that was yet, as Clive, aware of all the dirty tricks out there, was not one to say too much over the phone. They'd tapped enough lines themselves to know that one by now.

****

It was the early hours of a dull new day, not that John had any idea what the weather was doing on any particular day. His light was constant and artificial, though thankfully it was turned off during the night. Even then, there was a strip of light that came through under the door, and the machines around him had various lights on that never went off. Total darkness was simply not possible.

John had got used to this by now, his sleep was helped by the pain killers he was having fed to him through the drip, though these were already starting to be reduced as the worst of his wounds were beginning to heal nicely.

Lorna had been in briefly that morning to see John but was now preparing some new bedsheets for him. One of his leg wounds had made a mess on the bed covers the previous night so the sheet needed to be changed. She came back in, holding the small pile of sheets carefully in her hands, a smile on her face that defied the earliness of the hour. Due to a number of factors, John was a light sleeper, and over the last few weeks Lorna was fast becoming one herself.

She took away the dirty sheets, and with a little help from John who moved one way and then the other, they got the bed changed. He liked the smell of the new sheets, it must have been the washing powder, something about it taking him back to, as yet, unconscious memories. Maybe it was the same washing powder used in his childhood, maybe something much nearer? He could only guess. Maybe he just liked it for the here and now it represented.

He was gaining strength, he would get through this. This wasn't such an awful time after all. And he got to spend most of his time with Lorna, who was beginning to grow on him the more he got to know her. He wasn't sure what he really felt for her yet. There was so much of his life that he still didn't know about. But he knew already that he enjoyed her company. Her smile was often the first thing that greeted him, especially in the early days, when he'd first woken from those visions and hadn't known what to do.

Last night, now clear from any further visions, had given him his first dream. Nothing from the past, it was a combination of what had been around him for the past few weeks, as well as his books that he was starting to devour on a daily basis. And as Lorna made them both a hot drink and came over to him, placing his cup carefully next to his bed, he couldn't wait to tell her.

"I actually had a dream last night. We were in a space ship." She was taking a mouthful of tea so didn't say anything straight away.

"That sounds fun."

"It was kind of strange. My first dream in a long time, and totally different to the visions. I guess it makes the distinction clearer for me. The dream was quite short, fleeting really. I guess just a few moments. We were together on a space ship orbiting some planet. I don't think it was a real one. We were passengers. It was quite amusing really."

John was in very good spirits today and Lorna was happy about that. The previous few days had been tough, a lot of ground that had been covered. Now it was the waiting game: how long it would take for him to get up and about, how quickly he could start walking, carry his own weight. If he couldn't walk he wouldn't be able to get himself to where he needed to be, to do what everyone needed, and hoped, he would do. The longer it took, the more danger everyone was in. The situation on the base was increasingly unstable. An explosion, if not imminent, was an inevitable final outcome. That news was not public knowledge, nor was John's central role in the only solution. Both would be kept secret for as long as it was possible. It was hoped no one would find out, or at least not until long after the dust had settled and things had once again returned to normal. What normal looked like, it was unclear. Things had changed so much around them all, for so long now, that this was becoming normal. It was hard for Lorna to think of life beyond the hospital and yet, she told herself it all now depended on her actions and those of John. She kept herself from thinking the best, in case it might distract her, in case she missed something vital. There was no happy ending if things didn't work out as they had planned. And the plan was far from risk free. It was totally untested, unknown and all totally new. They had one attempt at it, and after that, if they failed, it would be the end. There was not one government projection that had anything but a disastrous outcome, if they were to fail with the program that John was so central to. The pressure they were all under was immense.

It was noticed how he followed her, how his attention was on her whenever she was in the room. How he'd look at her body when she wasn't watching him. John was certainly developing a thing for her, and this was reported to Lorna as one would report the weather. Everything was being used to their advantage. Nothing would get missed, no opportunity left anything but fully exploited. She was told to develop this, or at least fan his side more into flame. In herself, Lorna wondered, if push came to shove, what lengths she would actually go to. That thought troubled her. She was afraid of who she had become.

John was watching Lorna again and she was now more aware of it. He took in her chest. The uniform was working in that regard, a small amount of cleavage visible. Lorna tried not to be bothered by this, on some levels liking the admiration from a man, though it was far too soon for her to even be thinking like that. She hadn't even got to bury her James yet. There wasn't a body to bury, nor would there be. The area where he breathed his last was too exposed to the lethal poison that had killed so many thousands and would kill so many more. It wasn't the first time a patient had had a thing for his nurse, nor was it the first time it had happened with her. It was an all too common occurrence and sometimes meant she'd needed to swap with another nurse, someone less like the patients 'type'. With John, this was not an option, neither was their situation like those other patients. They had shared a very similar experience, even if that had been from different sides of the visions, but a shared history none the less. For John, the visions had been real. He was being told things that were to come. And he was to talk this through with his nurse, this angel he was coming to grow so fond of. For Lorna, she was to be there to listen. Aware of the basis of each vision, she was to help him feel grounded in reality, and to help him see his way through to outworking what the visions were showing him he needed to do. It was not as if John wasn't attractive to her. It was, as if in her head anyway, it was a totally inappropriate situation and any form of relationship, besides the patient/nurse one, was just not right. In this unique situation, she did understand the need to help develop a strong connection between the two of them, regardless of what that got called from John's side of things. She was clear how she felt.

The more she continued, the more hard nosed she became. It became a results situation. The ends would justify the means and over the next few days she'd surprise herself by just how far she'd take that thinking.

****

That same morning, a team of ten from an SAS base in the South of England, were deployed to stake out the hospital. The operation was to be covert in nature. It was best, as much as possible, to remain in the shadows and take note of anyone showing unwanted interest in the hospital rather than to be the obvious targets that others might work around. As yet, those others were a faceless foreign intelligence agency whose intention they were convinced was hostile. Two men stationed themselves some distance away, as another three made their way towards the outskirts of the hospital. A quick sweep of the perimeter was made, anti-bugging scanners were used. If any unconfirmed communications were being used, they'd pick them up. It was a very swift and military-like manoeuvre to the informed eye, but to the passer-by it would easily appear to have just been someone checking gas readings or searching for lost metal.

From their own vantage point, the African secret service team that was also watching the hospital, saw the arrival of the team, with three men getting out and walking around the building. They could recognise the work of fellow special forces and it was clear that they had arrived. The two that remained in the vehicle drove and based themselves at another prime position. It was the other option that they too had considered before focusing themselves on the main doors, their current position giving them that vantage point. They immediately turned off their communication devices, as the three man team some distance in front of them, started their scan.

Both the Africans looked at each other in silence, the girl behind the driving seat putting the key into the ignition and started the engine. They pulled away quickly, two SAS agents spotting a vehicle leaving, but there was nothing unusual about that outside a busy hospital. They drove off without raising any alarms, as the team of three continued their circuit. Twenty minutes later when the three men had circled the building completely, they broke into their individual positions. One guy headed inside to speak with the team stationed outside John's room, guarding him. Another went to work with the person monitoring the hospitals CCTV network, and another two went to set up the lock down of the hospital, with security screening machines moved into the main entrance, making coming and going a slow, more difficult process. Records would be kept and ID checked on everyone wanting entrance to the hospital. It was effectively now closed to outsiders. The remaining members of the SAS team, stationed outside, were keeping watch over the fire escapes at the back, as well as the only car park that visitors could use. The team would rotate around the clock, with another five personnel on hand to help with the change of shifts. It was an operation of the highest level, like that of a Presidential visit or an official engagement by the Queen. Preparation was key, as was staying largely undetected.

Now at a safe distance, the two African secret service agents who had just left the hospital reported in that British special forces had moved into the hospital. It only confirmed what they were already expecting. Somewhere in the hospital building this man was being kept. The British were either keeping very quiet about everything or, more likely, the patient was not yet in a fit state to talk. Until they could work out what exactly his state was, they could not fully decide on their course of action. The presence of the SAS, as it was rightly assumed to be, was only adding complication to the matter. They still had their shield: Clive and his team. They reminded themselves of this, and even more focus was to be given to that side of the operation. If Clive could be encouraged to make enough of a noise, maybe it would create an opportunity for them to sneak in, a good old fashioned diversion, even if Clive had no idea of his part in it all. And it did seem, from the telephone calls buzzing around so far, that Clive was getting closer. He was on the charge, and determined to get answers. Unknown to him, his life was very much in danger.

The Africans would keep watching, often close but staying in the shadows. Like the great predators that roam their continent, they were watching from afar, in the darkness. Watching and waiting. Ready to pounce at the slightest invitation. It would not be long before that window presented itself.

Chapter 19

The following morning at the offices of the newspaper, the two young reporters that Clive had sent to the hospital reported back. An hour's debriefing had just finished, a list of thousands of names spread all around the conference table that had been brought into Clive's personal office, taking much of the remaining space. In total, their investigation had been able to put about ninety per cent of the names to the patients that were occupying the beds. The truth, when they found it out, was shocking. Some patients were lying on sofas, or tables, even on the floor. Beds had run out as quickly as the hand gel had. It had been the least of their troubles. There was no way they could turn people away, it had been a miracle that they had made it that far in the first place. All the other hospitals nearby were in exactly the same situation. It was agreed that, for now, those stories should wait. They needed to focus on the ongoing disaster, with stories about hope and of hospitals that were going way beyond in their efforts to save life. No one needed to hear about basic, almost barbaric conditions, patients being found dead in beds unnoticed for two days. Blood that had not been cleaned up in a week. It was not unlike a scene from a horror film, something the two young reporters would never forget. Those stories would have to wait, if ever shared at all. This was war time recovery. That was the stance around the conference table that morning as the report was being given. Clive could see that the time in the hospital had had a traumatic effect on his two junior employees. Given the conditions, Clive had even more admiration for the fine work they'd been able to do.

A large scale plan of the hospital also lay open on the table. Green highlighters were used to indicate a room where the patient's name was known, and a yellow was used to indicate a room they were aware of, with no name for the patient. This accounted for a very high proportion of the space available, the assumption being that nearly every available room was now being used to house patients. Some of the communal areas had been spotted too: the canteen, the small staff rooms, including their rest areas. Toilets were clearly marked. All these rooms were coloured with a blue highlighter on the plans that lay before them all. Which left a small handful of rooms, all coloured in bright red. These gave them their most realistic areas of where John might be held. A few of these eight rooms that remained were small and in quite public areas. They had just been missed from the general search when the two young reporters had started going from room to room. What remained of the rest were more secluded areas, three really well protected rooms at that.

As lunch arrived, four boxes of fresh pizza being delivered from a nearby pizza place, they felt they now had their search area and, as a top priority, they needed to locate these eight remaining rooms. They would focus on the three central ones currently highlighted in red, to confirm or deny whether their man, John Westlake, was being treated there.

The call for the pizzas had been made forty minutes before, so when a small car pulled up, fresh pizzas being taken from the back seat, it was obvious who they were for. One of the African ladies watching the offices had been there to meet the driver, paying him in full for the pizza and taking them off him, herself walking into the building and taking the lift to the top floor. She was led towards Clive's office now and delivered the pizzas herself. There was an excited hum in the room as she arrived and walked over to put the pizzas on the main desk. Someone went to get some money from petty cash.

She got out her phone, as if to make a call, and took a photo of the highly coloured hospital plans. No one else noticed, they were absorbed in their work so the presence of a delivery driver did not attract their attention. She was given the money, and a small tip, and walked away with more money than she'd paid the driver downstairs, as well as a photo of the hospital plans which could now lead them straight to John.

She left the building unchallenged and went straight to her colleague. They looked at the photo quickly, happy at the outcome, and sent it straight on to HQ for them to print and distribute. The net was closing. Their moment was drawing closer. Still they needed to wait. Still they needed to be patient, for just a little while longer.

Later that afternoon, Clive himself went with one young female employee to the hospital. She was twenty three and he fancied his chances. Clive had always been one to mix business with pleasure, at least to try to anyway. His reputation was such that the others in the room knew he'd try something on when he announced he was taking her with him. She, for the most part, was unaware.

The journey to the hospital had been uneventful and they'd arrived and parked up as the afternoon was just starting to show signs of drawing in. The earlier warmth of the sun, that had baked them as they were getting into the car, had lost most of its intensity. They arrived at the main doors of the hospital and were surprised to see metal detectors in place; nothing had been said of these by the other two. Security was tight. It was the girl who spoke up as they both approached the guards.

"I'm looking for my brother, Michael Brown. The report online told us he was here. Dad agreed we should come straight away."

Clive looked at her, and thought to himself. 'Clever girl. Smart and attractive. She does have a future.'

They both went through the security scanners and signed into the visitor's book, Emma making it clear that she was to go first, writing her name neatly so that Clive could copy the surname. She passed the guy her ID and smiled at him. He seemed to like this and, while casually checking her ID, smiled back. Clive didn't have anything on him, of course, but played the part of the panic stricken parent well. He looked close to tears. They quickly walked off down the corridor, as the SAS guy came over to check how things had been going with the guard on duty. Since ID had not been confirmed on the male visitor, he had harsh words with the guard and set off to look for them both straight away.

Emma and Clive were working from their recollection of the plans of the hospital, though they did have a basic back up copy on a mobile phone in case they needed it. They had already covered their first target room, which was empty of patients; it was a small office supply store cupboard. Boxes of white printer paper took most of the space, not that there was much to start with. They mentally crossed it off in their heads. One down, seven to go. They were approaching the second of their target rooms, guards visible up ahead, when the SAS officer caught up with them.

"Excuse me, can I ask what you are both doing?" he demanded.

"We are looking for my son," Clive said, taking the lead.

"Can I see your ID, sir," he replied, no hint of this being a suggestion in his voice. This was an order.

"I don't have anything on me, I'm afraid. My daughter was in such a state when she called, hearing that her brother was being treated here. We thought he was dead. She just heard today. I came and got her straight away. What else was I meant to do?"

If they were father and daughter, he couldn't tell. Clearly she'd got her good looks from her mother.

"I'm sorry, sir, but I am going to have to ask you to leave."

"Excuse me?"

"I said you have to leave. You cannot be in here if you do not have any identification. This is a hospital. Not a shopping centre."

"Last time I was here, no one needed ID to visit family."

The SAS officer was already leading Clive by the arm. Clive was in no position to resist.

"What about me?" Emma said.

"You can carry on and find your brother," the officer informed her. She looked genuine enough. They were not the first people to not have ID whilst searching for relatives.

As they were approaching the front entrance, the SAS officer casually turned to Clive and said:

"What did you say that your son's name was again?"

Clive, for once, had no idea what Emma had said.

"Pardon?" he said, a little too hesitant.

"Your son's name. What is it?"

"Matthew," he said, making it up as best he could. The other guard looked up and shook his head. The SAS man turned and went after Emma, leaving the guards at the entrance with Clive. One turned to him and said:

"You're coming with us."

"I'm a journalist," Clive said, showing them his press card. "I'm just chasing a story, that's all. I'm not here to cause you any harm."

They noted down his name. Truth was they didn't want to make a scene. The same man said to Clive:

"I don't know what you are doing here, but hear me clearly when I say this. You are not welcome here, and are no longer allowed anywhere near this facility. If we see you back here, you will be in a lot of trouble."

At that moment, the other guard took a photo of Clive, the flash making him blink.

"You have no right to take my photo!" Clive

shouted. "I demand that you delete it immediately!"

"In here, we have every right. The safety of our patients dictates we monitor everyone who visits. And you have broken the rules and tried to get in here, for whatever reason you might have. You are lucky we are letting you walk out of here. If there is a next time, and I strongly advise against that, you won't be walking away. Now beat it!"

With that, they pushed him through the doors, helping him on his way. He kept his footing, and stood outside waiting. Three minutes later Emma was given the same treatment, her photo taken before she was also, a little more gently in her case, shown out of the door.

Their photos would be analysed and their identity would confirmed. As Clive and Emma walked away from the building, they were no clearer on what was happening, but their minds were racing with possibilities.

"I laid eyes on one of those central three red highlighted rooms," Emma said as they walked back towards the car. "There were two guards standing outside. I couldn't see anything inside. Whoever was in that room, they don't want anyone to find out."

"That's great work, Emma. Really good. I can see you going far. Why don't we go for a drink to celebrate. After all that, I bet you could do with one!"

She agreed and they went off in search of somewhere to get a drink, Clive enjoying the company and the challenge.

****

John was about twenty minutes into his latest session with the doctor in relation to his memory loss. They were now working through some exercises which, for a few people, would have already started producing some limited results. He wanted to see John feeling comfortable with the whole procedure first, before playing his trump cards. If those didn't work, then none of the exercises were likely to make any difference for John. So far there was nothing to suggest there would be any improvement.

At least it was less stressful than the morning's physiotherapy session had been. For the first time in weeks, Lorna, with the guidance and help of a physiotherapist, had attempted to get John to take his first steps since arriving there, but with little success. The lack of movement, compounded by the initial injuries to his legs and back, meant the muscles had started wasting. It was a painful and disappointing setback for John, though Lorna had felt that the physio, a younger but experienced man, had not been displeased with the session. Clearly, he'd seen this a lot in his line of work. It would just take time, effort and lots of mental strength. Lorna knew John had all these and she would certainly play her part in getting him walking again. They'd talked a little about it, but John was unusually silent in the minutes following the session. It was as if he was realising just how far he had to go. Getting out of the bed was clearly now just the start of the challenges that lay ahead. And of course, in the back of his mind, even walking was only one stage in where he was heading. At some point, as yet still unknown to him, he'd need his legs to walk the walk. The final one he'd ever do. A decisive one. A walk that, he hoped anyway, would save the lives of millions by making himself the sacrifice. Or so he'd been told through the visions. The more he thought about it, the stranger it all seemed. It was as if, with some gap now in time from the visions he had seen, his belief was starting to waiver. He would not let this be known, of course. Maybe it was natural to think that way, devoid of any connection to the events that he had been warned about. When faced with it, surely he'd be able to do it. But he'd keep these thoughts to himself. Lorna didn't need to hear this side of him. Not now anyway. He was not totally decided on if this was something he should talk through with her at all. He knew that she wouldn't understand. So he'd decided to bury it.

It was currently just John with the doctor, as the memory recovery session continued. He was much more talkative now, and needed to be too. The exercises, for the moment, needed his complete attention. Soon he'd need to allow himself to drift off a little, the doctor probing and prompting, asking things in such a way as to engage all areas of the brain. Just as someone might shake an apple tree to free some falling fruit, so the brain sometimes responds in kind, offering up all sorts of lost or hidden information. And sometimes, in cases like John's, there could be whole chunks of buried memory.

Forty minutes later they were finished with the latest session. John was now starting to feel the strain of the two workouts: one very physical, the latest mentally draining. Together they were now taking their toll on him. John needed to sleep and, as the doctor packed up, he was already drifting off.

The doctor wanted to have a word with Lorna but there was not much space just outside the door, even though the two soldiers moved a little. Instead, they both walked a short way down the corridor away from the guards, before stopping to talk with each other.

"I heard this morning was hard on John."

"Yes, but from what the physio told me, it was fairly normal under the circumstances. He said he'd seen much worse," she commented, before asking; "How are the memory exercises going?"

"To be honest, if something was going to happen, I would have hoped that there would have been some type of response by now, at least something from the exercises. Usually they prompt something. And for all my patients that have regained anything, they'd all responded better than John has so far. I'm not holding my breath."

Lorna felt for her patient at that moment, a level of care only a nurse can have in such intense circumstances. She wondered what it would feel like to remember nothing. If her memories of James, as sad as they currently were since his death, if those memories were suddenly gone. All the good times. The trips, the happy moments. What it felt like to be in love, to be loved. What it felt like to have him run his hands through her hair, how he held her head as they kissed. The little things. The important things. She couldn't begin to understand what it was like. And then that feeling came back. Added to all that he was feeling and experiencing, the emptiness of any memory he once had, they'd added their own images to his mind. A lie. The big lie. And this was now starting to resonate in her heart. Doubt was creeping in, the longer she was with him. She didn't love him. She was fairly certain of that, as much as she could be certain about anything. But she was starting to doubt if she could really do it to him, the more she got to know him, to like him. And that was a scary thought, and something she'd certainly keep to herself. One word of that to the team watching her and she was off the case, for sure. Probably wouldn't be allowed anywhere near the hospital. She'd seen the increased security, the more visible army presence. Though not really sure why, or what the threat was, she was certain that it was all for John. He was as heavily guarded as any President would be.

The doctor had been talking but she did not hear his latest question, until he repeated it, stopped, and then touched her arm.

"You really were a million miles away, weren't you." He was warm, smiling, gentle with her.

"I'm so sorry," she said, clearly embarrassed.

"Don't be, you must be so tired. You are with him constantly, right?" He too was aware of the increased security, the protection around such a high profile and yet normal looking man. It had taken a lot of checking and clearance for him to be allowed to see the patient. He'd been briefed, a little anyway, about the client before he'd first met him. He knew something of what was being hoped for. Of what, and who, John represented. And he was fully on board with it all. He too had loved ones, family now miles from where he was having to work. He wanted, as did so many, to live beyond it all. To have a hope. To have a future. John represented that. He was their best chance.

"Yeah, I've been with him since he first woke up. It's less intense than it was, but there is also more time now, and less to talk about. So we're venturing into new areas. I guess, if something does happen with his memory, that will at least give us a lot more to go on."

"It's not looking hopeful though, you picked that up, right?"

"Yes...I was listening to you, honestly." She smiled. She continued:

"Is there any hope that he will remember anything? They say in the final moments of life, it's comforting to have some memories to take you through to the other side."

"It's hard to say, but my gut feeling is that the exercises we're doing will provide limited, if any, recovery. We really need to see how the next two sessions go. I do have a few good options up my sleeve, but always tend to use these last, when the patient is already fully invested in the process, and relaxed with me."

"And after that?"

"After that, it depends. Like I've said before, with trauma patients, we look for trigger points. Photos, videos, anything that is a sensual reminder of what life once was. Family members even coming to see the patient. That can be hard though, with the patient feeling worried that the person in front of them is a total stranger, and the family member actually distraught from seeing their loved one in that state, often hostile to them. It's not always a great solution."

"And in John's case, it's not a viable option, either."

"Yes, I heard about that. The family have been told that he's dead. He should have been anyway. From what the team told me, everyone with him was killed. If they were to find out, then of course that would complicate matters."

"I think it would do more than that. As a parent, if you found your lost son, who you thought was dead, would you then let him willingly walk into something that would kill him, especially when he's telling you he's seen all these visions...?" She stopped. There seemed no need to go any further. They were also not totally alone where they were.

"I get you. So, as you see, the options are limited. I do have a final few exercises to work through with John, so there is always hope. In some exceptional cases, these have produced the desired results. My hunch, given the choice, is that the trigger points are his best shot."

Lorna smiled. She knew a lot about exceptions.

"The biggest exception of them all is lying in that room right there. Quite why he survived, I still do not know."

"Well, it's good for us that he did. At least we know there is hope. Have you heard the news from today?"

"No," she said, not that she'd heard that much of anything for about a week now. Her life had been the hospital.

"They say the reactors cannot last for much longer. Unofficially, I heard, they think it's a matter of weeks, if that. The radiation dust from them all has increased steadily over the last few days."

Lorna just looked at him; there was a finality in his tone, but the slightest sparkle of hope still left in his eyes. She wondered if he could say the same for her, at that moment.

"I guess that focuses the mind. We have a couple of

weeks, at best, to get this guy walking again. After that, who knows?"

Neither did. At that moment, neither of them knew what it would involve, what it would take. What it would cost them. They would just have to find out. And that moment was drawing ever closer.

Chapter 20

Clive slammed the phone down on his desk, clearly annoyed. He'd just had word that John's family had been told; someone had leaked to them the suggestion that John was still alive. It would ruin his scoop. However, what annoyed him far more than that was to think that someone in his team, a small one at that, could have been the source of this leak. It had happened many times before. To the young or inexperienced, hot news was just too good not to share. 'Careless Talk Costs Lives' had been the famous Second World War slogan in the UK. Never was a truer phrase spoken than in Clive's world of journalism. Usually it was rephrased to 'Careless Talk Costs Money', and often they'd add ' and Jobs' to that as well. They had not expected that in the present case the original statement would be the truer one. Lives were now at stake. And Clive was fuming. He stormed out of his office. To stay would be foolishness; he'd clearly do more harm than good. He needed instead to find out what had happened. If someone from his team had spoken to anyone, they were finished. Even if it had been Emma, nice as the drink had been with her, enjoyable as the kiss in the car had been when he'd made his move. For a while she had let it happen then she recollected herself and had stopped it. Maybe now, therefore, she was looking for an out, or looking for some form of come back? Some revenge? Well, if it was her, he'd find out. He always did. Just now, he felt like stringing someone up by their neck, to hang them so that the whole office got the message: on something this big, this important, this good, you don't go shouting your mouth off. You don't ruin the story before its time. Anyone doing that isn't thinking like a true journalist. They certainly aren't thinking like a team player. He was beside himself with emotion. He needed fresh air.

What he didn't know, was that no one had leaked

the news from his team. They were all too scared, as well as too immature, to really know the value of the story to the highest bidder. It had been in fact the secret service team from Africa. That morning, posing as reporters intent on bringing some good news, they'd knocked on the countryside front door of John's parents and spoken with his mother. Initially, she didn't want to talk, disliking the obvious intrusion. She was angry that the same people, journalists, were coming for more dirt, from the same filthy industry that had been responsible for killing her only child. Nearly having the door slammed in their faces, they'd simply asked her how she felt to hear of news that her son was alive. She'd frozen on the spot, and asked them to repeat what they'd just said. They'd played the part well, being the bearers of good news at such a difficult time for the nation. The information was given to the mother as to where her son was being kept. There was no more information than that. None was needed. Plant enough hope and they knew the mother would do the rest. It was another well planned distraction technique being employed by the African secret service team operating illegally in the UK. Their sole aim was to silence the possible truth that they'd been behind the accident. That, far from actually being an accident, it had been a deliberate attack; an act of war, no doubt, in their victims' eyes if ever they knew. What that Indian technician had done, when he went against their orders and sent out that final message from the probe, was to make them vulnerable. The Africans did not know why ever he had done that. He'd also gone missing since it had all happened. It was hoped that a team had got to him and made him pay for his actions, actions that could lead to a military show down if the British were to ever find out that this was no accident. The one final threat therefore, as they now saw it, remained with this freak survivor, John. And one way or the other, they needed to get sight of him. If it was through Clive and his team, they were happy. If it was through the family, that too would work out for them.

The two person team that had broken the news to the mother had remained in the shadows, watching the property. They were there to keep a track on her, to follow her. And sure enough, less than twenty minutes after they'd gate crashed the mourning of her lost son, she was seen leaving, overnight bag packed and placed in her car on the front seat next to her. They watched her back out of her driveway and head in the general direction of London. It would take her some time to get there, but they were now following her anyway. The passenger in the tailing car took out her phone and called ahead:

"She's on her way, as planned. Will be with you in around two hours, depending on traffic. We are following behind her. We'll call you when we get there."

With that, they finished the call. The net was closing. Soon there would be nowhere to go.

Clive had been making calls for the last thirty minutes. His usual sources, when stories had been leaked in the past, had revealed nothing. That was unusual. It might mean that it wasn't from his office, or was in fact from someone so senior that they knew Clive's 'go to' people, and had avoided them. That being said, none of those people were in his team; they were off the hook for the time being. Maybe someone else from the office had got wind of something and was doing their own digging? He'd keep close to his sources and see where it might lead. It lightened his mood somewhat to realise it wasn't a traitor in his own team and he went to find some coffee.

His usual lady friend wasn't answering her phone. He hoped she would later, maybe they could do something that evening. He was in need of some distraction.

As he was sitting down in his favourite local café, he was approached by two smartly dressed SAS agents, their appearance fitting with the other customers. To the watching eye, it was a natural, everyday business chat. Nothing to raise anyone's suspicion. Clive was initially hostile. They didn't say who they were but he'd come across the security service once or twice before. Those were the stories he'd get to tell the grandchildren one day, if he ever had any.

"What do you want?" he'd said. "Who are you? MI5?" Clive was keeping as calm as possible, and no one else in the café was taking the slightest notice, though he did try hard to keep his own voice down.

"Let's just say that we are watching you. What you are currently doing is now bringing you into our attention even more. You need to back off." The SAS man paused before adding, with a little more threat in his voice: "Why did you tell the family?"

"I didn't!" Clive barked back at them, a little too forcefully.

"Then you have a leak, and leaks in our line of business need to be shut down." They changed their tack. "You are a leak. And you are walking into something that you think you understand and yet have no idea about. We know you were at the hospital, with a young staff member who posed as your daughter. You were claiming to have a son there, but that is not true, is it?" Clive didn't respond. He didn't need to.

"This story stops here!"

"If you say so," Clive said, trying to make a joke. It didn't draw a laugh from either of the two suited men in front of him.

"Where did you get your information?" Clive wasn't about to reveal his sources, no journalist ever did.

"That's not your concern."

"It is precisely our concern if we make it our concern. If you want us to play hardball, we will. National security protocol means we can be in your office in no time. We can shut you down. We can put you in prison.

We can take your computers. Do you really want us that involved in what you are doing there at your little paper?"

He'd got the point. He certainly didn't want the British Intelligence Service anywhere near his office. He put his hands up, as if in surrender.

"Okay, calm down, will you? I'm listening. I'm here. Let's talk about this, shall we, before you jump in with both feet."

"There is nothing to talk about. Your source? Who fed you this lie that John Westlake was still alive? Who got you to dig into it? Where did you hear it from? I bet it wasn't from your usual contacts."

That was true, a fact overlooked by Clive, and one that he was now beginning to dwell upon. Maybe that source had leaked the news to his family? And if that was the case, there seemed little reason to protect them any longer. They hadn't played by the rules. He still had their cards on him in his jacket pocket.

"Look," he said, reaching into his pocket to get them. "They left me their contact details. It was two women, a couple of hookers if you believe what they said. They implied that John had hired them for relief. I certainly wouldn't have said no." This drew no response whatsoever from Clive's two companions. So he continued, "You are welcome to try and contact them. They are the ones who showed up and told me about the situation in the first place. I'd heard nothing from my usual sources. If I had, I wouldn't have been telling you now, of course."

They picked up the two cards that Clive had dropped onto the table and looked at them, as he was talking. The cards were rather generic looking, of very poor quality. The companies listed were also generic, meaning nothing to either agent. It was obvious that they were fake. Clive continued:

"They did ask me to call if I had news for them."

'The numbers might work, at least', they thought. The older of the two agents now put the cards in his pocket and proceeded to get up.

"Where does that leave me then?" Clive asked.

"Like we said, this is not a story. Stay away. I'd suggest, for your health, you take a break. Get away from it all. Let it go quiet, for now. In time, you can come back to the story. Once the situation has been stabilised. But if you continue, we have no choice but to get involved. We are having this conversation now to make that clear to you. You have been given your warning. There will be no further ones. Have we made ourselves clear?"

Clive said nothing, but nodded. They turned and left, as quickly as they'd arrived. Clive now sat back in his chair, cheeks puffed out, his body tired. He was wondering what he needed to do. Who had those two ladies been that had given him the story in the first place? And if it had been them, why had they told the family? Could he really just walk away? Would that be the best thing to do? It wasn't the first time the paper had been warned off. A few stories had brought similar reactions, though often they were run anyway. These other incidents had been before his time in his current role. This was his first personal encounter, and now, alone again, he wasn't sure. They'd been quite clear as to what would happen if he didn't back down. Something was going on, that was for sure. But was it something he really wanted to get his nose into? That was the real question going through his head as he left the café and made his way back to the office. Answering that question would show him what he needed to do. It was decision time.

****

John closed the book he'd just finished, his seventh that week. He was beginning to enjoy most of his new routine, unaware of what any other life had been like anyway. He guessed it wasn't quite as gentle as the one he was living now, though maybe gentle wasn't the word. His next physio session was due in a little while, and that would be anything but gentle. His first one had been so much harder than he ever thought possible. It was as much a mental exercise as it was physical. He had to will himself to do it, to move a little. That had not really happened last time round, but he hoped that today could be different.

He put the book back onto the piles next to his bed, two towers of books. With seven on the 'read' pile, it was now much higher than the four he had left to read. Soon he'd have to send Lorna off for more books. She'd probably need to take the books away soon anyway; one more and the pile would surely be a safety hazard. He laughed to himself about the thought that of all the hazards no doubt listed in some manual at the hospital, toppling books was probably not in there, yet.

He could only guess at what his life might have been like. He'd just finished seven novels, each one showing the lives of seemingly ordinary people, showing what they did, how they lived, where they went. John was living life through them at the moment. He was well aware of that fact, but actually felt it lifted him from his current situation and gave him ambitions for the future. He too was soon going to have a life once more. And walking out of the hospital, on his own two legs, was going to be the first stage of that. Reading was a very therapeutic exercise, one he intended to keep up.

He wondered if he had read much before. He couldn't see why he hadn't, he clearly enjoyed it. But he also realised he had the time now. In that moment, he vowed to read more, not knowing how much time he had left. It needed to be an essential part of his relaxation. There felt like nothing better than getting lost in a novel, a whole world of different people, lives that jumped from the page.

Lorna walked into the room at that moment, bringing him back from his thoughts. She came over to his bedside table and started moving the books he'd read.

"Thanks, I was getting afraid they might fall and crush me," he said, just about holding back a smile.

"Sorry?" she said, not totally in the room herself, now wondering what she'd missed.

"It's nothing," he replied.

Having taken the books over to nearer the door, ready to be moved away later, she came back, all attention, now with a smile on her face.

"So, John, today you have your second session of physio."

"Don't I know it!" He was joking with her, and she smiled back.

"Well, I'm going to make sure he doesn't go any easier on you today. Actually, maybe I'll ask him to push you harder."

"Good, that last session, after all, was rather lame. He needs to step his game up to keep pace with me, you know."

Lorna actually laughed out loud at this then gently placed her hand on his arm.

"Seriously, though, you can do this. I know you can, and I'll be here for you after. We can talk about how you feel, how it felt for you during the session, anything really."

"Thanks, I know I can count on you for a good chat. It's the one thing I am able to do quite well at the moment. That, and reading."

"Nonsense. You'll get there soon enough."

"But what if I can't walk? What if I never remember anything from before?"

"I don't think it will help you to think like that, John. Firstly, you do not have a broken back. Be thankful for that. You do not have any serious muscle damage, either, that would stop you from walking. Therefore, as with many other patients, it's just a case of using the muscles, and rebuilding strength where there has been some injury and limitation. It's a matter of time, and of course effort and hard work, than actual ability. You have the ability, you just need to engage it. And in relation to your memory, you are making new memories all the time. You remember those seven stories, right?" She pointed to the books. He kept his focus and attention, but didn't need to respond. She continued, "And you remember me. You remember the visions. Our time together here. Your brain, therefore, is not damaged so as to lose the ability to store information, it's just that, for some reason, your memory from before you came to the hospital has been lost. But either way, John, don't lose heart. Don't let one second of doubt stop you now. You've come so far, it's amazing to see you so healthy, and getting stronger by the day."

He processed what she had said for a moment, silent and contemplative.

"Why am I here, Lorna?"

"What do you mean?"

"I mean, what happened to me? How did I come to be in this hospital, with all these injuries, in the first place?"

She paused, calculating her answer for just a moment, before saying:

"If I am honest, I don't really know what happened to you or why you arrived in the state you were in," which was a half truth. She really didn't know why he had arrived in such a good state, not dead. He read it the other way.

She continued, "But as a nurse, that's not really my job, now, is it? I'm here to take you from where you were when you arrived, to the healthy, free walking man you need to be in order to leave this hospital. What has happened to you with these visions was something very special. Let's not forget that."

"Here's a question for you. Do you think I would have had these visions if I hadn't been so badly injured, and therefore here with you in the hospital? Would I have had them at home, for example, where ever that might have been?"

"I'm certain you had them because of the injuries." She was telling him the truth with this response, for sure. "Maybe the closer you are to death, the more aware you are of the spiritual side of life."

"Do you believe in all that stuff then?"

"Professionally, we are not meant to go there."

"Why not?"

"Good question. I don't know. They just think it's the way it has to be. This is Britain, after all. The 'tolerant' place where everything is accepted, except intolerance, and where nothing can actually get said!"

They both smiled at each other.

"But personally, what do you think happens when we die?" John said.

"I thought I once knew. I guess I had believed nothing happens, like most of the people around me believed. But then I'd never lost anyone. Now I hope I am wrong. I did once go to church. I don't know why we stopped. Just lazy really, I guess. And busy. But that busy doesn't really seem like it was worth it now, in the end. I'd have taken a less demanding job, with more time with James, if I had the choice now. What about you, John?" she said, diverting the focus of the conversation away from herself. "What do you think?"

"I'm a blank canvas. But I have seen beyond,

remember. This angel, or what ever he was. So yes, I guess I do believe in something."

Lorna wanted to say that it wasn't so, or that the vision at least didn't prove one way or the other. She couldn't, of course, and buried that urge instead.

They sat there in silence for a little bit. Then there was a knock at the door and the physio walked into the room, a smile on his face.

"Are you ready?" he asked, an energy and vitality to his voice that made John feel so weak.

"As ready as I'll ever be, I guess," John said, a smile appearing on his face. "Let's get this over with, shall we?"

Chapter 21

Clive had spent some time thinking about what he was going to do and wasn't any closer to working that one out, so had returned to the office and had shared his thoughts with the rest of the team. They were all surprised and also unsure what needed to happen. They'd all invested a lot of time and effort into the investigation so far. It was also true that for most of them it was just a job. They were getting paid regardless. For Clive, it was much more than that. It would have been his name on the front page article after all. His story. And now, that was not so certain. Consensus in the room, at least amongst the rest of Clive's team, was that they should back away, take the warning seriously and leave it all alone, for now. They still had all their information up to that point, so there would be the chance to publish it at a later stage. There seemed no reason to go so obviously against the instructions of the British Intelligence Service, MI5, or whoever they might have been. They were clearly getting into something far bigger than they realised, but that was what excited Clive. He was, after all, already aware of the bigger story behind the RAF base, the sole cause and reason for the whole incident in the first place. Instead of making the call right away, he wanted them to take some time to process it, and then they'd come back and take a closed vote. That way each one of them could vote with their heart, not as they thought the others in the room wanted them to. It was agreed that they'd each go away for a while. One would get some drinks, another some food. Pizza seemed the popular choice once again. They'd each go away for an hour before coming back, eating and then deciding whether to drop the biggest story they would ever get to work on, to pull out because of this threat from an unidentified group, one they presumed was in fact MI5.

Just ten minutes later they were leaving the office

and all going their separate ways. This caused a little concern for the watching African secret service team, who could only follow two members. So they split, one opting to follow Clive, an obvious choice, the other tailing Emma.

Clive stuck to familiar places. The local shop to buy some snacks, then on to his favourite café. It was the same place where he had been approached by the two British agents. His coffee was drunk in a less eventful fashion. No one seemed to notice him, though he was being watched. He finished, going over to pay his bill, flirting once again with the young waitress he was beginning to recognise. She responded in kind, but only to try to increase the tip he usually left. Nothing else about the man remotely interested her, but she wasn't going to let on. He was a customer, and he tipped well. That made him more than welcome.

Clive left the café just before one, heading for a local park. He liked to walk through there, the autumn colours still just about hanging on. While untouched by the incident, saved by its distance from the base, there was still the smell of burning in the air, and this was not the usual city centre smog. It was the burning columns of black smoke in the distance, a constant reminder, for those that could see it, of what had so recently happened. In the park, once he'd started walking in the opposite direction, it was at least possible to forget about all that, to imagine a much happier time, when the end of the world was not actually being predicted. Of course, even then, there were pockets of people, the non conformists, who ignorantly denied any such end as being in sight. Or even a possibility. As if their statement alone had any bearing on the actual, inevitable, outcome.

Clive was of a different understanding, because of what he already knew through John and what he had learned since. He knew the true scale of the disaster and what was about to happen. He was a realist, though not a fatalist. He was, therefore, looking to get on with life, as it now was, as best he could.

He had been walking in circles and criss-crossing the park for about thirty minutes. The woman tailing had at first thought that he was onto her, before it became clear Clive was actually just wandering, going no place in particular. He was so lost in his thoughts that, when the same African woman he'd first met a few days back stopped straight in front of him, he didn't immediately notice. Then he suddenly registered, seeing those same eyes, that same face. He paused.

"What are you doing here?" he said.

"We've been keeping an eye on you. And we now have our own message for you."

"And what would that be?" Clive said, looking around him, wondering if anyone else was watching, if there were others in her team, or was she really just on her own at the moment. He thought there must be others, somewhere.

"You need to run with the story."

"Sorry?" Clive said, not quite believing what he had just heard.

"You heard me. You must pursue this story until the end. You must find John and you must report this to the world. They need to know."

"Why are you saying this?" Clive was worried, scared even. "Why now?"

"You seem to be in some confusion about whether you want to proceed. I am just making it clear that stopping is not an option you have right now."

"And how do you know what I am thinking?" he asked. He was considering telling her how he'd been warned off and then remembered he'd given the two ladies up to them. So he quickly buried that thought.

"We know everything there is to know, Clive. And we want to help you to get this story. But so that you know the urgency of the situation, you need to go back to the office now, as they will have some news for you. And mark my words, if we do not see you going forward with this story right away, the news you hear will not have a happy ending.....and it will be the same for everyone working with you. And then, finally, it will be the same for you, too. Have I made myself clear?" She was only too clear and it sent a cold shudder down his back for a brief moment.

"Yes, you are clear. Tell me, who are you?"

She didn't respond to that last question, but with an all-knowing smirk, simply turned and walked away down another path heading towards a nearby London Underground station.

Clive rushed back towards the office, as sirens were already being heard in the distance. Arriving through the main doors, about ten minutes later, he was out of breath as he had been running for the last part. The lights from two police cars were flashing around in front of the building. Clive rushed in and asked what had happened.

"It's Emma. There was a white van, and as she was outside the front door, two men grabbed her and pulled her into it. She's gone, Clive. She's been kidnapped!" With that, the receptionist was in tears. Clive sank into the black leather sofa and was lost in his thoughts for a moment. He was thinking back to the park, and what the lady had just said to him. The words 'If you do not proceed, the news you hear from the office will not have a happy ending' ran over and over in his mind. 'And it will be the same for everyone in your team, and then the same for you too.'

"Oh God," he said aloud to himself. "What has happened?"

A police officer was now walking over to Clive, ready to ask him some questions. Clive had no idea what answers he would be able to give. This was all turning into a nightmare.

****

At that same moment, John's mother had just arrived at the hospital where she had been told her son was being treated. The journey had been a difficult one. She didn't like navigating her way at the best of times, and had got lost more than once. This had temporarily caused the car tailing her to lose her too; they were just not able to keep up with such erratic, irrational driving. But knowing where she was ultimately heading, they'd found her again and had called the team at the hospital just before getting there.

It had been a really emotional journey for her anyway. The feelings for her son, which had been wrapped in grief because of his death, now returned with this unheard-of hope, and that was a powerful feeling.

Her back was hurting from the journey. She really didn't like driving on the motorway, but hadn't had any choice that day. She just needed to get there. She stayed in her seat for a whole five minutes, composing herself, double checking the information to make sure this really was the hospital she was meant to be at. It all seemed to check out. She got out of the car slowly, stretching a little, straightening her back. There were still quite a few cars in the car park, but it was far from full. She made her way over to the main entrance, and was alarmed to see so much security there. She carried on in, the African secret service team watching from afar, not daring to venture in themselves, just yet. If they were lucky, she'd lead them to her son.

"Can I help you, ma'am?" came the question from the guard on duty just inside the front doors. She'd yet to go through security.

"Yes, I am here to see my son. I was told that he was alive, and being treated here. I'd been told he was dead, but someone told me he'd been found. I really can't believe it!"

"And what is his name, ma'am?"

"It's John Westlake. I'm Barbara Westlake, his mother." She proceeded to pull out her driver's licence card from her purse to prove the point. The guard looked through the records. He checked it a second time.

"I'm sorry, ma'am, but we have no one here by that name. Are you sure you're at the right hospital?"

She looked confused. The hope that was there started to slip a little further away from her. Had this been one terrible joke?

"Can you please check again! He has to be here. They told me he was alive!"

The guard didn't start looking again, he'd already done it twice and it was clear the guy wasn't listed there. Public records were now being taken from these new lists. Lists created by teams of volunteers, working around the clock to document each patient. The man from the SAS team came over to see what the fuss was about. The guard turned to him and said:

"Sir, this lady thinks her son John is being treated here, but we have no record of him."

He looked down at the lady's driver's licence, taking in her surname. He kept a blank expression on his face, his voice an even tone. No hint of anything came across to Mrs Westlake.

"Ma'am," he said, a gentleness in his voice that hadn't been there with the guard. She warmed to him straight away. "Can you tell me where you heard it from that your son was here?"

"What do you mean? Is he here then?"

"I think you've had that answer already, haven't you. But I wanted to check who had got your hopes up in such an awful way, to trick you into coming here? If it was someone we could find, we'd certainly make sure they never did it again."

"I...I don't understand," she said, tears pouring down her face. "I was dealing with it all as best as I could. We all were. And then these two journalists, I presumed they were, came to the door, disturbing us. I thought they were after some dirt, or something. But just as I was about to shut the door, they asked me how I felt to know that my son was still alive. They then gave me the information for this hospital. Said he was in D ward."

D ward was off limits, and was in fact where John was being kept. The SAS man kept his cool, and asked to look at the information. Instantly he could see that it had been put together by someone who knew their stuff. He recognised the signs. The extra information, the little clues here and there. Most people would write down the name of the hospital and an address. That was all. This had the marks of intelligence services at work, but whose?

"May I take this sheet of paper, ma'am?" he said.

"Please, call me Barbara," she said, through tears, handing over the sheet of paper which hours before had seemed like a winning lottery ticket, something that gave her son back to her. Now, it was nothing. "Are you positive he is not here?" she asked one final time, only looking at the man from the SAS, ignoring the guard altogether.

"Yes, Barbara, I assure you. I am sorry for what you must have gone through, but these people who told you this had another motive for doing so. Maybe they wanted to cause you more sorrow? I don't know. I'll hand this over to the police to look into. If they are doing this to lots of people, we need to stop them." He then added, for good measure. "Do you live alone?"

"Well, not usually, though my husband is away at the moment, in the north. He was there on business and hasn't yet come back. Why?"

"Well, it might be that they are intending to burgle

you, ma'am. Preying on people that have lost loved ones in the city, telling them a story to get them driving all the way to London, hours from home. Empty homes. I will notify the local police for you as well, though it might be too late.

"Oh my word. How could I have been so stupid?" She was in floods of tears, and in a rush to leave. She took her driving licence back, dropping it into her bag, and turned to leave.

Neither man said anything more to her. There was already a queue of other relatives waiting to get into the hospital.

Walking out of the hospital, she headed back to her car.

"It seems she didn't get in," came the call over the radio from one of the two teams now at the hospital from the African side.

"Damn it!" came the angry response. "What do we have to do with these people?"

"Shall we tail her?"

"Yes, follow her to see where she goes. If she sticks around, maybe we have another chance. However, don't go all the way back with her. I'm not sure it's worth it."

They pulled away just moments after she did; it was already five minutes since she'd left the hospital. She'd got back to her car, in tears, just standing there, keys in hand. It took her two minutes just to get back into the car, willing herself to shut the door of hope that had been so rudely opened again. She'd called her husband, but only got his voice-mail. She left a short message, ending with how sorry she was for leaving the house in such a rush. She really hoped nothing bad had happened.

In that time, the SAS guy from the hospital entrance had called to his team with what had just happened. They would analyse the information sheet they were given for any clues of its origin.

"Okay, we have her coming out of the hospital now,

walking towards her car," came the call from the other SAS unit stationed outside the hospital in the car park. It was their first bit of action for a long time. They watched her pull away, and then another car, which they hadn't noticed was occupied, also pulled away.

"Seems like she might have had a tail. We'll follow them. Please get someone to come and take our position. Over." With that, they too set off, keeping their distance.

****

At the joint MI5 and SAS task force HQ, they were working through the latest information that they had. They'd been sent a copy of the info sheet from the hospital, and a two man team were taking it all apart. It was clear that it had been well put together. It wasn't something done by mere amateurs. Another agent had also now brought in the two business cards that Clive had given them. All believed that the same team was behind both incidents, and links into further possible angles were being thought through as they spoke.

Flight records from all the airports were being processed and checked against the MI5 database. They were covering a wide range, not knowing when the team might have arrived in the UK, if they had not in fact been here all along. As yet, nothing to connect it all was showing in this regard. Word was also put out to the other countries which had close ties to Britain though it was clear the team were being played by some unknown outside force. So the British were being careful about what they asked. When the time came and they found out exactly who it was, they could bring others in on it all more fully, and hopefully those others would have fresh intelligence on the target that would help them close in on them.

It was clear that a concerted effort was being made to locate John. The fact that they knew about his existence was bad enough. The fact that they knew which hospital, and the exact part of the hospital, made it all even more dangerous. Quite what their angle was on it all, was anything but certain. Given the secret world from which the joint task force came, they assumed the unknown team was of hostile intent until proved otherwise. Everything was a threat. It always was. Until they could ascertain what the purpose was in trying to find John, there was an active kill order in place on anyone, regardless of who they were, if they posed a threat to the safety of John.

Calls were made to the numbers on the cards that Clive had handed over. Each call rang for a long time and was answered but then only silence. Both sides knew what this meant. The Africans, having given the cards to Clive, knew all the office numbers. So receiving an incoming call from another number, one that was not listed on any system they had, only meant bad news. And to the British, the cards were clearly not what they pretended to be. A team of three technicians went to work on the numbers, in tracking a location, or anything linked to the account. They would get answers soon, but not before the Africans HQ had been gutted and abandoned.

It was later that day that they made the connection, a young analyst breaking the news to the section heads in the main control room.

"Here, I've got it! The numbers are linked to an empty office in Chelsea. Nothing from the landlords, who'd never met the tenants, but the phone records tell us all we need to know. Very limited access now, most numbers are blocked and no longer working. But looking back, the office is rarely used. Last time was three years ago. A large trade contingent, including several political heads, were in London for talks. There were many calls from this office to the Nigerian and South African embassies."

"An African team?"

"Seems to be the very same ones that disrupted the talks we had over a year ago. No one with African connections had been invited to the talks. A team of people posing as waiters had infiltrated the system and were at the venue. Nothing important, it is believed, was lost."

"Okay, get me all known African agents working in Europe. We need names, faces, everything we have on these people within the hour. If they are the ones behind this, we need it ended, now."

"Sir, we've just heard from a team that they are following a car that was watching the hospital. It could be the people that told the mother her son was still alive."

"Okay, keep on them, and lets get backup in place. I want them caught and we can bring them here for questioning. We need some leverage with the Africans. They must be brought in alive!"

"Understood."

Orders were called out, five new teams were pulled from the SAS and transferred to the ongoing operation. They now had their target and it was just a case of picking them off, as quickly and silently as possible.

Chapter 22

Having had to flee their head quarters in a rush, the team of African secret service personnel that were currently working in the UK were making plans whilst on the run. They called out to let the teams know what was happening, agreeing to keep regular contact, but no longer to meet up as a whole, in case it would bring risk to the other members of the unit.

The field chief had been working in Europe, and mainly the UK, for decades. He was well known to MI5, but only now did the British security service fully appreciate exactly what his role entailed. His cover was blown and he would have to think about his own escape. What was most important in the meantime was seeing through their operation. Not having a secure base made things a little harder. Communications were now limited. Phone lines were not as secure as they would like, and therefore they would limit calls as much as possible, and use code when they had to. That way, it would restrict what was being understood. The British would need to break the code, or have the source text, in order to really understand what was being said and planned.

Little did they know, at that moment, that the SAS had successfully captured the two operatives who had been trailing Mrs Westlake. She was none the wiser, carrying on her journey back to the West Country and still trying to work out all that had taken place. She had not seen it when two cars behind her had surrounded and stopped a black saloon, armed officers suddenly all over the vehicle, stun grenades employed. An electronic blocking device had been enabled, shutting off all electrical equipment in the target vehicle, including the car itself, of course. It was over as soon as it had started. The two people in the car were handcuffed and masks were placed over their heads, as they were literally carried from their vehicle and placed into separate trucks which raced off into the night. The empty vehicle was attached to a truck and taken away later, to be tested in order to gain every last piece of evidence from its fibres.

Setting up what was, for all intents and purposes, a mobile field command in a local coffee house, the chief of staff for the Africans was currently looking through the plans for the hospital. They were the plans that had been obtained from the newspaper offices. It was good work, the colour coded system showing everything they needed to know. It was clear that the red rooms were their target rooms. From a security point of view, the three rooms on D ward made the obvious choice for keeping someone locked away. They were central, away from public areas and easily guarded.

When the watching African team had first arrived at the hospital some days before, they'd picked up traces of high level surveillance when they had scanned the hospital's electronic output. It was way more than the hospital would need, so it was correctly assumed that there was a mobile control room on site. It made sense for its location to be one of the three red rooms situated on the plans in front of them now. It also made more sense for this room to be adjacent to the patient's room, for easier video feeds. Only two of the three rooms highlighted in red were connected, sharing what seemed to be a small bit of wall space with each other, but nothing more. Emma, the kidnapped journalist, had been able to say that she had seen a guarded room when she had walked into the hospital. The larger of the two connected was the most obvious place to keep John. The smaller of the two connected rooms was more tucked away, accessed from another corridor entirely. She would not have got that far when she'd walked into the hospital.

All they needed was the chance to see the patient, and this, they reasoned, would be possible from the smaller control room which was separated from the larger room by a section of wall. It was highly unlikely that the smaller room was being guarded much, if at all. Why would it need to be? The occupants were just office personnel, not soldiers. They judged that this would provide them their best shot at John. One shot was all it would take.

A message was sent out to all field agents, with the latest plan of attack. They were to meet at the hospital that evening. Code Alpha Zulu. It was a kill order, and they all knew it. The two people watching the offices of the newspaper were also now leaving their post.

"What do we do about the girl?" came the coded message from another two who were holding her.

"Alpha Zulu on her. We can't leave any trail."

Both coded messages were received by the SAS team who were detaining the two operatives. They also had the source text, which had been taken from one of the agents. Neither had spoken, but the real interrogation had yet to start. They were sure they'd break them soon, though it might not be necessary. What they didn't know was where Emma was being held.

Clive had called MI5 quickly after the news had reached him, taking a huge risk himself. Once his identity had been confirmed, since they were the ones who had first made contact, they were ready to listen to what he had to say. They took what he said seriously, and by that time the true nature of the foreign team's operation in the UK was becoming known. Agents had been sent to the paper's offices, as security, and were keeping watch over the remaining team members. As of yet, nothing had been heard from them regarding Emma. MI5 had no idea where she was being kept. The white van used in the kidnapping had been found five miles from the scene, empty. It was being tested for clues, but that would not help them locate her now. CCTV at the place where the vehicle switch was made was not facing in that direction. It was one of just a few blank spots in the city's camera network, something only an intelligence service would know. They were clearly good at what they did.

It was feared that they would not be able to save the hostage. If the Africans were now fleeing, it was highly likely that they would kill her before they left. MI5 would be able to catch those responsible, seeing as they now knew where they were all heading, but only so as to bring them to justice. To find her now would be like looking for a needle in a haystack, unless the two prisoners started talking, or even knew were she was.

Nothing was said to Clive and his team, as they sat in silence for a while, the office in effective lock down.

Emma had arrived blindfolded at the place where she was being held, so she had no idea where she was. Stripped to her underwear, thinking she was about to be raped, she had pleaded with them not to hurt her. In fact she'd actually just been hand-cuffed and they'd taken the precaution of removing her clothes to make sure she wasn't wired. She was then left alone for a long time in relative darkness. She sat there, deep in her own thoughts, unsure of what was happening or why on earth she was being held. No one had said anything to her. She had no idea if anyone was coming for her. She had never felt so alone, or vulnerable.

Getting the order to kill her, the two agents looked at each other for a long moment, a game of rock paper scissors deciding who had to do the task. The butcher of the two lost, and straight away he started to fit a silencer to his hand gun. Like any athlete or sportsman, he was focused on his task, professional and swift. They could all take apart and then reassemble a weapon, in total darkness, in less than sixty seconds.

He stood up from the table in the kitchen, and told the other guy to start packing up, as they'd be leaving straight away. He walked down the corridor. The more slender agent heard the two shots fired quickly, and footsteps rushing back towards the kitchen. He was shocked to see a short Chinese man standing there before him pointing a silenced weapon straight at him. Immediately two shots were fired, killing the African agent instantly. He was dead before he hit the floor.

Emma heard what sounded like movement, and the clear sound of someone falling to the floor. Then a second sound of another person falling. The door to her room opened, and she could hear someone coming over towards her slowly. Whoever it was barely made a sound, apart from the noise from the wooden floor boards. She could hear the sound of a blade being opened. Her heart stopped. For a moment there was nothing, then her hands were grabbed and twisted, so that the blade could cut the cords keeping her hands tied behind her back. Her clothes were thrown onto her; it made her jump. Every sense was now coming alive. She had no idea what was about to happen. After what seemed like ages, she slowly lowered her blindfold, to see that she was alone. She looked around, but no one was watching her. She quickly pulled on her clothes and rubbed her wrists, there were red marks from the cords but no blood. She stepped out into the hallway, only then letting out any noise, a scream at the sight of a dead body, two exit wounds visible from the back of his skull, the body lying face down, a pool of blood covering the floor around him. She turned, and made it out of the front door. Still no one was around. Getting out to the road, she ran. Faster and for longer than she had done in years. To nowhere in particular, but anywhere was good. She was struggling to understand what was happening to her, what had happened. Who had saved her, and where were they now? Finally coming to a stop, she walked into the front entrance of a large hotel chain, only now beginning to feel safe, and asked to make a phone call.

****

It was the following morning when the government was informed of the African involvement in the ongoing operation. Those that had been involved in the energy deal, as well as the space program, were called together for an emergency session.

"Having told us the latest, what are we to read from their involvement in all this?" someone said, looking to the unofficial chairman of the meeting, the main political connection between them and MI5.

"I think their intentions are entirely hostile. Both Nigeria and South Africa have today issued withdrawal instructions to the majority of their embassy staff. Certainly both the ambassadors have left already. Official word is that it's the ongoing nuclear disaster and, as a natural precaution, while backing us to come through, they need to think about the safety of their own personnel as well. They pointed out that we did the same in Japan after the incident there a few years' back."

"And what's the unofficial line?"

"They are pulling out because we're onto them. They think that something we might be about to find out would warrant them all being outside of the UK."

"Are they after the plans for the power station? Is that what it is?"

"I guess that has to be their target."

"How in the world did they get wind of that?"

"Sir, with all due respect, only about a week ago, we had no idea that they even had a joint intelligence service capable of this level of espionage."

"Can we be sure that they haven't already got anything from us, seeing as they are already starting to leave?"

"It is still safe and secure, sir."

There was muted agreement around the six person table, that this was indeed still the case. Included within those six was a thirty six year old woman. At twenty nine, she had had the same level of ranking as people who'd worked their whole lives. A real high flier. Fluent in twelve languages, at the last count. She was born to a German father and Irish American Mother, but was raised in the UK. Travelling extensively, her father in the oil industry, she'd had the best of everything. Put through the most expensive private schools around, she had graduated two years ahead of her age group, with top marks. Oxford followed, with her doctorate taken at Cambridge in International Criminal Law, she was one of the elite students of her generation. She walked into a highly paid job in an international giant, spending four years travelling, with six month slots in Latin America, Africa, India and Russia, before being based for the last two years in Beijing, China. It was there that she was recruited into the Chinese Secret Service, and within months of that, was back in the UK, head-hunted for a military intelligence post, and six years later, was where she was today. One of just six people in that government meeting, and third in rank within the Chinese Secret Service.

Her worth to them was priceless. She'd already negotiated her fee for bringing them news on the power plant blueprints; cheap at five hundred million pounds. She really was as smart as she was attractive. And she always put both those qualities to good use, wherever possible.

****

The eight remaining members of the African secret service team currently operating in the UK had gathered just one mile from the hospital. The absence of the other four members of their team, who just had not shown up, spoke volumes. They were now all walking on very thin ice. Their final meeting had only been confirmed through an alternative channel, a last resort, but used when it was clear that two, and then the other two, of their agents had stopped responding. Neither of those two teams had anything important to give up under interrogation. They were lost to them now, casualties of war. It was noticeable how their chief just carried on, disregarding the fact that some of their colleagues were in trouble. It told them a lot about the man they were working under. They didn't like what they were learning, but had known others like him in the past. That sort tended to be the ones who got the most done.

The chief had the plans for the hospital open in front of them and was saying:

"This room here is our target area. We think it has minimal protection, if any. We will gain access from a venting outlet here," and he pointed to a mark on the map, which seemed to be in the same corridor as their target location. "From here, it's just a short distance to this point. When we get outside the door, we need to block all communications coming from the room, before taking it. They can't be allowed to report that we are there. Two of you will then watch the corridor, but if we want to get in and out without getting noticed, we are going to have to get this spot on. If we get trapped in there, I don't see that we have any way out."

He looked at each of his team members, four of them men, three were women. Each had been on such operations before, each one had killed someone. There was not a look of fear on their faces, but he could sense there was a growing awareness that they might not make it out again on this one. So much could go wrong, but with such a large hospital, maybe they could stand their ground until a deal could be reached.

The chief knew no deal ever would be. Their presence in the UK was totally deniable and no one in

Africa would admit to having secret agents there. He wasn't going to let them capture him. If bullets were flying, he'd make sure he caught one. It might even be from his own gun. He'd have that chat with all of them too, at some point, and if the situation arose. While there was still a slight chance, slim as it was, that they'd actually pull it off, he would keep it to himself.

Using the growing darkness as cover, the eight person team made their way to the edge of the car park, before running at speed for the back doors.

This was spotted by the watching SAS team, though they were a long way away, and unable to do anything but call in.

"We have seven, no eight, tangos approaching green four," the SAS coded message for targets running towards the rear doors of the hospital. "All call signs, standby, standby, standby. They are now climbing onto the roof. Standby, standby, go go go."

The command was heard by all of the SAS teams at the hospital, and they each took up their positions. Three more guys rushed through the main doors, weapons ready, to the shock and terror of the people close by. Visiting time was over, which meant far fewer people were around. The guard locked the doors, the other SAS man joined the three who had just entered and they raced to take their position.

On the roof, the eight people made their way to the main ventilation outlet, and using electric screwdrivers, quickly opened the hatch, dropping silently in through the roof. They lowered their bags last, the chief then coming down himself. There was a bit of piping to navigate through before they would be able to drop down into the corridor. Each made their way along smoothly, a stealth operation. Getting to the final hatch, they opened it outward, the door swinging soundlessly into the corridor below as the first agent jumped down, crouching as he hit the floor, looking left and right to check who was around.

There was not a sound, as the second and then third agent cleared the hatch. The bags were passed down before the rest of them made their way through.

Outside, the hospital was surrounded. Inside, the teams waited in position, line of sight constantly on the corridor outside John's room, from multiple angles. They certainly had the upper hand. Against eight, with the element of surprise, they knew these intruders didn't stand a chance. Still they waited though. The orders were clearly being repeated, over and over:

"Stand your ground, maintain position and shoot to kill."

Meanwhile the eight person team were unloading their bags. Weapons were ready, and the device that would disable all communications was set up. It was placed at the door, and then they fired it. The burst killed communications straight away in the room, as the lights flickered momentarily then went out. Within seconds, the eight had burst through the door. Shots were fired taking down the four people there who turned to see what was happening, their last vision being the killers entering the room. The silenced weapons made little sound. All the bodies were moved away and piled in the corner. Two agents stood guard at the door, an excellent line of sight down the corridor. They hoped it would remain as quiet as it was.

The chief looked at the desk of monitors and screens. The central screen showed a video feed of a person lying asleep in bed, monitors and wires clearly visible, though it was not possible to tell if they were still attached to the patient or not. He tapped the screen in delight.

"We have him. Lets get to work."

A measuring device was set up, to take accurate recordings from the room. They then marked a spot on the wall, clearing two of the screens from the right hand end of the table in front of them. One of the team then got onto the table, was passed a small electric drill and got to work on the wall. It was the type used to install spy technology, and by nature was silent. The wall, they guessed, was between fifteen and twenty centimetres, though they assumed that, as it was a non supporting internal wall, it was not solid. Still, it would take them longer than if they had a regular, power drill. That would be too noisy, of course. The longer they took, the bigger the risk.

The SAS teams were getting nervous now, knowing that their targets had been in the building long enough to have reached them, and yet there was no sign. No one had reported anything. The silence was sickening. What was happening? Where were they?

In the darkness on the roof, a lone figure made his way across the asphalt. Silently he clung to the shadows, reaching the ventilation funnel unnoticed. He descended, out of sight from any potential watching eyes.

In the control room, they were partway through most of the wall. The middle had indeed been a cavity. The wall was maybe just six centimetres thick on either side, and they were working through the final side. After five minutes they broke through, the drill coming free as the force of cutting through brick finished. Its operator pulled it back and a camera was pushed into and through the new hole. On a small portable screen, it showed a bed below them, on the edge of the room to their right. Someone was visible there asleep, the sheets wrapped around the raised body. Still there was silence. Nothing alarming was happening. Alongside the camera was now pushed a dart gun. It was highly lethal, the poison getting into the blood stream within seconds, its victim left with no chance. Taking one final check on the position, the operator loaded the dart into the weapon and pushed it into place.

"We are ready," he told the chief, who was standing

next to him watching the monitor, processing everything.

"Go ahead," he said, simply. The dart was fired, aimed at the leg and clearly hitting the mark. The sheets that were wrapped around would do nothing to stop the needle from connecting with the skin. At that moment, with all eyes on the monitor, the agent heard the thump, thump, thump of a high calibre weapon being fired with a silencer. He felt blood from the chief splash his face before himself taking a bullet to the leg. Each person of the eight strong team dropped to the floor, the chief having been shot in the head, the rest having been shot in both legs. All currently incapacitated. The room now silent.

The shooter then pulled a bag from his pocket, and dropped a load of identification onto the table. Names, ranks, serial numbers. Passports. Everything to tell those that would find them exactly who they were. Walking quietly out, he released a smoke grenade and climbed back up the ventilation shaft. As he was climbing back onto the roof, the smoke alarms were already going off.

On hearing the alarms, the SAS team in the main security room for the hospital were told it was coming from the back corridor.

"The control room!" they shouted through the ear pieces. "They're in the control room!"

Twenty minutes later they had secured the area and the alarm was switched off. SAS soldiers stood over the four bodies of the surveillance team, dumped in the corner like trash. Seven wounded men and women had been taken away under heavy armed guard, the eighth guy was dead from a bullet wound to the head. The documents were collected and passed on with the prisoners. It was a real intelligence coup. A high ranking spy killed and seven experienced agents down. Wounded but very much alive.

It was unclear as yet what had happened. No other weapon was found, certainly not the one that had grounded them all, nor any sign of who had done it.

The hole in the wall was discovered.

"Find out where that hole leads to, will you!" one man ordered. Two men, fully armed, headed off.

Neither of the two SAS men watching the back door saw anyone else come or go. They missed the Chinese secret service agent exit the roof, disappearing once again into the shadows, climbing back down the way he had sneaked onto the roof, and away into the night.

Chapter 23

That same day, Lorna had gone to find Alison, leaving the doctor once again with John. It would give her some time for fresh air and fresh conversation. She was finding that she was tending to go around the same circles with John. Lorna felt in constant need to steer the conversation in certain directions, usually to avoid other more complicated things. She just didn't trust herself with those subject areas.

Now alone with Alison, the evening light starting to fade slowly, she could talk freely. She could let off the steam, anger and frustration she was feeling, as could Alison. Both found themselves in very stressful, difficult positions. It was such a stretch from the usual job, which itself was demanding, that it made those times look like a vacation compared to the hours they were putting in at the moment. Alison too was feeling tired beyond compare. They walked for a few minutes, not really saying anything, just having a safe, quiet place to process their thoughts. If something came up that they needed to mention, they could tell each other. There was no need to keep a guard up here, no one was watching, they wouldn't be giving the game away by a careless word or phrase. This was their time to walk, talk, to be normal again. It wouldn't last for long, but they'd take as much time as they could, and would savour every moment, not knowing when the next chance would come. Getting to the edge of a line of trees that ran alongside the southern border of the hospital's grounds, they paused and finally started to talk.

"So, Alison, are things starting to calm down at all on the general ward?"

"You know, I really thought it would have done by now. Most of those that haven't died are in such a bad way, that they cannot leave. So they are taking up lots of beds. People can't die soon enough for the bed space we need."

She caught herself, realising how that sounded. "I didn't quite mean it like that."

Lorna was smiling.

"I get what you are saying. So, there's been no let up?"

"None at all. It's as if it is all happening again and again, fresh each day. People are only now starting to show signs of the radiation poisoning weeks after the incident. Many are fresh cases too, some are the rescue crews who are trying to contain the situation, and those that are clearing the crash sites. Some are those who ignored the calls to evacuate, too old or too stubborn to leave home. Many of these new cases are passing away really quickly. There seems little, if anything, we can actually do."

Lorna could hear the desperation in her voice now, that sense of loss, of despair, the fact that the years of training, and decades of combined experience counted for very little when faced with such an aggressive poison. Her main role, and that of all the staff in the hospital still working, was to ease the pain of death.

"What are the levels like?" Lorna said, asking about the staffing levels since the incident. They had been stretched to say the least when she was in the general wards just moments after the incident.

"I've not bothered to count. We are something like twenty five per cent from the normal levels, working one hundred per cent longer shifts with hardly any rest periods." In the past they'd worked up to ten hour days, or nights, with a rota of four days on and four days off. Lorna could only imagine the pressure they were all under. She knew it first hand, because though she was only working with the one patient, she had to be permanently on duty. At the beginning that had meant sleep for a maximum of about three hours at a time. That grew to about five hours as he progressed through the program. Now at about six, she felt a lot better. John was in a safe pattern, was coping well emotionally, and seemed to be fully invested in all that he needed to do. She now wondered how much longer she had with the patient. Soon, surely, she would be back on the wards as well. In some way, that thought brought slight relief, if only for a moment. She knew that for that to happen, she'd have to have sent John on his way to his death. A death he thought was his calling. In fact, it was just for their survival. She pushed that thought from her mind, for the moment.

"I can't begin to believe how tired you must be, Alison."

Alison turned to her, tears in her eyes. It was not just tiredness there, but grief. Sadness. Pure emotion.

"I've lost the ability to sleep. When I get the time, I just see the faces of those who are dying. My mind is crammed with thoughts. The staff room, as you know, has people coming and going all the time. They don't mean to be noisy, it's just I've become such a light sleeper."

Lorna understood that completely. Her first few days after the incident had been the same. Faced with such chaos, she didn't know how to fall asleep at the end of it all. She'd finally taken some pills to help with the matter.

"Look, I'll let you into a little secret, Alison. If you promise not to tell. I've been using some strong sleeping pills and there is a spare room, kept quiet, where I get to sleep. I think you need to try it too. It's away from people, away from all the noise. I've felt guilty having it all to myself, knowing what the staff room is like at the best of times. Why don't you use it tonight, to get some proper sleep. No one would disturb you, I'll make sure of it."

"Thanks," she said, still not sure what to say about it. She didn't know what would make the difference, and wasn't really too keen on taking pills to help her sleep. "Let's get some more fresh air, and we'll see."

They continued walking, the sun now on the horizon, evening drawing in fast.

"So tell me, how is our star patient doing?" Alison said, turning to Lorna, as if saying 'over to you, I've said enough for now'.

"John has started his physio. Getting him walking again is the main challenge now. He's currently in with the doc, his third session regarding his memory loss."

"Still had nothing from the past?"

"No, nothing. It seems uncertain whether anything will come back. Certainly now that things are not falling into place, it seems most likely, between you, me and the doc, that nothing will actually change. There is some more they can do, so until they've done it all, I guess we won't really know."

"How are the legs?"

"That's been hard, but a little more promising. At least we can see his legs, and we know where they are!" She was smiling at her attempt at a joke. "It was hard, the first session anyway. Always is."

Alison knew that only too well.

"But the damage is certainly not permanent," Lorna continued. "There is a lot to work with, and John did manage to stand up under his own weight last session, which was a huge encouragement for us all."

Alison nodded. She'd have loved to have still been involved in it all, but was not envious of Lorna. It hadn't been her doing, they'd both just been puppets in the system. She was happy with the success Lorna was having with the patient. She felt collective pride.

"Look, I think we had best start heading back," Alison said, indicating the growing darkness. "I would like to take you up on that offer for some sleep. I think I am losing the will to live."

Lorna looked over to her once senior colleague and saw the smile on her face returning.

"Sure, be my guest. Take as long as you need. I slept for a while during the day and I'll snatch what sleep I can tonight. John is going to need to chat about things anyway."

"Thanks, Lorna, you're a real friend."

As they walked back towards the hospital, Lorna thought through those last words. She didn't really have many friends besides Alison now. It was as if the disaster had forged stronger links, that this shared experience had made them closer, while her other friends seemed less connected now. Communication had a big part to play in that, as she hadn't really been able to speak to many people since it all started. None of them knew, as far as she was aware, about her James. She didn't even know if any of her friends had died. In the early days, when she was on the general ward, she'd wondered whether the next person in would be someone she knew. But there were too many, and that thought soon got swamped. But now, with her James gone, and John aside, Alison was the one friend she could talk to, and be herself with. With John, it was another matter entirely, as if it was another world. She was living in his alternative reality as much as he was. That became clearer the longer they went on.

Getting back to the hospital, now that it was very dark outside, they passed through security and went their separate ways, Lorna back to John, Alison for some much needed sleep. 'Maybe' she thought, 'I can finally get some hours of quiet that will make me feel at least half human once again.' Little did she know that she would not, in fact, wake up.

****

Security at the hospital had been tight all night and, to a large extent, they didn't really know what was happening. Two teams had been guarding John's room throughout the night.

Lorna had been with John when the incident had

happened, and though she'd heard a lot of activity, going out twice to check what was going on, they had been largely shielded from it all, so much so that Lorna had gone off herself to find somewhere to sleep, and only in the morning had been told what had happened.

The grief was like an ice dagger to the heart. Cold and biting, she was physically moved by the news that Alison was dead, killed in her sleep by unknown attackers. The news was horrific at the best of times, and now even more so. Had she been the intended target? Lorna was thinking about this, as she was on her way to a briefing meeting with a new group of specialists.

"What's happened to the others?" Lorna asked straight away; too many things were changing all at once.

"They too were affected last night," came the reply.

It was the tone of voice from this new stranger that told Lorna exactly how they had been affected.

"Oh God," she said, her hand coming up to her mouth, her body starting to shake. Someone placed a strong arm on her shoulder which actually seemed to bring some comfort.

"Look, Lorna, we don't have much time," they started. 'Why don't we have much time?' was what raced through Lorna's head, but she kept that thought to herself, for the time being.

"Last night was a shock to us all. We all lost someone we cared about. But we are certain the target was not Alison. They were here for John, and that is what worries us most."

"What?" Lorna said, a lack of understanding clear in her voice now. "I don't get it. Why were they after John?"

"Look, we really don't know. We've worked hard at keeping it quiet, keeping this whole operation a secret, but someone found out. And more than that, someone wanted John dead."

"Wanted? So the threat to John is gone now, it's over?" Lorna said, picking up on what they'd just said.

"We cannot yet assume that to be the case. John is still alive."

"You mean, they are going to come back?" There was genuine horror on Lorna's face. She didn't think her situation could have got any worse, bad as it was, and yet it just had. Things were now getting out of control, and people were getting killed because of it. Alison had been killed. She still couldn't get her head around the thought. She was convinced that she'd bump into her colleague somewhere around the hospital, that at lunch time, she'd find her and they'd go out and talk again. It was only hours since she'd seen her and she'd been fully alive and well. Lorna couldn't deal with the fact that she'd lost another close friend.

"Look, Lorna," came the tender reply, "you need to let us concentrate on the security side. Believe me, this is not going to happen again. We need you to concentrate on your role, the vital work and progress you are seeing with your patient. Last night has shown us that there is only so much time. The longer we leave it, the more risks there are."

"But who were they? Who are these people that would want to kill John? It doesn't make sense," Lorna said, thinking out loud.

"That, my dear, is the million dollar question. And believe me, before the day is out, we really hope that we will have those answers ourselves. For your safety though, we want to post a security team around you at all times, just to be careful."

"I thought I wasn't the target?" she said, not sounding too impressed with what they were suggesting.

"You aren't, it's just us being extra prudent. Clearly anyone involved in this operation is a target. Take the team that were working with you, for example. They happened to be in the wrong place at the wrong time, and now they are all history."

What they didn't tell her was that they were not the ones who had stopped the intruders. That in fact, they had no idea what had happened, and had it not been for the smoke alarms, the attackers might have got away altogether. It had been a wake up call of the highest order. Five people had been killed because of it: one nurse and the four person team monitoring John. Vitally, more through luck than judgement, John himself had not been affected in any way and was carrying on as before. Today would bring another round of physio, and further work with his memory loss.

Lorna left the brief meeting feeling numb. The loss of Alison only highlighted how little she had accepted the loss of James. It was ironic, at least to her at the moment, that there she was, surrounded by death on a daily basis, and yet so ill-prepared to actually deal with it herself. She'd sat with too many grieving relatives throughout her career, telling them to do things that she was unable to do herself.

She knew she'd have to work hard at keeping all of this from John. The slightest gap in her armour, and he'd be asking questions she couldn't possibly answer. No, she determined to herself as she walked the corridors back towards his room, she wasn't going to do that. Not now, not after all this time. She'd have to bury those thoughts. Hide them from herself, deny them the time to breathe or develop.

Walking back into John's room, her patient lost in another novel, she carried on as if nothing had changed. Keeping herself busy, doing the things that needed to be done. Anything to avoid reality.

****

At the secure military base somewhere in London, the seven wounded agents of the African secret service were being held, ahead of strong interrogation that would start in due course.

Kept apart from one another, none of them knew which of the others had actually survived and what, if anything, they were saying to the British.

The documentation had been thoroughly analysed. It was extremely rare for such materials to be carried around by a foreign hit squad on hostile soil. The MI5 and military personnel holding the prisoners knew this only too well. And yet the paper work seemed to check out, even if they were not in fact official original versions of the passports. They were forged, that was clear to see, though they'd been done well, and each document did indeed seem to belong to one of the people arrested.

Best guess at the moment was that an unknown ninth member of the team had done this to them, for reasons as yet unknown, turning in his own unit. No contact had been made, no messages passed on to them. The longer it continued, the stranger the silence became. What had been the intention and why leave it so late?

At Thames House, the home of MI5, teams were working through surveillance footage from around the hospital, leading up to the time of the attack, as well as immediately after it. Every angle was being studied, clues were being looked for that would give some understanding of what took place.

By mid afternoon, each of the seven prisoners had been taken for questioning. They were alarmed, in turn, to be confronted with their name and rank. How had the British found that out so quickly? Each had stood their ground. Besides knowing their name and nationality, nothing more was really gained. Officially, they were totally cut off. As expected, neither Nigeria or South Africa admitted to any knowledge of them. They appeared on no watch list or spy list. Nothing on either the MI5 or CIA system showed anything and the Americans were brought on board once the British were running into dead ends with their searches. The only person either intelligence agency had anything on had been the chief who'd been found with a bullet in his head at the hospital. The only one they could have leaned hard on, and the highest ranking officer, had been the one killed at the scene. Had that been planned, or was it just an accident? The CIA had quite a bit on the chief, and he was a well known and highly experienced African military general. He'd trained with teams in Nigeria as well as his native South Africa. Having first been posted to Europe about a decade before, it was widely understood that he was now overseeing the field agents for the secret service. He was not a risk, and therefore only a few notes were made in his file. Most teams based in Europe were there to watch threats that would come back to Africa, militant groups who would send squads to the African populations around Europe, especially to London and Paris. Groups who would recruit, train and send would-be terrorists back to Africa.

Sitting around trays of empty cups, the evening drawing in after a long day at Thames House, the MI5 officers were still keen to talk.

"So, the two big questions that remain are these: firstly, what were this rogue team of agents, presumably working for some African country, doing here, with an interest in killing John Westlake? And secondly, who stopped them, and why?"

There was a consensual nod around the table, yet no one dared to be the first to try to answer the question. Soon they hoped they would know, but they were not yet ready for what that answer might actually mean.

****

It had been one week since the incident at the hospital, and though still fresh in Lorna's mind, for the most part life had got back to normal at the increasingly understaffed hospital. Alison's absence was more noticeable each day, more so for Lorna than for anyone. It was as if the soul had gone out of the job now. There was no one for her to talk to, and the last seven days had been different. Not hard, as such, because it had always been that, but difficult to process, as she had no one to really talk with. So much of her frustrations she was having to choke down, burying them in a place she hoped they could stay indefinitely.

For John's part, he was totally unaware of anything having happened, and he'd been making some real progress, at least with his walking. Having taken his first few steps the other day, he was now able to cross his small room unaided.

His memory recovery programme was another story altogether. Having tried everything they could, it was agreed that for the time being, they would stop. There had been no change. The exercises had failed to make any difference, which was not uncommon, but still was quite a rare occurrence. All that was left were the trigger points, but these were not obvious, and also not possible for John. He'd have to accept the fact that he would not get any of his long term memory back. Instead he got to create his memories again by what he chose to do in life from that moment on. It was obviously a distant second best, but would have to do for now. John still held hope; he might one day discover who he had once been but the odds were growing longer against him by the day. At least he had his improving mobility to lighten the mood. Even Lorna was finding it a welcome distraction.

"So how does it feel like to be a walking man again?" she said when they were just the two of them once again, the physio having left after the latest afternoon session.

"I'd hardly call it walking, not yet anyway." John was smiling, almost laughing with her. There was real comfort, real warmth of friendship. If anything, she'd grown closer to him over the last week, something John too had become aware of, and was happy about.

"You'll be running before no time, you mark my words."

"Running? Me? Do you think I am the type?"

"Well, regardless of what you can't remember, I guess you can become whoever you want to be now, can't you?"

"I guess you are right, Lorna, I guess you're right," he said, before changing his tone a little, becoming more serious, his eyes more intense. "Do you think I will be able to take a walk outside? I mean in the fresh air. I've not been outside in, well, a long time. So much so that I have no memory of the outside world. It's as if I've only ever lived in this room. I really want to get some fresh air at some point soon, Lorna. Do you think you could arrange that?"

She had no idea but didn't want to let on.

"John, if you continue as you are, you'll be out of here in no time! Then you can have all the fresh air you want!"

"You really think so?" he said, as enthusiastic as a child being let loose in a sweet shop.

"Sure, why not? Your wounds are healing nicely. Maybe they'll be completely healed before the end of the month. You are starting to walk more, and strength will only build in your legs from here on. As long as you keep working hard at the sessions you are having now, John, okay?"

"Yes, ma'am," he said, a serious but amused grin appearing on his face, before it turned into a broad smile.

"How do you feel in all this, John?"

"What do you mean?" he said, his smile still there, but the question showing in his eyes.

"I mean, entering the real world with all the awareness of what has happened to you here. The visions, the knowledge of what you need to do."

"Did you have to remind me of all that?" he said, but wasn't angry. Of course she had to remind him, it was all she had left to do, but she didn't want to tell him that.

"As if I could forget," he continued. "Look, I guess in time I will know, right? I mean, at some point, something will tell me it's time. Something will happen, or I will see something, or maybe have another vision. I don't know right now, but I'm sure it will be clear. It could be years before it happens, it's not as if I have to just sit and wait. I might have my whole life to live. So it's not something I have to think too much about now, is it?"

"I don't know," Lorna said, not really sure why she was saying this. "I think, well, you've seen this now, so maybe it's happening sooner than you think?"

"Why do you say that?"

"Just a feeling. I mean, why reveal something to someone if it's years, or even decades away? How are you meant to carry on, knowing what you know?"

"I guess I see your point. So you think it might happen soon?"

"Sooner than you imagine, I bet. It's just a case of always being ready."

"I'm ready, as ready as I'll ever be, I guess." He sounded confident of that fact, and Lorna was certainly going to take his word for it.

"Tell me, if you would." He paused at that, Lorna turning to him, encouraging him on. "When it comes to it, in the moments just before, somehow, if it's possible, can you be there with me?"

Wow, she didn't know what to say. She smiled at him. Words were now forming.

"Of course I will be, John. I'll be right there with you. You only have to call, and I will come running. Don't have any fear about that."

"Thanks, that would mean the world." After he said this, there was a long silence, as each of them went into their own imaginings, churning through their thoughts, processing their feelings. It was not an awkward silence, far from it. They'd perfected the ability to just be silent with one another, knowing the good it was doing them both.

For Lorna, it enabled her think through what she'd just said, to justify it in her own way, if needed. It helped her get through each encounter, to hold her head high at the end of it all, knowing that she wasn't the monster that some of her thoughts were accusing her of being. She was far from a monster, she now reminded herself. She was just doing her job, a job that was vital for all. A job that would save the lives of millions of people.

After nearly five minutes, she got up quickly and continued with some work, making herself useful, but there was not too much that needed to be done. John also came back from his thoughts, picking up his latest book, the pages opening at the exact place he'd finished before. The old paperback showed signs that it had been a well read little book, which made it all the more appealing to John. Soon he was lost once again in the novel and Lorna took some things out of the door and down the corridor. The soldiers were standing on duty outside and another two teams were along the corridor as she got to the kitchen area. Finally she passed what had once been her sleep room and where Alison had been killed a week ago, the thoughts now coming back once again. Lorna had not been back in there since. Though the room had been closed for a few days following the attack, she couldn't bring herself to sleep in there when it had opened again, too saddened by the memories. Sleep itself was once again eluding her. She was now taking more pills than ever, but they were having little effect.

****

It was early afternoon as two figures made their way across a park on the furthest reaches of the city, where the buildings met the countryside. Here life seemed unaffected by all the death that had been happening in other parts of the city. The trees were still looking healthy, the air felt fresh. Around the vast park there were signs of life. Several people were walking dogs, a few children were playing in the playground, their mothers standing around, chatting. It wasn't cold, but the heat of summer had long passed.

On the far side, a long way away from the more public areas of the park, and therefore the listening ears, there were a number of benches. In summertime, these were often taken by old ladies, chatting away about the latest gossip, or artists, who would draw the city that stretched in the distance before them. Today, only one person was there, and the two figures working their way through the shadows quickly joined him, seating themselves beside him and not saying a word for a moment. One of them pulled out a small device from his jacket pocket, and switched it on. It was highly unlikely that anyone was listening in on them, but even if they were, the device they just switched on would make it impossible to hear what was being said, unless they were physically there listening.

In quick unbroken Chinese, they spoke amongst themselves.

"The seven Africans are being held by the British. Word is that they are buying the story and who they are, though they have no idea what they were doing."

"That will be sorted out soon, of course."

"And word on the patient?"

"Seems to be making progress. Should be out within the month. Probably less."

"And everything is in place for the final stage?"

"Yes, we are all in place. The British have no idea."

"Good, let's keep it that way. We need them to keep chasing these Africans. See if you can stir something up on those lines."

"Yes, sir." They started to get up, the meeting finishing as quickly as it had started.

"This has to go smoothly, we can't allow anything to go wrong now and we must get what we came for."

"Of course, sir, you can count on us."

"Good. You know, you are doing your country a great service. This will not be forgotten, comrades, this will certainly not be forgotten."

"Thank you, sir." With that, they were off, returning back the way they had come, splitting up for a time, keeping to the shadows, always out of sight, before meeting up again and getting into a car. The other man remained on the bench for some time, looking out over the city. He would return to the Embassy soon. His exit was imminent. He couldn't stay after word got out. He hoped his country would receive him well. There had been a lot of water under the bridge. But returning home to face the music was soon going to be the only option left to him. He hoped the good he had done would outweigh the rest. It was all he had to go on.

Meanwhile, in Nigeria and South Africa, word had reached them that their team had gone missing whilst on operation in England. It was clear to all that they had been captured, or killed. There was to be no rescue plan, no one would dare claim them. The British had started putting out feelers, looking for anything to connect them to someone, but as planned, their searches would come to nothing. The loss of the team was a real setback but because it was so well hidden it could not be traced back to them. Still, the Africans were on high alert. If their involvement in all this was known, they were sure the ramifications would be extreme.

Left without any operatives in the UK at all now, with three people in Germany, all they could do was to listen in, their bugs still giving them ears on the situation, if nothing else. The three agents in Munich were aware that they were already being watched. There was no way to get them over to the UK, it would be as good as admitting they were part of the same operation. The lack of any extreme action on the British side at least meant they had time. Clearly, no one yet knew how totally involved they were. Since it was likely to stay that way, they would be safe. If the British actually knew of what they'd done, surely there would have been action taken against them by now, or at the very least, some radio chatter about it. Seeing as neither had in fact happened, the control team of the joint Nigerian/South African operation was feeling confident. While their options to influence events in London were now limited, they were confident that they were still in the driving seat and had been directly involved in creating a much weaker Europe.

Chapter 24

At a joint meeting between all parties regarding national security, chaired by MI5 at Thames House, there was still no idea who was ultimately behind the attack on the hospital, which had left five people dead, plus one of the attackers. The seven remaining people, having been interrogated, had been taken by the Americans to a new terrorist holding facility, where it was hoped answers could be gained, in time. There, fewer regulations restrained the use of certain methods to break down an individual, and as it was just information they wanted, not information that was admissible in a court of law, handing them over to the Americans was deemed a necessary evil. Still, some around the table were unhappy, but it was already out of their hands.

As big a mystery as their motive in the attack, was who it had been that had stopped them. Still no one had come forward, the extensive study of surveillance materials had shown nothing, and none of the seven prisoners had given any hint that it was an internal traitor. No weapon was found that had been used to shoot the eight person team, despite an extensive search of the hospital and its grounds. It was a question that needed answering. It only made them more cautious, more aware, that there was far more to it all than met the eye. But it was impossible at that moment to understand more.

At best, the eight person team of various nationalities including British, were hired mercenaries, working at national level for the highest bidder. In their world, national allegiance changed from job to job, always available to those ready to pay for it. It was not unknown for such teams to be paid to hunt a group that they had just been paid to work for. Loyalty was a currency they didn't work in.

But what had gone wrong this time? How had they

got so far, gone unnoticed for so long, only to get turned over at the last minute? And what was with all the documentation, making identification easy? Clearly, that had been the intention, no one would ever go into an operation like that carrying their own ID on them. It just wasn't done. But someone had gone to a lot of effort to frame this team. And why leave them alive at all? They killed one guy and left the others with no fatal wounds. The head shot had been that of an expert marksman, with each leg shot clearly aimed at downing, but not crippling, the victim. Did that mean it was an inside job after all? Was it a level of professional courtesy that had saved the other seven? But surely with the ID left there, it was clear they'd all be taken in for questioning and not released any time soon, if ever. So it was almost a sentence, to have kept them alive. The suffering now would be much worse than a bullet to the head might have been.

It was a frustrating session, as more and more questions were asked around the busy table at Thames House, but few answers were readily available.

After another coffee break, the call was put into the government and the Prime Minister himself was fully updated on the situation, with a recommendation that the national security level be raised to the highest level. All airports and ports were put on alert. Everyone would go through the same checks, each passport being scanned. Teams were put in place to track the comings and goings, each person being given a risk assessment and the highest scores being kept for questioning. It would prove to be an unpopular action, but a media blackout was enforced. News of the extra security would only get out when people arrived back in their own countries. The team were not to know that by that time a new crisis would be under way and their complaints would get drowned out because of what was about to unfold.

****

  Lorna had been trying for most of the previous day to grant John's request about taking a walk outside. She had not had any success and the new day was bringing no change to the situation. It was deemed too high risk on both sides. John might see things that he wasn't ready to see. Outside the hospital, there seemed nowhere to take him that didn't show some sign of all that had happened. Clearly, he'd need to find that out for himself soon, but it was hoped that could wait until the last possible moment. From their side, it was an unnecessary security risk. In his room, in the confines of his small hospital bed, he was, in theory, much safer. There had been that invasion of people, the dramas of the previous week still very much etched on their minds, even if their star patient, John, was none the wiser. However, John was no fool. Unable to work out exactly what was happening, or had so recently taken place just around him, he had picked up a change in Lorna. Just something subtle, almost deep within her soul. There was a change, a sad one, and he was yet to raise the subject.

  So the team had declined Lorna's request for John to be given some time outside, though in principle the idea was a good one. Getting him walking more was certainly the direction they wanted to go, the ultimate destination they needed to reach. One long walk from John, his final walk, would change the world's situation for the better, it was hoped. He remained the last chance, the sum collection of the world's eggs in this one very small basket. And at the moment, this basket was now feeling very vulnerable. Out there, somewhere, had been people determined to kill John. They did not know if there were others out there but they feared the answer was certainly yes. Why they wanted to kill John, the last chance for salvation from this horrific situation, no one could work out.

Having had a night to think things through, and having herself taken some time to walk and think, Lorna came back with a fresh idea that instantly had traction with the team of people when she spoke with them again. Within the hospital building there were two enclosed courtyards, small square areas, that at some point the architects of the hospital must have thought were a really good idea. Now they looked dated and uninviting. The trees themselves were real, two small maples filled each courtyard, with a little pond as well, which was dirty and stagnant. Once there had been fish. Both were identical in size, twelve metres square. It wasn't much, but Lorna felt it could do. Certainly for John, who for as long as he could remember, had been in a small room. The outside courtyard would seem like the great outdoors. And would provide fresh air for the first time in weeks.

The courtyards were at either end of the building. One was therefore too far away, and too public. But the other was not far from his current room, at the quieter and more secure part of the hospital. There were a few rooms visible from the courtyard, but it was a hospital. What would John expect? If anyone saw him, it would not be obvious who John was. No one would bother him, of course, but John didn't need to be told why.

Lorna left the room pleased, feeling she'd won a small victory, while at the same time speeding up the final stages of this project she'd been pulled into. And yet, it was far more than a project; it was a man's life, and his days were getting shorter. If only he knew.

The team agreed to get straight on with preparations for the courtyard. Two members of the team left with Lorna, heading for the courtyard in question, making sure it was secure, and checking for any potential problems. There would be none. They agreed with Lorna, as they were going their separate ways, to let her know when John could come; a window of time to walk around the courtyard. Freedom, of sorts. Lorna thanked them, and sent them on their way. She headed back to John, stopping at a store cupboard to pick up some fresh bandages and bed linen, before entering his room, a smile on her face for the first time in some days.

"You seem happy today," John said, closing his book and returning it to the table next to his bed.

"And you'll be in a minute when I tell you the news."

"Go on," he said, his eyes focused on her in a warm and attentive way.

"You're going to get to go on a little walkabout outside, of sorts."

"Wow, that's great! What did you mean by the 'of sorts' bit?"

Lorna laughed.

"Yeah, well, it's just a courtyard within the hospital for now, but it's fresh air and a bit of nature. As soon as you can handle it, we'll make it happen." She felt that was the best way to say it.

"That's really good to hear. I think I am ready, but I'll wait until you think I am."

"I'm sure you're ready. We just need to do some more walking here. You've only managed about ten steps so far, I don't want to cause you more damage."

"I just want to smell the fresh air. This room kind of gets a bit stale after a while. No offence."

"None taken," she smiled back at him. She knew exactly what he meant. "Well, I promise you, the moment we get the chance, you'll be breathing some fresh air. Maybe the oxygen will work wonders for your legs."

John could tell she was joking and he smiled along with her.

"Maybe it can do wonders for your sense of humour too, Lorna." At this, she laughed out loud.

"Well, on that note," she said, changing the subject,

"I need to clean up your wounds again and give you some fresh sheets."

"I'm all yours."

Thirty minutes later she'd changed all the bandages and covered the bed in fresh sheets. His physical injuries were healing well. She'd had to put in two stitches on one wound the other day, which was now responding, but the rest were healing naturally, which had been unexpected when he'd first come in. Then, he'd been a mess of blood and flesh. Not all of it had been his, they'd later found out, but he had lost a lot of blood, and did have some sizeable wounds of his own.

Weeks later, he was now coming through, getting stronger by the day. With strength returning to his legs and more steps taken, health-wise he was progressing well. And soon he was to venture outside, which marked another important stage in his recovery and ultimate mission. Little did John know of what was resting on his shoulders at that moment but Lorna was playing her part at carrying that load right now. The better he got, the worse she felt. Then, it had been a distant prospect and she'd got involved and kept the illusion going. Now, it was a very certain reality, and those thoughts that had been nagging her for weeks were once again battling for control in her mind. Could she really send a healthy, recovering man, to his death? Could she really play her part in that, a central role, not a side role, as if caught up in something beyond her? As if she had no excuse? Far from it. She was active in playing out her part. And yet, once again, the counter-thoughts came. What choice did she have? Wasn't this all for the greater good, the good of the multitudes? Yes, that was why she was doing this. It wasn't for her, it was for them, the others. The faceless millions. It wasn't *just* for her, she finished. No, this was for something bigger. For life itself, a life she still wanted a part of, at the moment. She hadn't yet thought how that life would be, how it would feel. She would not let herself go there. Firstly, what would life be like without her James, whose death she knew she'd have to come to terms with when this was all over. That wasn't something she wanted to face right now, but it was there, none the less. And how would life feel with the knowledge of what she was willingly doing to John, her loyal and trusting patient? That was as hard a thought to deal with as was the loss of James. How could she go on, living a normal life, with the knowledge of all this? She realised thinking like this was futile and not getting her anywhere. Her steel and resolve would pull her through even though she knew these questions would return.

It was early afternoon when Lorna was told that everything was set to visit the courtyard. It was sooner than she thought, but she passed on the good news straight away to John who was eager to get outside. A wheel chair was brought for him, as there was no way he could make it that far on his own at this stage. Three minutes after leaving his room for the first time, he was being brought through the double doors that led out to the courtyard. Fresh air for the first time in his living memory.

On the way, Lorna had said very little. The hospital had seemed quiet, the corridors empty, though from the courtyard John could now see, on the higher floors, signs that there were other patients in the hospital. What hit John first was the smell. It was somehow familiar, but didn't resonate with anything in particular at that moment. He kept it to himself. Lorna helped him up from the chair and he took his first steps, in the semi outdoors, for the first time since before the incident. He managed to walk slowly over to the maple tree, its dark red leaves still clinging to the branches, though a few had fallen to the ground already. He reached out and touched one and it too came away in his hand. John let it fall slowly to the ground.

He was like a prisoner on day release. The simple things in life, like looking up at the sky, gave him the greatest pleasure. A large expanse of sky was visible, above the three floors of the hospital that rose around him in a perfect square. He was aware that it had been an hour since he had had lunch, which he was sure was given to him around one. And yet the sky looked dark. There was a darkness that didn't seem to fit, even if they had been in the depths of winter, which he was sure was not the case. The tree in front of him, isolated as it was, still had most of its leaves on. Deep inside him, something was starting to resonate but he could not pin down what it was.

Lorna was watching him, wondering what was going through his head. He was being unusually silent, but she realised it was a big moment for him. She'd been outside yesterday, and yet she too, in that moment, having had just one day in the hospital, was herself enjoying the fresh air.

She carefully wheeled the chair over to him and John sat back down.

"Is it alright if I just sit here for a moment?" he said.

"Yes, of course, take as long as you need." She knew they had about a twenty minute window. They'd been barely five. Clearly, he needed to build his strength up a lot more very soon to be able to make the walk he was expected to make.

John sat there in the hospital courtyard saying very little. He was taking deep breaths; each lungful of air seemed to be saying something to him and he was working hard to translate the message. It wasn't as yet coming to him.

Ten minutes passed. Lights went on and off in various rooms around him, each one obvious with the fading light of the courtyard which had no special lighting of its own. From somewhere up above, screams could be heard. John glanced up but couldn't see anything.

"That would be the maternity ward," Lorna said, the answer sounding true enough. In reality, that ward was housed in another building, far from where they were. It was of no real interest to John who returned to touching the tree.

"This pond certainly needs a bit of attention," he said, looking down at the pitiful excuse for a pond in front of them. When she'd first started at the hospital, it had been a nice enough looking body of water, with about a dozen different varieties of fish. Patients would take it in turns to feed the fish, it was deemed useful therapy for many, as indeed it was. Now, it just looked a mess, a sad reflection of the struggling times the hospital was in, which pre-dated even this latest catastrophe.

"Fancy doing some fishing then?"

"I'd be scared at what I might catch," John said.

"Well, I don't want you to catch a cold, so I think five more minutes and that had better be your lot for today, okay John?" She was aware their time would soon be up and didn't really want to cause any problems for anyone.

"Yeah, sure," John replied. "Can we come back here tomorrow? It's nice to be outside."

Lorna didn't know what the answer should be, but said anyway:

"Yeah, of course, John. Maybe you'll be able to walk around the pond next time?"

"Either that, or take a dip in it."

He sat there for another few minutes, breathing in the air, the light continuing to fade a little. He couldn't help but take it all in. When time was up, Lorna started to walk with the chair. Coming back in through the doors, it was as if inside, from his depths, his body screamed an answer to him. He did recognise that smell. The air, the smells around that had hit his nostrils as soon as he'd entered the courtyard. It was from the visions. He knew it was. And that made no sense to him whatsoever. He remained silent on the short journey back to his room, each corridor leading to another, each room looking the same as the last, until finally they were back at his room. The guards who normally sat outside his room, were at that moment out of sight as they had arranged. John was silent as he stood up from the wheelchair. It had been nice to escape for a while, though in that moment, his thoughts racing, there was something strangely comfortable with being back in his bed again. He said nothing as Lorna left the room, taking the chair away, greeting the two guards who had now returned to the corridor outside.

"That was strange," he said aloud to himself, no one else in the room to listen to him. 'That was really strange' he thought again, picking up a book from his bedside table, but for the first time in weeks, unable to read. His mind was too distracted to be able to focus.

Chapter 25

The following week went by quickly in the hospital. Overall, more patients had been arriving each day, death an hourly occurrence, with no let-up in sight. For John, the most important and well hidden patient in the building, it had been a week of great progress. Daily visits to the courtyard had been arranged, and the physiotherapy sessions had been stepped up in both frequency and intensity. Happening twice a day, the first before breakfast, and the second before dinner, John was now able to walk around the courtyard unaided, and was getting stronger by the day. It was thought, though untested, that he probably could walk from his room to the courtyard by now, which was about two hundred metres, maybe more. Certainly it was as far as they'd need him to walk at the RAF base, the Ground Zero of this potential world catastrophe, not far from the heart of London. His time had nearly come.

For John, the days were bringing more questions than anything else. He had not shared anything with Lorna, which was strange, he knew. It just didn't feel right to. Each day, in the outdoor air of the courtyard, enclosed and unnatural as it was, that same sense returned to him each time he came out through the double doors and breathed his first lungful of air; the smell was known to him. He couldn't see how any of this made sense. It didn't. How could a vision, something taking place in his mind, remind him of this smell? Maybe the vision was actually real, and yet he woke up in the hospital bed each time, even after that first one he remembered. It wasn't as if he was going anywhere else. Lorna was right there with him, each time he opened his eyes, she was there, smiling. Always smiling. It was his oldest memory of anyone that he had. Lorna, the smiling girl.

So how could he relate the air around him to those visions? And yet he knew it was the same. He knew this air. And the sky itself. Most of the week he'd come out in the afternoon. Twice he'd asked to come out later. On those occasions, it was naturally dark from being after sunset. He noticed how it looked in the confines of a small courtyard. He took in what light came through various windows, where the brightest part of the sky was. He worked out which direction was west. No stars were visible, but that was not uncommon. It was the afternoon light that gave him the most problems. Not night-time, because he'd now seen that, and yet there was something. Something was there, but he couldn't tell what. In this regards, it was different from what he had seen before. In the visions, there had been this darkness, something beyond the physical, a sense of foreboding and death. But John couldn't get away from the feeling that the smell of the air and the visions were trying to tell him something. What was it that he was picking up, a message from another place? Was this the start of what he had seen? He dared not even ask himself the question, he was afraid of the answer.

    Weeks ago, when the visions had finished, he was ready. He was 'all in' and would do what was needed. Now there had been this gap, this silence, this waiting. Prepared as he had felt then, now he was not so sure. He was no one's hero, that was for sure. He'd been working hard, and still could only barely walk for about ten minutes. Hardly the thing of comic book superheroes. Who was he kidding? He knew he would need to talk this through with Lorna. She was his only friend, and besides the doctor and physiotherapist, who he was now seeing twice a day, the only other person he saw and talked with. It was becoming noticeable, each time they made the three minute walk to and from the courtyard, that not another soul was around. No one. In a hospital so obviously busy, they never passed anyone. For John, who had spent most of the last month reading book after book, his own conspiracy theory was starting to build. Yet he had no idea what to make of any of it.

Lorna too had felt a distance growing between them over the last week and she couldn't put her finger on why. She guessed the healthier John got, the greater the reality grew as to what he might be walking towards. A healthy John meant an available John. That was her best guess at the moment. She too had to come to terms with what his recovery meant. The loss of Alison had really hit home over the past seven days and without anyone to talk to, Lorna too was processing things silently in her own head, increasing the distance between her and John.

Lorna was called into another briefing with the team who were watching over things in the background. They had started making preparations for what needed to follow. She was amazed, and a little disturbed, at how easily they were dealing with things, how matter-of-factly, as if he was just an aninal going to the slaughter house.

"There is one added complication," they said to Lorna, the tone changing completely, as a briefcase was placed on the table. Lorna remained silent.

"The base in question has been unapproachable, as you know. We've not been able to salvage anything, and yet there remains something very important that we need to recover. Something highly classified that is of great value to the country. And it exists only on the base. It will most certainly be destroyed in the ensuing explosion should John forfill his mission, so we need him to be able to recover it before that happens."

"What?" Lorna said, feeling that to ask anything more of John was taking a liberty, considering they were already tricking him into giving his life for them.

"Relax, he won't know anything about it. With this device..." he said, pulling a small black object like a mobile phone from the case on the table, before continuing; "...we can pull the data we need, as he is walking. It will happen automatically. He then just needs to leave it somewhere safe before continuing with...the operation."

"I don't understand?" Lorna said, confused at yet another thing being asked of her.

"When the time comes, you just need to make sure this is on him. There is even a small phone attached to it, so that it passes as a cell phone. We'll give him a wireless headset and you can speak with him as he makes the final walk. That will be a real help to him, I'm sure. We just need to make sure he drops the phone where we need it to be left. By then, it will have collected the data we need from the base."

"What is it that he'll be collecting, exactly?" Lorna said, as if standing on the side of John, making sure nothing else unethical was being asked of him.

"That's a matter of national intelligence, and believe me, not even we know what it is," he said, telling the truth. Lorna understood he was being honest with her, aware that they were all in this together and she was as much in the dark as the rest of them.

"Okay, I'll make sure he has this," she said, taking it from the man, who had locked it back in the briefcase it had arrived in.

"Keep this safe. We don't have another one," he warned.

"Okay, I hear you." In truth, Lorna thought they were being overly dramatic.

"It's state of the art software, you know," another added, not helping the overwhelming pressure she already felt. "We only had access to it a few weeks back, nothing else like it exists. Worth a fortune, no doubt."

"I'll keep it safe for you, don't worry." Lorna picked up the case and held it by her side. It felt no heavier than a small handbag. She imagined the device inside weighed nothing more than an average phone.

"This is all legal, isn't it?" she asked, but instantly

thought it would have been better to have said nothing.

"Of course. And it is as vital as the mission itself."

'Hardly,' she thought, but let it slide. How could some data be more important than the walk of one man, a walk of personal death, that would lead to the salvation of millions? Nothing was making much sense. She went back to her staff room and locked the briefcase away in a safety deposit box, which sat attached to the far wall. Previously, it had housed the strongest and most lethal drugs, locked away from would-be addicts.

She sat down briefly in a chair, taking a moment to just gather her thoughts. 'In for a penny, in for a pound' raced through her mind. "I guess I've come this far, so there's no turning back now," she said out loud, the words actually bringing some relief, as if voicing it took some of the sting away. It felt good. "And I can do this. I will do this. There is life for me at the end of the tunnel!" She was practically shouting now and she stopped herself. John was nowhere near, but it didn't seem wise to get too carried away. "Okay, enough of this and back to it," she said, walking out as she headed towards her patient once again, her John. 'No, he's not mine,' she caught herself, 'he's our John'. And she was smiling at the thought as she walked back into his room, her patient having fallen asleep, a book lying open on his chest.

****

It was the end of October, fifty six days since the incident at the RAF base on the edge of London. A London that had now changed dramatically since then, the four probes, each exploding with nuclear force, doing severe damage and causing much death. The official figures were not really known, the best estimates well below the reality. Hundreds of thousands of people had already died, and as many were terminally affected by the aftermath of the radiation poisoning. And yet even that colossal figure would be nothing compared to the death toll if the main reactors blew at the base, the six nuclear payloads getting more unstable by the day. They'd been overheating for fifty six days, leaking and fragmenting all the time, making the clean up and rescue efforts more hazardous by the hour. They were not far from exploding.

John, now mobile and walking for short periods, was ready. The moment had come. There was no time to lose, and it was vital that John was able to get to the base and shut the system down before it was too late. Getting the next stage right was vital. The country risked losing everything if they were to fail now. Masked from the media, the true nature of what might be about to happen was kept secret, for fear that the news would cause mass hysteria, panic on a global scale. The already struggling transport sectors would be overrun with people fleeing the country. There were not enough vessels to transport everyone, nor enough time. If news got out, the boats and planes would stay away entirely, trapping millions of people; the damage from that alone would be high.

And had news been leaked, they would have had to share their hope of a solution. But that would be a huge risk, the ethical consequences massive. Secrecy was therefore the country's best hope, which was why only a few people knew, and why it had been so alarming when a group of unknown assassins had stormed the hospital to hunt for a man they thought no one else knew existed. If there were others still out there, they didn't know where, or who they were working for. Security had been kept tight. The truth was they knew very little.

Lorna had been fully briefed that morning, that John was to be transported the following day. Hearing that the day had come hit Lorna hard. Sudden panic came over her, but she soon regained composure and focus, the reality and suddenness of the situation still shaking her. Having prepared for this moment, for what seemed like a lifetime, it was hard to comprehend that it was now here. Tomorrow, John was going to take a walk that would end it all, in a way. Of course, the radiation poisoning that had been affecting so many would still be a problem. People would still be dying, generations falling ill for decades to come. But the new cases would stop. The site would soon be able to be cleared and cleaned. The leaks could be plugged. And that, millions so far unaffected, meant everything. It meant everything for her too. Life, currently caught up in some bubble, as if frozen in time, could finally continue. Life could go on. A new day could start, a new season. And for the first time in weeks, as fresh and strange a thought as it was, it brought hope to her heart at that moment, for the first real time in weeks. She felt purpose, closure. It was the news that life was not all going to be as it currently was. That change was coming. Still, there were twenty four crucial hours to go, and she had to work out exactly how she was going to talk this through with John. How to communicate the news, how to explain things to him in a way that would make any sense. It was a moment she had turned over in her mind for a while but now the time had come, how could she do it?

    She thought this through as she made her way to his room. It was strange to think that, after tomorrow, she wouldn't be doing it again. She wouldn't be walking in to see John, in his room that was as much a prison as anything else. Strange to think that she wouldn't see John again, that from tomorrow this unlikely, but important figure, wouldn't play a part in her own life any more. That thought was now knocking with real emotion on the doors of her heart, as if trying to get in. Those had been kept shut long ago, with the loss of James. That thought too came back, that soon she'd have to open that up and deal with what was behind it. It was all coming home, how things were changing, would change, over the next few days.

Walking into John's room, she put on her best smile and, taking a deep breath, simply came out with a heartfelt:

"Guess what, John. You're ready to leave!"

John looked up from his book straight away, to check she wasn't joking, and when it was clear she wasn't, replied:

"Well, that's great news! Really? Wow, yes, certainly. I'm ready when you are!" Leaving the confines of a hospital room he knew well for a world he remembered nothing about was a concern, but he had spent too long there already.

"We'll have to do some final checks, just to make sure, completing the various bits of paper, but come this time tomorrow, you are a free man," she said, the 'free man' part only realising how bad it sounded once she'd actually voiced it. How could she call him that, when nothing about him was free? He belonged to them, to everyone. He was the one hope they were now counting on. The end of their nightmare. Anything but free.

"That does sound good to me!" he said.

Lorna turned away, so as not to show the emotion on her face at that moment, instead making it look as if she needed to work on something by the door, her hands refolding sheets that didn't need folding. She made herself busy for two minutes, just allowing her thoughts, her inner turmoil, to settle down, before finally turning back to John, who had just been lying there, watching her. She let that pass.

"So, how do you feel?" she said, finally.

"You mean, health wise?" he said, to which she nodded. It didn't really matter what she meant, as long as he was talking and they could move on the conversation.

"I feel good. My legs are feeling stronger, the muscles building again. The damage doesn't seem permanent, and the physiotherapist seems very happy with everything. I'm sleeping well, and more than ready to leave."

"Good," was all she could come up with. However, nothing felt good at that moment. She felt sick inside. Over the last week or so, they'd been drifting apart a little, as if subconsciously protecting themselves from each other. She didn't know what to make of it, nor why she'd felt like that. Lorna guessed the reality of what she was doing to him meant that she didn't want to be too emotionally attached. It wasn't sensible, and could risk everything. Things had now become too crucial to risk messing it all up.

"You'll be having one final session with the physiotherapist today, and the doctor would also like to see you."

"And will you be here with me today?" he said.

"Of course, John. Right with you, holding your hand if you need me to. Right here, as always."

"I'd love you to hold my hand," he joked, reaching over and grabbing her hand. She pulled away out of reflex, a silly reaction, before smiling at him, as if she was joking with him. He bought it and laughed back.

"Good, then today is going to be a great day. And tomorrow, I can't wait!"

"No, neither can I," she said, the words raw and real, ice cold inside, their real meaning shielded from John. 'If only he really knew,' she thought, the words burning into her now.

After lunch that same day the physio had been and he'd left wishing John all the best, like old friends going their separate ways. The same was true for the doctor, who was concluding his visit to John.

"You've recovered really well," he said, genuinely happy with John's condition.

"That's great. And my memory?"

"Like I've said before, John, it might never come

back."

"You've said that before, really?" John said, hiding the joke from his face, which was looking serious and concerned.

"Yes, John, I have. Are you saying you can't remember me telling you this?"

"Who are you again?"

There was silence for a time. Even Lorna came over now, a hand going over her mouth as an 'Oh my goodness' came through her lips. John couldn't hold his expression any longer and a deep belly laugh came pouring out of his mouth, as he watched their faces change, the humour currently lost on both of them.

"You had me there, John, for a moment," the doctor said, turning to Lorna, each catching the others facial expression for a moment. John spotted something there, something too serious for the situation, something not fitting with the joke he'd just made.

"You should have seen the look on your faces," John said, still laughing, pushing that last thought from his mind. "Priceless!"

"Well, really, John," Lorna said, only now breaking into a smile. Her heart had felt like it had stopped for a brief moment. Panic had threatened to creep in at the thought that his memory had gone, with all the knowledge of the visions, the program, everything he needed to do. All gone, all forgotten. Everything wasted. Hope gone. It was a terrifying moment of hopelessness, and it put things into perspective, just how much she really wanted this all to work out. She'd do anything for the plan to succeed.

"John, anyway...," the doctor said, starting to put things back into his bag. "It's been great working with you, and I wish you every success tomorrow...when you leave, every success for the future, what ever that might hold for you."

"Thanks, doc. You've been a great help. If I ever

hit those triggers you talk about, and my memory comes back, I'll let you know."

The doctor was smiling at this. He knew there was little chance of anything happening.

"You do that, John. You do that!"

And with that, the doctor patted John on the shoulder and left the room, determined not to look around, not to take one last look at the man that his hopes were pinned on.

Now it was once again just the two of them, as it had been so often over the last fifty six days. In the first two weeks, when John was fresh into the visions, and his wounds were at their worst, his waking hours had been very few. As the weeks had progressed, and especially once he'd come through the program, they'd spent much more time talking things through. He'd become an avid reader and had read a small mountain of novels at great speed as there was little else to do other than sleep. The books had taken him to new places, far away places, magical places, and some very strange places. They'd shown him love, death, sacrifice and sometimes betrayal, all feelings he, with his lack of memories, knew little about, though the visions had talked of his sacrifice. Love, too, was something he was now starting to feel. A love for the woman so much part of his present life, the only woman who filled his memories. And he wondered, deep down, what she felt about him, though he knew her own loss was still too real for her to even think about someone else. The age difference was something else as well. It was at best a one way fantasy, his dreamy nurse, cleaning his wounds, giving him bed baths, nursing him back to health. He was savouring every minute, aware that the final day was upon them both. He was not sure if he would even see her again, doubting if this would even be possible.

"What will you do after I'm gone?" John said, the innocent question initially catching her off guard.

"What do you mean? Who said you were dying?"

"No, I mean, tomorrow when I've left. What will you do then?"

"I think I'll take a long holiday."

"Yes, sounds about right. After working with me, you deserve it!"

"Indeed, I do. After all you've put me through!" The old Lorna was coming back now, she was smiling again.

"After all I've put *you* through," John said, with his own smile now too.

"Oh, it's like that, is it? You think I've been harsh on you?"

"It's been no gentle breeze, I can assure you!" John said.

"Okay, we'll call it even."

"Agreed. Look, I don't want to be forward," John started, his change in tone giving a hint at what was coming. "But seeing all we've been through together, the connection we've made, do you think, at some point, I could have your number and some day, when you've had your holiday, I could take you out to dinner as my way of saying thank you?"

"I think that could be arranged, John, yes."

"Good, I'd really like that. And maybe, in time, we could see a bit more of each other?"

"John..." she could see the look in his eyes. Those puppy dog eyes. "I really don't think that would be possible, you know."

"I get you. I just thought, seeing as you've seen me naked, it would only be fair if you returned the favour." John was smiling at her.

"I beg your pardon?" Lorna said, a cross between shock and intrigue appearing on her face.

"You've given me countless bed baths. Don't say you haven't had a peek when I've not been looking."

"I've done nothing of the sort," she said.

He put a hand on her hip, which she allowed him to do for a moment. No man had held her like that in a while. It felt good, her mind going back to days with her James. The intimacy they'd shared. But John was not that man to her, nor could he ever be that man, as much as he wanted to be. She touched his hand gently, but pulled it from her hip and gently placed it back on the bed.

"I'm sorry," he said, not knowing if he'd over stepped the mark with that.

"It's okay, John. It really is. Perfectly natural. However, I think I'd better go and get your dinner now. Big day tomorrow, you need to keep up your strength."

How little he currently knew. The next twenty four hours were to change everything.

Three Weeks Ago

MI5 had first been alerted to the fact that a trade was on the cards when a coded message was received through various diplomatic sources. Its content was checked, the call verified. Whoever it was, was being very careful to cover their tracks. But it was clear that the British wanted the trade. What was being offered to them was a piece of state of the art technology and they just needed to be the highest bidder. A drop off was arranged for the money, a tracker placed within the bag. They thought it was undetectable and would give them an understanding of who was behind it all, as well as safe guard their money, should something go wrong.

Three agents made the drop off. The bag was left in a very public place, people walking around, making surveillance very difficult. It also made following any potential targets almost impossible. Surprisingly out-foxed on this occasion, the bag of money, a cool million pounds, had already been picked up just after three in the afternoon.

The tracking device was discovered and removed. The contents of the bag were checked, happy that they'd got their money, they confirmed that the final drop off could take place.

Once more, MI5 received this confirmation through the same diplomatic routes, though a different path had been taken the second time. Whoever was behind it all was highly capable.

On the dot of four, a courier arrived at Thames House, from a London based courier firm. He had a small cardboard box with him, which did not give anything away as to its contents. It was handed over to the waiting team on the front reception desk, the courier himself taken to one side for questioning. His details were checked and put into the computer, much to his own annoyance. He was just an innocent delivery man, doing another job on a normal, fairly busy, working day; he knew nothing of where it had come from. The courier firm confirmed that the package had been dropped off the day before, hours before the first call had even been put into MI5; they were very clever. They knew the British would buy the hardware. By dropping it off before the call, it would be impossible to trace who'd made the order. Even that, of course, had been done by an unconnected person, just another piece in the puzzle.

The package was quickly taken through security at Thames House, screened for any unwanted devices. Nothing was found, and it was finally unwrapped on the main conference table, which was currently a scene of harsh words and short tempers. The ongoing national crisis was still in full flight. Sitting with them at that moment were two tech guys, brought in that day to give the latest purchase a once over, confirming what it was, and what it could do.

Taking out the small mobile phone looking device, the tech guys got to work on it straight away, as those around the table fell silent.

"It's genuine," came a startled statement from one of the two tech guys.

"I've never seen anything like it before in my life," said the other, having set up the simple test, the device performing as it should.

There was a collective sigh around the room, as everyone felt they could finally breathe again.

They'd just secured a highly advanced piece of technology that would come in very useful soon. It was an exciting breakthrough for them all.

Chapter 26

Present Day

It was now late in the evening of that final day in the hospital and Lorna was preparing John for his last night's sleep in his bed. A bed that had been his home for longer than he could remember. His usual cocktail of drugs were being prepared, together with a special drug. One that would put him into the kind of deep sleep state that he had been in at the beginning. He was again to have a vision, a very real and very different one this time. He needed to believe that it was now all happening. The television had been prepared, video feeds stitched together to make the early morning news look like real time events reporting on what was happening, and ready for when John awoke in the morning. It wasn't totally tidy, and was of course untested. But that was true for everything they'd done so far, and as far as they could tell, it was still all working.

She carefully injected John in his right arm, before bending down and kissing him on the forehead.

"Sleep well," she said, the words already fading, the dream-like nature of her goodnight kiss making him wonder if it actually happened. The drugs were taking their effect fast. Five minutes later, her patient soundly asleep, the cord was reattached into the back of his head, as it had been for all the visions so far, ready for later in the night, the early morning in fact, those waking hours when he would once again receive a vision. But this one would be like no other that he'd had before.

Lorna watched him for some time, actually stroking his arm for a while. She stood there in the silence, apart from the monitors that made their constant sounds which told her that everything was okay.

"John, I'm sorry for all this," she said out loud, breaking the silence in what was to be her own private goodbye. "I'm sorry for what you've been put through, all that has happened. I'm sorry about what will happen tomorrow. I'm sorry for the lies, I really am. And especially for my part in that. I hope you are able to forgive me, if you ever were to find out. I'm not such a bad person, though I'm not the angel you seem to think I am either. I just want to live."

With that, tears were running down her face. Great sobs pouring forth, crying like she hadn't done since the loss of James. Crying over the imminent loss of another man close to her heart. It wasn't love she felt, not love in the same way as she had with James anyway, but a different type of love. A connection, that was for sure. She felt connected with John in a very deep way, and knew that this connection would stay with her all her life, however long that would be. John only had one day, assuming everything went to plan. Normally, faced with death all the time in her job, it was hope they shared with patients. Hope of recovery, hope of better times. Rarely was the time of death known with any certainty. Of course, she'd dealt with many terminal patients in her time. But death, for them, came as a thief in the night. Not a surprise, but still sudden when it finally happened. John was quite the opposite. He was now the healthiest he'd been in the fifty six days since arriving, and yet tomorrow was to be that day. She left him at that moment, looking at him once more, deep peace upon his face, sleeping like a baby.

The vision came at around six in the morning and would last just seconds in real time, but seemed like much longer.

"Wake up!" came the call, as John suddenly opened his eyes, in that same large building he remembered too well.

"It's time!" came the second command; the voice sounded around him but it was unclear where it was coming from. Felix was nowhere in sight, nor was it his voice. This was something different.

"It's happening. Today! You have seen it already. You have been warned. You know what you need to do. Today is the day of salvation. Today is the day of your sacrifice. You have seen this, John, and you know what to do. Get ready. The world needs you. The world needs what you know. It's started, John. Watch the news. It's happening now. Now wake up, and do what you need to do. Wake up, John. It's time!"

The room went black, and that once forgotten feeling of falling returned with a force greater than he knew, as the room vanished and the sensation of plummeting returned again. He opened his eyes with a start. Lorna was not in sight but, hearing his call, she came running into the room. She'd been waiting in the corridor outside, unable to sleep. She had been crying for most of the night, though she tried not to show it at that moment.

"Turn on the TV!" he shouted. "It's happening today! I've had another vision!" There was a new urgency in his voice. She'd not seen it before.

She switched on what appeared to be live news feeds reporting on destruction and fire.

"Oh my God!" he said. "This is what I saw! It's really happening!"

His heart rate was racing, great drops of sweat were running across his forehead. Lorna came over and helped calm him, carefully disconnecting the cord that was attached to his head, freeing him from the last wires that kept him trapped. She knew that the effects of the drugs would wear off soon and his body would once again be his own. He calmed noticeably then images of a burning building filled the screen once again.

"I thought I had to stop this!" he said.

"Maybe you still can?"

"I need to get up."

He pulled himself around carefully, Lorna helping

him to get to a sitting position. He paused there for a while, so that he wouldn't get dizzy.

"I'm really scared, John," Lorna said, as John sat on the edge of the bed next to her.

"It's okay, it's all going to work out." John had no way of really knowing that, but he wanted to say something to Lorna. He could see there was something in her eyes. Fear maybe, but not shock. He was pondering that for a moment when she helped him stand, so that they were face to face. She kissed him gently on the lips, before pulling away. His body came alive, her kiss like touching the mains power supply. She kissed him again, passionately, pulling his head in to hers, holding it there for a few seconds. He was short of air but didn't care at that moment. It seemed like an eternity, like time was standing still, before she once again pulled away.

"I'm just so proud of you. I'm scared but full of hope all at the same time. All because of you."

"Wow," he said. "I'll do this for you, Lorna. I'll do this to save you. Do you hear me?"

"I do, John. And I know." With that, she kissed him again, much more gently this time, and less intensely, much to John's disappointment.

Ten minutes later John was ready, Lorna helping him put on his shoes, the first time he'd worn anything that heavy in as long as he could remember. The clothes themselves felt strange. Spending nearly two months in a hospital gown had been an experience itself.

The news from the television, constantly playing in the background, was reporting the doom and gloom. A helicopter was seen going down, though the footage had only been from the outside. They'd been careful, when putting the selection together, not to use anything that had been included in the visions. To have done so, they deemed, would have been foolish.

At five minutes past seven, John was ready to leave

the room. A room that he would never return to. All that faced him was lying heavy on his heart at that moment, but he was happy to have Lorna by his side. Their kiss would be the memory he'd take with him, when all others had been forgotten. He felt confused, he felt he was dreaming. But he was also prepared to play out the dream, as if life itself didn't matter any more. As if his life was already over. He was on his way to the winner's enclosure. On his way to receive his reward. And he was now starting that journey, with Lorna by his side.

"Here, take this," Lorna said, placing what looked like a mobile phone in his hands. There was a set of headphones already connected to the device, which hung down as she passed them to John. "This way, we can speak. You can talk with me all the way, even when we've parted company. I'll be with you."

"Thanks," was all he could think to say, taking the device, giving it a quick look over, before placing it in his coat pocket. The ear piece already in his right ear. Thoughts now racing full speed through his tired mind, questions he could not answer.

Three Weeks Ago

The bag containing the million pounds was carried in slowly, its bug and tracking device already stripped out some miles away. It was eventually placed on a small plastic table that had been pushed against a side wall. None of the furniture in the room matched; it was just a safe house, something put together very quickly. All countries had their own, countless thousands of homes and buildings around the world acting as havens in the midst of some of the biggest cities in the world.

Inside this particular one, along with the bag of money and the middle aged Southern European man who had brought it in, stood three other figures. High ranking security personnel and, as far as the British were concerned, unknown players in this unusual game.

"Has everything gone to plan?" one man said to another, in fluent Mandarin.

"Yes, entirely. They took the bait, thinking they had scored a real intelligence coup. The device has already been tested at Thames House."

"Very good. Let's keep a close watch on things."

"And what about these Africans?"

"They become the enemy, to the British. They do not know what is really going on, nor the danger this would do to the world if the situation here gets out of hand. They cannot be allowed to get to this John Westlake."

"But they are getting closer. We think they will attack the hospital. We've been tracking eight of their special forces."

The most senior Chinese official turned to a man who had been silent up to now, a man more used to the shadows. Their most experienced, and talented secret weapon. The offical said to him:

"I want you to tag these people, and if they make a move on this patient, you are to stop them. Do what you do best. Do not risk your own identity. I'd suggest getting them when they are already in the hospital. Leave most of them alive. We've forged some paperwork that will give their identity away. It will make the British focus on them, question them, torture them, no doubt. Kill the general. I've never liked him anyway. Now go."

The *Shadow Man* didn't say a word, taking in everything he was commanded to do, saluting, and then turning; he was gone. Vanishing into the shadows of that room, and away from sight.

"So now we wait. The British are certainly going to try their scheme, and sooner rather than later. Radioactive readouts from the crash site have been rising steadily for the last two weeks. News cannot be kept quiet forever."

"We have everything in place, sir. Everyone, and everything, is working as it needs to work. We'll be gone before they know what's hit them. They'll just be glad this situation has gone away."

"They'd better get it under control. Otherwise we risk losing what we came for, and if we are still in the country, should it all explode, we'd never get away. We'd go down with the whole thieving nation." He spat on the ground, as if even the words passing through his mouth brought a bad taste. "That cannot be allowed to happen."

"It will not be allowed, sir. You have my word."

"Good."

They broke from speaking between themselves, the language unintelligible to the middle aged delivery guy anyway, and said to him in perfect English.

"Thank you for your part in all this. Please, be our guest and take the bag with you for payment. The money is used notes, non consecutive serial numbers, as we'd requested. You've performed a good service for us. See that nothing ever gets said, otherwise that man you just saw leave will find you. If that happens, everyone you've ever loved will be shot in front of you. Do you understand me?"

"Perfectly," he said, unsure of whether he'd actually walk out the room alive himself. But he picked up the bag anyway, and made his way regardless, only checking over his shoulder as he left the main doors. No one was following. But he would certainly listen to their warning. With a million pounds, he would move far away from there, as soon as possible, and start a new life.

Present Day

It was approaching ten in the morning. John had been transported, at speed, through the streets, for what seemed like ages. The windows were blacked out, his identity kept secret. If anyone was out there watching him,

John was unaware of it. Lorna was holding his hand all the way.

In Berlin, as well as the capitals of Nigeria and South Africa, the African secret service were listening in, the only possible action left to them. Their bugs and devices, planted generously around the London, were still bringing in some information. They too were aware John was now on the move. Nothing had yet been said that would cause them to fear. The longer that continued, the better. British forces were not moving anywhere, their focus entirely on the UK, helping the recovery effort. As long as it stayed that way, the Africans would melt away into the background, making as quiet an exit as possible. The seven operatives held in an American terrorist camp were lost to them. If they could get to them now, they would, but only be to put a bullet in each head. Partly to end the misery, but mainly to stop the risk of one of them saying anything. Maybe one person would cut a deal, dropping everyone in it to save themselves. They could only imagine the Americans' tactics, playing each one off against the others, seeing who would be the first to take the bait. The longer they had them, the greater the risk.

The Chinese too were watching, far closer than the Africans, and much closer than the British who were still totally unaware of Chinese involvement.

MI5 were also watching the situation, of course. Brought up to speed only after the program had first been tested, they saw the potential straight away. There was a lot riding on the success of this mission and they would not allow anything to go wrong now. They watched the convoy working its way south. Half an hour ago they had crossed the lines that kept people out and were still one mile from the crash site.

"How do you feel?" Lorna asked John, breaking the silence, as the vehicle now slowed and worked its way around something.

"Like I'm in a dream, I guess." John had become noticeably more serious the longer the journey had been going.

"I know you can do this, John."

"Thanks," but there was nothing more he could respond. So he changed the subject.

"It's been a crazy few weeks," he said.

"It sure has."

"How long was it that I was in hospital, exactly?"

"Today was day fifty seven," Lorna said, turning to him, her hand on his left knee.

There was still so much John didn't understand. Why was he there in the first place? Who had he once been? His whole memory, short as it was, consisted of his time with Lorna, in that small hospital room, with the addition of those courtyard walks over the last couple of weeks. His mind drifted to that courtyard and the doubts that had arisen. Those questions, that confusion. He remembered the smell and the darkness, even though it was during the afternoon. He thought about that morning's television, the vision in his sleep, Lorna's constant care for him, and this high speed convoy, windows blacked out, through the streets of the city. The most telling thing had been Lorna's reaction that morning, or more to the point, lack of reaction. No one accepted something that disastrous that quickly. But she'd accepted it all as easily as she'd accepted the visions in the first place. It was what had drawn him so close to her right from the beginning. She had believed him. And yet, now, his mind was processing all this and coming up with some random thoughts. He fought those thoughts in that moment, so as to remain, mentally at least, in the car with Lorna. He still had more he wanted to say.

"I still have no memory of who I once was, but can I tell you, even though all I now remember is you, I wouldn't change that for the world, Lorna." He paused for a moment.

"So this is it..." he said, not sure how to continue. "This is the moment of truth. Do you think it will be exactly as I saw it?"

"They've proved true for you so far, John. You really were that Prophet the visions spoke about. I'm sure it will be exactly what you saw. Why wouldn't it?"

That made sense, while at the same moment making no sense at all.

"This is rather surreal, isn't it?" he said.

"What do you mean?" But she was starting to understand exactly what he meant already.

"I mean, you and me, in a car, going somewhere that weeks ago seemed to appear to me in a vision. If the visions are to be believed, the lives of millions of people are in danger, I mean, must already be in danger at this very moment. And I need to save them. Somehow, in me, for some reason, rests the ability to make a difference. It's more than just the knowledge of what is going to happen, there must be some divine force at work, or something?"

"Yeah, I guess," she said, not very convincingly. "But that's what makes me so proud of you, John. That, without even all the answers, you are willing to put yourself in that place, to make yourself available to rescue all those people. To save us." She couldn't bring herself to use the word sacrifice, or anything linked to death. It felt too raw to her at that moment, and she didn't know how she'd handle it.

"But I'm about to die," he said, as sudden and sombre as that.

"Yes, you are, John," Lorna said, a tear in her eyes, but her voice was steady, it still had energy. She was surprising herself.

"Have you thought about what happens after death?" John said.

"No, I don't think I have really."

"And yet, you must have been around it for so long, working as a nurse as you are? Doesn't that seem strange to you?"

"Not really. My work is dealing with the living. What happens after death is not really my domain."

"I guess not. I guess for me, I really have to think about it. It's not something I can put off, is it? Getting to terms with what is about to happen, for me, is a big part of getting through it all."

"I wonder if there is nothing."

"How could there be nothing?" he said, wanting to dig a bit, for the first time obviously coming at something from the opposite side to Lorna.

"I mean, most people don't believe in anything after death, so I'm just saying."

"Do they really, though, or is that just the easy answer? What do you believe, Lorna?"

"I don't believe there is anything, John," she said, all too automatic. She was being less guarded now in her responses, as if the further they got from the hospital, and nearer to the conclusion, the less it mattered. That time was too short, too pressing, to waste it picking her words carefully. And yet she'd walked right into John's trap.

"How can you say that, Lorna, when you've been with me through these visions? These premonitions. How could you still say there is nothing more than the physical?"

"Those are different," she said, again without thinking, speaking off the cuff, and instantly realising what she'd said. A silence fell in the car at that moment. It was an awkward silence, one that Lorna desperately wanted ended with every fibre in her being. But she didn't have anything clever to say. She feared John was piecing it all together, was processing things in his mind now. What was he thinking? What conclusion was he coming to? The silence dragged on for a few minutes, and it wasn't as if they could spend that time looking out of the window since the windows were blacked out on both sides.

John was continuing to puzzle over it all. Everything in him was telling him something wasn't adding up. Some deep sense, an unknown, or forgotten, ability maybe. Stitching the pieces together; the odd phrase here, an expression there. The surroundings, the sounds, the smells. It was all starting to paint a slightly different picture from the one he had been led to believe, but he couldn't put his finger on exactly what it was, or what was happening. It was as if his subconscious thoughts were pressing through in order to become conscious. Thoughts that could then affect his actions.

Finally John turned to Lorna and, moving close to her, whispered quietly in her ear:

"Is this a game?"

She turned to him suddenly, slight shock on her face, but she was able to control her response quite well.

"What?"

"Is this some kind of game, some kind of reality show?" he said, still whispering in her ear.

"I don't know what you mean, John. This is really happening, this is now, and this is urgent."

It was all beginning to sound staged, scripted even. He'd have gone on questioning, had it not been for the car stopping at that precise moment, and the instruction being given that they were now there. They were as far as they could go in that vehicle, and a change was needed. A side door of the vehicle was opened and light poured in, but it was from flood lights, not sunlight.

What stood before them was like no scene either of them had ever seen before. Lorna felt physically sick. This was the closest she'd been to where James had been killed, and until that moment, she'd had no idea it would have such an effect on her. Fear engulfed her for a moment, and she instinctively gripped John's hand even harder. He felt the squeeze, which was actually beginning to hurt, and he understood this was no game. He could see the fear in her eyes.

Still two miles from the crash site, there was already a vast field of debris lying before them. Buildings stood destroyed, cars burnt out. If this had happened that morning, a lot had changed since then.

Just at that moment orders were given from somewhere behind.

"From here on, Mr Westlake, you need to go in this special armoured vehicle. It will take you most of the way, and it will keep you and your driver safe from the radiation. Ms Brookes, you need to stay with us."

Lorna turned to acknowledge the instruction.

"Ms Brookes, is it? I've not heard you being called that," John said.

"That's because I'll always be Lorna to you, John. Or 'that nurse who wouldn't leave me alone'. But I think Lorna is shorter."

They both smiled. It was Lorna who spoke next.

"Can I travel with John?" she asked, turning to the man who had given the instructions just a moment before. He looked at them both, before granting permission.

"Be my guest. Only John is to get out of the vehicle, mind you. Here, put this on."

He passed her a hideous looking chemical suit. It was yellow and had a hood that wouldn't have been out of place on a deep sea dive.

They both got into the second vehicle, much more military in design, making the moment even more sinister. But now, here she was, returning to the place where her husband had died. Returning with another man, a man that loved her, and in her own different way, she too loved. He was here to make the site safe. Finally. The last two months had been the most stressful of her life. Nothing could compare.

They were joined in the back of the vehicle by

another soldier, who wasn't wearing a suit, so they presumed, correctly, wouldn't be joining them for the journey. Instead, he handed Lorna a small telephone, which he attached to the outside of her suit, the hood already having its own built in speakers and microphone.

"Now you can speak to each other through the phone," he said, before turning to John and saying:

"It's vital, that once you've walked around the south side of the building, you leave this device on the ground before you continue. This device cannot go in with you. Do you understand?"

John nodded, not bothering to give a civalised response to what he felt was a daft request. He was about to give his life and they were concerned about a mobile phone. Although he was sitting next to her, he called Lorna with the phone, as the vehicle pulled away slowly, and her voice came through clearly over the noise of the engine.

"So this is it, I guess? Thanks for coming with me," he said.

"It's important for me to be here, with you...." She said, pausing, as if not knowing what to say next but wanting to continue. "It's the first time...I mean..." but she didn't know what to say.

"This is where James died, isn't it!" John said suddenly, the pieces finally starting to slot into place.

Even through the yellow hood, he could see her facial expression, near panic appearing for a while, then a tear. She wasn't going to lie any more.

"Yes, it is," she said simply; no other words seemed to fit any better.

John did the maths in his head very quickly. Her James had been dead before he'd first spoken with her. That had been one of the first things he'd picked up from her. That sadness behind her happy, outward demeanour. But if he had died here then, and this was her first time back, there was no way that this had all happened like they said it had overnight. The damage alone, what he'd seen when they changed cars, had been there for a long time. The burnt out buildings and cars had long been extinguished. This was some game.

"This hasn't just happened, has it?" John said.

Lorna sank deflated in her seat, as if all hope had been knocked out of her in that moment, like a boxer taking two heavy blows to the head, one after the other.

"I don't know what to say," she said. She felt exposed and very vulnerable, alone for the first time in the process, with no cameras watching her. She was unaware that MI5 were listening in on the conversation, although they were unable to actually communicate with her, just listen. They too were shocked at what John had just said. Were things about to fall apart at the last minute?

"Well, why don't you start with the truth. Tell me what is really going on."

Without a second thought, Lorna launched into the whole thing. In the five minutes it took the vehicle to navigate its way slowly through the debris that made movement difficult, she told him the whole truth. She left nothing out, explaining how she'd been fetched with James, the last time she'd seen him, all that then happened. Alison and the other patients. The first time she saw John. Everything. He was most fascinated to hear about why he had stood out, why he'd been picked. Why he'd been found alive. He asked what he'd been doing on the site, but she didn't know, which was the truth. No one knew. He was just a lucky survivor. She explained what she knew about the chemical make up, the protection in his body that had soaked up and destroyed the radiation poisoning, that was killing so many. That this would keep him safe now. She explained about the danger from the power plant. That if it exploded, everyone would die. She'd die. She assured him that if it was shut down, the problem would end, it would go away. The country would survive, would continue, would recover. She told him how he would also die anyway, if nothing was done. If it wasn't from the radiation poisoning, it would be from what followed. All life in the UK would be dead. Most of Europe would be affected. There would be no food, no clean water. No power or transport. He'd be stuck here, with no way of getting away, and no one coming to rescue him. The fallout would be too dangerous. Weather patterns would change. If starvation or thirst hadn't killed him, the colder weather would. A freezing cold country as nuclear winter set in. That today wasn't about him making the choice between life or death, but between dying with the millions, or dying to save the millions. It was a genius line of reasoning and the listening ears at Thames House could not have scripted it better if they had tried.

John was blown away by it all. At some level, especially since the courtyard experience, it all was starting to fit together now. It made more sense. And the element about being a sacrifice, even if packaged in a lie, was still true. He could still be the hero, if he chose. Dying alone from hunger or thirst, or even the cold, didn't sound at all appealing, compared to an instant death once the safety shut off at the troubled base was activated.

When Lorna had finished, there was an eerie silence. The vehicle had long reached its spot. It now just sat there like a metal dragon, deciding its own fate. Those listening at MI5 headquarters, as well as those in Berlin, Africa and Beijing, were all speechless, waiting in a state of anxiety for what would come next.

"Thanks for being honest with me, Lorna. That is your name, isn't it?"

"Of course it is! Lorna Brookes. My husband James was killed just as I said. Everything I've told you about myself is true. I don't want to lie to you any more, John. I'm sorry for doing this to you. I just needed hope."

"Hope? It was all a lie though?"

"It is genuine hope for me. For us all. It's real."

"Why didn't you just tell me?"

"I don't know, that wasn't my decision. I was pulled in once you'd already been entered into the program. You were already in the hospital before I heard about you. Would it have made a difference?"

John thought about that for a moment. Truth was, he had no way of knowing. He'd felt a hero before, on some noble quest. Special. Now it was all a mask, a facade, and he didn't like what he was seeing behind it all. Lorna, of all people, had been central to this episode, this betrayal. Yes, he felt betrayed, and he wasn't afraid to admit that. But what good would that do?

"It was just wrong," he said.

"I know. And I'm sorry, John. I really am. But the clock is ticking. There really is a crisis and it's a few hundred metres away, around that building. If this thing isn't stopped immediately, we all die."

"So we all die!" he said, a little too rashly. He regretted it immediately, but didn't let it show. This wasn't how he wanted to play it.

Lorna started to cry, her resolve giving way. For too long she'd hidden behind this hope that John would end it all, that she'd get to live through it. That there was light at the end of the tunnel. Now, in this moment, she was having to quickly come to terms with her own death.

"You're right, John. I don't deserve to live. I'll take this suit off right now, if you want. I'll step out of this vehicle with you and go as far as I can." She made as if she was about to take off the hood, getting the response from John she had hoped she would.

"No, stop! Don't do that. You don't need to do that."

She paused.

"It's up to you. Do I get to live or die today. If you don't make this walk, I might as well take this suit off. I'm as good as dead. Why wait any longer?"

"Okay, you've made your point," he said, pausing briefly. "I loved you, you know."

"I know, John. And I'm sorry."

"Sorry? Why do you say that?"

"Because you loved someone without knowing what I was doing to you. Without knowing who I really was."

"Isn't that just it. Didn't we both become new people during those days in my room. Around my bed. Me with no memory, forming new ones all the time, determining who and what I was to become. You, fresh from loss, starting over again. Growing who you were to be by doing what you were doing. Isn't that who I fell in love with? The you that is sitting before me now. The you that has nursed me back to life. The you that kissed me this morning."

"I know..." she said, blushing a little, but not embarrassed about it one bit.

"Tell me, Lorna. If it had all been different, would we have had a chance? You and me, I mean?"

"If it had all been different, I would never have met you. And I wouldn't be a widow."

"Yes, of course. That's a clever way of not answering my question. And, for what it's worth, I forgive you."

"What?"

"I forgive you. I don't want you leaving this place feeling I blamed you for all this. So I forgive you. I'm making this choice, in my own mind, knowing all that you know. I'm choosing to do this to myself, not you. So I forgive you."

"John, I don't know what..." and she slumped in her chair even more, tears pouring down her face, her whole body shaking, as if a great weight was being released from her shoulders at that moment. They were tears of sadness, but also tears of hope. Great big drops of hope pouring down each cheek, as she sat there, barely able to see John through the mist that was forming on the inside of her hood from all the moisture, but at that moment it didn't matter. John was going to take the walk and was doing it of his own free will. She wouldn't have to carry on with life knowing what she knew. And that was a great weight lifted from her. It meant a fresh start really was possible.

"Look, I know you really need to go now..." she finally said after a few moments of composing herself. "I wanted to tell you in person, as I've told no one yet, and really don't know what it means. I am pregnant with James' baby, and if it's a boy, I'll name him after you."

John looked down for a moment, as if weighing up that last statement, before he looked up again, more determined that she'd ever seen him.

"Then that does it. That's the hope I need that you are coming through this. If you are pregnant, and I really hope you are, then that's my motivation, right there. My memory will live on. I won't be this forgotten stranger that didn't even know who he was himself."

Lorna was crying again, but these were tears of joy. She wanted to kiss him again, to thank him, but that was not possible with the suit on. To take it off would be to risk exposure. That would endanger any child that might be there, though she was still unsure if that was the case. Though she'd never missed a period before, she knew in trauma situations it was very possible that her own body had shut down. Even carrying a foetus during this time risked severe damage to the unborn child. She had been exposed to many cases of radiation poisoning.

Without saying any more, John opened the door, placing a hand on Lorna's suit, where her knees would be, and said goodbye. She wanted to hug him but he shut the door, and banged on the driver's door for it to get moving again, which it did after just a brief pause.

Movement was a little bit slow and there were huge piles of debris lying around, but without a suit to slow him down, John made his way, getting to a clear patch as he circled the main building. The instruction came from Lorna that it was now time to leave the phone before he continued on. What could she possibly say to him in that moment that would mean what she wanted. As John got to the spot, he saw a crumpled white news van, and buildings around, and instantly memories started pouring in.

"Wow!" he shouted, real surprise in his voice.

"What is it?" Lorna asked, concerned that he might be showing signs of being affected by the radiation.

"I remember! It's all coming back to me. I was a reporter. I was here! Right here! I've seen the van, and it's caused me to remember, just like the doctor said! My name is John Westlake, and I was a reporter for the newspaper. I remember it all!" Thoughts and memories were flooding his mind now, as if the flood gates of some great dam had been ripped open, great force pressing these images from his past through to his mind. He remembered a Doctor James Brookes. He remembered what he was doing to him, how he was tricking him.

"Oh Lorna. I think I met your husband!" He didn't dare say how.

"What? How do you know?"

"I met a Dr James Brookes at this base once. Maybe three months ago."

"Oh John, I can't believe that you met James!"

The guilt was starting to build. He felt wrong causing all that pain to Lorna's husband. He was a good man caught up in a nasty scam. Suddenly, John realised he wasn't such a nice man himself. Then the flashes came from the moments before the crash.

"Hold on, I remember something else. Right from the moment of the crash. Lorna, are you listening to me?"

"Yes, John, I'm right here."

"There was a message. We were tracking news from the base, I had it bugged. And seconds before the probe hit the ground there was a message. It sent a message to the base."

"What was it?"

The tension around the world at that moment, in secret little pockets where listening ears were eavesdropping on this private conversation, was unbearable. In Beijing, they wondered what was going to be said. At Thames House, MI5, who were recording this message as well as listening in, were shocked at what they were now hearing. And in Africa, their worst fears were about to be realised.

"The message was that this was no accident. It was planned. Someone crashed the probes on purpose and made them detonate. It was an act of war. This was no accident!"

"What does this mean?"

"I don't know, Lorna. But you need to let them know. Tell them what I've told you. Make sure they know. I had a device at home. It was recording everything. That will verify what I've just told you. The message will be there. It has to be. I saw it just before the explosion. It's the last thing I remember before the crash. Make sure they know, Lorna. I'm putting the phone down now. I love you!"

With that, John placed the phone on the ground. Never before had he felt so alone, and yet never had he felt such strength, such purpose. This was his moment. Maybe it wasn't the end he'd imagined, but he knew who he was now. He'd done plenty of bad things, but maybe he'd come good in the end. Maybe he'd be remembered as the hero after all.

Making it to the safety shut off, without any further delay, he pulled the switch. There was the sound of rushing liquids, something far off, before the noise increased. The danger was growing, being released. He'd done it. For a moment nothing happened. There was silence. Stillness. Before the whole building erupted, a huge explosion throwing debris and smoke high into the air. The ground shook. Two miles away, where Lorna stood watching from afar, she saw the fire ball.

She lowered her head, and wept.

Chapter 27

The Days That Followed

At the RAF base, the intensity from the fires had died down considerably. Clean up crews had been working around the clock to close down the area. Radiation leakage had stopped, the final actions of John had been a complete success. There was already word of him being given a posthumous knighthood. Nothing much could be salvaged from the site, and there were certainly no bodies to bury. Those that had fallen there, including James and John, had been burned up in the fires that followed the safety shut off, if not already in James' case. It was an untested system with many flaws. The heat generated over weeks of usage resulted in the explosion that killed John, whilst making the site safe for everyone else, the nuclear risk dealt with. Final word of the lack of bodies had not yet reached Lorna, but she hadn't expected either of them to be found, anyway.

Most urgent now for the MI5 and government personnel on site, was the recovery of the recording device which John had been using as a telephone, and which he'd left in the safe area before continuing on his final part of the walk.

Finding the device undamaged, they collected it and handed it to a couple of the tech guys.

"It's empty!" came the instant alarm from one of the technicians.

"Don't tell me that! Find it!"

"He's right, sir. It is empty. Nothing is on this device."

"Where does that leave us? I thought you said this thing worked! We paid one million pounds for it for Pete's sake!"

"It does work; it is working. Look, its collecting data from all your telephones and devices now."

And true to form, it was. Information, contacts, numbers. They were all appearing on the screen in front of them; the group of agents and government officials recognised their own details appearing briefly on the screen. Then, after about ten seconds, it vanished.

"Look! It's wiped it! Oh no, shut that thing off quickly!" and without explaining any more, the technician switched it off as fast as he could.

"What is it?" asked someone from the governmental team, himself a senior figure in the country.

"It's stripping out the data and sending it on somewhere. We've been tricked."

"What do you mean?"

"I mean, who ever sold us this, has taken everything. They've got the lot. We've got nothing."

"The blueprints for the power plant?"

"They've gone. It's all gone. We've lost them."

"Damn it!" screamed the head of MI5. This might be enough to bring down the whole government with it.

"There is a joint task force meeting this very minute looking at what military response we are to make against this act of terrorism," said the senior government figure. "I'm due there later today. I cannot take them this news, that we've had this information stolen from right under our nose. Give me something to take to them! That's an order!"

And with that, he stormed off. The meeting was over.

The truth was, they had nothing to go on. They didn't know what had happened. They could only guess, and wait. Soon, it would be clear who had taken all the information. How they responded to that information, was as yet unknown.

****

In a small room on the second floor of the Chinese Embassy in London, four men and one woman stood around a small table, smiling at one another.

"We have the blueprints back?" the most senior figure asked.

"Yes, it's all here. And we got a bonus too. MI5 contacts, code names and a lot more, plus most of the government's code names as well. The device pulled the information from them all as they came to check it. We've shut it down now. They can't trace it back to us."

"Good. It's worked perfectly. Now we must take this back to Beijing. You've done well, each of you. We need to make our exit now."

As always, one member of the team stayed in the shadows. The *Shadow Man* was their most prized asset, their secret weapon. He would be the only one staying behind. He would be their expert eyes on the grid. If anything needed doing, they'd send him a coded message, and they knew he'd be able to get the job done.

The room became empty, people going their separate ways. There was a scheduled diplomatic flight leaving later that day, it was a normal event, having been planned for ages. It made perfect sense for them to all be on that flight. Still, no chances would be taken.

Walking down the stairs, the senior man spoke to his comrades one last time.

"You have done me proud. There had been a great crime done against our Motherland, when the British stole from us these most valuable blueprints. They've been struck a blow. Next time, they will think twice. But each of you have distinguished yourselves. You can hold your heads up high. The Supreme Commander will want to see you personally, it will be your greatest honour. Our finest hour. I salute each and everyone of you. You have done us all proud."

And with that, he gave each of them a hug, which

was highly unusual. Protocol could be put to one side, just this time, given the circumstances.

Their exit raised no problems. Airports around the country were starting to open again, the movement of people continuing as it had done before, even if life still felt sombre. Just after four o'clock that same day, the Chinese jet took off, heading home, with a stop in Dubai to refuel on the way. They were clear, they were gone.

A new team would be bought into the Embassy the following week, fresh faces that knew nothing of what had taken place. And left behind, should he need to be called into action, was their Shadow Man.

****

The discussion with the military subcommittee had been heated, to say the least. There were warmongers on both sides of the party line, political enemies who now found surprising alliances. Others, though, wanted a steady response, a thought through course of action, based on sound understanding.

Data from John's hidden recorder had been recovered, his story verified. It made perfect sense that those behind the hit squad on the hospital, the seven who had been captured and were currently being held in an American prison camp, were working directly for whoever had sabotaged the launch of the probes. The data was being analysed for what it could give them. Any ideas, any clues.

There was strong pressure being put onto the Prime Minister to declare war. British battleships - the HMS Ocean and Defender - were already sailing south from their Portsmouth base, heading for the coast of Africa. They would be joined by others very soon. At the moment it was just a precaution. The Americans, unlike the way they had reacted after 9/11, were suggesting caution rather than attack.

War was in the air. This had been a calculated attack on the UK, that had been intended to wipe them from the face of the Earth. They had been saved by one of their own, John Westlake, who had stepped in and stopped it. Newspapers that decades before had been so anti the wars in Iraq and Afghanistan, were now leading the call for action to be taken against those responsible.

The Prime Minister had yet to speak to the Queen. If war was to be declared on anyone, it had to be after consulting with her. That was the protocol. Even in times of chaos, procedures would be strictly adhered to.

News that the power plant blueprints had gone missing had been very disappointing, especially to the Prime Minister. Totally unaware of the origins of the plans in the first place, he'd seen this project as legacy making. He'd be the man seen as creating a future for the nation through his time in charge. Now, there was little he could do. Was war to be his lasting legacy? He thought about other leaders, his predecessors in the UK like John Major and Tony Blair. Men who had taken the nation into a war fought on foreign soil. This war had already come to England. London would take years to recover from these terrorist attacks, as they were now being called. That was the one thing keeping the PM from declaring war. If it was the actions of a single terrorist unit, regardless of how big they were, that was one thing. New tactics would be needed to fight back against that. But if it was found out that this was the act of a nation, or group of nations, then in his mind, it was no longer an act of terror but an act of war. The ships were on their way. Britain had the fire-power to win any war fought in Africa. And someone, soon, had to pay. It was just the work of the intelligence community to tell them who it was that was ultimately responsible.

In a quiet part of the garden, away from the tensions of the conference room, the Prime Minister and Foreign

Secretary walking slowly, deep in conversation. Friends for a long time, the PM was glad he had an ear to share his thoughts with.

"How did we not see this coming?" said the PM, talking about the loss of the blueprints.

"They used the smoke-screen well. We were so distracted with the incident, we didn't see it coming. No one did."

"And we had good reason to. The nation's existence rested on what happened at that base. It had to be our focus. Tell me, was it an opportunist or was it all planned?"

"That's a very good question. One I've been thinking through myself a lot. There are a number of mysteries to all that has happened over the last month. Holes in our knowledge. The device was clearly a plant. The money was never traced; however well it had been bugged by our guys, they were better. We never did know where it came from; we thought we were onto a winner. But we played straight into their hands on that one. My question is, how did they know we had the blueprints in the first place?"

"Tell me, Michael. Is there anything I need to know about the origins of those plans, that might bring some light to the situation? Anything that affects the actions I might have to take shortly?"

"It's probably best you don't ask that."

"I see. That's what I feared."

"There's also the question of that team we snatched. Names, passports, the lot. Seven wounded but alive, one killed. Who shot them? Who planted that data on them? How did they know where they were when we didn't?"

"Yes, I see there are more questions than maybe we will ever have answers for. Tell me, should we go to war over this?"

"Honestly, I don't know. The country has lost

hundreds of thousands of people through this nuclear disaster. That is a huge loss, a national crisis. To fight a war is to risk more life lost. Yet not to respond might appear to say that we are broken. That anyone can do this to us and get away with it. It's a tough call, and one I don't think, in all honesty, we are ready to make. We need a little more time."

"That's what I think too. There seems to be no problem with getting the ships into place. We've sent two ships south already. Maybe the threat of war will give us some impact in the region? Some friendly countries offering us up exactly who it was behind this all. Who knows?"

"Who knows, indeed. Look, what ever you decide, I'm with you. But I think it's time we went back inside, and continued the discussions. We need to present a united front. The last thing we need is the opposition spouting off how you are not doing enough to protect this nation."

Nothing more was said, as they made their way back inside. Already, nearly five hundred miles south, in the North Atlantic Ocean, two British navy ships were making their way to the north west coast of the African continent. It was hoped, that by the time the giant vessels got much further, a clear decision would have been made about what they did next.

****

For Lorna, the last few days had been difficult, and quite a blur. She'd gone through several meetings, counselling sessions of sorts, aimed at helping her speak, to get things off her chest. They hadn't done as much good as she'd hoped. In truth, her final conversations with John had been the biggest release.

Now she was walking through the front door to her home for the first time in over two months. In some ways the house suddenly felt very homely. Naturally there was dust and a stale smell. It had been left empty for a long time but there was something comfortingly familiar about it all. Standing in the hallway, a wedding photo hanging on the wall, Lorna just stood there for a few minutes, looking at the picture, taking in the memories.

James was dead.

She was going to have to deal with that. Just as she'd had to deal with so much other death around her recently. Alison, a colleague who became a real friend throughout it all. And of course John. A man she owed so much to, and even at the end, faced with the truth behind the lies, he'd continued. He'd done what was asked. She remembered in that moment that John had said he'd once met James. She would have loved to know how that had been, but there was no way to find out. Still, it was a nice thought in her mind, to think of these two men, who'd both had such an impact on her life, talking with each other. She was sure they would have been friends. Lorna turned from the photo and all its associated memories and walked into the kitchen. It was relatively clean and fresh. Outside, the garden was a mess. She'd have to get someone in for that, it wasn't her thing. That had been James' domain. Lorna realised in that moment that she would miss the little things as well as the big.

Over the next twenty minutes, she walked into every room, slowly taking in each moment, allowing the memories of good times to come and have their say. She was going to deal with her mourning in her own special way. And though there was sadness, the loss of someone she loved dearly, there was hope too. The same hope that had brought her through this whole experience, through the chaos. Hope that had enabled her to keep going where others might have stopped.

When her mini tour of the house had finished, she went back downstairs, and made herself a cup of tea.

Sitting in her chair, her favourite one, she felt a glimpse of happiness. She was home. Yes, it was now about living life in a different way. But it would be life to the full. Looking out into the garden, forgetting all its untidiness, she saw her future. She saw into the years to come, and they were going to be good. Nothing could ever be as bad as the experiences she had just been through. The future was hers now to discover, and more than that, to live.

She placed her tea back on the table next to her chair, a smile on her face. Smiling. The 'smiling girl'. Next to her tea sat a plastic pregnancy tester, the blue lines on it clear even from where she was sitting. It was not just herself that she needed to think about now.

<<<<>>>>

Please leave a review on Amazon!

Let's Connect!
Facebook:
www.facebook.com/TimHeathAuthor

Twitter
@TimHeathBooks

Coming Soon

The Tablet
The Shadow Man

ABOUT THE AUTHOR

Tim has been married to his wife Rachel since 2001 and they have two daughters. He lives in Tallinn, Estonia, having moved there with his family in 2012 from St Petersburg, Russia, which they moved to in 2008. He is originally from Kent in England and lived for eight years in Cheshire, before moving abroad.

Printed in Great Britain
by Amazon.co.uk, Ltd.,
Marston Gate.